THE
PRINCE
OF
SECRETS

ALSO BY A.J. LANCASTER

The Lord of Stariel

THE PRINCE OF SECRETS

STARIEL: BOOK TWO

A.J. LANCASTER

To my weird, wonderful, and numerous family members,
none of whom are in this book, I promise.

THE LINEN CLOSET

T HE CAT WASN'T in the linen closet. His Royal Highness Hallowyn Tempestren, the secret fae prince and newly minted steward of Stariel Estate more usually known as Wyn, frowned down at pristine and, above all, *unoccupied* white sheets. Crouching, he checked the lower shelves, but the closet remained conspicuously cat-free. It seemed unfair that the cat should *not* be here now, given the number of times she'd managed to sneak in to sleep despite his best efforts. Where in the high winds' eddies was she? Wyn could locate any mortal in the house in about thirty seconds, but the cat still eluded him after half an hour of searching.

Straightening, he clicked shut the closet door and considered where else in the labyrinthine Stariel House might appeal to a sly she-cat about to give birth. The long, empty shape of the hallway held no answers. Gas lamps cast a yellowish light, combining unpleasantly with the aged pink-and-green-striped wallpaper. A gap where one of the curtains hadn't been closed properly showed a thin rectangle of darkness. He straightened it absently, thinking.

Perhaps the bedrooms? Plumpuff—one of the children was

responsible for the name—had a typical feline talent for inserting herself wherever she was least wanted. Wyn could readily imagine her choosing to have her kittens in the middle of one of the aunts' beds. Of course, the problem was that the house boasted an alarming number of bedrooms, in various states of habitability, spread sporadically over four floors and two wings. It would take time to search them all. Too much time.

He shifted from foot to foot, weighing his options, then sighed and with some reluctance reached out with his leysight. He rarely invoked it to such an extent, but it came easily, almost eagerly, to his call. The world sharpened, the lines of magic that criss-crossed this land sparkling with colour and the layers of Stariel and under-Stariel swimming before him, a beautiful and yet unwelcome reminder of the difference between himself and the people he served. They were human; he was not.

Stariel grumbled as he scanned the leylines for a hint of the cat's location. Wyn wasn't bound to this land and Stariel knew it. However, he had its lord's permission to be here, so usually it would simply cast a metaphorical eye over him, shrug, and move on. Not tonight, though. Tonight, Stariel crouched over him as he sifted through the currents of power, making them as stiff and uncooperative as chilled dough. He fought the urge to hunch under the unfriendly, disconcertingly focused presence.

It *could* be just the season affecting Stariel's mood. It was only six days until Wintersol, and it was natural for the land to be slow and reluctant to wake until springtime. It could also be that Wyn's magic was stronger at this time of year, and something about that had set Stariel bristling. Stormcrows knew faelands could be strange and arbitrary about such things. But had it been this bad in winters past? Had it felt this personal? He couldn't remember if he'd ever pressed the land for information near midwinter before.

Of course—there was one *other* thing that could explain a change in Stariel's attitude; its new lord. *Though I wasn't expecting*

Hetta's influence to increase Stariel's hostility towards me, he thought wryly. Perhaps his kissing skills could use more practice, in the slow, teasing wind of... He tugged his thoughts back from that distracting direction. Later. Right now, he needed to focus on finding the cat.

With an effort of will, he widened the net of his leysight, and his senses expanded through the house. Stariel resisted, frosty and intractable, only grudgingly giving up the locations of its inhabitants. The Valstars had ruled over Stariel for a millennium, and the land was far more attached to them than it was to Wyn, who'd been resident not quite a decade. Ten years was an eye blink to a faeland.

He pressed harder but still received only a hazy impression of the many lives within Stariel House. Most of the Valstars had returned to the family home for the Wintersol celebration and were spread through the interior like so many fireflies. The servants were largely down near the kitchen at this hour, though he didn't need Stariel to tell him that. If he strained, he could make out the no-nonsense tones of Cook giving orders.

But no cats.

Wait—the merest skitter of claws kneading at an already threadbare windowseat: the library. Wyn set off along the hallway with long-legged strides, as the library was at the opposite end of the house from the linen closet. There wasn't much time left. New life always affected the fabric of reality to some degree, and the atmosphere of the house had already begun to shift.

He caught snatches of conversation as he went. From the red drawing room came the sound of the aunts competitively comparing children. In the adjoining room, a good portion of the adolescents were playing cards, ignoring their parents' conversation. The crack of ivory balls distantly to the southeast told him that some of the older Valstar cousins were playing in the billiard room. He took care not to be seen, for he couldn't afford the potential delay. He didn't need magic for that: speed, stealth, and superior hearing worked just as well.

It took him only a few minutes to reach the library. The room's domed roof loomed overhead, the light-spells along the walls throwing ornate shadows into its curve. It was the only room in the house that warranted the use of the more expensive technomantic creations over gas lamps, because of the fire risk. They pinged oddly against his senses, like little blank spaces in the world, something he'd long since decided was a side effect of that specific branch of magic combining with the mechanics of mortal technology. Technomancy wasn't a magic the fae possessed.

He didn't need to guess who had activated the light-spells, for he could hear Marius Valstar speaking from the windowseat at the far end of the library. His stride faltered for a beat, but he mastered the urge to avoid Hetta's older brother and instead slunk towards him between the rows of bookshelves. Marius was reading to some of his younger relatives, voice warm with affection. Reading to children always put him in a good mood; perhaps he would forget to be angry at Wyn.

Wyn rolled his eyes at the over-optimistic thought. Of course Marius would simply *forget* that Wyn had lied to him for nearly ten years about who and what he was. It wasn't so much the masquerading as a human servant that had upset Marius. It was that Wyn had been deeper in Marius's confidences than anyone else, and the reverse had turned out not to be true.

Even if Marius *did* suddenly forgive him for that betrayal, there was another good reason for him to be angry at Wyn, though he didn't yet know it. Wyn's thoughts turned to Hetta again, and he couldn't stop the smile that came to his lips, even as a cold band settled around his heart. Perhaps it was better that Marius didn't know his sister and Wyn were...entangled. After all, it might end soon enough. It *should* end soon enough. The band tightened, the cold spreading over his rib cage.

Marius nestled into one of the windowseats, his dark head bent over a book and spectacles slipping down his nose. Two young girls sat together at the other end of the seat, Marius's cousins Willow and Violet. Their teenage brother Daffodil—their mother had a penchant for botanically themed names—evidently considered himself too old for stories, which he'd made clear by leaning against the wall as if about to walk away. His expression, however, was equally as enraptured as the two girls'.

A grey cat curled on Marius's lap, and Wyn's focused sharpened. It wasn't the cat Wyn was looking for. Stariel had deliberately misled him. No time to mull over what that might mean. Instead he began to mentally shuffle through the locations of the other windowseats in the house.

Marius was reading the tale of an ancestral Valstar and his encounter with a gaggle of mischievous waterfae who'd taken up residence in one of Stariel's mountain lakes. The subject matter seemed a little too topical to be accidental. Marius knew Wyn was fae, but most of the Valstars still didn't. Wyn had never asked those who knew his identity to keep it a secret, but so far they had. Was Marius reconsidering? They could all change their minds at any time, and that left Wyn vulnerable. It itched at him, the need to take control of the situation, but so far he'd managed to resist the urge to do so. He owed them that.

How many windowseats were there in the house? Twelve? Still far too many to search in the time he had left. He tried to narrow them down. <Please,> he asked Stariel. <Give me something more. This is important.>

"Did Sydney *really* meet fairies in the sheepfold lakes?" Willow asked as Marius finished. Since it was a Valstar story, it had featured their ancestor easily outmanoeuvring troublesome lowfae. Wyn doubted the real tale had been quite so straightforward.

"It's just a story," Daffodil said to his sister from his position against the wall. "Everybody knows fairies aren't real."

The comment briefly distracted Wyn from his mental pleading. Daffodil and his siblings hadn't been at Stariel when Hetta had matter-of-factly told her family that the fae *were* real and revealed the imposter Gwendelfear. Evidently the information hadn't yet spread to those family members who'd been absent for the reveal. Surprising—usually anything with even a whiff of scandal to it whipped through the family like wildfire. But then, with Lady Sybil, Lady Phoebe, and Mr Gregory all refusing to acknowledge the matter, the information would travel more slowly. Those three were usually key nodes in the information network.

Marius looked up and jerked in surprise as he spotted Wyn between the bookshelves. Then he bared his teeth in an edged smile.

"I don't know. What would you say, Mr Tempest? *Are* fairies real?" The two girls turned and exclaimed to see Wyn.

Wyn gave Marius a flat look before he turned to Willow and smilingly asked, "What do you think, Miss Willow?"

Willow had dark, bushy hair and the Valstar eyes, solemn and grey. They held a spark of defiance as she answered.

"Mama says that the wee folk *are* real, that they're just hard to spot. We always put out milk for brownies on full moons."

"It's just a tradition," Daffodil broke in. He shoved his hands in his pockets and hunched. "Mama just likes the tradition." He glanced between Marius and Wyn, looking for support. "It's just old wives' tales. Harmless."

Wyn blinked. He hadn't known that about the milk. Of all Grandmamma Philomena's children, Aunt Maude was the one who followed her mother's lead the most when it came to old superstitions, but he hadn't realised she'd passed it on to her own offspring.

"Old wives often know more than you'd credit," Wyn said neutrally to Daffodil. He nodded at Willow. "And better to be safe than sorry, no? Perhaps one day you'll be glad you curried the brownies' favour."

Marius frowned, but just then Aunt Maude came into the library, clearly on the hunt.

"Ah, there you are girls, Daffy," she said. In short order she bustled all three children out of the room. She paid no more attention to Wyn than if he was an item of furniture, which in a way, he was. *The fringe benefits of servitude.*

Wyn was about to move on with his search, but Marius spoke first:

"So…if I leave saucers filled with milk outside your door, will I secure your favour?" His tone was light, but there was a note of accusation in it.

Wyn let out a soft breath of amusement. "I've no particular fondness for milk, Marius. I'm not a brownie."

There was a pause. "That's not an answer." Marius held his gaze, chin tilting. Marius had recently worked out that Wyn couldn't lie. Ever since then, he'd been pushing.

Are you ever going to forgive me? Wyn wanted to ask but refrained. Marius's anger was entirely justified, and a masochistic part of him was glad of it. Stormwinds knew more Valstars *should* be angry at him for the way he'd deceived them, for the fae wrath he feared was coming because of him. *I will leave*, he reassured himself. *I will leave before it comes to that.*

"Very well," he said, straightening. Toe-to-toe, Wyn was only an inch or two taller—the Valstars were a lanky bunch—but with Marius seated, he had the advantage. Advantage? He had to take a moment to quieten the uncharacteristically aggressive urge to intimidate. The tide of the darkest season rode him hard at this time of year, but he was neither lowfae nor lesser fae to be ruled by such instincts. "Yes. You would. The giving of a gift invokes an obligation on the part of the receiver. However"—he held up a finger—"the nature of the obligation varies according to the value of the gift. Given that I am already obligated to your family for sheltering me, that I have previously sworn an oath to protect Stariel and its inhabitants, that I am not particularly fond of milk, and that you could supply it at no cost to yourself, the additional favour I would owe you would be insignificant." He shrugged. "Also, I'd prefer not to have to clean up saucers of milk outside my door when someone knocks them over." An inevitability, given the number of children running around the household right now with the family home for Wintersol.

In the thoughtful silence that followed, Wyn's attention strayed to the fabric of the windowseat, which was beginning to fray along the edge where Marius most often rested his feet. Wyn made a mental note of it, adding it to his already long list of things there was never quite enough money or magic to remedy. But perhaps, if his and Hetta's meeting at the bank this week went well, they would have more funds for maintenance soon. If that didn't happen before he left…well, he'd simply have to write down the most urgent needs for the new housekeeper. The one they hadn't employed yet. *There is still time*, he reassured himself, though that reminded him of the cat, for which time was definitely not in plentiful supply.

Optimistically, he sent another mental plea to Stariel for information, or at least to let him have proper access to the leylines. The faeland ignored it as it had all the previous ones.

"You can't keep running," Marius said suddenly, changing topic in his characteristically abrupt fashion. "How do you expect us to accept you if you can't accept yourself?"

Wyn snapped back from thoughts of upholstery and cats. Marius's grey eyes bored into him, curiously penetrating, as if he could see all Wyn's intentions laid out like stars on a moonless night. This was the other reason he'd considered avoiding him; Marius was prone to flashes of uncomfortable insight.

"I beg your pardon?" Wyn said at last. "I believe our definitions of 'running' may be different, if remaining in one location for nearly a decade qualifies as such."

Marius's expression didn't change. "You're not human, Wyn."

Wyn laughed. "I'm aware, as you so often insist on reminding me." He gestured at the storybook Marius had been reading from. A grossly inaccurate painting of a puckmere featured on the cover:

for starters, that species of lowfae tended to view clothing as entirely optional rather than an opportunity to play dolls.

Marius had the grace to look embarrassed, shoving the story-book to the side. He opened his mouth, about to say more, but there was no time for it, so Wyn spoke briskly before Marius could.

"In any case, have you seen a cat? *Not* that one." He indicated the grey cat on Marius's lap. "A calico. The children call her Plumpuff."

A peculiar expression crossed Marius's face. "You're looking for a cat."

"Yes. Have you seen one?"

"No. But why in Simulsen's name—"

"Then forgive my rudeness, but I must be off. Time is short." And he slipped away from the library, leaving Marius staring bemusedly after him.

MIDWINTER KITTENS

W YN HADN'T WANTED to involve Hetta in this affair, but time was running out and he could wrangle no further help from Stariel. The faeland grew obstinate when pressed, holding the leylines to ransom, and he was reluctant to summon more power and try to force the issue with Stariel being so belligerent.

Hetta was much easier to find than the cat. He was always aware, to some degree, where she was, the taste of her magic so familiar that he could swing towards her as unerringly as to due north. Human magic didn't generally have individualised signatures, but the Valstars had fae blood in their ancestry. It had been enough to give Hetta's magic distinctive notes of coffee pricked lightly with chilli even before she'd succeeded to the lordship of Stariel. Since her ascension, her magic had mingled with Stariel's, deepening in complexity. In this season, crushed pine and frost dominated, and Wyn followed the shape of it through the house. Hetta's signature was brighter than old Lord Valstar's had ever been. Was it simply the difference between Hetta and her father, or a sign of some deeper change in the land now that the ways between Faerie and Mortal were open once more?

Hetta was in the stillroom with her grandmother. Wyn opened the door and crashed into its characteristic wall of scent, the pungency of lavender and rosemary interlaced with a thousand other herbs. He always found the room disorienting, impossible to distinguish the smell of magic from the mundane. It tended to give him a headache if he stayed too long.

Pausing on the threshold, he took the opportunity to drink in the sight of Henrietta Valstar, Lord of Stariel, in the moment before she noticed his presence. She was bent over a tray of jars filled with one of her grandmother's remedies, carefully screwing on lids. A small crease formed between her brows as she concentrated, and the sleek ends of her auburn bob slipped forward, shadowing her face.

Everything that she was—fiercely loyal, deeply pragmatic, often impulsive, occasionally whimsical—shone from her like starlight, heart-stoppingly beautiful. Hetta had returned to Stariel two months ago after a six-year absence. A faked Choosing Ceremony had made her lord-in-name shortly after her arrival, but it had not yet been a fortnight since she'd become lord-in-fact. This thing between them now, deeper than their long friendship, was newer still. Wyn had never intended for it to happen. *But apparently my ability to resist temptation could use work,* he reflected as he watched Hetta's deft motions.

The thought that was never far from his mind these days rose without prompting, as did its accompanying silent vow in response. The wrath of two fae courts *would* descend on him, sooner or later; he had to keep that from affecting Stariel and Hetta, whatever it took. Ice twisted in his chest.

Hetta looked up and saw him. Happiness lit her grey eyes and splintered the ice into something soft and painful. *How did I ever think I could resist her?* Her lips were painted the same colour as spring roses, her eyelashes blacker and longer than usual. She'd been out for most of today, meeting with the village council, and she was still dressed to impress.

"My Star," he said. It was an old address for the lord, and his preferred one for Hetta when others were present. "I would ask for your assistance."

"Is that what we're calling it now?" Grandmamma Philomena said cheerfully from the end of the stillroom. "I don't know who you two think you're fooling." The elderly but spry matriarch wandered over to Hetta and patted her arm. "Leave those to me, m'dear. You'd better go 'assist' your boy." She twinkled at Wyn.

"Thank you, Grandmamma," Hetta said, ignoring the comment. She came around the worktable towards Wyn, and he followed her out into the hallway.

He shut the door. "Clearly, we're doing a terrible job at being discreet."

Hetta shrugged, but her eyes danced. "I said nothing. You know how Grandmamma is."

"I do," he acknowledged. Fortunately, Lady Philomena was inclined to keep her secrets; she liked having something over her less-observant descendants.

Hetta plucked at his lapel. "I'm assuming you pulled me away for a reason?" Her lips curved mischievously. "Though if you want to find a private corner somewhere and…*talk*, I have no objections."

Her eyes had darkened to the deep grey that heralds storms. One hand rested above his collar, against his pulse, and he drew in a deep breath, caught by the intimacy. The warmth of her called to him, even through all the layers of clothing separating them, and his body hummed a note of pure yearning.

The cat. *Remember the cat!* The cat seemed entirely beside the point at this exact moment, but he managed to shake his head. "Another time."

"All right." Hetta let her hand drop. She looked slightly

disappointed, which provided a small, smug bolster to his vanity. "What did you want me for, then?"

"I'm looking for a cat. I need to locate her as soon as possible. Can you ask Stariel where she is? A long-haired calico. The children call her Plumpuff."

Hetta's expression echoed her oldest brother's recent one. The two siblings had a similar bone structure and the same way of arching their narrow eyebrows when they thought you were being ridiculous. Amusement twitched at the corners of Hetta's mouth, but she merely closed her eyes and reached without demanding an explanation.

The nuances of magic around her changed, and he knew she was immersing herself in Stariel. She opened her eyes, her expression blank, and when she spoke, there were echoes of the faeland in her voice, deep and alien: "*The cat is in the room of paper ways.*"

She shook her head, the blankness fading. "She's in the map room. Of course she is," she said in a more normal tone of voice. She gave a sigh of resignation. Hetta, Wyn, and her cousin Jack had covered practically every surface in the map room with paper yesterday, trying to translate Hetta's instinctive knowledge of the estate into one that other people could also read. Likely Plumpuff had made a nest of it.

"Are you all right?" He hadn't liked the way Stariel had dominated over her momentarily.

She waved his concern aside. "It's more difficult, searching the house. It seems to occupy more dimensions than the rest of the estate. And I'm always worried I'll concentrate too hard on the wrong part of it and find out something about one or other of my relatives that I'd rather not know." She smoothed down her skirts. "Right, shall we go find your lost cat then?"

"You do not need—"

"Oh, but I do. And you can explain to me why you're fretting over this feline while we walk. And also what you did to make Stariel so grumpy with you."

The map room was on the third floor and in the north-east corner, which meant the quickest way to get there was to go down to the ground floor, cut across the courtyard outside, and then climb the internal staircase of the northern tower. Stariel House had been built and added to by a succession of Valstars, and it showed in the inconvenient layout. The chaotic nature of the house reminded Wyn a little of the court where he'd grown up, though the actual architectural style of ThousandSpire was utterly different, built to accommodate both greater extremes of climate, especially the scorching hot dry season, and the winged nature of its inhabitants, the stormdancers.

Giving in to temptation, he took Hetta's hand as they crossed the dark courtyard, safe from prying eyes, Hetta's small, soft hand at odds with the strong-willed woman beside him. The night was black as pitch, and the air sank bitter teeth into them, the promise of ice on the wind. Hetta huddled against the shelter of his taller form as they hurried across. Above them loomed Stariel House's three towers of varying heights, one of which pre-dated the rest of the house. Again, he recalled the spires of his homeland; he couldn't seem to escape reminders of his nature tonight.

"Well?" she prompted when they'd reached the bottom of the northern stairwell and he still hadn't spoken.

"The cat is about to have kittens. In fact, she may already have had them."

"Kittens in midwinter," Hetta mused, then frowned. "Is that usual?"

"No. That is just one of the several reasons why I believe the father may have been catshee."

"A fae cat?" she asked. "Those are real?"

Of course Hetta would have heard of catshee; they were common enough in Northern folk tales.

"Yes. They're a type of lowfae and usually wyldfae as well—swearing allegiance to no court. They go where they will."

"Do they usually mate with normal cats? I mean, I assume all our other cats aren't secretly fae?"

He grinned as he held open the door at the top of the stairwell. "They *go*," he emphasised, "where they will." Hetta laughed, and he clarified. "A lot of mortal cats have a bit of catshee in their lineage somewhere. They're one of the more fecund kinds of fae."

"There's some problem with all of this you're not telling me, though," she said as they rounded the last corner in the corridor that led to the map room. "Stariel's native wyldfae have never worried you before; why should half-fae kittens throw you into such a dither now?"

"I'm wondering if it's merely coincidence that led one of the catshee here at this time." It wasn't the whole truth, and Hetta's raised eyebrow as she pushed the map room door open said she knew it, but she didn't press.

The map room was a round corner chamber in the north-eastern tower, part of the oldest section of Stariel House. He quickly scanned the room, which was lined with shallow shelving units and dominated by a central table, and found the cat on the windowseat. Hetta drew back the curtain that separated the windowseat from the room and revealed Plumpuff amidst a nest of what had until very recently been neat stacks of paper.

She gave a small sigh. "The dratted creatures always know precisely how to cause the most trouble." But her expression was tender as she took in the three tiny kittens, all black as soot. Plumpuff was entirely pleased with herself, washing her progeny calmly as they wriggled. She looked up placidly and meowed.

Hetta quirked an eyebrow at him. "Well?"

He tasted the kittens' nature. "Catshee indeed," he said, wishing it were otherwise.

"Well, fae cats or not, they can't live in my map room," Hetta said firmly. "I'm pretty sure Marius left a crate here somewhere that I can transport them in. Where would be best to relocate them to?"

"The kitchen," he suggested absently.

Hetta went to the other side of the room, looking for the crate. Wyn bent to study the kittens. Their eyes were screwed tightly shut, features soft and indistinct. They nuzzled at their mother, the instinctive drive of new life towards that which will sustain it. To his leysight, they glowed, though more dimly than they should.

It was because they were dying, of course.

Even as he watched, the energy of them faded a little more. The power of the spell he'd set to repel housefae bore down on the tiny lives with inexorable force. The spell kept wyldfae from entering Stariel House, but the kittens had bypassed it, transported in their mother's womb. Now they were trapped within the spell's bounds, and it was killing them.

It could be a coincidence, finding that loophole in his spell. After all, what would three half-fae kittens gain anyone? But he hadn't survived his upbringing in a brutal fae court by believing in coincidence.

He should let the kittens die and keep his spell intact. Stariel's native lowfae and any roaming wyldfae would remain excluded from the house and so would any spies amongst them. The spies would be for him, of course, now that the fae knew he was here. He balled his hands into fists. Who was he trying to protect? These kittens had been born here, in Stariel. They were *Hetta's*. They had more right to be here than he did.

The kittens mewled; tiny, feeble things rustling softly in their paper nest. He could read distress in the currents around them. They were only kittens. What did it matter if they died, if it made him safer? It was the rational choice. He should be strong enough to make it.

His father's voice echoed in his ears: *"You are weak, Hallowyn."*

There was no greater weakness than sentiment, for the fae.

He reached out and stroked a single finger over one small black kitten. Its fur was thin and velvet-soft, but it shivered away from the touch, no doubt connecting his scent with the spell that was killing it. He pulled his hand back. "*You are weak.*" His father's words beat at him as he extended his will.

The tension around the kittens, that slow and deadly drain of life, abruptly snapped free. Plumpuff started to purr, and Wyn patted her on the head before rising. The kittens began to nurse, the tiny sparks of their life-forces steadying.

Hetta stared at him from across the room, the crate dangling from one slender hand.

"What," she said in a low voice that had hints of Stariel in it, "did you just do, Wyn?"

THE MAP ROOM

HETTA STARED HARD at Wyn as rain and spice permeated the air, as if the map room were suddenly at the centre of a bizarre thunderstorm. The magic he'd worked had altered the atmosphere of the house on some fundamental level, and Stariel bristled with hostility towards him.

<Stop that,> she told the land firmly, pushing its attention away from Wyn. <You're fond of him, remember? I know his secrecy is trying, sometimes, but this reaction is quite out of proportion to the offense. He's our *friend*.> Friend wasn't quite the right label anymore, but she hadn't found a new one yet that didn't sound either silly or premature.

Stariel didn't answer in words. It was too big and too old and too complicated for that. Instead, she felt it muttering, a guard dog reluctantly standing down. It worried her. Had she inadvertently caused this new aggression? There was so much she didn't know about being lord!

"I'm trying very hard to keep my temper at your apparently incurable tendency to hoard secrets," she said to Wyn as he knelt next to the kittens.

Sometimes Hetta could read him as clearly as a neatly typed play script, but other times, like now, he went still and blank and showed no emotion at all. *Going fae*, she'd mentally dubbed it, though he kept his human shape. She'd seen him in his true fae form only once.

Even through her exasperation, she couldn't help appreciating the graceful way he rose to his feet, fluid as a stag. The warm brown of his skin gleamed in the light from the room's central lamp— the house hadn't yet had elektricity installed—and made strange shadows in his white-blond hair.

"I deactivated a long-running spell of mine," he said, carefully choosing his words. "It was to repel lowfae and keep them from entering the house. It was killing the kittens."

Hetta frowned. "How long has this spell been in place? Since Gwendelfear?" Gwendelfear had been a fae from one of the two warring courts out for Wyn's blood. She'd smuggled herself into the house in disguise and been responsible for both courts learning of Wyn's residence at Stariel.

"No," Wyn said. "That would have been a much more useful spell. This one, I'm afraid, only worked on lowfae. Gwendelfear is lesser fae—my spell was never designed to keep her out. Lowfae are small things, largely without much intelligence, although they can be powerful in some cases. Many of the lowfae are also wyldfae and owe allegiance to no court."

Hetta came towards him, stopping to place the crate down on the windowseat beside the kittens. "So fae cats are lowfae; Gwendelfear was lesser fae; and you are greater fae. Are there any additional flavours I should know of?"

"I am royal fae," he corrected. "Though 'flavours' makes us sound like types of ice cream." He paused, lips twitching. His face was all spare angles, beautiful and remote. The only bit of him with any visible softness was his lips, a sensual promise that Hetta knew first-hand held good. "You look about to make some remark regarding 'tasting'."

"I do not!" But of course, now he'd said it, her attention drifted to his mouth again. When she hastily raised her gaze, his russet eyes were brimming with laughter. It woke an answering fondness in her, saccharine as candy-floss. How could she resist him like this, full of warm irreverence that transformed his alien beauty into something infinitely more attractive? But she knew how Wyn worked; if she let him, he'd only slide away from her questions. So she prodded him sharply in the chest. "Stop trying to distract me. How long has this spell been in place?"

The laughter faded from his eyes, and he straightened. "A little less than ten years. Since I arrived at Stariel." He hurried on before she'd fully absorbed the ramifications of that statement. "That was part of my rationale for removing it. It was originally intended to reduce the risk that one of Stariel's wyldfae would discover my identity and spread the news to those who might bring it to my father's ears. Obviously, that is no longer a risk. My father knows I'm here now." He looked past her to the uncurtained windows, though there was nothing to see in the darkness. He'd gone very fae again, the prince briefly replacing the steward.

Part of his rationale, he'd said. It wasn't hard to guess what else might have influenced him, not when he reached out absently to pet Plumpuff's ears. The three tiny bundles of black fur squirmed next to their mother. Hetta could hardly be angry at him for saving them, though she still wished he'd told her earlier about this spell of his.

"How is it that you always manage to find a way to turn these things about so it's impossible to be properly angry with you by the time you've explained yourself?" she complained.

"My excellent kissing skills? My dark and tortured soul, which makes you long to comfort me?"

She laughed but grumbled, "You aren't as winsome as you think." Some of her earlier anger began to return as she thought of the length of time he'd been holding this secret close. Ten years!

The stillness drained out of him, taking the sharpest of his edges with it. "There's a spell on the henhouse to keep the foxes and stoats away." The words burst from him in a sudden torrent, as if he couldn't get them out quickly enough. "As well as the lowfae. Brownies love eggs and will steal them if they get the chance. And there are spells on the carpets to help keep the dirt out. Actually, a surprising number of my spells have to do with keeping things out or keeping things in. There is a cooling spell in the pantry—"

"Just how many spells do you have whirling away out there?" she interrupted him.

"Ah, of what order of magnitude?"

She gave him a very speaking look.

"I'm not trying to be difficult, Hetta. But it might be easier to ask Stariel to simply tell you."

Hetta closed her eyes and reached. It took a few false starts to explain to Stariel what she wanted, but once she had, the land responded so eagerly that she had to pull back from the sudden influx of information. She put a hand on the wall to steady herself, her head ringing. <More slowly, thank you,> she instructed the faeland. She and Stariel were still working on their communication; it wanted to please her, but it had difficulty grasping the smallness of humans.

To her relief, the land understood, and the avalanche of knowledge slowed to a more manageable trickle. She frowned as the information came to her. Wyn's magic was *everywhere*, and it was magic wholly unlike her own, or like any human magery she knew. Hetta herself was a master illusionist, had worked most recently in a theatre in Meridon before Stariel had chosen her. Illusion was a magic largely used for entertainment—including some very *adult* entertainments—and was consequently looked down on by polite society. Though there were a variety of other human magics, from the common technomancy to the rare mediation, all had known bounds and rules within which they worked. Wyn's magic was something altogether different, something out of tales. Or, she thought with a start, like the magic of Stariel itself.

Stariel's magic didn't fit within the neat parameters of human magic that Hetta knew, but she'd never really questioned it before. Its magic might be old and strange, but Hetta's family had been used to that strangeness for centuries. *But it's just as much fae magic as Wyn's*, she thought, trying to decipher the wefts of Wyn's spells. Wyn had told her Stariel was built on an accord between Hetta's distant ancestor and the High King of Faerie.

Some of Wyn's spells were obvious. The one in the dairy was to keep milk from spoiling. Around the household lay a great many of a cleaning nature. She paused to pick at one in the linen closet, deciding eventually that it was to repel moths.

Reaching out with her land-sense like this was oddly satisfying, like stretching a cramped muscle, and knowledge began to come to her faster as her focus widened. It didn't feel as if she were being told new information by someone else. Instead the knowledge welled up inside her, immediate and complete, as if each area she focused on was merely a prompt for her to remember things she'd only momentarily forgotten. Her head throbbed, the pain increasing until she gave up on trying to hold on to the details of every 'memory' at once. Slowly she mastered the trick of it, learning to let the knowledge fade as she moved on to each new, tightly defined area. The headache ebbed. *I suppose there's only so much space in a human head*, she thought wryly. *Like a cup beneath a running faucet.* It was probably for the best; being aware of every ant's location moment-by-moment would be overwhelming rather than useful.

Reaching the village, she found spells of warmth on some of the cottages, which, Hetta reflected guiltily, still weren't properly insulated. They had yet to secure a bank loan to begin the necessary upgrades.

She couldn't tell what every spell was for, though they all felt benign enough. A few of the village gardens had spells affixed to them, but not all. Similarly, individual trees in the home orchard. Other spells were larger and more powerful, strange and tasting of storms. <It's all right,> she told Stariel when it became something between frustrated and downcast in its inability to translate in a way she could understand. <Luckily us humans have our own ways to communicate. Us fae and humans,> she corrected.

She opened her eyes. Wyn was carefully lining the crate with discarded paper. "What are all the ones on the children for?"

He kept his eyes on his task. "Three years ago, in January, two of the village children who'd been out playing didn't return from the forest before nightfall. A blizzard came in very suddenly. By the time we managed to rouse Lord Henry so he could find them, the smith's daughter had died of cold."

Stariel was a very large estate and entirely wild in parts. The Lord of Stariel could locate anyone within the estate's bounds, but the old Lord Valstar, Hetta's father, had been a drunk. If he'd fallen into a stupor, waking him enough to understand what was needed would've taken a long time. Too long. Her stomach twisted.

A clean, cold anger burned in Wyn's eyes for a heartbeat before he tamped it down. "They're locator spells. But they too are now rendered superfluous. I don't doubt your capacity to do your duty, Hetta. I will undo those as well, if you wish it."

"After that tale, I don't know how I could." It seemed a sensible safeguard, but it still made her uneasy. There was so often an edge of secrecy or manipulation to fae magic—Wyn's magic. *He's not human,* she thought for the thousandth time, trying once again to merge the two halves of him, the old, trusted friend and the strange fae prince. Which one was she attracted to? Even as she posed the question, she knew it was a foolish one. Wyn wasn't two people, and it wasn't as if he'd developed a whole new personality overnight.

He'd always been a study in contrasts: secretive and manipulative; kind and dry-humoured. And yet, something *had* changed, between them if nothing else. It had only been a few days since they'd kissed, irrevocably exchanging friendship for something she didn't yet have a name for, but already she could see complications sprouting in all directions. What was she going to *do* with this infuriatingly attractive man and all the baggage that came with him?

Something of her emotions must have shown, because he left the crate, rose, and wrapped his arms around her. She went willingly, tucking her head under his chin, letting her anxieties melt against his reassuring solidity. He smelt of clean linen and soap, with a hint of rainstorm and a spice she couldn't quite place, similar to but richer than cinnamon. Her mind supplied the name after a pause: cardamom. That familiar mixture had always been his, but she'd only recently realised that some of it wasn't real scent at all, but how her senses perceived his magic. Human magic didn't have a smell. It might as well have been a symbol of their entire relationship; something she'd always known about him given suddenly new connotations.

Magic or not, it was still a highly appealing scent, and she gave a little sigh against his chest. "I understand why you've kept so many secrets in the past. But we can't go on like this, with me continually blindsided by things you ought to have told me sooner. I have wider responsibilities now, and this isn't just about me and you." Which one of them was she reminding?

She felt him nod, his arms tightening around her. "You're right."

"You know it irritates me when you won't defend yourself," she told him, looking up and lacing her hands behind his neck. Her hands were ungloved, bare fingertips brushing against his skin and the silken strands of his hair. "How are we ever to have a proper fight if you just give in all the time?"

The corner of his mouth twitched. "Very well. In my defence, I am new to this…" he fished about for a word, "this sharing between us. And the spells are largely old." He smiled then, slow and full of wickedness. "But don't tell me you want to fight, Hetta, when you are clearly angling for something else entirely."

With slow deliberation, he pulled a handkerchief from his pocket and raised it to her lips, carefully wiping away the remnants of her lipstick. Her breath caught.

As she'd hoped, he bent and kissed her. He was so careful, so controlled, and only when they kissed did he ease the tight leash he held on himself. Not completely, of course, but there was a hint of wildness in the curve of his mouth, a fierce, tantalising edge of temptation. Some devilish part of her was determined to see him cut free of restraint, and if she couldn't make him lose his temper then perhaps she could drive him mad with lust.

The latter option also appealed for entirely non-altruistic reasons. Frequently, Hetta had found, men kissed merely as an eager prelude to more intimate relations. Which Hetta didn't object to, but Wyn kissed like they had all the time in the world, as if kisses were an end in and of themselves, a slow, languorous drug burning deliciously through her whole body.

She fumbled at his bowtie, feeling there was altogether too much starch separating them. Wyn made a noise low in his throat, half-laughter, half-growl, and then he picked her up and swung her onto the high map table so that her legs dangled to either side of him. A pile of paper crashed to the floor. They both ignored it, and she fisted her hands in his shirt, pulling him closer, her heart dancing a frantic rhythm.

They'd forgotten to shut the door to the map room.

This oversight became apparent as two of her cousins traipsed into the room one after the other and then froze in similarly staggered fashion.

4

UNWANTED RELATIVES

"**H**ETTA!" HER COUSIN Jack exclaimed. Hetta had a good view of his face past Wyn's shoulder; his brows nearly merged with his hairline in shock. Her cousin Caro wore a similar expression. Hetta had a fleeting impression of seeing double, as Caro had the same true-red hair as Jack and both her cousins had flushed nearly the same shade.

Wyn broke away, stripes of colour high on his cheekbones. In the unguarded instant before he reassembled his composure, he looked gratifyingly unravelled with his hair mussed and bowtie hanging loose.

Hetta remained awkwardly perched on the map table. Was there any point pretending she and Wyn had been engaged in some innocent lord-and-steward consultation? Deciding that there wasn't, she grinned impishly up at her cousins.

"Oh, do go away. Can't you see I'm busy?"

Jack spluttered something inarticulate, but Caro, her eyes round and brim-full of questions, said, "Fair enough. I think I'll look at the waterway maps some other time. Come on, Jack."

But Jack wouldn't be shifted. Caro shrugged helplessly at Hetta and trotted out alone. There was a pause while they all listened to her footsteps recede. Wyn went and shut the door behind her, rearranging his bowtie with quick, neat motions. When he turned, his armour was firmly back in place.

Jack shot him a venomous look. "What the blazes do you think you're doing?!"

"Reciting poetry," Hetta said acerbically. "Honestly, Jonathan, if you don't know what we were doing, I'm not going to explain the facts of life to you."

Jack went even redder, his mouth pressing into a hard line of disapproval.

"You know what I mean! You can't carry on like, like—" Jack whirled on Wyn. "If I found anyone else canoodling with my cousin, I'd ask when the wedding was, but there bloody well better not be a wedding in the offing here, *Mr Tempest*."

Jack knew Wyn was fae. He'd known it for years before Hetta, something that still irked her. Hetta's own father had told him, expecting Jack to follow in his footsteps as lord.

"Canoodling?" Hetta repeated incredulously. "You sound like your mother! I truly don't see what business this is of yours. Go away."

She and her cousin had only recently reached an uneasy truce after they'd had to work together to unravel a plot against Stariel. Hetta had a feeling she might've just undone that. But she was less concerned with Jack than Wyn. He'd gone distant and unreadable again, but she knew what he was likely thinking; his ambivalence about remaining at Stariel had been increasing with every day since her lordship, and her dashed cousin's untimely interruption would be making him recalculate.

"You know what I mean! It's not—you can't go round acting like a..." Jack's indignation faltered in the face of Hetta's cold stare.

Wyn's demeanour had also grown frosty. "Do go on. Acting like a what, exactly?" he asked in a soft, dangerous tone.

But though Jack was hot-headed, he wasn't a complete fool. "Don't you try and turn this back on me. How long has this been going on? Carrying on like bloody dogs in heat! I thought you had some notion of honour! I don't know what your people think is acceptable, but you can't just—"

"Don't worry, Wyn hasn't deflowered me," Hetta interjected, bringing Jack's diatribe to a screeching halt.

Jack turned an even deeper shade of red but didn't back down. He could be tiresomely persistent if he saw something as his duty.

"Well. Good," he said stiffly. "Because it's not like you can marry him."

"That privilege was given to a very comely stagehand five years ago," Hetta continued as if he hadn't spoken, sick of Jack's prudery. *Honestly.* "Steven, his name was. Or was it Stefan?" She slid off the map table, dusted off her skirt, and said with false sweetness, "No, it was definitely Steven. He had lovely blue eyes." She draped an arm deliberately around Wyn's waist. He put a hand over hers, presenting a united front without hesitation, and her heart gave a fierce, happy squeeze.

Jack was, for once, speechless. Hetta had evidently so offended his sense of propriety that he couldn't even look at them, fixing his gaze on the far window instead as his throat worked, trying and failing to form speech. Eventually he grit out, "You always ignore things you don't like, Hetta, but you can't just please yourself and pretend it affects no one else this time. You're the lord. He's not even human."

Hetta glared daggers but Jack ignored her and turned to Wyn. "If she won't see the sense in it, then you'd bloody well better. Whatever this…thing…is between you, it needs to end now."

Wyn's voice was still clipped and cold. "I make you no oaths, Jonathan Langley-Valstar, but I would remind you that I made an oath to your uncle to bring no harm to Stariel. I do not intend to break it." His hand on Hetta's tightened. "And now I would ask you to leave."

Jack rocked back on his heels, eyes narrowing. Wyn rarely made demands. But to Hetta's surprise he nodded curtly, turned, and left without another word.

Wyn dropped her hand and went to the door again, closing it with a soft click for the second time. The room echoed with a pleasant absence of angry relatives. As if the silence were an entrance cue, the wind rattled at the windows.

"You lied to him," Hetta observed. There was no possibility of Wyn breaking his oath to her father, since it didn't exist anymore.

He leaned his head briefly against the wood, his back to her, and didn't bother to refute her statement with the technicality that he'd said nothing untrue. Wyn couldn't outright lie, but Hetta had begun to realise that you could lay out pieces of perfect truth to create wholly false pictures. She didn't disapprove, exactly, since she'd probably do the same in his place, but it had made her pay more attention to what Wyn *meant* rather than what he *said*.

"I would re-take the oath in a heartbeat if you would but let me."

Wyn's oath to her father had ended when he'd died. Oaths were a serious business for fae; they lost power if they broke them. Hetta didn't like the idea of imposing a magical obligation on her friend; a broken oath had already hurt him once, and she didn't want to be the means for it to happen again.

"Well, I'm not accepting any such oath. I don't want us to be liege lord and supplicant." There were already quite sufficient complications between them without adding that on top. Hetta might technically be his employer, but at least he wasn't magically bound into that role.

"Neither do I," he said, turning away from the door. As he did so, something beyond her caught his attention. "Get out!" he told it sharply.

She turned too but caught only a flash of movement as something scuttled away, impossible to recognise. <What was it?> She leaned on Stariel for the knowledge. "A wyldfae," she answered herself. She could feel the little creature hurrying away from the tower, through the cavities in the walls.

"A brownie," Wyn agreed. "The wyldfae are already investigating the house." His eyes were distant. "That brownie will likely spread the news of our relationship to half the wyldfae on the estate before noon tomorrow."

"Jack and Caro won't tell anyone, though." A hope rather than a certainty, but far more important than whatever brownies thought of her and Wyn. She crossed the distance between them and put a hand against his chest. "What Jack said—"

"He is right."

She stiffened. "He's *not* right, thank you very much! If you dare say that you've dishonoured me or any other such ludicrously old-fashioned sentiment, I shall singe your eyebrows off!"

He blinked down at her. "Oh. No, of course I don't mean that. I mean...I'm not human."

Several retorts sprung to her lips, but she waited for him to explain himself instead. Outside, hard drops of rain began to hit the tower.

He spoke softly, as serious as she'd ever seen him. "It's not human scandal that I fear the most. I fear what it may mean for Stariel if my past catches up with me. And I fear it may not be a matter of *if* but *when*. Perhaps it's merely paranoia to worry about those catshee kittens...but perhaps not."

"And I said I would fight the fae for you if need be." She could expel fae from Stariel, if his father sent them again. But it was the wrong thing to say. His jaw tightened. "Have I wounded your pride?" she asked, somewhat fascinated. She didn't think she'd ever managed to offend him before, or at least he'd never shown it if she had.

He grimaced. "I'm a damnably proud creature, apparently." He reached out to tuck a tendril of Hetta's hair behind her ear. "It irks me, that I bring so much trouble with me. I should much prefer the reverse, that my presence should bring you only gain."

She appreciated the honesty, but still said frankly, "I'm worried your martyrish tendencies will make you decide you need to leave for my or Stariel's own good." She didn't try to hide what she thought of that.

He stilled, fingertips warm against her neck. "I…cannot promise you that I won't." He looked miserable. "Sometimes it would be nice to be able to lie."

The words spilled out before she could snatch them back: "I won't forgive you if you leave." Her heart hammered; it felt too much like an ultimatum. She shouldn't be issuing ultimatums when this thing between them had barely begun, should she? But if he had to tell the truth, then so should she. And she couldn't pretend she'd accept that sort of betrayal. Not from him.

Oddly, his expression softened. "I know. And I'm glad of it."

Plumpuff meowed plaintively before she could ask exactly *why* he was glad about her giving him ultimatums.

"Very true," he said past Hetta's shoulder to the cat. "I should transport you and your offspring somewhere better suited to your dignity."

Hetta sighed, not as reassured as she'd like to be. "And I'd better go and make sure Caro isn't intending to announce the lord's scandalous affair with the steward to all and sundry." She had mixed feelings about keeping their relationship under wraps. It was certainly nice to avoid the storm of judgement and scandal while everything was still so new and uncertain. But it couldn't go on like this forever, and part of her already chafed at hiding what she felt.

"Thank you," he said solemnly.

"Don't thank me yet, because *you* get to talk to Jack." Hetta had a fair idea of her own temper. Wyn was much less likely to burn her cousin's hair off, and, more importantly, much more likely to talk him round than she was.

His mouth twitched. "Very well. I will talk to Jack."

MINOR DOMESTIC CRISES

W HEN WYN FINALLY left Hetta, Jack had gone to bed. Wyn frowned at his door, annoyed more with himself than its occupant. The house was quietening, at least half of the Valstars having followed Jack's suit. The other half consisted of mainly the teenage set, who were over-excited by the presence of so many of their relations and likely would not be done till the wee hours.

What, precisely, was he hoping to achieve here? 'Here' in the metaphorical rather than literal sense, for it was clear he wouldn't be seeing Jack until morning. On the brighter side, that meant Jack had calmed down enough to sleep on it, and a calm Jack was unlikely to tell anyone what he'd seen without speaking to Wyn first. Indirect action wasn't in Jack's nature unless he was in a towering rage. It was one of the things Wyn liked about Jonathan Langley-Valstar, even if the fae would count that as a weakness.

On the less bright side...he set his shoulders against the wall, folded his arms, and brooded down at the hallway runner, trying to map out possibilities and consequences. He didn't want to leave

Stariel, or Hetta, but the fae didn't forget debts, and now they knew Wyn's location there was no chance they'd let the matter rest. King Aeros would be weaving some plan to make his errant son pay the price of his broken oath. Probably in blood. But exactly how would his father choose to strike, now that Hetta's lordship had secured Stariel's borders? And most importantly, *when*? The revocation of the Iron Law might have made Wyn somewhat lower on his father's list of priorities—or the reverse. Wyn swallowed. He hoped it wasn't the reverse.

Surely he would have until after Wintersol, at least? That would give him time to tie off the worst loose ends: employing the new housekeeper, securing the bank loan. And he was sure between them he and Hetta could cajole her cousins into keeping what they'd seen to themselves until then. When—if—he had to leave, he didn't want Hetta to have to face a storm of scandal alone. The cold in him deepened, as if his heart were keeping time with the night.

A tiny, insubstantial sound at the other end of the hallway drew him from his strategising. Wyn stiffened but didn't otherwise give any sign he'd heard it, his senses telling him it was another brownie without the need to turn and look. Was it watching him specifically, or just exploring its new territory? He made a mental note both to make sure the pantry was secure—the little creatures loved to steal food—and to remember to put out milk for them now that they had the run of the house.

He waited. After a few seconds, he felt the tiny flicker of the lowfae's presence move on, beyond the reach of his senses. Just exploring, then. Wyn let out the breath he'd been holding, shook his head at his paranoia, and went to seek his own bed.

THE MORNING BROUGHT WITH it a hundred small tasks requiring his attention, and Jack slipped out of the house before Wyn could catch him. Jack's land-sense was stronger than that of most of the Valstars, and he frequently sought refuge in the estate when his emotions were unsettled. Probably not a good sign, but Wyn was busy enough to be glad of an excuse to delay the conversation.

Stariel House was chronically short-staffed, and there was more work than usual just now with so many Valstars home in the lead-up to Wintersol. Once Stariel acquired a new house manager, the burden of everyday domestic organisation would fall to them, but currently there was only Wyn, land steward, butler, and house-keeper rolled into one. Wyn liked being useful, but even he was beginning to feel stretched somewhat thin. Fortunately, his steward duties were not as taxing in this season as they would be come spring, but they still added to his workload, particularly as he was still deciphering the full extent of the previous steward's dishonesty and preparing to plead Stariel's case to the bank.

He spent a few precious minutes checking his domestic spells that filled the gaps between staffing and maintenance funds, recharging them where necessary. The surfeit of seasonal power eddied around him, oddly energising, leaving a cool, scentless taste on the back of his tongue like ice chips melting. His work drew Stariel's interest, and he again had to resist the urge to hunch under the weight of the faeland's prickling hostility.

Had Hetta's irritation with him manifested in the faeland, or was Stariel's attitude all its own? ThousandSpire hadn't always shared his father's moods. It had been fond of Wyn, despite King Aeros's contempt. This could be the same—Stariel acting independently of Hetta's feelings on the subject. *Stormcrows, I hope so.*

He blew out a breath and went downstairs to the servants' hall to begin to address the day's usual assortment of small mishaps, each one unique and yet somehow cumulatively as predictable as clock-work. Today's specific ones involved one of the maids being called away on a family emergency and the hall boy managing to sprain an ankle on his way downstairs to the morning staff meeting. Wyn rearranged schedules and workloads and managed to prevent the hall boy injuring himself further—an achievement in and of itself, since the boy had *no* sense of self-preservation. He sent him off to see Lady Philomena; Hetta's grandmother dealt with minor medical complaints among the staff and family both.

Current crises averted and meeting adjourned, Wyn found himself alone in the servants' hall. A long wooden table ran down the room's centre, and Wyn smoothed a pattern on it, trying to settle the unease that had scratched at him since last night. These days, his place was at the table's head—or at least it would be until they found a new house manager; the steward was set apart from the rest of the hierarchy—but his gaze lingered on the seat the hall boy had recently vacated. That's where he'd begun, years ago when he'd first come to the estate, terrified someone would see through his mask, see he didn't belong here. But no one had, and now the memory of the decadent gold-and-gem-crusted dining rooms of ThousandSpire, filled with the jostling, varied shapes of greater and lesser fae, seemed far stranger than the plain, empty one before him. *I belong here now*, he reassured himself. He might not be human, but he was closer to it than King Aeros would ever be, and Father could not change that now, could not erase ten years of history.

The back of his neck itched, and he caught a flash of movement from the corner of his eye. Hmmm. Another brownie. Wyn didn't believe in coincidence, but before he could investigate, the door burst open and the senior housemaid entered in a rush.

"Sorry, sir, but one of the pipes in the lavender bathroom has burst."

Wyn rose with a wry smile. Imminent flooding took priority over curious brownies.

The burst pipe was just the start of a procession of minor domestic crises, and both Jack and brownies remained unaddressed as the

day drew on. Late afternoon found Wyn opening the back door
into the stableyard for the weekly grocery delivery, reflecting that
after this, at least, he ought to have a moment spare.

"Mr Jones, precisely on time, as always," he said in greeting.

The grocer had his hands in his pockets, and he rolled his lips
around warily. His taller son stood behind him, eyes bright.

"Wasn't sure I'd be dealing with you this week, Mr Tempest.
Heard you'd gone up in the world." The tone was friendly; the
subtext, barbed.

Wyn smiled warmly at the pair, unsure what to make of said
subtext and feeling his spare moment beginning to evaporate. "Lord
Valstar has indeed appointed me steward. Were you worried I'd be
too full of myself to speak to you?" He shook his head. "I hope I'm
never so top-lofty. I shall depend on you to tell me if you fear I'm
becoming so. Besides, it would be madness to offend the man who
makes the best sausage in the county."

The grocer didn't soften, the mention of Hetta tightening his
mouth into a hard line. Did he disapprove of Hetta's lordship? But
the grocer wasn't a particularly political man, and he hadn't seemed
bothered when she'd first ascended. Had something changed?

Wyn tilted his head. "You've known me for many years now, Mr
Jones. Is there something amiss that I can help with?"

The reminder of Wyn's length of service eased the line of the
man's shoulders. "Naught but unpacking the cart, same as usual."

Ah. The man was worried by Wyn's *relationship* with Hetta. Had
he terribly misjudged both Caroline and Jack's ability to hold their
tongues? But no, neither of Hetta's cousins would choose the local
grocer as their confidante. Which meant…had news of his and
Hetta's indiscretions gotten out of the house in some other way?
Or was the grocer's wariness based on something else entirely? Idle
speculation, perhaps? Hetta and Wyn's old friendship was no secret,
and Wyn *had* recently been promoted on her say-so.

Wyn was set to delve deeper into the matter, but as he stepped over the threshold into the stableyard, Stariel *pounced*, and the ground shifted abruptly under his feet.

He stumbled. A mortal would have written it down as clumsiness, but Wyn wasn't clumsy. With some difficulty, he followed the grocer to the cart, and the disturbance moved with him, altering the position of stones, subtly raising or lowering the ground level as he stepped. *My own personal earthquake.*

He sent a stray thought at the faeland. <Have I offended you somehow? If so, my apologies.> It didn't answer; neither did it cease trying to trip him up.

Maybe it would stop if he ignored it? He tucked his clipboard temporarily into the cart for safekeeping and picked up a crate in its stead, adjusting his feet on the unstable ground. The grocer gave him a strange look; he supposed he did look rather like a cat on a hot tin roof. He ignored the look and began the journey back to the house while attempting to keep up a façade of relaxed friendliness, peppering his conversation with as many sideways references as he could to his long history of service here, to Hetta's commitment to duty. *I am a person of competence that you know and trust; Lord Valstar is part of an ancient and respectable bloodline. There is nothing to worry you here, regardless of what you may have heard.*

It seemed to be working, even though it was hard to keep hold of the thread of conversation with Stariel's ground-shifting antics distracting him. He breathed a sigh of relief as he crossed the threshold again; at least Stariel kept its game restricted to the outside. Stormwinds knew what it would add to the house maintenance bills otherwise.

He stowed the crate securely in the cellar and hesitated as he went to step outside again. Maybe Stariel would be bored with its game now? But as soon as he crossed the threshold, the ground once more began to shift, subtly but surely, like walking on the back of a living, moving creature. Picking up a bag of potatoes, he leaned heavily on his leysight. Using that, he was able to predict Stariel's small leyline warpings before they occurred, moving his feet one step ahead of the faeland, as if they were partners in the world's oddest dance.

<I will not apologise for kissing Hetta, if that's what this is about.> He was sorry for so many things, but it wasn't in him to be sorry for that. Was this jealousy—if it *was* jealousy—normal when one courted a faeland's chosen? Had his mother had to deal with this from ThousandSpire when she'd met his father? His thoughts shied from that thought like a raw wound; he didn't wish to think of his mother.

Stariel's presence intensified.

Wyn froze. Belatedly, it occurred to him that deliberately provoking *an enormous and inhuman magical entity* was perhaps not his most brilliant idea. He hugged the potatoes and compacted his magic as small as it would go, trying to appear harmless. In hindsight, perhaps he should have simply fallen over and let the faeland satisfy itself. A curl of suicidal rebelliousness stirred at the thought.

The minor leylines twitched ominously, and he held his breath. Would the faeland escalate? His magic coiled restlessly under his skin, and he pushed it down more firmly lest it be taken as a threat. Despite what his foolish Wintertide instincts insisted, he could *not* challenge the might of a faeland. *I am harmless and familiar, no threat at all to you. You know me*, he tried to channel towards Stariel.

Thankfully, Stariel appeared to decide that since Wyn did *technically* have permission to be here, more active opposition to his presence wasn't allowed. The faeland grumbled, but its attention grudgingly shifted away, the ground settling sullenly under his shoes. Thank the high winds' eddies. His muscles slowly unknotted themselves, his heart beating abnormally fast.

"All right, sir?" the grocer said behind him.

"Ah, yes, thank you. Woolgathering." He shook himself and his burden back into motion. Together, they finished unpacking, and by the time the grocer and his son left, Wyn thought he'd managed to reassure them that Stariel House had not become a den of incompetence or alarming mortal morals. Though why precisely had they needed the reassurance?

Once the pair were safely out of sight, he let his mild expression fade and frowned thoughtfully in the direction they'd taken. The grey-brown of the long driveway curved around Starwater towards the village, and the wind ruffled small white waves in the great lake's surface. He would like very much to know the details of what people were saying about Hetta—about Hetta and *him*—on the wider estate, particularly if news of their indiscretions *had* somehow gotten out of the house.

Which meant he needed Lottie, one of the housemaids. She had a penchant for anything that smacked of intrigue. And she might even be the source of the gossip, if she'd witnessed something. He and Hetta had been careful, apart from last night's incident, but Wyn knew well how invisible servants could be. The main problem was that he couldn't simply *ask* Lottie for an update on the current state of gossip on the estate. An indirect approach was called for.

He went in search, noting the flicker of movement in the corner of his gaze as he did so. *Soon*, he vowed. Too-interested brownies had not yet reached the top of his priority list, though they were rapidly advancing on it. First, gossip.

He located Lottie and the cook, Clarissa, down in the kitchens, cooing over the kittens.

"I trust all the bedrooms are made up, Lottie?" he asked as he came in. The last of the Valstar relatives arrived today, and it had been a scramble to get enough bedrooms liveable in the short timeframe. Old Lord Valstar hadn't invested much in maintenance of the house. Hetta was determined to change that—had in fact scheduled a meeting with the bank for tomorrow—but in the meantime, they managed as best they could.

Lottie started at his words and rose from her crouch with one last pat to Plumpuff's head. "I was just about to start on the Lavender Room, sir. Did you want me to make up old Lord Valstar's room?"

"Yes, thank you." He'd cleaned it out after the old lord's funeral, but no one had since slept in it. "It's time enough. Put Lady Cecily and Mr Frederick in it. Don't bother with the Lavender Room. The leak is stopped, but it's best left unoccupied until the plumber arrives."

"Yessir." Lottie straightened her skirts and was halfway to the door when he spoke to the cook.

"I would ask for your opinion on something curious, Mrs White. I was speaking with the grocer just now and he made certain insinuations regarding my recent change in job title." He let himself sound puzzled rather than alarmed.

Definitely the housemaid had contributed to the spread of something; Lottie froze like a rabbit caught out after dawn, eyes blowing wide.

The cook pulled herself up, bosom swelling with righteous fury. "He never suggested you weren't fit for the job!" She whirled as if to move out in search of the grocer and forcibly change his mind. Clarissa had known him since he was a youth at Stariel and still considered Wyn in a faintly maternal fashion, despite his now elevated position. He could speak to her more freely than he could to the housemaid. Stariel was relatively informal, as great houses went, but the servants' hierarchy was still nearly as intricate as that of ThousandSpire. *Who knew growing up in a fae court would be such excellent training for managing a mortal household?*

"He's left already," Wyn assured her hastily. "I hope I was able to give him some reassurances as to my commitment to this household." He frowned, putting a trace of worry into his words, and picked up a dish cloth. He began drying some of the luncheon dishes. "I'm not sure where he came by his notions. I hope they're not widely held." He raised a quelling eyebrow at Lottie, who was still standing mid-kitchen, blatantly eavesdropping.

Lottie started. "Sorry, sir." She hurried out of the kitchen but didn't carry on into the house. Wyn heard her pause out of sight but still within earshot. Good: he wanted her to hear his conversation with the cook.

Clarissa heaved a sigh and pulled out a large lump of dough. "Well, I don't hold with gossip," she said—fortunately, being mortal, she could tell such a whopping untruth without any ill consequence. "And I don't know what's got into his head. Anyone with sense can see you're just as qualified as Mr Fisk was—and more!" She scowled at the memory of the former steward, who she hadn't liked even before it came out that he'd been stealing from the estate.

Wyn chuckled. "Thank you, but my ego doesn't require stroking on such a front. I am confident enough in my abilities. I'm more concerned that I may have inadvertently offended someone or other without realising."

"It's just narrow-minded Northern folks. Some of them are as foolish as hens when it comes to newcomers."

Wyn paused to stack the dish he'd been holding. "I admit I had hoped nearly a decade of service might put me outside that category." Northern countryfolks' attitude towards change had more in common with the fae than they realised.

"You'd have to be born here, I'm afraid, to qualify for some," Clarissa admitted. "But don't worry, the novelty will wear off once people see your promotion had nothing to do with favouritism."

"Favouritism?" He heard Lottie take a sharp breath outside the door, but it hadn't been audible to Clarissa, who kept kneading the dough in practised motions.

Clarissa eyed him. "Well…everyone knows you're friendly with Lord Valstar. Not that anyone's suggested there's anything inappropriate with that!" she hurried to reassure him, which he didn't find particularly reassuring.

"I have known Lord Valstar for many years. I've no doubt she will be an excellent lord." He carefully transferred the completed stack of dishes to the correct cabinet. "And I intend to fill the role of steward to the best of my ability. I hope you're right that I am merely the novelty of the moment."

Clarissa looked relieved at this response. "Besides," she added, "anyone who knows you knows you've not a scandalous bone in your body. And if they don't, I'll certainly tell them so. It's not as if you're one for chasing skirts or anything! You might as well be one of those monkdruids." She heaved a sigh at the thought. Wyn had no doubt she would've liked to matchmake him with someone or other, given the least encouragement.

"Er...thank you for your defence of me, Clarissa, although I think this conversation itself may be veering into inappropriate territory." The rebuke was a gentle one because she'd known him for so long, but he wasn't about to encourage open speculation on his love life.

Clarissa grinned but acknowledged his point with a nod.

That Clarissa thought him asexual wasn't an accident. Greater fae naturally exuded a charm designed to attract, but he'd solved the problem by twisting that allure sideways. He still attracted people, but it was with a platonic appeal, a low-level suggestion saying: *I remind you of your uncle/brother/friend/child.* It had seemed wise to avoid the complications that came with the non-platonic sort of attraction, given both his nature and position here. *Yes, and what a marvellous job I've done at avoiding those complications, as it turns out,* he reflected.

However, at least Clarissa's comments meant none of the staff had *seen* him kissing Hetta. That made things simpler. No low-level suggestion would override the evidence of their own eyes, not unless he resorted to full-blown compulsion, and he would *not* compel his staff.

"Well, I hope I can rely on the staff to squash such rumours." He wrinkled his nose. "It will be harder to persuade a suitable housekeeper to take up residence if we appear to be an unbridled hotbed of scandal."

"Do you want me to have a word with the girls?"

Wyn shook his head. He knew she would regardless, and he meant his next words for Lottie. "I hope that's not necessary. They're a sensible bunch, and they do this household credit, and so I shall tell the prospective applicants." Perhaps that might spur the housemaid to be more thoughtful about what stories she spread in future, though he was probably being overly optimistic. Ah, well. There were far worse faults than gossiping, and it was useful to know *who* could be counted on to spread information quickly.

Clarissa sighed. "When are the applicants coming for the interview?" she asked, although she already knew the answer.

"After Wintersol."

"It'll be good getting another body. I don't know how you manage half of what you do. And how you're supposed to do Mr Fisk's job now besides. It's not right to run you ragged!"

"I am not run ragged," Wyn said firmly. "Though I admit I will appreciate the help." He tilted his head. "I don't suppose I can persuade you to reconsider?" Wyn had tried to persuade both Clarissa and the senior housemaid to take up the position, for it was hard to get staff up here, and he was unsure of the quality of the applicants, but both had been resolute in their refusal.

"No," Clarissa said, thumping the dough for emphasis. "I'm in no time of life to be haring around managing servants. I'm happy as I am: chief cook and bottlewasher."

"A most excellent bottlewasher," Wyn said, earning a laugh. "And a most excellent cook." He bowed. "Now I must leave you. The accounts won't do themselves."

He made sure not to cross the kitchen too swiftly, and the housemaid had removed herself by the time he passed through the doorway.

Now he just needed to deal with the overly interested brownie following him.

6

HOUSEFAE

WYN TOOK A circuitous route to the ballroom and pretended not to notice he was being followed the entire way. The Wintersol Tree stood in one corner of the large room and, sure enough, the children had already knocked several of the decorations off since the morning. The low-angled rays of the setting sun sparkled as they hit the stranded ornaments. He rescued them while observing the housefae out of the corner of his eye.

Now, was this unnatural amount of attention simple curiosity or something more sinister? Were there spies from his father's court among them? Or from the Court of Dusken Roses, whose princess he'd vowed and then failed to marry? *If so, I hope they enjoy hearing about my stellar potato-carrying abilities.*

It struck him, suddenly, that Lottie's mother was exactly the old-fashioned sort who would put milk out for brownies, and that brownies loved to gossip. Now that the High King had revoked the Iron Law, he could no longer depend on Faerie and Mortal gossip remaining separate. Sooner or later, the two would cross over. *Stormcrows.*

The central heating system didn't run through this room, and its two glass walls made it frigid when it wasn't filled with people, but it wasn't the temperature that sent a chill through him. Information was power, in Faerie and Mortal both. What if his father found out exactly what this estate—and more importantly, its lord—meant to Wyn? What if he chose to strike at Wyn through Stariel because of it? He leant down and picked up a stray ornament, curling his fingers around the fragile construct of wood and ribbon. His father must not find out that Wyn was…attached. At worst, he must assume Wyn was using Hetta for his own ends, that the relationship was cold-blooded political strategy on Wyn's part, that there was nothing here that could be used against him. *And that I will cut ties and leave without compunction if and when necessary.*

He swallowed and carefully replaced the ornament on the tree, outwardly oblivious to anything else. The evergreen was symbolic of immortality to Prydinians, supposedly keeping dark spirits away during the lengthening nights leading up to Wintersol. Wyn had wondered more than once if the tradition had roots in Faerie; several types of darkfae disliked pine. The sticky resin scent bloomed in the air as his fingers brushed the tree's needles, reminding him of Hetta's magic. She'd been busy today as well, and they'd been unable to find much excuse to be in each other's company. How had her conversation with her cousin Caroline fared? It could hardly have gone worse than his own as-yet non-existent one with Jack.

There! He caught a flash of movement under one of the many chairs lining the edges of the ballroom. Brownies, like many lowfae, were quicker than ferrets.

He was quicker, obviously.

Spinning away from the tree, he reached under the chair and hauled the brownie out by its scruff.

"Eep!" it squawked as it struggled, little fists flailing against his fingers. It wasn't foolish enough to use its claws. It also wasn't a brownie. Urisks were related to brownies, but the solitary creatures tended to favour the outdoors. What had brought this one inside?

The urisk was entirely androgynous, about the length of Wyn's handspan, and heavily furred. Its lower half ended in neat goat-like legs, while its upper limbs had tiny hands with retractable claws. Its face was faintly goat-like, with a wide, flat nose and large, tilted eyes that burned with a feverish desire to escape as it writhed.

"Lemme go! Lemme go!"

"Why were you watching me?" Wyn asked it, a thread of power colouring his voice. The instinct to dominate over the smaller fae was so strong that the compulsion was done before he could think better of it. Hetta would be disappointed in him.

The urisk answered without hesitation—not that it could do otherwise: "They want to know!" The tufts of its ears twitched. Wyn didn't even need to ask the next logical question, his power subconsciously swelling out and magically flattening the poor creature into submission.

"Everyone! Everyone wants to know everything! In FallingStar and out. It's good currency. Didn't mean no harm! Just watching! You're not even doing anything interesting now anyway!"

"Names," Wyn asked grimly.

"Some faraway courts. Ten Thousand Spires. DuskRose. That's all I know! That's all I know!" The little creature trembled in fright.

"You are of FallingStar," Wyn told it. That was how the fae knew Stariel: The Court of Falling Stars. "You should show more loyalty to your lord than to spy on her people."

"*You're* not of FallingStar. And we've no reason to be loyal to the mortal lord when she's banned us from the house for so long."

Always, unintended consequences. "She wasn't responsible for that. *I* was. You have her to thank for your free run of the house now. Tell the other housefae that I will put milk out for them every evening if they stop following me. Otherwise I will be forced to take..." he paused for effect, "*alternative* options."

The urisk's ears flared in surprise. It probably hadn't expected Wyn to let it go at all, but he placed it gently on the ballroom floor after delivering his threat. It didn't need to know it was a toothless one.

It looked up at him, eyes big and wary, then decided to take its chances. It fled, tiny hooves skittering on the smooth surface. Wyn watched it go. He needed, he thought with a sinking feeling, to talk to his godparent.

7

FEATHERS AND SHIRTS

I N THE USUAL way of things, Wyn would be waylaid by fifty-seven different people before he reached the front door. Of course, since right now he wouldn't mind putting off speaking to his godparent, the house was deserted, even when he detoured to the cellars to collect a suitable gift.

The grand entryway echoed as he changed his shoes for boots more suited to the outdoors and let himself out. His normal point of egress was at the back of the house, but although he might mentally bemoan the lack of distractions, he was committed enough to his chosen course not to actively derail it by attempting to exit via the kitchens.

He pulled up a simple glamour as he walked across the lawns. They were damp with dew, the day already darkening. Would it be better to leave this until tomorrow? But tomorrow he needed to leave early to drive with Hetta down to see the bank manager, and he needed more information before they left the safety of Stariel's bounds.

One of the few advantages of living in the fae courts—and to Wyn's mind, there were few indeed—was that clothing there was designed to accommodate the various needs of shapeshifters. Here, in the Mortal Realm, it was either destroy his shirt and coat or remove all his clothing from the waist up. Reaching for his bowtie, he recalled Hetta's nimble fingers, and a ghost of that sensation spun around him as he untied the strip of material and unbuttoned his shirt. Mortals were curiously body-shy, compared to the fae, but he'd observed that that seemed to only add to the allure of showing skin.

How would Hetta react, should she happen to wander into this part of the estate right now? Or in a few moments more, when he shed his mortal form? His musings, which had begun to grow heated, came to an abrupt, chilly halt.

He shook his head to clear it, using the cold as a focus. He'd chosen a sheltered spot in a stand of trees beside Starwater, but the air was still sharp in the deep shade. Ice shards glittered in the lake's surface. He wasn't as susceptible to the cold as a human, but in his mortal form he wasn't completely immune to it either, and it was nearing the heart of winter.

Shifting to fae form didn't require effort so much as...relaxation. Warmth spooled out through every sinew, followed swiftly by *elongation* as he unfurled his wings, taking satisfaction from the flexing of bone and muscle. Even in shadow, the silvery-white feathers glimmered, the weight of them both familiar and strange. He reached a hand up to touch one of his horns, idly considering the smooth, metallic texture, the slightly heavier feel of his head as he turned it this way and that. This was his native form, and yet he'd spent the last decade in his more human one, growing from youth to adult. A few weeks ago, when a draken attacked, he'd assumed his fae form for the first time in years.

Again, he wondered what Hetta would think of him like this. She'd seen his fae form only once—during the draken attack. They hadn't discussed it, but afterwards he'd felt her subtly withdraw from him for a time. Sometimes he caught her looking at him as if imagining the space around him filled with feathers. *I suppose it's unreasonable to expect her to accept me like this without a blink when this form is strange even to me now.*

"Ah, Marius," he said aloud to the silent lake, remembering his friend's words. "Why must you be right so frequently?"

He folded his shirt and coat into as neat a bundle as he could and tied them about his waist for safekeeping before making his way down to the lake edge. Away from the trees, he spread his wings, wrapped his magic around him like a cocoon, and launched into the sky. He was far too large a creature with far too wide a wingspan to defy gravity from such a starting position, and he drew on the magic of his birthright to aid him. It was a magic peculiar to the stormdancers—the greater fae of the Spires—bearing him upwards for those first few vital downstrokes.

The air resisted his efforts, chill and unhelpful. He had to struggle for height, leaning on his magic further, and his wings protested at the unaccustomed exertion. It grew a little easier as his muscles warmed and he gained enough altitude to take advantage of the headwind.

Disused senses flared to life: an awareness of wind currents, pressure, and the moisture content of the air. Colours swirled, beyond the limits of human eyesight, and a glorious awareness of magic set his skin afire. The dual nature of Stariel—mortal estate and fae court—became a thousand times more apparent than usual.

He had keen senses even in human form, but this was to that as a sunshower to a hurricane. The tight anxiety in his chest eased, replaced with sparkling wonder, and he let out a delighted laugh. The ground fell away, a patchwork of brown-and-green muddy fields spread before him as he climbed higher and higher. Buildings became picturesque miniatures of themselves, and tiny doll-figures shepherded equally doll-like sheep. The bright blue-green of the Stariel evergreen woods took on the appearance of cake decorations. Across the lake, the pale stone of the Dower House drew his eye, a central feature in his and Hetta's current plan to persuade the bank to lend them funds. Would it be worth circling it, to see if a birds' eye view would give better insight into the repairs needed before it could be rented out? But he resisted the temptation to procrastinate; there was an already neatly totalled list of repair estimates in Hetta's desk drawer.

The air was thin and difficult, with winds at cross-currents, absent of the warm, lazy thermals that made for effortless gliding above the rocky needles of Ten Thousand Spires. He had to fight for every downstroke, muscle rather than magic, clawing height from the chilly mountains inch by inch.

It was glorious.

He angled his wings, tacking one way then the other and resisting the wind's efforts to turn him about as he arrowed towards the Indigoes. Progress was slow, but heady anticipation kindled in his chest as he imagined the rapid, wild descent on the return journey, with the wind at his back, rushing straight down the mountainside.

Exhilaration took a beating when he landed in a clumsy tangle of limbs where the hilly terrain of the northern Sheepfold grew into the rockier feet of the Indigoes. *I am sadly out of practice.* He straightened himself out, uninjured but glad both of his glamour and the spot's isolation. In this season there weren't even sheep here to witness his ignominious landing; they'd all been moved to lower pastures for the winter. Thank the high winds' eddies—he suspected no amount of princely poise could cover rolling in the dirt like an upended chicken. *A dignified prince indeed*, he thought wryly, fastidiously shaking his wings to free them of loose stones and bits of grass.

Calling up a bit of air magic to help with the task, he folded his re-smoothed feathers back into place—and paused. His hand moved almost of its own volition, plucking one of his secondaries free with a tiny prick of pain. The feather lay in his hand, silvery-white, and he stared at it for longer than he should have before shaking his head. No. What was he thinking? He could not give Hetta one of his feathers, not when he hadn't committed to staying. *And not least because she'll think it a very odd gift*, he reflected. It was an old, rarely invoked stormdancer custom, denoting a trust deeper than mere intimacy.

He stuck the feather in his trouser pocket. Feathers were not the issue right now. He'd chosen one of the highest altitude shepherd's huts as his destination. It was as unoccupied as he'd hoped, but he didn't go inside. Instead, he made his way to a patch of dying grass in the lee of the hut. The wind stirred the lifeless blades, ruffling his coverts with its cool touch, promising snow.

Despite his elevated position, Stariel House wasn't visible, hidden by forests and the folds of the landscape, but he wasted a moment gazing in that direction anyway. Hopefully, Hetta would forgive him for what he was about to do. Storms above, he hoped *Stariel* would forgive him.

Before he could change his mind, he inscribed a rough circle around himself in the grass with the end of a sharp stick. To fae that did not have permission to enter Stariel, the land exerted a repelling pressure that grew weightier the longer one resisted it. To lesser fae, it was as impenetrable as a literal wall. To the greater ranks of Faerie, it was permeable, but only at great cost, and only if Hetta wasn't actively forcing her will down upon the invader. Wyn had been exempt from that pressure for nearly all his time at Stariel, first by the permission of the old Lord Henry, then by his daughter's.

Now Wyn extended that exemption with an effort of will, until it blanketed the space inside the circle. He sent a mental apology in the direction of the faeland. It wouldn't like this, and he could feel its presence already gathering around his little piece of magic suspiciously.

"Lamorkin," he called. "I summon thee. Lamorkin! Lamorkin!"

There was power in the names of fae, and in this case there was an additional bond between him and the fae he summoned. He invoked it as he called, throwing the name along with his will out along the bond. He must remember to teach Hetta to set the spells that would prevent translocation into the estate, but it was convenient that there was no such spell in place right now or his summons could not have worked.

He waited, and the bond pulled tight. A faint popping noise like pressure equalising against his eardrums, and then he was no longer alone in the circle.

The fae he'd summoned gave a slow and deeply unsettling smile, showing pointed teeth. "Why hello, my dear Hallowyn."

"Hello, Godparent," he said.

8

LAMORKIN

LAMORKIN WAS CURRENTLY presenting the appearance of a short, blue-skinned androgyne with slate-grey hair that matched the colour of their teeth and long claws. Since they were a shapeshifter without a primary form and took pleasure in disconcerting their audience, this was far from the strangest shape Wyn had seen Lamorkin in. Consequently, he merely bowed the correct degree of acknowledgement. Lamorkin pursed their bluebell lips, slightly piqued at his lack of reaction.

"Nearly ten years without a word, and now you summon me twice in one moon, princeling." Their voice, which was usually the same no matter what shape they took, was high-pitched and oddly resonant, as if they were speaking from more than one voice box simultaneously. They were also prone to making a complex clicking noise when in thought that no human was capable of reproducing. Lamorkin made such a sound now, their beetle-black eyes taking him in in rapid flickers. "Have you brought me a gift to compensate me for your rather abrupt summons? I was occupied elsewhere."

"Please accept this as thanks," Wyn said, holding out the bottle of sloe gin he'd brought with him from the house. Fresh bread was traditional, but Wyn knew his godparent's taste better than that.

Lamorkin's eyes gleamed, but they accepted the gift with unhurried grace. It disappeared with a similar pop to the one that had heralded Lamorkin's arrival.

"Well, now. I'm pleased to see you haven't forgotten your manners entirely, living with the mortals. Now let me look at you. You didn't give me time to properly examine you last time. You were far too rushed for a godchild who has not seen their godparent in years." Last time had been a few weeks ago, after the draken attack. Wyn had been desperately in need of information on the state of the fae courts. Prior to that, no one in Faerie had known his location—not even his godparent.

Lamorkin made a show of walking a slow path around Wyn, keeping inside the boundaries that he'd drawn. Wyn kept his expression impassive, though he greatly disliked having Lamorkin at his back. Habit, more than anything else; if Lamorkin had meant him harm, he'd have died ten years ago, on his father's orders.

"Well," said Lamorkin when they'd completed their circuit. "Well, indeed. Grown, haven't you? Perhaps time spent in the Mortal Realm wasn't so foolish a choice after all. You have changed much, letting yourself be subject to mortality." Their eyes slitted. "I see your blood feathers are starting to grow in. Very like your sire's they will look when they are finished."

Wyn flinched, an infinitesimal movement that most of his mortal friends would've missed, but Lamorkin caught it. They smiled a shark-tooth grin of satisfaction.

"You have grown too trusting," they said, shaking their head. They meant, of course, that Wyn was out of practice at hiding his reactions after so long away from the fae courts. The fae lived for such signs of weakness.

Wyn was too preoccupied by Lamorkin's comment about his wings to answer. He knew he resembled his father—a bit of knowledge so familiar he'd thought it lacked any power to hurt. But the news that his wings had begun to sprout his father's distinctive red patterning...it hit him bitterly, a betrayal he hadn't anticipated. King Aeros's wings were the same silvery white as Wyn's, except for the blood crimson of his primaries, a difference that Wyn had always found reassuring. But a stormdancer's colours sometimes changed as they aged. 'Bloodfeathers' was the term for the final stage of mature plumage.

He resisted the urge to fan his wings around to see the change for himself. It would be a futile exercise anyway, if the new feathers were starting between his shoulder blades; the change clearly hadn't yet reached even as far as his secondaries based on the untouched feather he'd plucked earlier, which meant he'd need a mirror to check. It didn't stop him imagining the change in his minds' eye, a thin line of small red feathers stark against white. How long till his bloodfeathers came in fully? *Even if they do eventually match Father's, it's only a superficial change*, he told himself sternly. *It means nothing.* But he wasn't sure he could've said the words aloud.

Lamorkin began to move again, pacing the boundaries of the circle that kept them from crossing over into the rest of Stariel.

"Hmmm." They made a liquid gurgling noise in their throat. "Busy, busy, boy, I see." Their shape began to distort with their restlessness, smooth blue skin growing lighter, scalier, fingerbones shifting so that what had been relatively human-shaped appendages now appeared as many-jointed as millipedes. Lamorkin wriggled their still shifting fingers in satisfaction as their ears migrated upwards on their skull, becoming long and floppy for a few seconds before drawing upwards and hardening into horned protrusions. It was always thus with one of the maulkfae; they changed as often and as easily as breathing.

"I would ask for your advice, godparent," Wyn said politely, standing as still and straight as he could manage under their appraisal.

The maulkfae paused and tilted their now serpentine neck to one side. Their beetle-black eyes narrowed, framed by poisonous green scales that transformed into tiny feathers as he watched. "I give nothing for free, boy. This you already know."

"Yes, godparent," Wyn said, not letting a trace of the frustration he felt into his voice. "But you have already been paid for your advice and protection."

"Not *limitless* advice and protection," Lamorkin argued, but they seemed pleased with his words. Lamorkin had always appreciated a certain degree of assertiveness, so long as it was tempered with respect. And, in their own deeply strange way, they were probably as fond of Wyn as of any living creature. A line of green feathers grew down from their eyes up and around their ears, darkening in hue and lengthening into graceful, decorative plumes.

"Not limitless, no," agreed Wyn. "But as far as you are able, if I ask it and it does not endanger you. So you agreed to my mother."

Lamorkin made another oddly liquid sound of satisfaction. "Your mother. Yessss. The price was paid."

Wyn didn't like to dwell on exactly what his mother had bargained. She'd never told him, and she'd disappeared before he'd been old enough to pursue the matter. Lamorkin, too, would not tell him. He suspected the price had been high. Godparents were rare and valuable. Traditionally, only royal fae both needed and could afford to bargain for them. Children were rare for greater fae and even more so for royal fae. But ThousandSpire was an exception, its bloodline unusually fecund. By the time Wyn had been born, King Aeros was of the view that he had sufficient children that any one requiring a godparent to reach adulthood was not worth the expense, so Wyn's mother had made the arrangements for her sixth child entirely herself. The wider court thought Wyn without one; one of his earliest memories was of his mother explaining to him that he must never reveal otherwise. He wondered, sometimes, if all his siblings had such secret godparents.

"I hope you've been well in the time since our last meeting."

Lamorkin's cheeks crinkled as they smiled, their mouth now much wider than it had been. "And that is why you are my favourite, Hallowyn. Your good nature will probably be the death of you, but it is so refreshing to be welcomed with such sincerity!"

"I do try to please you."

They laughed, a beautiful, disturbing sound made of harmonics and echoes, like a hundred songbirds trapped in a cave. "Oh, oh! I have missed you, clever one! But what a fuss you have caused."

"Will you tell me exactly what kind of fuss I have caused of late?"

Lamorkin paused in their circling and bared their teeth in wicked pleasure. Their body began to elongate, and two bony knobs protruded out from their spine. They had played this trick before, so Wyn wasn't outwardly discomposed when less than a minute later he found himself facing a fair approximation of King Aeros. Of course, his father's skin didn't ripple constantly, and nor did he have the habit of twitching his fingers as if unable to keep from intermittently testing his finger-joints. The key difference, however, was that King Aeros's eyes were burnished gold rather than the beetle black of the maulkfae.

Lamorkin extended their newly grown wings tentatively, the movement limited by the size of the circle. They glinted silver and crimson in the sunset. Lamorkin could have broken through Wyn's circle—it wasn't a construction designed to withstand forceful opposition—but then the full weight of Stariel's displeasure would fall on them. Already Wyn could feel Stariel's attention growing, aware that something was amiss within its borders. Hetta was probably getting a hell of a headache from it, he thought with a twinge of guilt.

Lamorkin spoke. This time it wasn't in their usual too-complex pitch, but in a voice that Wyn hadn't heard for nearly a decade and hadn't missed.

"It seems the old adage remains true, though I had begun to doubt it: 'The same storm that sinks ships brings unexpected treasure.'"

The King of Ten Thousand Spires had a deep, rich voice, and he spoke with a precise accent that was—if one set aside what he might be saying in it—pleasant to listen to.

Wyn swallowed. It was hard to remember that it wasn't really his father standing in front of him.

Lamorkin-Aeros went on, and it became clear that he was replying to someone, though Lamorkin didn't bother to reproduce the other side of the conversation. "Hmmm. Your proposal has merit, Rakken, though I am inclined to prefer Aroset's suggestion. We shall see." Lamorkin-Aeros chuckled, a bright, happy sound. "But in any case, perhaps my youngest will not be such a disappointment after all."

It became clear that was the end of the little display, for Lamorkin tilted their head and began to shift their form in earnest once more. White and red feathers became layers of delicate spines—completely impractical for actual flight, but still quite fetching—growing over Lamorkin like a cloak.

Cold that wasn't due to the weather crept down Wyn's spine so that he had to fight the urge to huddle into his wings.

"My siblings," he said. Aroset was the heir presumptive, second-oldest but first in cruelty; Rakken was third in line, the most ambitious and probably the most ruthless. Wyn doubted he would enjoy either of their schemes.

"Yessss," agreed Lamorkin.

"Do you know what either of them are proposing?" Was his father playing them against each other, dangling favour as the reward for whichever of them could strike at Wyn first? It wouldn't be the first time King Aeros had encouraged that kind of game. His heart sank. Did his siblings want him as dead as his father did? *All* of them? "And what of my other siblings?"

Lamorkin shrugged. "It's a fair warning, Hallowyn."

It was. Maulkfae were bound by their own peculiar rules; they had told him what they could.

Wyn paused. "Is there any way to free me from my oath to DuskRose's princess?" Before he'd fled, he had promised to marry Princess Sunnika. That had been before he'd realised his father planned to murder him and pin the blame for it on DuskRose, neatly providing an excuse to reignite the war between the courts. By fleeing, he'd broken the oath between him and DuskRose's princess and given both courts a strong motivation to retrieve him—dead or alive. On a personal level, the broken oath had also fractured Wyn's power.

"Yessss," Lamorkin said, clearly enjoying themself.

Wyn's lips twitched at the very fae bit of humour. He had walked straight into that. "Please, Godparent, tell me what you know about those ways." Before Lamorkin could speak, he held up a finger. "And I know you are about to say that my death will free me, but whilst I always appreciate your sense of humour, I'm in some kind of haste today." He gestured at the world beyond the circle's bounds. "Stariel grows increasingly upset at my bending of its boundaries. So I would ask you to take pity on your impatient godson."

Lamorkin pouted. "You are no fun, Hallowyn. I have years' worth of mockings to work through."

"And I do look forward to hearing them another time."

Lamorkin frowned at him, as if they were certain that Wyn was mocking them but couldn't quite figure out how. They fluffed up their spines, much like a sparrow settling into a dust bath, and grumbled, "Oh, very well then. But you cannot ask me to speak in straight lines entirely, my princeling. It is against my nature."

Wyn inclined his head.

"If you reject the solution of your own death, there are always other parties to consider," Lamorkin said slyly.

He frowned. "Princess Sunnika? Even if I were the murderous sort, that would not free me of my oath. If anything, it would only break it more resoundingly than before."

"I wasn't speaking of DuskRose's princess."

"Then who—oh, you mean my father," Wyn said with a sigh. "My own oath-debt will still stand, but the one affecting ThousandSpire will no longer hold, since it was between my father and DuskRose's queen. Which would free me of some of the political consequences of my broken oath, at least." He shook his head. "That is not a path open to me, godparent, although I thank you for the suggestion." Lamorkin had no true moral compass—like many of the older fae—so it was useless to try to explain to them why Wyn could not murder anyone, let alone his own father.

The Lamorkin nodded graciously. "Of course. You cannot reclaim the power that is your birthright that way."

Wyn didn't bother to refute this assertion. "Is there another way to heal the broken oath? Short of marrying Princess Sunnika," he added, to prevent Lamorkin's otherwise inevitable response.

"You could persuade DuskRose to voluntarily release you from your half of the promise," Lamorkin said, their eyes gleaming in appreciation as they found the loophole he hadn't closed. If DuskRose were even willing to negotiate, they would demand a high price to absolve him of his oath. Wyn had already considered that angle but had failed so far to think of anything he could offer DuskRose that might tempt them. Not when Wyn's broken oath tilted the balance in their favour in the war against ThousandSpire.

"Thank you, godparent. And other than that?" Patience, Wyn had found, was the key to a great many things.

Lamorkin tilted their head to one side. They were now covered with thick, luxurious black fur, with small, bear-like ears. They had shrunk in size so that they had to look up to meet Wyn's gaze. "If you wish for more power, you had not yet passed through the Maelstrom when you left the Spires."

"I had not thought..." Wyn trailed off, unable to find a proper ending to his sentence that wasn't false. The Maelstrom was a permanent magical storm at the heart of ThousandSpire. Legend said that it bestowed power upon those it deemed worthy. In reality, it mainly bestowed death.

Lamorkin ran their shining claws through their coat, letting out a little murmur of pleasure at the sensation. "You *had* thought, my Hallowyn. But you are afraid." Abruptly, they straightened, growing taller. "You are right to be afraid. You cannot survive the Maelstrom by playing at being human."

"What makes you think the Maelstrom will grant me any more power than I possess now?" Wyn countered.

Lamorkin made a disparaging sound. "There are no guarantees with such matters, foolish princeling. This you know. You asked for possibilities; I have given them to you."

Wyn shook his head again, the churning, lightning-shot clouds of the Maelstrom rising in his mind's eye. "I cannot reach the Maelstrom even if I wished it." Portals were the main magical method of moving between two locations in Faerie, but even if he'd been able to find an appropriate resonance point here in the Mortal Realm, the Court of Ten Thousand Spires had perhaps the strongest wards against all types of translocation in all of Faerie, built up over the years of its war with DuskRose. Trying to link to anywhere inside his home faeland was like hitting a wall of solid diamond. And he would never be able to reach the heart of ThousandSpire overland, not before his father detected his presence. It was a relief to have these excuses to fall back on.

At this, the maulkfae smiled, and it was again a disturbing gesture filled with far too many teeth. "Ah, but this I *can* help you with." Their fingers twitched, and after a second, something appeared in their palm. They held it out to Wyn, who didn't reach for it immediately. "Sensible, untrusting child. But take this gift. It will not harm you."

Wyn eyed the object they were holding out warily and didn't take it. Harm was a very subjective term. "What will it do?"

"If you whisper the name of the Maelstrom to it, it will take you there. And back again," they added in an impatient tone when he was still reluctant to take it, "if you whisper FallingStar to it. It will work but once in each direction."

He took the object, which turned out to be a deep red stone in the shape of a teardrop, hanging from a long silver chain. It hummed only slightly to his leysight, the spell so cleverly coiled it was nearly undetectable. It was a reminder of the strength of Lamorkin's magic, of the value of his mother's bargain. A translocation spell contained within an object—a small, portable object, no less—was uncommon enough to be impressive in and of itself. But one powerful enough to penetrate the wards of ThousandSpire? Wyn closed his fingers around the cold stone with a shiver of unease.

"Thank you, godparent," he said, after convincing himself that he was thankful to be given an increased number of options.

"Always so sincere," Lamorkin said fondly, reaching out to touch his cheek with the tip of one claw. "Now, since I have been so very helpful, are you going to tell your beloved godparent what you've been doing since I last set eyes on you?" A particularly fierce blast of wind penetrated the lee of the hut, making their feathers dance.

The cold tried to reach fingers beneath his own feathers, but he still held an insulating skin of magic about himself. Wyn smiled. "I think you have a fair idea, godparent. There's no one like you for knowing all the gossip that flows into the courts."

They clucked. "I would hear it from your own lips. Courting a mortal! Mortals almost always spell trouble for faekind. I do not understand your fascination with them."

"One particular mortal, godparent. They are not interchangeable, you know." His heart pounded. Lamorkin knew about him and Hetta; the courts knew about him and Hetta. Suspicious grocers suddenly seemed utterly trivial, the time he thought he'd have left here slipping away inexorably as the tide.

Lamorkin harrumphed. "They might as well be. I cannot approve of this. Why, you will age if you stay here in the Mortal Realm. You might live only another century! A mere blink."

Wyn smiled, thinking of his human friends' reactions to hearing a century spoken of as a short span of time. "I'm aware. Doesn't the romanticism of it move you, a little?" he added slyly.

His godparent narrowed their eyes. "Don't be impertinent, godchild."

He bowed his head. "Indeed, godparent." A gust of wind rattled the nearby shepherd's hut. "I believe you will like her, my mortal."

"The queen of this unnatural realm," Lamorkin said thoughtfully.

"Yes, although 'lord' is her preferred term."

"You're a fool, Hallowyn." The exasperation in their voice made the echoes more grating than usual.

"Isn't that why I am your favourite? You appreciate a difficult task, and this may be the most difficult one yet, to help me come through this with my skin intact."

"I should have asked your mother for more," they grumbled.

Wyn reached out a hand to clasp his godparent's fluid one. "I'm very glad you came. I had missed you."

"Hmmm," was all they said, but he could tell they were pleased. They stepped back and repeated, with what Wyn considered unnecessary emphasis: "You will never pass through the Maelstrom if you insist on playacting as human." Then, with only that faint popping noise to give warning, they disappeared.

Wyn let the circle crumple in on itself as soon as Lamorkin left. Stariel roared into the vacuum, alert and outraged. It sniffed him, dissatisfied but still respecting the permissions Hetta had given him to be here. The weight of its inspection made the hairs on the back of his neck prickle.

The amulet lay heavy in his hand, gleaming darkly, and he considered flinging it into some deep crevasse. Then he sighed and put

the thrice-cursed thing around his neck. It was never wise to scorn
a maulkfae's gifts. He flexed his wings experimentally; they ached
only slightly from the journey up here, and the return would be
much easier, with the wind at his back. But before he could take
off, the crunch of footsteps had him swivelling towards the sound.

Jack came to a stop a few feet from him, hands tucked into the
pockets of his great coat, and gave him a speaking look.

"Any minute now," he said, "I expect you're going to explain
what you're doing up here inviting fairies in and setting Stariel
into a panic."

9

COLD CONVERSATIONS

ETTA MIGHT BE the Lord of Stariel and therefore the person who commanded the power of the faeland, but Wyn had overlooked one important fact. *All* the Valstars were connected to Stariel and, excepting Hetta, none more strongly than Jack. On the up side, this meant he no longer needed to track Jack down for that conversation they were supposed to be having.

"Ah. Yes," Wyn said intelligently.

"How are you not half-frozen?" Jack frowned at Wyn's bare chest. "It's making *me* cold looking at you." Jack was dressed far more appropriately for the weather, bulky with layers. The ends of his woollen hat—one of Lady Philomena's creations—were tucked under his thick scarf so that only the tips of his brilliantly red hair were visible.

Jack's faithful dog, Shadow, wagged a tentative tail at Wyn, tilting her head this way and that at his wings. Eventually she decided that despite his altered appearance, he was the same person who could occasionally be counted on to bring her titbits, and she bounded towards him. Jack's frown deepened, but he didn't call her back.

Wyn's godparent's words about playing human still rang in his

ears, but there didn't really seem to be any alternative. He shifted
to his mortal form and immediately felt the bite of the wind. Icy
air washed down his spine, vulnerable without the shield of feathers. Hurriedly, he pulled on the shirt and coat he'd tied to his belt
for this purpose, smoothing himself back into some semblance of
mortal respectability.

Jack hunched against the cold and gave Wyn a distinctly unimpressed look. "We may as well go into the hut, since we're up here,
and then you can tell me what in blazes is going on." He turned and
stumped towards the small shepherd's hut.

Shadow nuzzled Wyn's kneecaps apologetically before sprinting
after her master. Wyn followed. The wind grabbed hold of his gar-
ments as he stepped out of the lee of the hut, cutting off abruptly
as he entered the single stone room. It was only a little warmer than
outside; no one had been inhabiting the place for some time now.
He didn't shut the door, since the shutters fitted to the windows
made that the only source of light. Shadow lay down next to the
cold hearth and perked her ears expectantly at the two of them.

There was a rough wooden table and stools inside the hut, but
Jack made no movement towards them. Instead he leaned against
one wall and folded his arms, fixing Wyn with a penetrating stare.
He had the same grey eyes as Hetta—the colour common among
the Valstars—and his expression briefly mirrored hers; disconcerting, as they didn't usually look much alike. Hetta and Marius both
took after their father, with Lord Henry's more narrow, angular features. Jack had a square jawline that he tended to jut out when he
was being stubborn, which was often. His thick brows were a shade
or two darker than the bright red of his hair, and they were currently pulled together in a harsh hawk's scowl. There was more than just
disapproval there; Wyn had the sense he was being weighed.

The silence of the room deepened, and Jack's scrutiny took him
back to a memory, years ago, of the first time they'd gone together
to the pub in Stariel-on-Starwater, the largest village that fell within

the estate's bounds. They'd been youths then, Jack the only person other than Lord Henry who knew Wyn's true nature. The secret had sat badly with Jack, and yet it had also made Jack feel some degree of responsibility towards him.

That night, Wyn had been anxious to fit in. There had been a good-natured arm-wrestling competition that Wyn would've been content to merely watch, but Jack was having none of it. So Wyn joined in and, carefully and with extreme good cheer, lost more than he won. This made him popular, and he found himself being declared 'a good sort'. Jack, too, had appeared to be enjoying himself. It was only later, as they were making their way back to the house long after nightfall, that Jack drew to a halt and said rather abruptly, "It's not good sport to lose on purpose."

Wyn had a hard head for liquor, but mortal alcohol hit rather more strongly than its fae equivalent.

"What?" he'd said, at a loss. He didn't understand Jack's anger; it had been a frivolous competition with nothing riding on it. He was fae—of course he was stronger than mortal men, but it would've been foolish to flaunt that. But Jack dragged him over to a tree stump next to the path and insisted that they go again, burning with some fierce emotion. So Wyn pressed Jack's forearm down onto the stump as if it were willow wand.

"Good," he'd said, grimly satisfied, and stumped back to the road, only a little unsteady on his feet.

"Did that make you feel better?" Wyn had asked, his tone light, as he tried to work out what was in the other man's mind.

Jack's mouth had gone hard, all signs of inebriety replaced with sudden, shocking sobriety as he weighed Wyn up. "Do you always do whatever you think will make people like you better?"

"In general, yes." Wyn intended his answer to come out teasingly, but instead it fell like a confession into the darkness. He waited for Jack to take umbrage, but instead Jack threw back his head and laughed and laughed.

"Well, at least you're honest about it." Then he'd slung an arm around Wyn's shoulders, drunken camaraderie returning. Wyn had thought the unsettling conversation over, but before they parted, Jack had fixed him with a pointed finger and said, quite seriously, "Don't ever lie to me because you think I'll find your answer more pleasing."

And Wyn had said, just as seriously, "I will not." He'd meant it, though it was impossible not to when he was physically incapable of lying.

And now they were here, adults rather than half-grown youths, but the expression on Jack's face was the same as it had been all those years ago, as if Wyn were a puzzle he couldn't decipher.

"What," Jack said eventually, "was that *thing* you were talking to?"

"That *person*," Wyn said, with a curl of disapproval, "was fae. My godparent, to be precise." How strange, to guard a secret so closely for years and yet find that he could release it with such ease. But it was a secret with no value here in the Mortal Realm, and certainly not to the Valstars.

Jack's fierce expression faltered. "You have a fairy godmother?" He reflected on his own words and gave a bark of laughter. "A fairy godmother!"

"More or less."

Jack's eyes narrowed. "For goodness' sake, speak plainly. I've no patience for your word-spinning tonight."

Wyn gave an ironic bow. "Very well, I will clarify: when I said I was speaking to my godparent, I meant exactly that. My godparent is a natural shapeshifter, not limited to a single 'true' form. Nor," he added, when Jack looked no more enlightened than before, "a single 'true' gender. So 'godmother' is not entirely accurate." That wasn't the whole reason, but if Wyn attempted to set out the full nuances of fae culture on the issue, they would be here all night.

"Oh," said Jack. Then, to Wyn's surprise, he added, "like your High King, then."

"Ah, not quite." Wyn had told Jack about the High King several years ago, on a night when the pair of them had been unusually inebriated on sloe gin. Jack had made a disparaging remark about the Southern monarchy and then, in a fit of abnormal curiosity, asked, "I don't suppose there's a fairy king, then? Or queen." Not wishing to explain his own relationship to royalty, Wyn had told Jack about the High King while he grinned with drunken affability. He hadn't expected Jack to remember.

At Jack's flat look, Wyn gave a faint smile. "I'm sorry, Jack. I'm not intentionally trying to exasperate you. Although it seems I exasperate you very well without trying—stormwinds know where we might end up if I was deliberately attempting to thwart you! The High King is a shapeshifter, yes, and also not limited to a single gender or form. But he generally prefers to assume either a male or female gender and remain as such for long periods of time." *And occasionally others*, he didn't add. "At present, he is the High King, and has been for at least two decades, in mortal time. Before that he was the High Queen for approximately half a millennium."

"But how—" Jack looked torn between disgust and fascination, then abruptly remembered he was supposed to be interrogating Wyn. He shifted irritably. "Damme if I know how you do it, but you always seem to slide away from the subject at hand! Why were you talking to your godparent, regardless of sex? And how did they get into Stariel? I'll wager you had a hand in that."

"I was seeking information about the current state of the fae courts. There is something going on, though I seem only able to catch the edges of it."

Jack straightened, and Shadow responded to the alarm in her master's stance by rising and going to butt her head against his knees. "They can't attack us here, though, can they?"

"No, but consider how many of your kin do not usually reside within Stariel's bounds. Or how often you are not within them yourself. Stariel is not the world."

Jack ruminated on this, fondling Shadow's ears. "It's about you," he said slowly. "The fae want you."

"I'm afraid so."

Jack shook his head. "How is this good for Stariel, Wyn? Or for Hetta? What about your oath to protect the estate?" He huffed. "Not that it's not a relief to know you *can* be selfish, but did it have to be this?" He sounded more exasperated than angry as he answered his own question. "Of course it did. You never do things the simple way, do you?" He wrinkled his nose. "But really—Hetta?"

"Are you questioning my taste?"

"Your sanity, morelike."

"I had heard that proper mortal etiquette was to sing your female relatives' praises and then threaten to skewer potential suitors, rather than to suggest said relatives are not worthy of courting," Wyn pointed out, amused.

"Aye," Jack agreed, his lips curving despite himself. "Consider yourself threatened then." He sobered, crossing his arms and settling his weight back against the wall. "Normally I'd say it's your own business, but…blimey, Wyn. It's an unequal match. You must see that?"

Wyn tilted his head. "Unequal for which of us?"

"Both," said Jack. "I mean, how does this end? You can't marry her, and you can't *not* marry her once the news gets out. And it will."

"Why *must* I marry her? Why *can't* I marry her?" Wyn said, deliberately obtuse. They could argue over the mortal reasons for 'must', but Wyn alone knew the reason why he *couldn't*, curse the ties that bound him. What were Jack's reasons? Did the prospect of scandal and the fact that Wyn was fae matter to him so much? Or did he too fear that any connection to Wyn would only endanger Hetta?

But Jack didn't rise to the bait. Instead he surveyed Wyn through narrowed eyes. "Because I'll bloody well shoot you, otherwise."

Wyn laughed, taken by surprise.

"I mean it, Wyn. End it. The sooner the better. Or you'll break her heart when you leave. Don't tell me you want that."

Wyn froze, feeling a desperate longing to be high above the Indigoes again, with the world made small and simple below. "What makes you think I plan to leave? Stariel is more home to me than anywhere else in the world."

"You'd be that selfish, then? Bring fairy politics and monsters down on all of us? See Hetta suffer the scandal of being seduced by a servant—you know that's what they'll say. Or try and pretend to be human for her sake?"

A little riled, Wyn retorted, "I have pretended well enough, for ten years. Besides, humanity is relative. You know that the Valstar line already lays claim to fae blood through your original forbear. Tell me, how human do *you* feel?"

"More human than you," Jack said, eyes flashing.

Abruptly, Wyn regretted his temper and attempts to needle Jack. They were only thinly disguised ways to direct his own guilt outwards, and Jack didn't deserve them for trying to protect his cousin and family. Wyn raised his hands in submission. "I'm sorry—I should not have spoken so. It is only that I am…somewhat sensitive about the topic."

Jack glared at him. "That's exactly what I most dislike about you, Wyn. You can never just have a proper row, can you? Sometimes what you need is a good row."

"If my affability offends you, I am sure one or other of your relatives will be happy to oblige you with an argument on any number of topics."

"Affable, my ass. Don't think I haven't noticed you've made no promises to break things off with Hetta."

Wyn was silent.

"Damn your feathery hide," Jack grumbled. "I can't force you to make the right choice, but I'm not going to run to the rest of my relatives, if that's what's fretting you. *I'm* not going to be the one responsible for dragging my cousin's name through the dirt." He glared at Wyn to make sure he understood exactly who Jack *did* hold responsible for that. "But I won't put your secrets over Stariel's safety if it comes to it."

"I would not ask you to."

They made their way out of the hut, the air between them sharper than the icy winds.

WHEN WYN RETURNED TO the house, he found Hetta had gone out for a driving lesson with Marius. He stored Lamorkin's amulet securely in his room under wards, glad to have it no longer on his person; he hoped it would remain sealed in its box forever. But he couldn't keep from turning his godparent's warning over as he navigated the convoluted route back down to the steward's office. His preoccupation nearly caused him to collide with a person rounding the corner at speed in the long hallway, and only his quick reflexes saved them both.

"Sorry—"

"My apologies—"

They both spoke reflexively and then faded into silence as their eyes met.

Caroline was usually a very self-composed young woman. Just at this moment, however, her usual prim composure wobbled. Colour washed over her cheeks, nearly as red as her hair. She was no doubt recalling the previous evening.

What had Hetta said to her? Was she about to repeat Jack's

censure? If so, it would be for mortal rather than magical reasons, since Caroline didn't know Wyn was fae and Hetta hadn't enlightened her. He knew this with ironcast certainty. People looked at him a little differently, once they knew.

When in doubt, show none. He nodded his head in acknowledgement. "Miss Caroline."

A crease formed between her brows, and she looked him up and down as if trying to decide whether to say anything or not. The hallway wasn't an ideal location for a private conversation, and Wyn stretched his senses, checking no other mortals lurked around corners within earshot. Thankfully, there were none.

"It may ease your mind to know that Jack has already had words with me." Maybe he could avoid the *third* conversation of the day in which someone mistrusted his relationship with Hetta.

The corner of her mouth twitched. "Did they have any effect?"

He spread his hands. "I assure you, I do not wish to taint Hetta's good name." *Yes, and wishes are for children, as Father would say.* But perhaps the sentiment would prompt Caroline to promise she'd say nothing of this to anyone else. He moved his weight subtly to suggest that they might each continue on their way now if she were willing.

Caroline didn't point out that refraining from kissing her cousin in the first place would do a lot more good than wishing. Instead, her frown deepened, and to his surprise, she looked concerned rather than disapproving.

"No, that's...I mean, I'm sure you don't." She opened her mouth, shut it, and then opened it again before saying in an undertone, "Be careful, Wyn. Hetta's not petty, but, well...she *is* your employer, if this goes badly."

Cheeks flushing, she turned away and walked briskly past him. He stared after her, torn between amusement, sentiment, and affront. Caroline was worried he'd lose his *job*, if his affair with Hetta went public? *That* was not a turn of conversation he'd predicted. *I am a fae prince! Employment is the least of my concerns!* he had the egotistical urge to shout after her.

He shook his head. Unreasonable to be annoyed that she thought him only the role he'd played, and yet he was. Annoyed—but also oddly touched that she cared about his wellbeing in such a fashion. Warmth filled him like sunlight, throwing the glittering fragments of his dishonesty into sharp relief.

At least, he thought philosophically, Caroline's concern meant she'd probably keep the affair to herself for the time being. He continued to his office and unlocked the door. The steward's office was a more battered version of the lord's study, owing in part to the fact that old Lord Henry had not had much time for bookwork. Wyn had recently moved his headquarters to it from the housekeeper's office on the ground floor, readying that room for its hopefully soon-to-be-appointed occupant.

There was a note resting on the desk:

> *To my most provoking steward—*
> *The linesmen finally sent through their quote. I've been through the accounts with a fine-tooth comb, but by my reckoning we're going to need to borrow quite a sum. Do you mind checking my figures—though I fear you too will come to a similarly deplorable conclusion.*
> *Hetta*
> *P.S. Don't think that we aren't going to have words about whatever it was you were doing up in the Sheep Fold!*

He smiled fondly at Hetta's handwriting and found her calculations neatly laid out on a scrap of paper next to the ledger and the linesmen's quote for installing phone lines and elektricity to the house. Making himself comfortable in the leather chair behind the desk, he got to work.

Wyn had always liked mathematics. Growing up, his interest in the subject had been tolerated but not encouraged; mathematics wasn't considered a particularly princely skill. Using it now to further Stariel's interests filled him with deep satisfaction. His father would hate the idea of his son performing such a service. Wyn was self-aware enough to admit this added to his enjoyment.

He took less satisfaction, however, in coming to a similar conclusion to Hetta as to the sum that would need to be found. They were going to see the bank manager in Alverness tomorrow. For cultural mortal reasons that even ten years in this realm hadn't been sufficient to make him fully grasp, the bank had been reluctant to entrust Stariel's finances to purely feminine hands—hence Wyn's recent appointment to steward after Mr Fisk's treachery.

The major problem was going to be cashflow, as they'd already known, but if the drainage scheme they'd planned increased the rate of return on the lower flats and they could refurbish the Dower House before midsummer…he sank into a hypnotic world of numbers, where every problem had a clear, crisp solution. Outside, the sky shadowed to indigo.

The footsteps were as familiar as his own pulse, which quickened at the sound, and he knew who it was even before she knocked. Hetta came in with sparkling eyes and cheeks and lips reddened from the cold. She wrinkled her nose at the accounts book.

"My calculations match yours," he told her, rising and coming out from behind the desk. "How was the driving lesson?"

"Good, thank you." She met him halfway, her palms smoothing over the lapels of his coat. He leaned into the touch, and some bit of tightness he hadn't been aware of carrying unwound itself. "Though I think I alarm Marius sometimes. Hopefully I don't turn your hair white tomorrow." She reached up to tousle his hair, smiling. "Although how would we tell? Now, what in Simulsen's name were you doing up in the Sheep Fold before? It made my head ring."

"My apologies." He told her about Lamorkin.

There was a pregnant pause. "Remember our previous discussion regarding secrets?" Hetta asked with some exasperation.

"This was actually me trying *not* to keep secrets from you," he said sheepishly. "Though I now see that it perhaps would've been better to tell you what I intended *before* summoning my godparent. I am sorry; I am making a terrible start at this transparency business." The bone-bred instincts of Faerie to avoid revealing vulnerability were of no use to him here; he needed to be less fae, for her.

Her lips curved. "Well, it's not as if your ingrained tendency towards secrecy is a *surprise*, but do try to get out of the habit sooner rather than later." She interlaced their fingers and folded them matter-of-factly onto the seat beneath the window. Wyn had no objection to this arrangement, though he kept his ears pricked for sounds from the hallway, not wishing to be caught twice in two days for the same transgression. "All right, tell me about this godparent of yours."

The weight of her leaning against him sparked yearning and something hotter, darker, and entirely not appropriate to his office. It felt like flying; it felt like falling. He met Hetta's eyes, and the exhilarating thing he could not control seemed to expand between them.

Desire. Wyn named it silently, this sparking awareness of spaces and forms. Naming it didn't lessen its power, but then it wasn't a sensation born of magic, was it? And desire wasn't its true name, not at root; it sprang from a deeper emotion, one he would *not* name, not to Hetta, not yet, not when he could not promise her he would stay.

"Lamorkin is my oldest ally," he began instead, taking a firm grip on his instincts, his vanity thankful for how unruffled he sounded.

When he finished telling her the whole of it, she frowned past him, towards the lake, painted gold and black in the last sun's rays. "Should we still be going outside the estate boundaries tomorrow if the fae are up to something?"

He had been wondering the same, but... "We could delay, but

for how long? Lamorkin's warning was so vague, with no indication of timeframe. I admit I do not like it much either, but we will be surrounded by iron all the way to and from Alverness, and we mean to be back before nightfall." And Stariel needed to secure more funds for its future; he couldn't jeopardise that.

"Well, I'm not precisely helpless if we do run into trouble," Hetta said thoughtfully, unfurling her fingers and summoning a small ball of fire to hover in the centre of her palm. The glowing orange flames danced, throwing flickering shadows across her skin before she snuffed it out.

Wyn's magic coiled restlessly in response. "Neither am I."

GRIDWELL'S BANK

THE NEXT MORNING, Hetta got into the kineticar accompanied by an uncharacteristically quiet Wyn. She wasn't sure what lay at the root of his pensiveness—fae machinations or domestic concerns—but she let him have it anyway, busy with the mechanics of starting the engine and fiddling with gears. Marius had been a thorough if slightly anxious teacher, and she felt confident enough as she carefully manoeuvred out of the converted garage. It was nonetheless reassuring to know Wyn could take over if she faltered.

It was a good day for driving, fine and clear. Wisps of cloud striped the brilliant azure sky, and the dew sparkled on the grass along the driveway. There were some hiccups during the first few minutes of their journey, but she hit her stride soon enough, and they curved smoothly away from the house. She beamed at the view in triumph. If only every part of lordship were this straightforward!

"You should applaud my skill, you know," she said lightly, "or I'll begin to fear I'm doing something wrong."

He smiled faintly. "You drive well. I thought you would." But he remained abstracted, his gaze unfocused as he leaned against the

window. The kineticar's configuration required some minor con-
tortions on his part, not being designed for someone of his height.

They didn't speak as she slowed to pass through the village of
Stariel-on-Starwater, carefully steering the vehicle through the
rabbit warren of turns. It was relatively quiet at this hour, but Hetta
still waved at the few inhabitants they passed. She only recognised
a couple, and it made her feel like a terrible lord. Wyn, of course,
knew all of them, and absently supplied her with names when
she asked.

This would be the first time she'd left the estate since being
chosen. As they approached the border, her grip on the steering
wheel tightened. She knew their location relative to the border as
precisely as she knew the limits of her own body, though there was
no physical marker, only empty road. She slowed the car as they
drew near that invisible line until they were only crawling. Bracing
herself for the loss of sensation, she edged over the estate boundary
and let out a startled breath.

"I can still feel it! Stariel. It's fainter, but it's still there! The
bond, I mean. Do you think it will weaken with distance?" She
mentally tapped the bond; it was like hearing someone move in a
distant room, knowing they were close without being able to see or
speak to them.

"I do not know, I'm afraid. Perhaps," he offered.

"Hmmm," she said as she accelerated, not sure how she felt about
this development. Before becoming lord, her connection to Stariel
hadn't existed outside the estate. It was disconcerting to find that
now she couldn't truly escape from it. Even more disconcerting,
however, was not being able to sense the world around her now
they were driving on non-Stariel lands. It made her feel oddly blind.

Brown-and-grey farmland stretched to either side of the road. To
the west were the distant purple shapes of the Indigoes; to the east,
the Saltcaps. Weak winter sunlight watered the landscape in pale
yellow. Hetta didn't even notice Wyn's continued silence, caught

up in her own ruminations on the nature of lordship, falling into a hypnotic trance of road, steering wheel, and wide blue sky.

"The general population of Stariel apparently thinks me some kind of monkdruid," Wyn said eventually.

Hetta broke out of her trance with a startled laugh and risked a quick glance at him. The sunlight limned his profile in gold, turning his white-blond hair into pale flame. His focus remained on the road ahead, but there was something to the shape of his mouth that told her he was both amused by his own dry humour and waiting for her reaction. It was an expression she'd seen him adopt a lot over the years, though only when they were alone.

"I was wondering about that, actually. Here you are, infernally beautiful, and yet I've never seen anyone so much as flutter their eyelashes at you. It's intentional, isn't it?" He was silent, and she sighed. "I'm going to be angry at you again in about thirty seconds, aren't I?"

"Well, you *did* express a wish for more anger in our relationship," Wyn pointed out. He snuck a look at her. "Infernally beautiful, did you say?"

She briefly took her hand off the gear stick so she could poke him in the shoulder. "Don't let it go to your head, vain creature. All right then. What's the explanation this time for what I assume is some nefarious use of magic?"

He explained about fae allure. "It's a form of minor glamour native to greater fae, something we do without conscious thought. It makes us appear, perhaps, a little more... fascinating than we would be otherwise."

"A sort of magical lipstick?"

He chuckled. "It's not a bad comparison." He told her about skewing his so as to subtly discourage romantic interest, and she laughed at the cook's resulting glum assessment of his lovelife. "It's possible I overdid it," he added ruefully.

It was again an uneasy glimpse into the more concerning aspects of fae magic, but it also explained something that had been puzzling her until now. Wyn might maintain an entirely proper manner with the household, but no degree of professionalism should be able to transform over six feet of broad-shouldered male with the features of a woodland god and shining silvery hair into something as staid and unalluring as an elderly butler.

"So why hasn't it affected me, then?" she asked.

"I think it did, before you left. When you came back, it's possible your own magery gave you immunity." He paused and confessed, with some sheepishness, "But also…I wasn't trying as hard as I could have not to be attractive to you."

She laughed again, a giddy lightness swelling in her chest.

ALVERNESS WAS THE LARGEST city of any size in the far north; even the former Northern capital of Greymark was still many miles further south. The wide river Ess bisected the city, and the distinctive shape of the distilleries lining its edges woke mixed feelings of nostalgia in her. She'd done her schooling here until the age of sixteen, attending a boarding school for girls during the week and catching the train back up to Stariel every Friday night. It had been a relief to be away from her father, and a handful of the other girls and teachers had proved much-needed kindred spirits—but the rigid lessons and narrow assumptions of what her future would be had felt like a cage inexorably closing around her. She had a fleeting thought for the weight of duties and expectations of her new role, and a steely determination filled her. Stariel wasn't a cage, and she wouldn't let it become one. Bringing some degree of modernity to the estate was the first step in establishing that, shaping her own destiny rather than being shaped by others.

Gridwell's Bank was an impressive building on a paved street near the city centre. Hetta parked the car successfully after only two attempts. She took a deep breath before getting out of the car, settling her nerves into place.

Wyn held a briefcase containing accounts books and their notes. "Our numbers are solid," he murmured, his eyes full of calm confidence. At least her steward had faith in her, even if his judgement couldn't be considered objective by any stretch.

"Yes," Hetta said, to herself rather than him. The bank's ornate stonework still loomed down at her, solid numbers or not. She rested her gloved hands briefly on top of the kineticar's iron, summoning her courage. At least they hadn't met any malevolent fae on the way here, and the formal, mundane busyness of the bank was reassuring. "To battle, then."

He nodded, lips curving. "My Star." She watched with some amusement as he assumed the role of rigidly correct steward, every inch of him radiating aloof competence. They'd agreed beforehand that this approach would be best; the bank manager was conservative.

The bank lobby was filled with hushed industry, rustling paper and the click of shoes on the polished floor. Bank tellers looked out at the world through screens of special glass designed to see through any attempts at illusion, which made Hetta feel self-conscious even though she wasn't illusing anything at present. Even her lipstick was real. She was the only woman currently in sight, and she fleetingly regretted having worn skirts rather than trousers. But no, she was here for Stariel, and that was more important than tweaking the noses of old-fashioned bankers. Straightening, she reminded herself that she was the ruler of the North's oldest estate, and she had every right to be here.

They were shown into the bank manager's office only ten minutes after arriving, which Hetta took as a good sign. When she'd lived and worked in the great Southern city of Meridon, she hadn't even been *able* to open a bank account in her own name, even after waiting on the bank's leisure for a lot longer than a mere ten minutes. Lord Henrietta Valstar evidently held more clout with such institutions than Hetta the no-name illusionist.

The bank manager, Mr Thompson, rose from his desk to greet them. He was a short, stout man with spectacles, perhaps fifty years of age. Mr Thompson knew well how the estate's accounts stood, for he'd been instrumental in discovering the previous steward's skimming. Wyn and Hetta had built a painstaking case for a loan since he'd last met with Hetta.

Mr Thompson addressed his remarks chiefly to Wyn, who gently deflected them back to Hetta. There was no malice in him, but it didn't make his paternal attitude any less irritating.

After the pleasantries were done, Mr Thompson did finally address himself to her first rather than last, cocking his head to say, "I am pleased that you've been able to fill the steward's position so quickly after that rather unfortunate business when last we met. However, I wonder if you will allow me to satisfy myself as to Mr Tempest's experience, since Gridwell's needs to assure itself that Stariel's finances are in competent hands?" He smiled, though it didn't reach his eyes.

"Of course," Hetta said. "That *is* why he's here with me today."

Mr Thompson hesitated. "I should like to talk with Mr Tempest alone."

Anger flared, but she wanted this interview to go well. Stariel was in dire straits, financially, thanks to the efforts of the previous steward.

Wyn gave a minute nod. He would back her whatever she chose, but he thought she ought to let Mr Thompson have his way. She thought of Wyn's warming spells on the cottages, and of the elektric streetlights of Alverness. She could sacrifice a little pride if it meant securing a loan for Stariel's future, she told herself sternly, even if it made her want to do something childish like set Mr Thompson's in-tray on fire.

"Very well," Hetta said crisply. This was just *one* compromise, not surrender. Once they'd secured this loan, well, she would show Mr Thompson exactly how unwarranted his prejudice was. She'd dashed well make Stariel *thrive* under her management. In a minute or two she'd be able to remember all the nobler, more altruistic reasons for wanting this, but right now the most important one was so she could have the petty satisfaction of waving her success in Mr Thompson's face.

Mr Thompson nodded, as if it hadn't occurred to him that she might *not* agree with his high-handedness. "There is a very fine tea room opposite the bank, if you do not care to wait in the reception room downstairs, where you are most welcome, of course."

Hetta had to bite her tongue to keep from telling him what she thought of being so dismissed. "I shall return in half an hour then."

Mr Thompson's expression told her that he would've liked to send her away for longer, but she ignored it, giving Wyn a fierce look on her way out. She just hoped he knew what he was doing.

HETTA IGNORED THE TEA room and chose instead to wait in the pub around the corner, purchasing a broadsheet from a newspaperboy before she did so. The pub was of the traditional sort found in every village, all low ceilings, dark wood, and gleaming taps, the smell of smoke and ale impressed into the walls. In Meridon, cocktail bars and dance halls were in fashion. While Hetta heartily endorsed the trend towards lighter, airier spaces playing modern music and serving delightful fruity drinks, there was something reassuring about a pub of this sort, which probably looked exactly the same now as it had five hundred years ago.

Warm air washed over her as she entered, and Hetta loosened her scarf with relief. The taproom was well lit with the new elektric lights. *We must get those installed in the village*, Hetta thought fiercely, feeling a bit better about giving in to the bank manager's request. If all went to plan, by next winter Stariel would have them too.

Hetta was quickly ushered through to the lounge bar, where cheerful orange flames danced in the fireplace. She chose a seat at a table nearest the warmth, pulling off her gloves as she sat and asking for mulled wine. She stared blankly at her bare hands, her mind still back in the bank manager's office. It was difficult not to think about the fact that Wyn could compel people if he wanted, though she wasn't truly worried he'd give in to the temptation to do so, not when he was so uneasy with that side of his magic.

Unless she asked him to.

The thought drew her up short. *Would* he compel the bank manager, if she asked, if mundane logic failed? This would arguably be for the greater good. But she'd always be able to argue that now, as Stariel's lord, wouldn't she? If she started justifying things for that reason, where would she stop?

With a wisp of regret, Hetta let go of the idea. Deep down, she knew it had only ever been an idle fantasy anyway. Quite aside from the slippery slope it represented, she remembered what had happened with John Tidwell. Compulsion had stopped the immediate harm he'd intended—blackmail—but had also driven him to act in anger, injuring Hetta's younger half-sister Alexandra in the resulting accident. Besides, relying on ethically questionable fae magic probably wasn't a good way to begin her lordship, she told herself sternly.

The barmaid arrived to put down an earthen mug brimming with spiced red liquid, startling Hetta from her musings.

"There y'are, miss," she said. "Just the ticket for a day like today. You can feel the snow coming. Maybe we'll have a white Wintersol!"

"Maybe, though I hope it will hold off for today!" Hetta said, not correcting the girl's address. It woke the same familiar-and-yet-not feeling Wyn did. He wasn't all that had changed since her lordship. "Thank you."

She wrapped her hands around the mug and brooded into the flames. Without thinking, she reached out with her land-sense, and mentally stumbled when only the tiniest ping of acknowledgement came in response. It felt like trying to catch something with numb hands.

On the one hand, lately there had been moments when she hadn't been sure if her own emotions were mere reflections of Stariel, and it was reassuring to know for sure that here and now her thoughts were entirely her own; on the other, well, she'd grown used to the convenience of exerting her will and receiving instant information.

She spread her newspaper on the table, seeking distraction. Its pages were full of politics, gossip, and local affairs, mostly centred on Greymark, the largest Northern city. Alverness got a few lesser mentions, but more, she saw with amusement, than Meridon, Prydein's capital, even though it dwarfed both Northern cities by an order of magnitude. North and South had been united under one crown for three hundred years, but one could be forgiven for thinking it had been only a few days.

Hetta had never paid much attention to politics, Northern or otherwise, but one article about the disagreement between the Lords Conclave and the Greymark Worker's Union gave her pause. Stariel was the oldest and one of the larger estates in the North. Although its wealth had dwindled, the idea of Stariel—isolated, traditional, riddled with folklore—still held a certain amount of sway in the common psyche that probably had political capital, if Hetta wanted it to.

Her father had kept himself apart from politics, rarely attending the Northern Lords Conclave and casting his vote by proxy if at all. It had made it easy to forget that her responsibilities extended beyond just Stariel. But…perhaps there might also lie the answer to her increasing number of questions about her lordship. The gods knew very few people outside of Stariel realised quite how magical the estate was; could there be similar isolated estates whose rulers Hetta could ask for advice? Wyn might know if there were more human faelands, and perhaps Marius would have an idea of any relevant folklore about other estates. She made a mental note to ask them both, and to check when the Conclave was due to meet next. She had a funny feeling they needed to ratify her membership or some such bureaucratic nonsense.

"Lord Valstar!" a deep male voice enthused from behind her. Before she could do more than glance up in surprise, the speaker had pulled out the chair opposite and seated himself across from her. He held a wine glass lazily in one hand. "I hope you don't mind the intrusion."

She stared at him. He was familiar and yet she couldn't recall his name nor where she knew him from. But how could she have forgotten someone like him? For he was extremely good-looking, with rich brown skin, knife-sharp cheekbones, and a strong jawline. He wore his long dark hair tied back, the colour glinting with warmer, almost metallic tones in the firelight. She'd given both heroes and villains his sort of face and manner at the theatre—roguish heroes, and villains of the kind people secretly swooned over even as they condemned them. But it was his eyes that struck her most; vividly, unbearably green and filled with keen intelligence. She would have remembered those eyes, but they sparked no recollection. Why, then, did she have the sense that she'd met him before?

"Forgive me," she said, "for though you seem familiar, I cannot recall your name."

He laughed. He had a decadent laugh, dark and sinful as chocolate. It was the sort of laugh that made one feel both effortlessly witty and anxious to continue being so, just for the chance to hear it again. It struck another chord of familiarity and yet, again, she was certain it was the first time she'd ever heard it.

"It would be extraordinary if you did, since we have not met before, Lord Valstar." The green of his eyes brightened. "I will try not to be insulted by your sense that you have met me before, for I know where that must come from."

"Do you?" said Hetta, mystified. "Please do share this insight, for I'm quite at sea. You seem to know who I am. Will you introduce yourself?"

"No, I think not," he said decisively, putting his wine glass down. "Not yet. He will be able to tell you well enough, and I don't care to air my name about for those who might be listening at present." He leaned back in his seat, an air of 'your move' about him.

His expression didn't betray much as his gaze flicked over her. In another man, the assessment might have been sexual, but this one felt like he was toting her up, calculations turning behind those green, green eyes.

Hetta raised an eyebrow at him. She knew he was expecting her to demand answers but saw no reason to gratify him. Instead she completed her own assessment: almost unnaturally good-looking, expensive tailored dress, an air of command, extremely arrogant, oddly familiar, and reluctant to speak his name aloud.

A fae.

On the heels of that insight came another, and she wondered that she'd failed to see the resemblance until now. She mentally filled the space behind him with vast feathered wings, unable to help speculating what he looked like in his true form.

Her heart pounded, but she took a calm sip of her mulled wine and willed herself to convey only polite interest. If Wyn could do it, then so could she.

"There's a strong family resemblance, Your Highness—is that the correct address?" she said, proud of how steady her voice was. She'd intended to startle him, and serve him right for being so deliberately obtuse, but he merely gave a slow, satisfied smile.

He inclined his head regally. "It is, Lord Valstar."

Would he know if she reached for her pyromancy? Wyn had a sixth sense for magic, and she wasn't sure how far that fae ability extended. She was keenly aware that her last encounter with Wyn's court had involved a winged monster trying to eat her and Jack. If only she stood on Stariel's lands!

Wyn! If his brother—he *had* to be one of Wyn's brothers—was here, what did that mean for Wyn? He had five older siblings, he'd told her, but she knew nothing else about them. Except that they were definitely not one big happy family. Was this a diversion while the others attacked?

The man's smile widened, as if he knew precisely what she was thinking. Abruptly she was done with her pretence of calm, done with this game.

She stood, her chair thudding back. "I have no patience for cryptic. Explain yourself or I'm leaving."

The man didn't react to her sudden show of temper. He took another sip of his wine and viewed her through half-lidded eyes. "You should not be so hasty, Lord Valstar, for I'm about to offer you something." He reached into his coat pocket and drew out a stoppered vial with a flourish. Whatever it contained was impossible to see through the elaborate worked metal of the container.

"Where I come from," he said, "there are places known as dark-sinks." He twirled the vial thoughtfully as Hetta wondered why in the nine heavens he was giving her an impromptu lesson on Faerie geography. "Unpleasant places, darksinks, and nearly infinite in their variety. In one such location there lives a type of creature known as a lug-imp. It has a painful and poisonous bite that is deadly to those who have broken oaths."

Wyn. Wyn, who the fae Gwendelfear had called *oathbreaker* with venomous repetition.

"Ah," he said as Hetta scrabbled at the table for balance, dizzy with sudden fear. "I see you know someone who meets this description." His smile turned wolfish. "Yes, lug-imps are a singularly foolish choice for the Mortal Realm, where promises are made and broken with distressing regularity, but"—and here he shrugged, the gesture eerily similar to Wyn's when he was pretending something didn't matter— "one does not always get one's way."

She had to find Wyn. She drew fire into her veins until it crawled under her skin, straining for release. Usually Stariel gave her own natural abilities a boost, but the trickle from the land was thin and sluggish at this distance. It would have to be enough.

She turned away, but the fae stopped her with a hand on her forearm, strong as iron. She hadn't seen him move.

"I said I had something to offer you, Lord Valstar." He relaxed his grip on her arm and tilted the metal vial in his other hand, drawing her attention to it. "This is an antidote to the venom of the lug-imp, which you may need today."

She couldn't stop her instinctive movement towards it, but he'd pulled it out of reach before she'd done more than raise her arm from the table edge. No one in the pub reacted to their altercation, and Hetta felt a shiver of unease. *Is he using just glamour*, she wondered, *or compulsion?*

He tsked, settling his weight back in his chair. "You mistake me, Lord Valstar. I am no philanthropist, to give something for nothing." He passed the vial from hand to hand with what Hetta considered quite unnecessary flourish.

"What do you want? Stop spinning this out like the villain in a bad melodrama and tell me, for Simulsen's sake!" She had no patience for this game when deadly fae monsters might be attacking Wyn right now.

His eyes flashed, and his smile grew slightly edged. "And what if you do not like my price?" he asked.

"Then we'll see if I can *make* you give it to me," she said acidly. If he wouldn't give her the vial... Wyn was at the bank, only a block distant. How long would it take to run there? Surely she would've heard some outcry if a tide of venomous monsters had already descended upon the building?

He relaxed suddenly, all charm and sunny smiles. "Ah, but I do not want you to do that, so I shall set my price low." Hetta nearly stamped with impatience when he met her eyes. "A kiss: that is my price."

"Fine," she snapped, taking a brisk step closer. She would have leaned down, but he was suddenly standing and several feet away, laughing, his eyes glittering like poisoned emeralds. It was that chocolate-rich laugh again, warm and delighted, wrapping around her despite her irritation. *Is this what Wyn meant by allure?* she wondered.

"Oh, I can see why he likes you, Henrietta Isadore Valstar," he said. And then, before she'd quite realised what was happening, he'd taken hold of one of her hands and brought it solemnly to his lips. He pressed a brief, chaste kiss there. "It is done." And he held out the metal vial.

She snatched it from him in case this was all some bizarre trick, but he made no move to stop her. She stared at him.

"Go," he said gently, making a lazy shooing motion.

She turned and shoved her way out of the pub and into the cold afternoon, vial clutched in one fist. The gods save her from all melodramatic fae bar one.

11

LUG—IMPS

"ARE YOU AND Lord Valstar lovers?" Mr Thompson asked as soon as Hetta had left them alone in the office amidst black-and-white furnishings and rigidly ordered bookcases.

Wyn had to give the man credit for being so blunt. Particularly since he'd made sure to position a heavy desk between the two of them before insulting Wyn. And it *was* an insult. Prydinian culture had strong things to say about intimacy outside of marriage, particularly for women.

Where had Mr Thompson's suspicions come from? They'd been evident in his demeanour since Wyn and Hetta arrived, which was part of why Wyn had acquiesced to his request to speak privately. But how had such gossip reached so far outside of Stariel when even there only the faintest murmurings were beginning? The back of his neck prickled. The whole thing smelled of fae intrigue, but how had they gotten this mortal involved? And for what purpose?

Wyn fixed Mr Thompson with a superior look, channelling an inner monologue to help convey the proper degree of frosty hauteur:

You are not only a mortal but an ordinary one. I am a prince and my loyalties run deep. You dare to question my conduct?

"I am going to pretend you did not make that remark," Wyn said, each word sharp as splintered obsidian. "And I suggest you do likewise. You may question my facility with accounts, my experience at management, or my commitment to ensuring Stariel's prosperity, but I will not tolerate aspersions on my character or on Lord Valstar's."

The short man laced his fingers in front of him and leaned forward. He probably thought he was doing a good job of intimidation, but Wyn had been on the receiving end of stares from far more terrifying creatures than middle-aged bank managers.

Mr Thompson persisted. "You have been with the Valstars for nearly ten years, and you started as one of the under-servants, am I right in thinking?"

"That is correct." Interesting—Mr Thompson must have a strong basis for his suspicions, stronger than mere idle hearsay, to pursue them so doggedly.

"And now you are steward—that's a commendable rise in position in roughly a decade, wouldn't you say?"

Wyn chose to smile coldly. "Are you suggesting I was trading bed-favours with Lord Henry for all that time? For it was he who appointed me butler and then later house manager. Or did your rather impertinent question refer to the new rather than the old Lord Valstar?"

Mr Thompson choked. "No, no, of course I wasn't suggesting that." His face crinkled in disgust, but he didn't back down. "But you can't deny your rise in status is decidedly odd. What was your background? Who recommended you for the position?"

Wyn spread his hands. "Merit, and the difficulties of attracting experienced staff to such an isolated estate. I recommended myself, Mr Thompson. I realise that Mr Fisk's performance has made you anxious to reassure yourself about the new holder of his office. But it seems to me that the simplest way to do this would be to let me take you through the estate's current accounts and our future plans. The most immediate issue, you will see, is cashflow." Wyn pulled the first ledger from the pile and opened it. "This is the tenancy records and expenses for the estate, both for the village proper and the tenant farmers. I am proposing to keep separate records in the future, as the nature of each is quite different and in the past issues have been obscured because of the conflation of the two. I have done some preliminary estimates of the most urgent works required in the village and how the outlay might be offset. As an initial venture, we are proposing to see to the most urgent repairs of the Dower House so that it might be leased out and thus provide a regular rental income. Here you can see our calculations..."

He had judged correctly; Mr Thompson was a man who respected numbers and those who understood them. Suspicion still lurked beneath the surface, making him aggressively question every suggestion Wyn made, but Wyn hadn't overstated his abilities. He was new to this role, but he *had* been managing the household accounts for years. He also conceded with grace where he was wrong, subtly flattering the older man's experience. But he was not often wrong.

"The per-metre rate for putting in the elektricity lines seems lower than I would expect," Mr Thompson said.

"It is. Lord Valstar spoke to the lines company, and they were willing to reduce the installation cost due to the large nature of the job and the fact that no trenching work will be required."

"Why not?" Mr Thompson asked, and then answered himself before Wyn could. "Lord Valstar's land-sense." The subject brought Mr Thompson's suspicion back in full force, though Wyn still wasn't sure why. Exactly what had he heard about Wyn and Hetta—and from whom? The bank manager narrowed his eyes. "One hears of such things, of course. It must have been strange for you, accustoming yourself to the peculiarities of Stariel Estate."

Wyn shrugged. "One grows accustomed."

There was a soft knock at the door, and a maid entered carrying a tea tray. From it wafted a pungent and instantly recognisable scent. Wyn only just managed to stop his instinctive jerk away, the smell burning in his nostrils.

"Will you take tea, Mr Tempest?" The eyes of the maid were guileless, but Mr Thompson's held a thread of anticipation. He leaned forward, watching Wyn closely for a reaction.

"Thank you, we will," Mr Thompson said quickly. "Both of us." The maid poured them both cups, set one down in front of each of them, carried the tray over to the side table, and left without further ado.

Wyn eyed the liquid and thought furiously. Mr Thompson was a great deal more than merely suspicious of Wyn's motives. Wyn needed to act quickly to reassure the man, so he picked up the delicate china cup without hesitation and faked a sip. The bitter smell jangled unpleasantly, sending a wave of disorientation through him, and he put the cup down with a clatter and a moue of disgust. He misjudged the act slightly, and a splash of hot liquid spilled into the saucer.

"What kind of tea is this?" he demanded. Did Mr Thompson really think he could serve yarrow tea without comment? Any normal mortal would notice the strong taste. The tea might have made a lesser fae drop their glamour to reveal their true form, but Wyn was no such thing.

"Yarrow," Mr Thompson said, disappointment making his mouth droop.

"Well, I cannot say I care much for it," Wyn said firmly, pushing his cup aside. He repressed the urge to stride to the window, lift the frame, and hurl the entire tea tray out. The smell scratched against his eardrums. Yarrow wasn't like iron—it didn't negate fae magic so much as interfere with Wyn's sense of the world.

I can do this, he told himself. He could sit here with the stench of yarrow reverberating through his skull and argue over interest rates. His thoughts moved strangely, billowing like fog as he tried to concentrate. The yarrow meant something...Mr Thompson had deliberately served it to Wyn.

Which meant he suspected what Wyn was. Which meant... someone had told him? Or had he simply guessed? There were people in the North who still held to old superstitions, even though the High King had only very recently lifted the Iron Law. The same High King who had told ThousandSpire and DuskRose to marry their children and cement peace. Focus! The High King was not important right now. Interest rates!

No, wait...not interest rates. Yarrow! Why had Mr Thompson served him yarrow tea? Concentrate!

Mr Thompson was speaking seriously of percentages now, Wyn having passed his little test. Wyn latched on to the numbers with grim determination. It was easier to calculate cumulative interest at three-and-a-half percent over five years than it was to pull himself through the chain of logic necessary to deduce Mr Thompson's motives. He could do that later, away from the yarrow's mind-fog.

Wait—something snagged at his him, and he unconsciously reached for his leysight, trying to draw meaning from currents garbled by the yarrow. The plant must have been plucked at high noon at midsummer, to have this much potency. But even through the disorientation, something made his feathers stiffen—wait, he didn't *have* feathers currently. Did he? It would be so much easier to think in his native form.

No, he mustn't change forms. That would be a terrible idea: Mr Thompson would *definitely* know he was fae then. He stifled a giggle. But underneath the influence of the yarrow, deeper instinct struggled to communicate, like a flare sent up amidst vast, roiling stormclouds. He found himself staring at the great ornate mirror frame above the sideboard. Swirls of gilded leaves and roses were worked into the design. Was it important? His reflection showed eyes slightly more vibrant in colour than they should have been—fae bleeding through.

Roses...Mr Thompson broke off in mid-sentence as Wyn stood, strode to the window, and pushed up the sash. Great quantities of cold, clean air sucked inwards and, more importantly, great quantities of yarrow-tainted air sucked *out*.

He could finally taste what the yarrow had been masking. Aroset's magic—crushed rose petals and copper amidst the storm-scent that was common to all his father's line—seeping into the room through the mirror-frame. That was all the warning he got before the mirror's surface rippled.

"Get down!" he yelled at Mr Thompson as the portal opened. The short man had begun to rise in protest, but at this he froze, mouth falling open in surprise to be so shouted at.

The other side of the portal was dark, but Wyn still couldn't quite believe where it connected to until the first lug-imp came lumbering through on too-small wings. Surely even Aroset wouldn't connect a darksink directly to the Mortal Realm? But there was no denying the smell of her magic nor the species of darkfae coming through the portal.

If an insect and a toad had a grotesque terrier-sized child, that child would be a lug-imp. Their bodies were ovoid, head joined to body without any discernible narrowing at the neck. The first through the portal gaped wide jaws as it caught Wyn's scent, showing a mouth over-stuffed with razor teeth. Its tiny wings had to beat so fast to keep it aloft that each individual flap blurred into a thrum.

It made a beeline for Wyn. Of course. It *would* have to be lug-imps, wouldn't it?

"*Avanti!*" Wyn cried. The air thickened obediently, and the lug-imp's rush slowed as its wings met resistance. It was only partially effective, as the lug-imp quickly compensated and began to push forward again, like a swimmer through jelly.

Mr Thompson stood at the end of the room furthest from the door. The ornate mirror hung halfway along the wall opposite Wyn by the window. With the lug-imp's path temporarily slowed, Wyn could try to dart around it towards the door to escape, but that would leave the bank manager alone with a swarm of darkfae. Had Mr Thompson broken any promises?

Three more lug-imps wriggled out of the portal, snuffling as they came through. Two eagerly followed their compatriot towards Wyn, but the third picked up a different scent and made straight for Mr Thompson, its eyes burning a bright and sickening yellow. Well, that answered that question.

Wyn lunged towards the bank manager, who was reaching for the tea tray. Mr Thompson triumphantly hoisted the teapot, removed its lid, and awkwardly threw the contents at the lug-imp. The lug-imp simply diverted its flight path away from the spray of liquid and, quick as a hornet, rushed at Mr Thompson's legs.

Mr Thompson cried out, and Wyn dove, tearing the lug-imp away, his heart pounding. Had it broken skin? Would its venom have the same effect on a mortal as a fae?

The lug-imp writhed in his hands, its skin reptilian and moist, and tried to sink its teeth into Wyn as well. Wyn drew back his arm and hurled it at the wall. It hit with a sickening crunch, knocking accounts books from the shelves. Slowly, it got to its stumpy feet, its wings hanging at a broken angle. It growled and began to lurch towards him, teeth snapping angrily.

The injured lug-imp was the least of his worries. More were pouring from the portal every second, the thrum of their stunted wings loud as a kicked beehive. How long could Aroset hold the portal open for? Wyn released another surge of air magic, sending a trio of darkfae crashing into the windows, shattering the glass and tumbling one out into the afternoon. Drat. There would be mortals out there—mortals who made and broke promises without a second thought.

And Hetta. She would be out there too.

Working magic in his mortal form was clumsy, and he was out of practice with storm magic besides, but he grit his teeth and grasped after the stray lug-imp with fingers of air, sweeping it back inside the room. The distraction cost him—another lug-imp took the opportunity to swarm across the floor, underneath his thickened air shield, and sank its fangs into his calf.

Pain lanced from the bite, bright as fire. He tried to tear the lug-imp off but couldn't get a grip on its slippery skin. Its fangs sank deeper, and the pain ratcheted up a notch, a knife twisting in his leg. Whirling, he took up one of the heavy accounts books and knocked the lug-imp loose.

He stumbled backwards to lean against the bookshelves, leg threatening to crumple. Mr Thompson was in worse straits. The bank manager had lost his footing at some point and sat, panting, with his back against the desk, white face pulled in a rictus of silent agony. Evidently lug-imp venom *did* affect mortals.

"Dammit!" Any strong emotion could fuel elemental magic, temporarily at least, so Wyn balled up his pain and shoved it into his spell, the winds singing in response. He needed to close the portal. To do that, he needed to get past the swarm of angry lug-imps, held at bay only by the wind he had summoned, and increasing in number by the second.

Dare he summon lightning? The thought of frying the swarm in front of him was grimly satisfying. But it was too great a risk. Lightning was difficult to handle at the best of times, and he was out of practice and in his mortal form besides. He would likely electrocute the swarm, himself, and anyone else in the building.

Mr Thompson was the first problem. The bank manager curled forward over his injury, practically insensate. How fast would the poison act? Wyn made his way to the other side of the desk, fending off lug-imps with a combination of gusts of wind and a heavy accounts book. The desk was a sturdy piece, difficult to move even with inhuman strength, and the action left him briefly unable to defend himself. He kept the air currents shifting, but the lug-imps were surprisingly able fliers, and another starburst of agony radiated out from his shoulder as one managed to get close enough to bite. He shoved the desk against the wall, trapping Mr Thompson underneath it in a wooden cage that would hopefully protect him from further injury, and turned. The lug-imp at his shoulder clamped tight, and he had to use both hands to wrench it free. Ligaments snapped as he forced its jaws apart, and it released with a high-pitched screech of pain, its lower jaw hanging unnaturally loose.

The pain was incredible, the venom pumping through his system with every heartbeat. He took the pain and diverted it once again into his magic, filling the office with an angry whirlwind. The light-fitting swung in dizzying circles, shadows dancing in its path. Lug-imps thumped against bookshelves and into the ceiling, only to get up and throw themselves towards him again. Little warning fires lit behind his eyes—he couldn't keep channelling the pain into his magic forever, not without consequence.

Wyn limped through the whirling air currents towards the portal, where the squat bodies of more lug-imps were still emerging. The frame's ornate design dug into his hands as he grasped hold of it and yanked. It resisted with more strength than the simple nail it hung from should have possessed, but he persisted, even when a lug-imp's muzzle came through right by his arm and latched on to his forearm, its teeth digging deep into the muscle until he feared they'd reached bone. His magic shook with the effort of repurposing the pain.

With a cry of triumph, he pulled the frame free of the wall and brought it down hard on the floor, stomping his heel into it for extra measure. The glass broke, taking the connection with it. It wasn't the most elegant way to dismantle a portal, but it sufficed.

He tried to shake the lug-imp off, but it just clamped harder, refusing to surrender its prize. He hammered it against the wall where the mirror had lately hung, but he could feel his strength ebbing away as the venom reacted with his blood, draining power.

Black spots appeared on the edges of his vision as he kept dashing the cursed lug-imp against the wall, struggling to simultaneously keep his air shield up, the winds shifting. At least no more lug-imps would be coming now the portal was deactivated. That left only twenty of the things, all straining to reach him through the tempest, yellow eyes bulging. Only twenty. He could do this, though he was already shaking with the effort it took to keep them all from coming at him at once. With a crunch, he at last managed to make the lug-imp on his forearm release its jaws, but it was only temporarily dazed and quickly rose, flinging itself into the air and attempting to take another chunk out of him. He dodged, reflexes slower than they ought to be.

There was only one choice, really, so he took it, shedding his mortal form between one breath and the next. Wings unfurled, forcing their way through his shirt, the fabric ripping as feather and bone extended. Everything became sharper and more confusing at the same time, as new senses flared to life and were bombarded by the cacophony of magics in the room. The energy that he had struggled to channel in his mortal form suddenly flowed properly, like a leaking bottle abruptly coming unstopped.

Unfortunately, the pain was also fiercer in his native form. He snarled at the horde of lug-imps in the vague hope it might intimidate them. It didn't.

His blood sizzled with the venom, making him fully aware of how unstable a mixture it was. But it was easier to twist the pain into magic, into the flows of air, which was fortunate, since his wings made him a much larger target for the lug-imps. He snapped back his primaries just in time to avoid a lug-imp colliding with the outer arch of his wings. Whirling, he let storm magic wash over his feathers and out, gusting the lug-imp off course.

This was when Hetta arrived.

The door slammed open and she stood there, expression determined rather than surprised, still wearing her hat and scarf, the coffee and frozen pine of her magic eddying around her.

"Cover your eyes!" she cried.

He shut his eyes and flung up his arms, both anticipating what she was about to do and wondering how she'd guessed that lug-imps were particularly sensitive to light. But she was, after all, a master illusionist, weaver of light. Perhaps it was simply an obvious tactic for her regardless.

Even with his hands covering his face, white seeped through the cracks between his fingers, leaving after-echoes on the insides of his eyelids. The lug-imps shrieked in sudden pain. When the light faded, he opened his eyes to find them disoriented in their blindness, blundering into the furniture and glancing off the walls.

He met Hetta's eyes. Rage burned in them, rage driven by terror. When she summoned fire, it wasn't fed by Stariel but by that rage. Pyromancy was elemental magic, could be fuelled by emotions in a way most human magic couldn't. It came from Hetta's long-distant fae ancestor; he should probably tell her that at some later point, when they were not in the middle of a fight, when the world didn't quiver so badly.

Together, they dealt with the remaining lug-imps. Hetta's fire-balls made a cleaner death than Wyn's systematic crushing, and he wished briefly for his sword, though it had been years since he'd held it.

Wyn stared down at the last lug-imp under his feet, realising dully that it was done; the lug-imps were all dead. Round brown bodies and charred bones littered the room like grotesque fallen leaves. He let the winds die. The pain, diverted for so long, screamed back with a vengeance, and at once he was aware of every bite and scratch, of the venom churning violently in his blood as it pumped its way through his veins.

Then Hetta was at his side, feverishly touching the wounds on his arm and shoulder. She was trembling, and he allowed himself to put his arms around her, burying his nose in her hair. Safe. She was safe.

She pulled away. "They bit you!" Her voice was higher than usual. "I have the antidote!" She was pulling a vial from her coat pocket as she spoke. The already tangled threads of fae machinations multiplied. "Your brother," she said as he swayed with pain and confusion, trying to make this new piece of puzzle fit. "He came to the pub I was in and said he had the antidote to the venom of those things. Take it!"

Wyn pulled himself together. "No, I don't need it. But Mr Thompson will." He stumbled to the desk, spikes of agony shooting up his leg. "He's under the desk," he explained.

"But they bit you—and he said their venom was deadly to oathbreakers." The vial was clutched tightly in her fist, her gaze riveted on the blood dripping down his arm, drenching the tattered remains of his shirt.

The desk was heavier than it had been before, and in the end he had to shuffle it away from the wall inch by inch. "I have my own antidote," he said. "But I dare not use mine on Mr Thompson unless there is no other choice."

He bent and dragged the bank manager from under the desk, propping him against the wall. He was semi-conscious, but the movement roused him, and he stared at Wyn with puzzlement that slowly changed to fear as he processed what he was seeing.

"Fairy!" he rasped, struggling away.

Wyn turned back to Hetta. "What did my brother say about the antidote? His exact words."

"That it was the antidote to the venom of the lug-imp," Hetta recited.

Wyn held out his hand for the vial, and Hetta relinquished it with reluctance.

"You're sure?" Her eyes were dark with worry.

"I am sure." He caught Mr Thompson's face and forced open his mouth. The bank manager protested feebly. Wyn ignored him, tipping the entire contents of the vial into his mouth and then holding his lips closed until he swallowed. Mr Thompson shuddered, and then the tension went out of him all at once as he slumped into unconsciousness.

"Is that supposed to happen?" Hetta brushed past his wings to kneel beside him. Wyn slid the bank manager into a more comfortable position on his side.

"I don't know how badly lug-imp poison affects mortals," Wyn admitted. "The antidote will have neutralised it, but his body will still need to heal. It was probably only the pain keeping him conscious."

"Why are you still in pain, then, if you've taken the antidote?" Hetta picked at his sleeve where blood dripped from his forearm. "We need to get this cleaned and bandaged." Her expression grew thoughtful as she took in the jumbled disorder of the room, the smashed window, the broken and scorched bodies of lug-imps, and Wyn's feathered appearance. "This is going to be somewhat difficult to explain."

GLAMOUR & ILLUSION

RUNNING FOOTSTEPS GAVE them a split-second's warning before the door burst open, revealing the same maid who had so recently served Wyn and Mr Thompson tea. Both he and Hetta reacted instinctively, and so Wyn wasn't sure whether it was his glamour or Hetta's illusion that kept the maid from seeing his true form. He met Hetta's eyes, a sliver of wry amusement at the shared impulse passing between them. Perhaps it was for the best that both had been cast, since his glamour was a sketchy effort, and he knew illusion took time to craft well. But the combination held, or possibly the wider scene of destruction proved sufficiently distracting.

"Merciful Mother Eostre!" the maid exclaimed, hands briefly covering her mouth in horror. Her wide eyes took in the remains of the lug-imps, the ruined mirror, the strewn books, the curtains billowing in the freezing air from the smashed window, and finally came to rest on Mr Thompson's slumped form. "Mr Thompson!"

"Madam!" Wyn said firmly when it seemed the maid might go into hysterics. He didn't dare stand in case it disrupted Hetta's illusion. But he got the maid's attention. "As you can see, Mr Thompson requires medical attention. Please go and send for the doctor at once."

"But what happened? What are…" She pointed to one of the crushed lug-imps, which was oozing yellowish blood into the carpet.

Hetta stood, briskly brushing lint off her skirt as she did so. "Bad fairies, obviously. A surprise, I know—one so rarely sees them outside of tales. But it's not important right now; what's important is that Mr Thompson urgently needs a doctor."

"Fairies," The maid repeated faintly. Her gaze flew to Wyn, seeking some alternative explanation, but he merely nodded. "Oh, you're bleeding too, sir."

"I'll take care of that," Hetta said. "The doctor?" Her commanding manner seemed to reassure the maid, who took a deep breath.

"I'll be back right quick, Lord Valstar," she said, nodding and disappearing back out the door.

Hetta sagged in relief and let the illusion drop. Wyn rose. He had to lean against the wall to do so, leg protesting against taking his weight. Every muscle screamed as the shift in position washed fresh venom through his system.

"I can see through your glamour," she said with some surprise, tilting her head.

"It would make sense," he said, seizing gratefully on the distraction from the dizzying effects of the venom. "Faelands give strange and unpredictable gifts to their rulers, but they're often related to the person's base magic." And Hetta had been a master illusionist before she became lord. "You call people's innate ability to see through illusion the Sight—we call it the same for those who can see through glamour. Stariel may have gifted you both types of Sight now. You could check." Human mages learned to use magesight in order to see the weaves of their own—and others'—magic, but unlike the Sight, it was an active rather than passive ability.

Hetta frowned, and he knew she was releasing her grip on her magesight. She blinked. "You're right. Hmm." Her gaze grew intent, and he felt her re-weaving the illusion around him. Human illusion and fae glamour might achieve the same effects, but they used different means. Illusion meant shifting light; glamour had no physical basis and relied on twisting a person's perceptions. Humans without the Sight could use specially made glasses to see through illusion, if desired, but such devices were useless on fae glamour.

"Sit on the desk," she told him. "I'm going to find some water and bandages."

He sat, too tired to argue, feathers brushing the desk. It made him oddly uneasy to feel the heavy presence of his wings but not to be able to see them out of the corners of his eyes. If he moved them too quickly, he could see ripples in the air, showing glimpses of silver as Hetta's illusion warped. He could not see his own horns, of course, but he assumed they would create similar distortions if he turned his head too quickly.

Mr Thompson's breathing was definitely easier, and his colour looked better. He appeared, for all intents and purposes, to be deeply asleep. That was something, at least. *Though it may now be slightly more difficult to convince him that I'm a trustworthy steward.*

The ornate mirror frame lay in a pool of fractured glass. Wyn eased himself off the desk with a wince and went to it. Lifting it a fraction, he breathed in the copper, old-fashioned roses, and storms that made up Aroset's signature. His sister had made no attempt to mask her magic.

However, the smell of Aroset's magic was stronger than it should've been with the portal broken. He followed it, creeping his fingers along the edge of the frame until they snagged over something that shouldn't have been there. A single crimson rose petal mocked him and helped explain how Aroset had been able to create a portal here. Portals were much easier in unclaimed lands, but there still had to be some kind of resonance between two places for them to work. No matter how hard a bargainer Mr Thompson was, Wyn didn't think his office would resonate with a darksink. It was still a mark of Aroset's power; none of his other siblings could have positioned a portal so perfectly nor have held it open for so long, resonance-link or not.

He crumpled the rose petal in his fist and had just limped back to the desk when Hetta returned with a wave of excited and interested parties. He checked his impulse to take charge, for Hetta had things well in hand. *Stariel chose true*, he thought, a warm and complicated ache in his chest as he watched her.

In short order, Mr Thompson had been removed to a couch in another room to await the arrival of the doctor and Hetta had procured a basin of warm water and a pile of bandages and summarily dismissed everyone. Wyn sat quietly throughout. The temperature inside Mr Thompson's office was now effectively the same as that outside, but he didn't particularly feel it. Stormdancers had to be relatively immune to cold, to reach the high, freezing heights above the spires.

He rolled up his trouser leg without being asked and let Hetta fuss. She cleaned the wound matter-of-factly while he unbuttoned his ruined shirt and wrapped it around his forearm in a temporary bandage. Hetta's gaze slipped up to his bare chest, and he felt an uncharacteristic urge to preen.

"Will these need stitches?" she asked, pulling her gaze back and dabbing carefully at his calf. The water stung.

"The one on my wrist might," he admitted. His makeshift bandage was already stained crimson. "It's the deepest, and the venom slows my normal healing rate. But I doubt we'll find a needle not made of iron."

She paused and bit her lip but didn't press. Through the open window came the occasional sound of vehicles and the low chattering of people passing below.

He sighed and waited until she had wrapped his calf in a long white bandage and moved on to his shoulder. "You want to know about the antidote." He had to lift his left wing slightly so she could reach the bite properly, and the intimacy made his heart stutter. Or perhaps it was merely blood loss.

"You said you had your own antidote already, but how did you know to bring it with you? What is it?" Hetta scowled at his shoulder.

"I didn't," he said. The puzzle pieces still didn't fit. "My brother, the one you spoke with, can you describe him?"

Patience wasn't one of Hetta's particular virtues, and she let him see she wasn't impressed with his evasiveness, but she answered nonetheless.

"Tall, long dark hair, your cheekbones." Her lips curved. "Good-looking. Very green eyes."

He stiffened, accidentally knocking the cloth out of Hetta's hand. "Sorry," he apologised, re-settling himself. A bubble of pained laughter forced its way out.

"Wyn?"

He couldn't seem to stop now that he'd started, silently shaking with dark amusement.

"Wyn, if you don't tell me what in Prydein is going on this second, I'll—I'll pluck your dashed feathers!"

"I'm sorry. It's..." He tried to get his breath, but her wrathful expression set him off again.

She dropped the cloth and cupped his face in her hands, damp fingers warm against his skin. The touch centred him, stilling the threatening hysteria. "Wyn. Tell me," she said gently.

He took a deep, shuddering breath. "Thank you. It's just—Rakken."

"Rakken?" she asked, picking up the cloth and going back to her task.

"Rakken is who you met at the pub. *Not* the same person who sent the lug-imps." He repressed another burble of mirthless laughter.

"Though he must have had a hand in persuading Aroset to send them." Oh, damn Rakken's dark sense of humour. "He probably thinks this is all incredibly funny. Though, on the brighter side, at least one of my siblings doesn't want me dead."

"I'm afraid I don't get the joke."

"Lug-imp venom is deadly only to those who have broken their oaths. Aroset sent them as a message as well as a weapon of assassination."

"Aroset?"

He'd never told her the names of his siblings. They felt simultaneously foreign and familiar on his tongue. "Aroset is second-oldest, the most powerful, and the most vicious. She is my father's favourite. Rakken is third in line. He is…ambitious. Manipulative. Ruthless. Subtler than Aroset, who probably thinks that sending lug-imps to kill me is the height of sophisticated subtext."

"I'm still not seeing any cause for hilarity," Hetta said flatly.

"It's…well, Aroset sent a creature she thought would be deadly to me, but she also sent one whose venom I specifically have an antidote at hand for. Which Aroset didn't know, but Rakken at least suspected. Giving you that vial was both a back-up, in case he'd guessed wrongly, and him telling me that he set this entire thing up. Which means he thinks there's some political advantage to be had from my being alive even though my father ordered me dead." He pulled his feathers tight against his body and added in a low voice, "And he was testing to see how easily he could manipulate you through me."

Hetta understood the implications of that immediately. "I'm not going to even pretend to be sorry for coming to your rescue."

"What did you bargain for the antidote?"

She shrugged. "A kiss on the hand, as it turns out."

He mutely held out his own hands, and she placed hers palm up in his. Lifting them, he could detect no malevolent magic, just the faintest trace of drenched citrus: Rakken's signature. "It's"—*all right* was wildly untrue—"probably a good sign. He must want to be on cordial terms with you, otherwise he wouldn't have let you off so lightly." And what did *that* mean, exactly, that Rakken thought he wanted credit in his ledger when it came to Hetta? Undoubtedly nothing good.

"You still haven't told me what the antidote is." She squeezed his hands in gentle rebuke.

He released her hands and gave a deep sigh. "The blood of a virgin," he said, raising his eyes to the ceiling. "Which I happen to have a plentiful supply of. And which my brother undoubtedly thinks is a hilarious thing for me to have to point out to you."

There was a beat of silence.

"Oh," said Hetta. Then, "Well, I did wonder if you might be."

He turned to find her wringing out the cloth. "Dare I ask?" He repressed a wince as she reached for the deeper wound on his wrist.

"Honestly, Wyn, I've known you for years, and I've never seen you show particular interest in anyone in that way. Which you did say just this morning was deliberate."

"Not anyone...just one person, actually." Part of him shied from revealing that, the sheer depth of his vulnerability when it came to Hetta. Oh, she could hurt him so badly if she wished.

She looked up, eyes shining. "So your 'condition' is, in fact, my fault?" she teased.

"You assume I was referring to you? How do you know I have not been hiding a deep passion for your Aunt Sybil all these years?"

Her lips curled up at the corners. "Are you embarrassed? Your feathers are fluffing up."

Had it really been so long since he'd taken this form that he'd lost his ability to conceal his physical tells? Thank the stormwinds it was Hetta who stood before him and not someone who would take advantage of the lapse. He forced his coverts flat and said lightly,

"Well, I was worried you wouldn't think it one of my more appealing traits. Fortunately, it's a relatively easy condition to rid oneself of, or so I've been led to believe."

Hetta laughed. "You're still extremely appealing, rest assured." She frowned down at his forearm, where red was seeping through the white crepe. "Though it would be significantly better if you weren't bleeding everywhere. I can't seem to get this to stop."

Wyn wasn't worried. "I've healed worse."

He realised his mistake when she looked up, horror-struck.

"Yes, yes, I know: poor Wyn and his tragic upbringing. It's not news, Hetta—it's not even *interesting*. Please desist looking at me as if I were an abused puppy. It's a blow to my already bruised ego. Think of how smoulderingly attractive you find me, rather. I *am* half-naked, after all."

"Half-naked, half-hysterical with pain, and *bleeding*," she told him fiercely, and he knew he'd made her angry. Better anger than pity.

"Well, I *am* profusely sorry to be bleeding, if you were seeking an apology," he said.

Hetta's anger burned like gunpowder, explosive but short-lived. She glared at him and then it all drained out of her, exasperation taking its place. "Oh, how dare you put me in a temper when you look so pitiful. I can't rail at you when you look like you're about to faint."

"I will endeavour not to do so then." The pain was indeed making him light-headed, but he smiled, soft and fond. "I like it when you rail at me."

She laughed again, though she tried not to. He'd always liked her laugh, the way it bubbled out of her in helpless, girlish eddies. "Be serious for a moment," she said, wrapping another layer of bandage tightly around his forearm. "Your brother is playing a very unfunny game, and if this is what it's like when he's *not* trying to kill you, I'd rather not stick around to see what the sister who *is* trying to kill you does next. We need to get back to the estate."

Wyn too would be easier with Hetta safely back on her own faeland. "I agree. But first—"

He found he had to close his eyes in order to concentrate properly. The magic flowed sluggishly in response to his tired will, but Hetta's gasp told him he'd been successful. When he opened his eyes, the winds had gathered all the lug-imps and every bit of his blood within sensing range into an ugly, throbbing globe of air.

"I would appreciate it," he panted, "if you would burn that."

Fire pulsed from Hetta's hands, and he spun it into the wind-ball. The flames burned white-hot for a second, temporarily lifting the temperature of the room despite the open window. Only a few fine ash flakes fluttered free when he let the winds die. They settled onto the carpet, pale grey against the darker material.

He slumped forward, fatigue seeping into his bones.

"I've never seen anything like that," Hetta said, staring at the space where the globe had been. "How did you do that?"

With her eyes bright with delighted inquiry, the resemblance between her and her scholarly brother Marius was suddenly more pronounced. This was a side of her he'd never seen up close; Hetta had spent years studying magic, but she hadn't returned to Stariel in that time, and the stories of her studies had come via letter.

"Sympathy and air magic," he said. "I am fae; they are fae. Like calls to like. And I am a stormdancer: controlling the winds is our primary power."

She practically glowed with excitement. "How do—hold that thought," she said, giving herself a shake. "It's hardly fair to quiz you when you're like this. But we're definitely going to try this again when you're recovered."

Wounds be storm-tossed; he pulled her into a one-armed embrace, ignoring the protest from his shoulder.

"You'll start bleeding again!" she protested, but he didn't care.

He kissed her because he couldn't resist; because she was so lovely with her coral-pink lips; because she looked at him like he was rare and glorious; because he couldn't help his heart from squeezing with agonised happiness at the sight of her; because he was sure it couldn't last. He was falling, too hard and too fast, and he couldn't stop it, didn't want to stop it. The warm curves of her pressed against him, and his whole body thrummed like a struck tuning fork, pain fading to a mere background note.

I love you, he wanted to say but didn't. It wouldn't be fair; he couldn't say that to Hetta and then leave her. And perhaps not saying it would make it somehow not true, when the time came. He gazed into the depths of her storm-coloured eyes. *But probably not. After all, that didn't work at any point in the last decade, did it?*

"You're a very disobedient patient, you know," she said to him, a little breathily. She lifted her fingertips to his mouth, rubbed her thumb over his bottom lip, and held it up stained coral pink. "I forgot I was wearing lipstick. You'd better wipe that off or the next person to turn up will know exactly what we've been doing."

He fished a handkerchief from his ruined coat and did so. The room was still a mess of dislodged books and broken glass, but far less morbid without the corpses of the lug-imps.

"Can you stand?" she asked.

"Are we planning to disappear without a word, leaving rumours to sprout in our wake?" he said, easing himself off the desk, stretching his wings out slightly for balance. His injured calf burned and wouldn't bear much weight, but: "I am moderately certain I can limp out of here."

"I know you like to be in control of things, but you can't control everything, Wyn. Let them figure it out for themselves. I don't particularly care what stories they tell so long as I'm standing on Stariel soil before nightfall." She gave him an inscrutable look, and he realised suddenly what an odd picture he must present: bare-chested and bandaged, standing unsteadily with wings half-furled. *Not human.*

"I would like to see how Mr Thompson is doing first," he said. "I hope the antidote worked, but I'd rather know for sure we aren't leaving a dead bank manager behind. For one thing, that might make securing a loan substantially more difficult."

Before Hetta could answer, the door pushed open again to reveal the maid with an older woman in tow. The maid held a bundled shirt.

Wyn reacted faster this time. Hetta's illusion would probably be sufficient so long as he stayed still, but why take the chance? He pushed the image of himself in mortal form at both women's minds. The effort left him sagging against the desk, wishing he hadn't decided to stand up.

The maid looked around wildly for the lug-imps and seemed both reassured and worried by their absence.

"I burned the bodies," Hetta explained. "It seemed like a good idea."

"Oh," said the maid faintly. Her gaze went interestedly to Wyn's bare chest and stayed there, and he realised his usual aura of asexual reassurance had come completely unravelled. Bother. "I've brought one of Mr Stewart's spare shirts—he likes to change after cycling to work." The maid coloured and gingerly picked her way across the room, holding out the item of clothing. Wyn thanked her as he took it from her, and her flush deepened. She turned hurriedly back to the other woman, who was still standing on the threshold. "The doctor's with Mr Thompson now, but this is Mr Thompson's wife. She's a—" The maid wrung her hands in a little gesture of helplessness.

"I'm a herbwoman, and something of an expert on the fae. I usually have dinner with my husband on Wednesdays," the older woman said crisply. She clutched a large brown handbag firmly under one arm, and her eyes narrowed as she took in the scene before her.

"How is your husband, Mrs Thompson?" Wyn asked.

Mrs Thompson replied to Hetta rather than Wyn. "We managed to wake him briefly, but the wound required stitches, and he is vastly fatigued." Her gaze flicked not to Wyn's face but to the expanse of his wings. Her mouth drew a hard line. "Lord Valstar, might I have a word with you alone?"

Interesting, and much too coincidental; Mrs Thompson had the Sight, and that wasn't exactly a common gift. She had to be the reason for Mr Thompson's old-fashioned belief in the fae, and more than likely the source of the yarrow tea as well. But what had made the Thompsons suspect Wyn in the first place? He had a glum feeling that at the end of that thread would lie one or another of his relatives, though their motives remained opaque to him.

With enough power, he might be able to press against her mind sufficiently to force it to see only what he wanted her to see, slipping from mere glamour into compulsion, but he doubted he could do it without damage. A mind could only bend so far before it broke. Besides, he was weak as a day-old kitten just now.

"I'd rather not leave my steward alone just now, given his condition. I'm afraid you'll have to speak to the two of us together," Hetta said cautiously. "I assure you, he is eminently trustworthy."

Mrs Thompson harrumphed. Then a sudden gleam of triumph came into her eyes, and she turned on Wyn. "For goodness' sakes, boy, why don't you put that shirt on?"

How in the High King's name was he going to achieve that? Human clothing wasn't designed for a being with wings, and she knew it, the bloody-minded matriarch.

He took a deep breath and changed. Usually it was hardly any effort at all to shift forms, but he automatically reverted to his fae one when his reserves were running low. He healed faster in full fae form, mainly because the energy currents were easier to channel. Going against that instinct was akin to battling a headwind, and he became acutely aware of the venom in his veins, of the damp puddle of yarrow tea in one corner of the room still jangling unpleasantly against his senses.

The shift, when it came, settled unsteadily, as if his wings lurked just beneath the skin, ready to unfurl at the slightest provocation.

The room wobbled, and he was glad of the excuse to lower his head under the guise of wrestling with the shirt. His fingers moved thickly, and when he finally got his arms through the sleeves, he stared down at his chest and the long line of buttons in despair. *I am a prince*, he reminded himself. *I will not be defeated by buttons.*

An eternity later, he looked up to find Mrs Thompson watching him with a lot more uncertainty in her expression. Better than outright hostility, he supposed. He wagered she hadn't before encountered a greater fae who could change shape rather than just concealing themselves behind glamour. Perhaps it would be enough.

Enough for what? he asked himself fuzzily, and then couldn't hold his thoughts together well enough to answer.

"If you don't mind," Hetta said, "I'm in something of a hurry to be gone from here. I want to be back at the estate before nightfall."

"Oh, but your steward must surely need to see the doctor?" Mrs Thompson squinted at Wyn, as if that would make his wings reappear. "He doesn't look well. He may need stitches."

Her words fell slowly in his ears, turning to meaning one syllable at a time. Stitches. Iron. Any needles the doctors used would be made of iron. Nausea rose in his throat as he imagined the metal piercing him.

"No, no stitches," he said, trying to lean as much of his weight against the desk as possible without being too obvious about it. The hard wood against the backs of his legs put pressure on the bandage, a dull ache. "I am fine. Hetta's done a fine job patching me up."

Both Mrs Thompson and the maid stared at him, and he realised he'd accidentally used Hetta's pet name. He was woozier than he'd realised, to make such an error. But too late to take it back now.

"Would you leave us?" Hetta said to the maid. "For I'd like to hear Mrs Thompson's words and be off as soon as possible."

The maid nodded; her eyes were alight with curiosity as she left. Wyn considered whether he had the energy left to power an anti-eavesdropping spell and reluctantly concluded that he did not.

Eavesdropping maids were a problem, weren't they? Like Lottie the housemaid. Couldn't blame them, though; he would eavesdrop too if he thought the information worth it. Grey mist danced on the edges of his vision, and feathers itched under his skin, straining for release. But he mustn't. Why mustn't he? It was becoming harder to remember.

The room swayed gently, the carpet curiously unstable under his shoes. Glass shards glittered in the fibres. It would be a nightmare to clean them up—the poor maid. Why did he keep thinking about maids?

Mrs Thompson was rummaging in her handbag. "I'm afraid you have been deceived, Lord Valstar."

MRS THOMPSON

HETTA DIDN'T HAVE much patience for the bank manager's wife—she was too worried about getting Wyn back to the estate before his siblings sent their next lot of monsters. Why had he changed back to his mortal form, taking her illusion with it? She wished he'd stayed sitting on the desk; he swayed like he might faint, looking much worse than a few moments ago. Blood had seeped through the bandages on his forearm, spotting the new shirt red.

"Lord Valstar!" Mrs Thompson recalled her attention.

"Sorry, Mrs Thompson. Do go on." How long would it take them to make it down to where the kineticar was parked? Maybe that's why Wyn had changed—he definitely wouldn't fit in his fae form.

"Your steward is not as he has presented himself. He's not a mortal man at all, but a fairy!" With this proclamation, Mrs Thompson drew forth a container from her handbag and marched forward to fling the contents over Wyn. The liquid splattered onto his face and shirt, smelling strongly of herbs.

Time froze, followed by everything happening at once. Wyn's

eyes widened. Then he lost control of his form, wings spiralling free
with a great whoosh of air as he crumpled. Hetta tried to catch him,
but Wyn was a tall man, and the breadth of his wings made him
bulky as well as heavy. Hetta managed only to help him fall to the
floor in a controlled fashion.

"Wyn!" What had Mrs Thompson thrown at him? Tiny dark
flecks shimmered on his skin and the wet remains of his clothing:
iron filings. The pressure of his wings had largely shredded the
shirt. Again.

Wyn's pupils had shrunk to pinpricks, and he shivered like a
nervous horse, rubbing violently at the wetness on his face.

"Quickly, Lord Valstar, get away from the creature!" Mrs
Thompson snapped.

"What was in that mixture—" Hetta began, trailing off as Mrs
Thompson pulled an ornate pistol from her bag and aimed it stead-
ily at Wyn. It happened so quickly that Hetta didn't have time
to react. Wyn shoved her away, wind and magic stirring, and the
gunshot rang out, deafening in the small space. Acrid gunsmoke
filled Hetta's nostrils, but she took no notice of it, flying across the
room to bat the weapon out of Mrs Thompson's hands.

The woman smiled with grim satisfaction, but it faltered in the
face of Hetta's anger. "It's for your own good, my lord. They can
enchant the mind! He'll lose his hold on you once he's dead."

"Get out!" Hetta snarled. Fire ran in little rivulets down her arms,
pooling in her hands, and she let it blossom into hovering fireballs.
At least she'd left her gloves in her pocket when she'd run here from
the pub, or they'd be a scorched mess by now. "Get out!"

Mrs Thompson turned and fled, but Hetta knew she'd be back
with reinforcements.

Hetta let the fire snap out, fear spiking as she turned back to
Wyn. The bullet had hit him on the upper curve of his wing, and
blood ran thick and fast from the wound, staining white feathers
dark red and dripping into the carpet.

"Cherries!" he gasped, trying to rise.

This comment was so extremely odd that it jolted Hetta out of her rising panic. She pulled off her scarf and rushed forward, trying to stem the flow. Scrabbling one-handed around on the desk, she found the leftover bandages. Then she looked helplessly down at the wing under her scarf. Where would she even start bandaging? The feathers were tightly interlocked, but perhaps she could wind the bandages between them somehow?

"Cherries!" he said again to Hetta. "Candles!"

"You're not making any sense," she told him, heart pounding. Even if she got his wing bandaged, how could they escape before Mrs Thompson returned? How would Wyn fit in the kineticar in this form?

Wyn shook his head like a dog shedding water. "I can smell her magic," he said, gritting out each word. Frustration burned in the russet of his eyes, and she knew he was having as much difficulty making his words coherent as she was deciphering them. "She's here."

"Whose magic?" But then she could smell it too—cherries, just on the peak of ripeness before they tipped into rotten. Cherries and, strangely enough, beeswax. The only magic she knew that had a taste was fae magic. Hetta pressed her scarf more firmly against Wyn's wings and grimly let her pyromancy simmer up.

Cherries, full and sweet, flavoured the air so strongly that Hetta could almost taste them. The air warped slightly and, with a faint pop, a fae woman stood in the room with them.

She was short, with the kind of ample hourglass figure and lazy sensuality that made men stop and stare. Her smooth, flawless skin was a shade or two paler than Wyn's, and she had hair that began at its roots as inky black and ended as cherry-blossom pink at her waist. But it wasn't her extraordinary hair colour that marked her as fae, nor her unnaturally symmetrical features. No, it was the black, cat-like ears that peeked through her hair, and the long furry tail that curled out from her spine in a skewed question mark.

Midnight-dark eyes swept over Hetta and Wyn. There was something feline about the angle of them—or maybe that was just the general effect of the ears and tail. Paired with full lips and a dainty nose, they gave her a mesmerising kind of beauty.

Wyn's magic rose, mingling with the cherry and beeswax, until the air smelled like a wet orchard. Even Hetta, with her lack of familiarity with fae magic, could tell there was something wrong with Wyn's.

"Settle your feathers, Prince Hallowyn. I am not here to harm you," the fae woman said. Her voice was low and sultry, amusement tinging her words. "My, you *are* having a bad day. Though you've grown since I last saw you." Hetta didn't like the proprietary way her gaze ran over Wyn.

A sudden wind rustled the discarded paper strewn around the room, though it didn't lift a single glossy strand of the fae woman's hair. Hetta's skin tingled, and that sense of approaching storm increased.

"If you can even summon lightning in the state you're in, you're far more likely to kill your lover than me," the fae woman remarked coldly.

"Who are you?" Hetta demanded, resisting the urge to stand protectively between Wyn and the woman. "What do you want?"

"I am here to do you a favour," said the woman, teeth flashing in a sudden smile. She moved swiftly, faster than Hetta could follow, her fingers abruptly digging into Hetta's wrist, her other hand resting just below the injury on Wyn's wing. "You may thank me later."

Darkness exploded, the world turning inside out. Time lost meaning, and it might have been five minutes or five seconds later when light returned, leaving Hetta dizzy and disoriented.

When the world had righted itself, she stared in disbelief. They were next to the road just outside Stariel's borders, beneath the naked branches of a roadside cherry tree. Wyn lay in a crumple of feathers and blood, eyes blazing with fury. The fae woman was nowhere to be seen.

"Who was that?" Hetta asked, though she already knew. There was really only one person it could be.

"That," said Wyn, his voice tight with pain and anger, "was my fiancée. Princess Sunnika."

14

UNUSUAL COMMUNICATIONS

Hetta knew about Wyn's engagement and knew that breaking it was why he was hunted by two courts. But the tale had been so fantastical—warring fae, princesses, and so on—that she hadn't given much thought to the actual physical woman he'd been engaged to. Wyn had also failed to mention his former fiancée was spectacularly beautiful. That shouldn't matter, in the grand scheme of things, but it somehow did.

It was going to be hard not to dwell on it later, but she didn't have time for it now, not with Wyn bleeding into the muddy verge. She hurried to his side, trying not to slip on the soft ground. He made an incongruous picture of broken elegance, the sunlight glittering in his hair and feathers. She'd thought his wings pure white, but now she noticed a line of bright blue feathers close to his spine, sparkling like sapphires where they weren't obscured by blood.

Before she reached him, Wyn winched his wing in and tied Hetta's scarf around the entire thing. *So that's how one bandages a wing.* The scarf had originally been a periwinkle blue design patterned with intricate white flowers. Now it was mottled dark with blood.

"How did we get here?" she asked, dropping to her knees beside him.

"Teleportation. The greater fae...of DuskRose...have that gift," he panted. Mud and grass smudged his primaries, and blood smeared the remains of his dripping shirt. The scarf-wrapped wing gave him a lopsided appearance.

"Do you know what she wanted?"

He shook his head and pulled clumsily at his wet shirt-sleeves, trying to unbutton them. Hetta pushed his hands away, taking on the task herself. Her knees pressed into the mud, damp seeping through her skirt. Each inch of material she lifted away from his skin made him suck in a breath.

"What was in that mixture?" she asked softly.

"Yarrow. Vervain. Eyebright." He lapsed into a tongue she didn't know to list the rest. "I do not know the local names for those." His words were thick and slow, and when she'd freed him of his ruined shirt, he scrabbled at the soaked bandage on his forearm with shaking fingers. Hetta didn't like to remove it—he'd lost so much blood already. But he tore at it feverishly until she stilled his hands with her own and unwound the bandage for him.

When she'd removed the last of the herb-soaked material, Wyn sagged in relief, eyelids fluttering shut for a second. A fine tremor ran over his skin, but when he opened his eyes he'd regained a measure of his usual composure.

Blood was welling up where she'd removed the tainted bandage, the lug-imp's bite deep and raw. Hetta made a rapid decision and pulled off her coat, setting it impatiently aside. The coat was too thick to wrap effectively, but her blouse would do. It was the work of seconds to undo all the buttons. She wore a slip beneath that left her shoulders bare, and the cold wind bit at her skin in the time it took to shrug back into her coat. She began to wind the thinner material around his arm, an absurdly frilly bandage.

"I am ruining a lot of clothing today," Wyn murmured. His gaze strayed to the expanse of skin visible above the low neckline of the slip but unfocused as she tightened the makeshift bandage. "We need to get inside the boundaries."

Hetta looked towards Stariel. The estate lurked just on the edge of touching, so close she could feel its eagerness for her return, but she doubted Wyn could even stand unaided, and she wasn't strong enough to carry him by herself.

"Wait here," she told him.

He gave a weak smile. "As you wish, my Star."

She stumbled onto the road. This was a back way, to the north of the main road that passed through Stariel-on-Starwater. The train track that ran nearly precisely along Stariel's eastern border was only a long stone's throw away.

Gravel scattered as she ran towards the boundary, clutching her hat securely to her head. *"I can heal wounds that would kill a mortal man,"* Wyn had said once before, and she hoped it held true now, even with wounds made with iron bullets. It was hard to keep a firm handle on the alarm threatening to rise up and choke her. She'd never seen Wyn so disoriented before. That worried her nearly as much as the blood loss.

Sheep raised their heads to watch her from the field beside the road and, with the sudden skittishness typical of their kind, abruptly took exception to her running, turning and bounding away. The air held nothing but the earthy mix of sheep, grass, and mud, but she couldn't help searching for a hint of something out of place, in case it was all the warning she got. A sudden croak made her start, but it was only a crow perched on the low dry-stone wall. The road angled up to meet the train tracks, and she launched herself over that final hurdle.

As soon as she crossed the bounds, gasping, her awareness expanded. Energy surged through her, bolstering her magical reserves, as if she were a sagging balloon suddenly swelling with air. Stariel nearly knocked her over in its enthusiasm, metaphorically trying to lick her face and rub itself against her, like a large and exuberant dog.

<I'm glad to see you too,> she told it, before delving deeper into the estate. Stariel caught the taste of her emotions and vibrated with sudden alarm and fierce protectiveness. Where was the danger? It would rain down retribution on anyone thinking to invade its territory.

Hetta sunk willingly into its hyper-alertness. She would need it for what she was about to attempt. Her body faded from her awareness until she was a creature of soil and forests and groundwater and a thousand tiny moving parts. A web of bright sparks scattered across her surface: her family. All the Valstars had at least a bit of the land-sense, a connection to Stariel, but some had it more strongly than others. What did she need? For a moment, she struggled to remember her intentions, too deeply immersed in the land. She clutched towards the brightest point of the web on instinct. *Jack*, she thought. That must be Jack.

But it wasn't Jack. Two feminine minds started at the sudden touch, their identities becoming apparent as Hetta's focus tightened: Hetta's half-sister Alexandra and her cousin Caro. Alexandra's pen poised above a blank piece of paper and a drop of ink fell from the nib in the time it took for Hetta to realise they weren't who she wanted.

Hetta drew back with a mental squeeze of apology and tried again to convey to Stariel who she was looking for: *Jack*. She tried to think how Stariel would know him: stocky, red-haired, blunt, and dutiful to his roots. She visualised the mile-eating way he walked, the whistle of him calling his dog. Something in her scrambled description set off an echo of recognition in Stariel, and the land eagerly zeroed in on a different spark.

<Jack!> she flung at him as his mind lit up in surprise. She didn't know if it was possible to communicate this way, but if anyone were connected tightly enough for it to work, it would be him.

There was a pause.

<Hetta?!>

It wasn't speech, not really. Communicating with Stariel had given Hetta some practice at interpreting a wordless flow of meaning. This was a more quick-silvered version of that, Jack's thoughts fast and darting as minnows compared to Stariel's. Jack was a tumble of incredulity and worry, demanding answers and offering assistance all at the same time. How was she doing this? Wonder shimmered through their connection.

Hetta tried to parcel up what she wanted into something communicable, distilling the image as she'd learnt to do as part of her illusionist's training: Wyn, lying bloody and broken against the muddy-green of the verge, the train tracks in the distance. <Come here. Help.> She visualised a great string connecting Jack to her current location and flung the image at him. Concern shivered through the connection, but he'd understood. She hoped.

Disentangling herself from Stariel was difficult, her own anxiety making the land swarm up in a misguided attempt to reassure her. Two feet, she had two feet, warm inside their boots. The texture of her stockings prickled against her toes. No, that wasn't her toes; the prickliness was the swish of pine needles in the southern forests. She tried to locate her hands but found instead the intricate threads of waterways joining, forming the major tributaries to Starwater.

Stariel had senses she had no name for—the tiny ripples of air currents as a robin flitted from branch to branch, the heavy saturation of the soils in the sheepfold, the ebb and whirl of magic within its borders—so she tried to focus on the sensations that were purely her own: the slanting sunshine of winter afternoon warm against her cheeks, the cold air filling her lungs, the loamy scent of countryside, and the small shifting of gravel under her boots.

Finally, she opened her eyes. The sun had moved. How long had she been standing there, lost? This couldn't be normal lordship behaviour. She would've noticed her father caught in mindless reverie. The need to find a teacher scratched at her again.

Wyn! She spun and looked down the sloping road. Her last rush to the boundary had carried her a little past the train tracks, thank the nine heavens. There were only two trains a day this far north, and the later train wouldn't pass this spot for another few hours, but it still made her shiver to think of herself standing mindless and vulnerable on the line.

Wyn was still sitting when she reached him, and it struck her all over again what an awkward position it was for a winged creature. His eyes were closed, and he didn't react to the sound of her approach. The brown of his skin was washed out to a sickly beige, the lines of his face stark. The smell of rain on dry earth hung around him, fragile as spider webs.

"Wyn?" she said, worried by his intense stillness. "You'd better not be unconscious. I shall be very annoyed with you if you are."

His eyes snapped open, russet flecked with brandy-gold. "I should like to avoid that," he said, voice oddly sluggish.

"I've summoned Jack." She paused. "Why did Mrs Thompson shoot you? It seems a rather excessive act. Don't tell me our bank manager's wife was working for your brother."

"I don't…know," he said. There was something dreamlike about his expression. It worried her, but his words were coherent enough, if more slowly spoken than usual. Had he done some kind of fae thing to push back the pain? "But I don't think so. It doesn't make sense for Rake to try to kill me after working so hard not to. Especially not so clumsily."

"You and I have an entirely different understanding of what constitutes trying to kill someone," Hetta disagreed. "What about the other one? The one who sent the lug-imps?"

"Aroset?" He shook his head. "She would never send a mortal to do the deed. I suppose it could be one of my other siblings."

"I'm never going to complain about my familial disagreements again," Hetta vowed, wringing a small smile from him. He looked so worn that she couldn't bear it. She flung herself at him with extreme carefulness, wrapping her arms around his chest and burying her face against his collarbone. She trembled and simultaneously cursed herself for such foolishness. *He* was the one injured, not *her*! But he'd been shot, and it could've so easily been much, much worse. She kept replaying the sound of the gunshot and his sudden flinch as the bullet hit. She hugged him tighter.

Wyn kissed the top of her head, his good arm coming around her. "They haven't killed me, Hetta. And I don't intend to let them," he said softly, stroking small circles between her shoulder blades.

"Good," she said without lifting her head. "You're forbidden to die on me, you understand?" She breathed in the warm scent of him, that dust after rain smell mixed with spice. That and the warm solidity of him finally eased the cold dread she'd held ever since Rakken told her about the lug-imps.

He murmured wordless reassurance, but his pulse was too fast and erratic against her cheek. It quivered through her, closer than her own, and her insides re-tied themselves in painful knots. He might not be dead, but he certainly wasn't all right. Hetta wasn't used to dealing with this intensity of emotion; never in her past affairs had she suffered this stomach-clenching fear of loss. She didn't much like it.

He leaned his head against hers. "Oh, my love, I'm sorry. You cope so well that I forget, sometimes, that this isn't what you're used to." Her heart gave an odd squeeze at the endearment. She'd known, of course, but he'd been *so* careful not to say it. He didn't seem to notice his slip, which worried her more than anything else. "Will you help me stand? We should get to the border."

Hetta pulled herself together. "I don't think you should move. If Jack has an ounce of common sense, he'll bring the pony cart."

"And I don't think we should stay here where we are vulnerable for any longer than we have to." He must be tired indeed to disagree with her so bluntly. "I've amused you," he observed.

"It's the sight of you trying to be all calm and collected when you're nine parts unconscious," she said, getting to her feet. The angle gave her a close view of his horns, and he stiffened under her appraisal. He wouldn't admit it unless she made him, but she knew he hated her seeing him like this. "Can you stand? There's no point in us arguing about it if you can't."

"Do I get some credit for trying to argue, regardless?" he asked lightly. She refused to smile, and he admitted, "I don't know. My leg is…painful. But I would rather suffer that tenfold than stay here as a sitting duck any longer."

She'd prefer them to be within Stariel's bounds too. How much time had passed since she'd summoned Jack? Had he even understood what she wanted from him?

"All right," she said reluctantly. "But let me see if I can find a stick or something first."

Some minutes later, with the aid of a flimsy piece of poplar that was all she could find, they managed to lever Wyn up off the ground. Fortunately, he'd been injured on the opposite leg to his shoulder, so he could sling one arm around Hetta's shoulder for balance.

They proceeded by inches. Wyn was no lightweight, and he could put no weight at all on his injured foot. By the time they'd gone three yards, Wyn was panting and shaking with the effort and Hetta was regretting giving in. How could she have forgotten how good he was at masking discomfort?

"This isn't going to work," she told him, coming to a shambling halt. "We should just wait for Jack."

It took him several seconds to reply as he caught his breath. "But we…have…come…so…far!"

She ignored this attempt at levity. "You're going to faint in another minute at this rate," she said grimly.

"Possible," he admitted, face pale. The movement had made his wounds start bleeding afresh, seeping through all Hetta's makeshift bandages. There would be no salvaging her blouse or scarf. Thin rivulets had worked their way down his left forearm and over his hand to end in scarlet drips at his fingertips.

Hetta made a decision. "Impending fae attacks be dashed. Sit down before you fall down!"

He would've tried to argue with her, but she shimmied her support out from under his shoulder and he folded heavily to the ground. He glared up at her, the clear affront in his expression making her heart squeeze with worry; it wasn't usually so easy to read him.

Hooves clattered against gravel and Hetta spun, hope burning in her throat. It was Jack, driving the pony cart, but he wasn't alone. Her cousin Caroline and her brother Marius sat in the cart, wearing matching shocked expressions. Marius's was because of Wyn's injuries. Caroline's was because of his wings.

IRON

WYN BORE THE reveal of his nature to yet another Valstar philosophically. Or at least as philosophically as possible under the circumstances, which wasn't very. Every breath grated muscle and bone against the iron bullet. It made it difficult to care much what people thought. Stormwinds curse iron! It tangled through his magic, making it impossible for his body to heal as it should. He'd sunk into a meditation before, carefully cordoning off the pain, but the strain of moving had broken that temporary mental block.

The horse snorted at Wyn as Jack pulled the cart to a halt, but the animal was familiar enough with him not to shy away. Instead it stood, huffing disapprovingly at his wings.

"Good…afternoon," Wyn panted. He was suddenly conscious of the mud sticking to the tips of his primaries. From his ungainly seat, he couldn't raise his wings high enough to keep them free of the dirt. Would it be easier to bear being so exposed if he were at least clean?

His thoughts tumbled back and forth like stones in a polisher's barrel. Caroline's face was too composed. Had Jack warned her? Marius was frozen. Please let this not be another reason for

Marius to be angry at him. He had bungled that relationship so badly already.

Caroline was saying something to Hetta, and then they were all getting out of the cart.

Marius was saying something to him as well, but it was hard to concentrate over the searing agony of the iron. Why were they all milling about so? They ought to go back inside Stariel's borders where they were safe. He tried to tell Hetta this, but the words came out garbled and he had to repeat himself.

"The border—we need to go."

"Yes, but not until I've stopped the bleeding again. Caro's brought the first aid kit from the house, thank the heavens."

He watched, oddly detached, as Hetta removed the makeshift bandage from his arm. It had come loose as they walked, and the wound had re-opened. His fingers were tacky with drying blood. Hetta began to wind a fresh white length in its place, taken from the first aid kit. The large case stood open on the roadside, glittering with jars, instruments, and bandages. Something snagged at him, difficult to grasp as fog. If only the iron weren't in him, poisoning his blood.

The iron!

"Need to get the iron out," he said, scrabbling weakly for the scarf tied about his wing. What was the word? "Forceps."

"The bullet!" Hetta understood, thank the Maelstrom. "It's still in you."

There was a cacophony of voices. Marius demanded to know who had shot him and Jack swore, while Caroline matter-of-factly said something about steady hands, but then he lost track until Hetta untied the scarf and emptied a canister of what felt like liquid fire onto his wing. Agony exploded, white-hot as the heart of a star. He fanned out his wings in instinctive response, and the movement jolted the iron ball. Lights danced across his vision.

Hetta. Her hands were on his face, anchoring him, and he

brought his good arm up to twine his fingers with hers. He was gripping too tightly, but he couldn't make himself let go, not with the sharp iron of the forceps digging into the arch of his wing.

It took forever and no time at all. He couldn't tell. There were only his harsh breaths and the piercing wrongness of the iron, Hetta's hand and the low sound of her voice as she murmured comfort. He couldn't make out the individual words, but he held fast to that stream of reassurance. A long disused part of his mind flared to life, the part that knew how to survive even when pain made that seem impossible, and he coiled in on himself, a pebble in a river of torment.

Then suddenly it was done, and the world righted itself. He became aware that he was shaking and forced himself to stop, though he couldn't bear to relinquish Hetta's hand quite yet. Her eyes were a paler shade of grey than usual, lovely as dawn mist. She had her back to the sun, and it brought out the red in her auburn hair.

Sheep baa-ed in the distance, the sound curiously grounding. It was second nature to test the air for hints of magic, but there was only the lingering fragrance of cherries. If there were any fae present, they were well hidden. But of course they would be—both Aroset and Rakken were skilled enough to mask their signatures if they wanted.

"Thank you," he said. Caroline was calmly wiping the forceps and packing up the first aid kit. She'd been the one to remove the iron ball with the steady hands of someone used to handling dangerous chemicals. Caroline worked as an assistant in a chemical research laboratory at Knoxbridge University in the South. Both her parents were academics, committed to open-minded liberalism but not the sort to believe in such old-fashioned things as fae. Caroline didn't seem to know what to make of the situation, her expression carefully blank. Perhaps she was recalling their earlier conversation in a new light.

He began to struggle to his feet. "We need to get inside the bounds." His balance was off with one wing bandaged tightly to his body. Would his injured leg bear his weight? It didn't matter; he would hop if he had to.

Jack put a hand on his uninjured shoulder and stopped him. "Bloody hell, Wyn. Give yourself half a minute at least."

"No," he said. "I will take as many minutes as you like once we are a hundred yards down the road and safely inside Stariel. Help me up."

Jack muttered something decidedly uncomplimentary under his breath, but he did as Wyn bid and hauled him to his feet. Wyn grit his teeth at the movement. It was hard not to think about how he must look when they were all so clearly unsettled by it, his inhumanness. Caroline's eyes kept flicking up to his horns and then away, as if she were trying not to be rude.

Jack dealt with his disquiet by covering it with bluff humour. "Gods, you weigh half a tonne like this," he said as Wyn leaned on him for balance.

"An exaggeration. But let us get me into the cart before your strength gives out. I don't wish to overtax you."

Jack lost his self-consciousness for long enough to glare at him.

Marius fluttered about, wanting to help but not quite sure how. Like Caroline, his gaze kept darting in and out, simultaneously fascinated and not wanting to stare. Oh, Marius, well-meaning and indecisive as always. Strangely it made Wyn's mood lift. He knew how to deal with Marius when he was like this.

"If you get in the cart, I would appreciate a hand up," Wyn said to him. Marius nodded, nerves settling a fraction, and moved with alacrity to follow the instruction.

It was an awkward and painful business, but their efforts ended with Wyn successfully on the wooden bench inside of the cart, hunched over and panting. Hetta scrambled up to sit beside him. He appreciated that she was trying to pretend his appearance didn't bother her while in front of her relatives, and he almost slung an arm around her before remembering that he mustn't.

Jack got the cart moving with a crunch of gravel. Wyn gripped the wooden bench tightly, his wings instinctively trying to flare out for balance. The small movement sent a jolt of pain ricocheting down his spine.

"All right," Marius said. "Who shot you?"

"The bank manager's wife shot me," Wyn said conversationally. "For some reason, she thinks I am fae."

Caroline made a small sound, a giggle quickly stifled, though her gaze didn't lift from inspecting her feet, which she'd apparently decided was the safest way to avoid rudeness. Marius didn't smile. His fingers stiffened where he held on to the rough wood of the bench, and he frowned at Wyn's bandaged wing. "Will you be all right?"

"Unless something else unexpected happens, yes."

"Where did you leave the car?" Jack spoke from the driver's seat.

"Alverness," said Hetta. "We were transported back here by magic."

Jack took his gaze off the road long enough to frown at Wyn. "How is that possible?"

"DuskRose. Many of the greater fae of that court—the shadow-cats—can teleport. Magically transport themselves from one place to another. It usually only works within line-of-sight. I didn't know Princess Sunnika had the strength to shift multiple people over such a distance. She has grown in power. Before this I would've said only Queen Tayarenn had that capability." It chilled him, knowing that Princess Sunnika had that kind of range. The innate ability to teleport was a rare gift amongst fae—hence the power wielded by the shadowcats. Unlike other types of translocation magic, it could be done without any prior preparation and didn't depend on establishing a resonance link between locations, at least over line-of-sight distances. That flexibility made it deadly in battle.

Caroline was nearly vibrating with curiosity and blurted out,

"DuskRose? Princess Sunnika? Who are these people?" Her gaze lifted, meeting Wyn's for a second, and he caught the next question that she just managed to avoid verbalising: *What are you?*

He was about to explain when copper bloomed on the back of his tongue and the hairs on his neck rose, with static rather than cold. He jerked and banged his bandaged wing painfully on the side of the cart. *Aroset*. Where was his sister's magical signature coming from?

"Get us over the boundary, Jack," he said urgently, scanning the surrounding fields. "Now." Jack, bless him, didn't argue, and clucked to the horse. The cart's pace increased.

Wyn took a sharp breath as he spotted his sister. She must've stepped from a portal at that very moment, for her presence suddenly blazed to his leysight. When had she become so adept at portals? How had she located a resonance point so quickly? That faint feeling of charge increased, and Wyn gathered up his fraying magic. Could he divert a lightning strike if she made one? They were so close to the boundary, to safety, but Aroset was fast as a snake.

She didn't strike though, in those few heartbeats of vulnerability, merely watched through narrowed eyes, crimson wings flexing with indecision. *Father must have told her not to attack Stariel's lord*, he realised. *She doesn't want to risk hitting the others.* But apparently whatever orders Father had given Aroset on that front weren't a strong enough disincentive, for he saw her posture shift and felt the crackle in the air that signalled an attack. He braced, but between one breath and the next they crossed the boundary that marked safety, and Stariel hit him with the force of a wrecking ball.

Stariel was old and vast and so, so powerful, and the full weight of that power abruptly pressed down upon him. He gasped, throwing up shields instinctively, trying to make himself as small and insignificant as possible. That only angered Stariel further, and it ripped through his shields like tissue paper.

Hetta's commandment reverberated to his bones. <Stop!> she flung out. He'd never been more in awe of her, standing between him and that vast force, not one fibre of her being doubting the faeland would obey. It did, but grudgingly, curling away from him, suspicious and snarling.

He looked back, but Aroset was gone. He realised all his feathers were fluffed up and quickly un-fluffed them, slumping in sudden exhaustion. His blood still fizzed unpleasantly from the lug-imp venom, and the bullet wound ached dully, but at least they were safe. For now.

"Who was that?" Marius asked. "And what was that from Stariel just now?" His land-sense wasn't strong, but apparently Stariel's reaction had been such that even he'd felt it.

"My sister," Wyn said. He was so tired, swaying to the rhythm of the cart. He wanted desperately to shut his eyes and let himself sleep. "She's trying to kill me, but she can't cross the boundaries without Hetta's permission. And Stariel…"

Hetta came to his rescue. "I don't know what's gotten Stariel's knickers in such a twist, but I intend to figure it out. Wyn can explain himself later—he's had rather a bad day." She began to tell them what had happened. Wyn shut his eyes, letting her words wash over him, his awareness narrowing to the warmth of her body so near to his.

He didn't like the description of her meeting with Rakken. It was easier to think without the iron in him, and the conclusions he drew were everything he'd most feared: the fae using him as a bargaining chip against Hetta. Sunnika, though…the stormwinds knew what her motivations were. He doubted they boded well.

High King's horns, but he needed to sleep. He'd made too many mistakes today already, and he feared making more through fatigue. He slit his eyes open to find Marius watching him grimly. Wyn couldn't really blame him.

This road approached Stariel House from the north-east, and they had just come into sight of the building when Wyn marshalled his strength and changed. His tiredness increased tenfold, and he felt blind and deaf after so long in his fae form.

"I thought it took longer for you to heal in this form?" Hetta said under her breath. She still wore her hat, and it shadowed her face as she looked up at him.

"Hmmm," he said noncommittedly.

"Well, you're right that it'll cause less of an uproar this way," she agreed. "But I think you do them a disservice, assuming they won't accept you if they know."

"How do your wings heal if you magic them away?" Caroline asked suddenly.

Wyn smiled. "How do you know where your hands are when your eyes are closed?"

"Are they still there, then?" Caroline searched the space behind him as if expecting to see feathers.

"No. I'm a true shapeshifter."

"Oh." Caroline's eyes burned with a thousand questions, but she abruptly realised he didn't wish to answer them.

Marius, however, had no such compunctions. "What do you mean, a true shapeshifter? And why—"

"Oh, leave him alone, Marius," Hetta said. "And give him your coat."

Wyn was about to protest that he didn't need it—he wasn't cold—but Hetta poked him gently in the ribs before he could say so. The two siblings glared at each other across the cart, genuine irritation on both sides. Usually the two of them were close, and Wyn would be damned if he came between them. "Hetta, I don't need—"

"Oh, for goodness' sake, Wyn, stop being such a martyr," Marius snapped, shrugging out of his coat and passing it across.

Wyn's gambit had worked to defuse the tension between Marius and Hetta, the only downside being that now Marius's ire was firmly redirected back at Wyn. He eased himself into the coat, praying that he wasn't about to wreck a *fourth* article of clothing for the day. It was hard not to feel like the universe had taken a pointed and personal dislike to him donning human attire. He was broader in the shoulders than Marius, particularly when bandaged, and the material pulled tightly at his back. Hetta was right though; it did give him a marginally more respectable appearance, which he now realised had been her intention.

The rest of the journey was almost peaceful. The air seared with the weight of meaningful looks and unspoken words, but no one was sinking their fangs into him or trying to shoot him, and for this little space of time he could relax. He ought to be thinking of what to do when they got to the house, but he knew without asking that Hetta would take care of it, and he was tired enough to let her. And surely he could defer deciding what to do about the fae until he'd slept, at least?

You are weak, Hallowyn. It was weak, to pretend he didn't already know what he must do now that his father had set things in motion. His hourglass had run dry.

Their arrival created a minor uproar. A gaggle of Hetta's relatives waited at the entrance to the house, framed by the two stone creatures that guarded the front steps. They were, ironically, statues of lowfae, though none of the Valstars would know the live equivalents. Perhaps that would change, now the Iron Law was no longer in place.

Hetta muttered to Jack, "Wonderful job at sneaking off quietly. Just wonderful."

"Don't blame *me!* You're the one who set Stariel in a dither! You're bloody lucky I got away with only these two!" Jack jerked his head back at Caroline and Marius. "I'm sorry if I was more worried about saving your skin than being discreet."

There was a pause.

"I'm sorry, Jack, that was horribly ungrateful of me." A quiver of wry amusement laced Hetta's voice. "I've just realised that half my relatives weren't here last time we explained the whole the-fae-are-real business. Well, at least I shall have more support this time. Just think, eventually we may get to the point of being able to shout 'wicked fae have attacked!' without having to stop and explain ourselves. What a marvellous concept."

"I'm not sure I look forward to shouting 'wicked fae have attacked' on multiple future occasions," Wyn couldn't help saying. He thought of the maidservant in Alverness and of Mrs Thompson. "But you are right—better to explain now than wait for rumour to catch up."

Hetta's voice was soft. "Does that include you?" Alarm thrilled through him. He couldn't make himself confirm either way, but she read his lack of answer for what it was and sighed. "It's all right. This is your secret, Wyn, and I won't *make* you reveal it."

Self-loathing dug sharp claws into his chest. He was being unfair to Hetta, to all the Valstars. But he was so tired, and he shied from the thought of the uproar that revealing his identity would cause. Besides, he would be leaving anyway, so what was the point?

There was a hubbub of voices as they approached, and the Valstars crowded around the cart as Jack drew up.

"What in Prydein is going on, Henrietta?" Aunt Sybil, Jack's mother, demanded.

"Wicked fae have attacked, I'm afraid, Aunt," Hetta said airily.

Aunt Sybil pulled herself to her full height. Since she had a tendency to dress all in black, the effect wasn't dissimilar to a crow puffing up. "What did they want?"

This caused a ripple of reaction in those Valstars who hadn't yet been informed of the fae's existence.

Before Hetta could answer, her half-sister Alexandra cried out, "What's wrong with Wyn? Are you all right?" She looked both very young and very earnest as she pushed her way forward. Her brother Gregory, her elder by two years, echoed the question, though suspicion lurked in his expression. Both knew of Wyn's nature, but their different experiences with the lesser fae Gwendelfear had made Gregory leery of all fae and Alexandra too trusting.

"I have been most adequately bandaged," Wyn assured them both.

"He needs to be in bed," Marius disagreed. "Hetta will explain. I'll help you into the house, Wyn."

Hetta gave her oldest sibling a speaking look but sighed. "Yes, you do need to rest, Wyn, before you fall over." She turned her gaze towards the minor horde before her and declared, "You had better all come with me into the hall, for I've something to say to you all."

Curiosity cut through the crowd like a pike, but they didn't immediately follow Hetta's direction. Instead, they fluttered around Wyn as Jack and Marius helped him out of the cart, interjecting concerns and suggestions for his well-being, as if they truly considered him one of their own. It filled him with a soft and oddly painful sensation.

On the ground, he leaned against the cart, testing his wounded leg with a barely repressed grimace. Hetta scrambled out of the cart to stand beside him.

"Throwing me to the wolves, Hetta?" he asked her in an undertone, eying Jack and Marius.

"If I wanted to do that, *you* would be the one about to spend the next hour arguing with my entire family," she shot back. "I have every confidence in your ability to handle yourself." She didn't touch him, not here with all her relatives watching, but her eyes softened. "Don't let your martyrish tendencies get the better of you. Go and collapse somewhere. You look terrible." She raised her voice and addressed her various relations more generally. "No, Marius and Jack are quite capable of helping Wyn into the house, and he doesn't need you all here as an audience. Come along!"

It was a relief to be away from the scrutiny of all those eyes, but it did leave him at the mercy of Marius and Jack, neither one of them particularly kindly disposed towards him at present.

"I'll get a cane for you," Marius said after a pause. By the time Jack had helped Wyn up the entrance stairs, he'd emerged with one of cousin Ivy's spare walking sticks. Ivy had been born with a malformed limb that gave her an occasional limp. The stick was a little short for him but still helped greatly with his balance, though he wobbled like a new-born kitten. The venom was slowly losing its potency, only murmuring in his blood now, but negating its effects had sucked his reserves dry.

Jack and Marius exchanged glances. "You'll never get up all the stairs to your room," Jack said matter-of-factly.

Wyn shook his head. "I will. I would rather be in my own room. I will hobble up there by myself if need be."

"Aye, and go through the pair of us as well if we try to stop you?" Jack said dryly.

"Well, I would prefer not to."

Jack muttered something uncomplimentary under his breath, but the two men walked with him as he made his painstaking way into the house, each of them ready to lend a hand if Wyn faltered.

In a more formal house with more staff, there might have been stricter rules about who lived where. But Stariel House had been understaffed for years, and for nine-tenths of the year it was underpopulated as well, with the Valstars spreading out to pursue their various interests elsewhere. The current stress on bedroom availability had more to do with rooms being in good repair than in existence. This meant that Wyn had had a relatively open field when it came to selecting a room. His was the only occupied chamber on his floor, in the high attics of the old west wing, too cold and draughty to attract much interest from anyone else.

"I've never understood why you choose to room in that draughty garret," Jack grumbled as they made their way up the entrance stairs one slow step at a time. Wyn found it easiest to progress with one hand on the banister and the other leaning on the walking stick, transferring his weight up each step in undignified hops. Each jolt made him grit his teeth, and he had to stop halfway and rest.

"I don't mind the cold," Wyn said truthfully.

"It's the fact that it has a balcony," Marius said suddenly. "You like knowing you can escape if need be."

Wyn smiled. He found Marius's complete inability to prevent himself from blurting out his intuitions as he had them at turns exasperating and endearing, but the familiarity of it just now steadied him. "I do like having access to the sky," he agreed softly. Even though he hadn't flown for years before recent events had necessitated it—a denial he wasn't sure he could repeat, with the glorious memory of soaring above the Indigoes still fresh in his mind, untainted even by his ungainly, unpractised landing.

He'd thought the two would plague him with questions and accusations once they got him alone. Marius was dark with hurt and ruffled sensibilities, and it would be like him to choose the worst possible moment to air these. Jack, too, wasn't a tactful man. But they both held their opinions back, though the weight of them was nearly tangible.

He must look terrible.

By the time they reached his 'draughty garret', Wyn was blurry with fatigue and deeply grateful that they hadn't taken advantage of him. Stormwinds knew what he might say, pain and fatigue loosing his carefully guarded tongue. But they were being strangely considerate, despite the anger he could sense in them both. That warm and complicated feeling lodged in his throat again; it was so very *human* of them.

He did as Hetta had bid and collapsed onto his bed. Fleetingly, he wondered how she was coping downstairs before darkness billowed up to meet him.

CARNELION HALL

CARNELION HALL WAS the largest room in the house, though it shrunk when filled with Valstars and assorted others—Hetta noticed one of the maidservants loitering at the back, attempting to look busy. Everyone was waiting for Hetta to speak, though not quietly, of course. One couldn't have three or more Valstars in one place and expect any degree of quiet. The half of the family who already knew about the fae were busily explaining this to the other half, with varying degrees of fact and tact, and the half that hadn't known were reacting according to their natures.

Hetta fiddled with the top button of her coat, reassuring herself it was done up and hid the fact that she was missing her blouse. She still felt oddly naked.

"I know one may *think* one has witnessed something with one's own eyes, but the eyes are actually extremely unreliable instruments," Uncle Percival said to a glowering Aunt Sybil. "Why, one of my colleagues, a professor of psychology, reports that…" His wife punctuated his increasingly tangential speech with firm nods, clearly waiting for a pause in which to insert her own professional opinion. Caro didn't join in her parents' academic musings and instead shrugged helplessly at Hetta.

"My nan used to tell me about fairies as big as carthorses, with teeth as long as my arm!" the housemaid was saying enthusiastically to Hetta's half-sister Alexandra. Her eyes grew round. "Do you think that was one of the ones that attacked Mr Tempest?"

Alexandra bit her lip. Hetta didn't hear her response, but she suspected it was a negative. Alexandra had met the fae Gwendelfear, after all, who hadn't in any way resembled a carthorse.

Prior to inheriting the lordship, Hetta hadn't had much occasion for public speaking, and yet since her ascension she seemed constantly called upon to do so. She moved to stand in front of the large fireplace in the centre of one wall. Opposite, racks of swords and banners hung, ageing monuments to ancestors she couldn't readily name. Taking the battle accoutrements as a prompt to begin her own campaign, she straightened.

"Right," she said loudly. There was a susurration of shushing. Hetta tried not to fidget as the room's attention crystallised. "So… as you've undoubtedly gathered, the fae are real. As some of you already know, we had an encounter with them before, not long after my father's funeral. You may remember our houseguest, Miss Gwen? In truth, she was the fae Gwendelfear, come to try and take advantage of my newness to my role."

This was only a half-true and carefully pruned version of the actual story. The Choosing Ceremony had been deliberately sabotaged, so that Hetta had only appeared to be lord when in fact she wasn't. But only a handful of her relatives knew that and, as Hetta had since been chosen for real, it seemed best not to re-open the case.

There was some resistance to her statement, but when Hetta looked pointedly at Aunt Sybil, her aunt grudgingly confirmed, "It's true."

"We saw off Gwendelfear and another fae monster, and I had hoped that that would be the end of it," Hetta continued.

"Gwendelfear helped us, though!" her half-sister Alexandra piped up. Heads swivelled towards her, and she blushed. "I mean…"

"She did," Hetta allowed. "The fae can be good or bad or not, much like regular people." She ought to encourage that idea; it would make it easier for Wyn if the day ever came when he let himself be seen. "And today one of the fae from Gwendelfear's court came to our aid when another lot of fae attacked Wyn and me at the bank. Both the bank manager and Wyn were injured in the attack."

There was a beat of silence, followed immediately by Uncle Percival objecting. "My dear Henrietta, whatever may have happened, your conclusion cannot be correct. Fairies!" he scoffed.

Hetta ignored him. "At this point, I must ask you not to leave the bounds of the estate. You all know Stariel's magic, but you probably don't realise that it offers protection against the fae. This is a precaution only, and I'll be doing my best to bring this to a quick resolution." Did she sound too much like a pompous government official? But maybe that was a good thing in this case; people took officials seriously, didn't they? And she had to make her family understand the danger, whilst also not unnecessarily alarming them or setting their backs up, as she seemed to constantly do. *Maybe I need to check if one can purchase manuals on speech-giving.*

"You can't mean that!" Aunt Sybil spoke this time. "And I don't know what's going on, but why has this become such a problem now? We never had this trouble when Henry was lord." There was a general rumble of agreement. "You clearly don't have a clue what you're dealing with!" Aunt Sybil pronounced, warming to her audience.

"I have more of a clue than you do!" Hetta snapped back before she could help it. Hetta could hardly be blamed for the fae coming back to the Mortal Realm for the first time in centuries—something her father hadn't had to deal with! *Though these particular fae aren't here because of some general change in the world,* she thought guiltily. They were here specifically because of Wyn. Maybe a more selfless lord would consider giving him up, for the good of the wider estate; Hetta already knew she wasn't that lord. She'd already lost her old life and dreams to Stariel's lordship; she'd made her peace with that, begun to construct new dreams on Stariel's foundations. She accepted her position would mean making necessary sacrifices sometimes, but there had to be some room for the individual woman's wants amidst the vastness of the estate and all its people, didn't there? If she didn't fight to hold on to some bit of selfishness, she feared the estate would swallow her up until only Lord Valstar was left.

And Wyn isn't a necessary sacrifice anyway, she thought firmly. Setting aside her personal feelings, the estate would find his loss most inconvenient. And if they could sort out the business between him and his father's court, wouldn't it be good for Stariel to have one fae they could trust on their side?

"Well, how are we supposed to help when you've clearly been hiding things from us?" Aunt Sybil demanded. "How long has this been going on?"

Hetta bristled. "The attack just happened today! And you've known the fae existed for the same amount of time that I have!" More or less.

Aunt Sybil changed tack, huffing. "Well, why haven't you sought an expert? What about Lord Penharrow?"

Lord Angus Penharrow was their neighbour, and the person responsible for sabotaging the Choosing Ceremony. He'd been courting Hetta before she found out what he'd done. Only Jack, Marius, and Wyn knew this; the rest of the family only saw that something had soured between Hetta and the neighbouring lord. Probably Aunt Sybil thought Hetta was just being missish.

"Penharrow Estate," Hetta said through gritted teeth, "is less magical than my left foot, and so Lord Penharrow is possibly the person least qualified to offer advice on this matter. Please, if you are aware of any *magical* estates that might offer us some insight, do share, Aunt."

But her other relatives piped up with their own questions. She'd lost control of the room. Caro watched her intently, and Hetta realised that she was waiting for her to reveal Wyn's secret. Temptation gripped her. What would happen if she told them all, here and now? Would their affection for Wyn outweigh the shock of the revelation? But she shook her head curtly at Caro. She wouldn't force Wyn to choose the path she wanted.

How was he doing now? Surely Jack and Marius wouldn't have let him climb all those stairs up to his chamber? They wouldn't be so foolish, she reassured herself, even if Wyn was. They would have put him somewhere sensible on the ground floor.

"Well, thank goodness I invited Lord Featherstone to visit after Wintersol," Aunt Sybil was saying, abruptly jerking Hetta's attention back.

"You invited who? And what does that have to do with the price of peas?" Hetta said. The country metaphor came out without thinking, to her shame. Gods. If she wasn't careful she'd end up sounding just like the elders on the village council, as unintelligible as sheep when they really got going.

"Lord Featherstone's mother is one of my old school friends," Aunt Sybil said, as if this explained anything. "I haven't seen her in years—she married the old Lord Featherstone in our first season and moved away to his estate out in the Isles—but we correspond." Her expression softened briefly. "In any case, it has been clear to me for some time that you are in no way prepared to rule Stariel, and my friend suggested that her son might have some advice to offer, as Featherstone is known for magical peculiarities also. Lord Featherstone often visits Greymark after Wintersol, and I invited him to stay with us for a few days on his way down."

Hetta stared at her aunt, annoyed both by her high-handedness and the fact that she was actually offering something potentially helpful. Hadn't Hetta already wondered if there were other estates like Stariel? Although she suspected Aunt Sybil might have been driven by other motives entirely. No doubt she'd like to see Hetta married off to some faraway lord, leaving Jack to rule in her absence for large chunks of the year.

"I appreciate the forward notice of houseguests," Hetta said, unable to keep the bite from her tone. "And I'm happy to receive any advice Lord Featherstone has to offer on the subject. In the meantime, however, if you must go outside the bounds, I would like you all to take one of the anti-fae talismans Grandmamma prepared last time when we had our previous troubles with the fae."

"What anti-fae talismans?" Uncle Percival demanded.

"Won't that offend the good fae?" Aunt Maude asked. She was the most superstitious Valstar and seemed faintly smug to have her beliefs vindicated.

"I'll need to make more," said Grandmamma. "But you're fortunate that I've a few done up already." She burrowed about in her basket and pressed a small pouch into Uncle Percival's chest until he had no choice but to take it from her. She handed the next one to his wife, humming cheerfully. "Willow, dear," she said to one of Hetta's youngest cousins. "Do you mind passing these out?" Willow took them from her grandmother, eyes wide. Grandmamma peered around at the rest of her relatives, who were all staring at her. She pointed at four of the cousins at random. "You lot, come upstairs to the stillroom and help me." Then she turned and swept out of the room, but not before making sure her chosen minions had obeyed her command. They did, slumping after her half-dazed, half-amused.

Hetta would've liked to slink after them, but when she tried she was immediately set upon. Questions came from all sides, though frequently her relatives didn't wait to hear the answer before cross-interjecting opinions at each other. Which turned out to be a blessing in disguise because after five minutes they were all so embroiled in debate with one another that she could escape.

The cooler and uncrowded air in the entrance hall was a relief. She took several deep breaths, closing her eyes to collect her thoughts. Two concerns jockeyed for prime position. The first was the need to seek out Wyn and make sure he was all right. The second was much more mundane: she was famished. Magical energy had to come from somewhere, after all. Kitchen first, she decided; then Wyn. Then a change of clothes.

She was halfway across the entrance hall when Marius and Jack came down the stairs from the floor above.

"What did we miss?" Jack asked.

"Much as you'd expect. Grandmamma is distributing anti-fae talismans. I've told everyone to stay within the borders for now."

"How did that go down?"

Hetta gestured towards the hall. "You're welcome to see for yourself. I, for one, am going to the kitchen to get something to eat."

Jack contemplated the open door to Carnelion Hall and the low hornet-buzz of noise that sounded from it, squared his shoulders, and marched down the steps.

"Where did you put Wyn?" Hetta asked the two men. Marius was still standing halfway up the main staircase, frowning at Hetta. He didn't appear to hear her question, but Jack grimaced on his way past and said, "His bedroom." He shrugged at Hetta's disapproval. "*You* try arguing with the feathery bastard when he's set on something." And he disappeared into Carnelion Hall without waiting for her to reply.

Hetta wasn't sure she liked Jack's new nickname for Wyn. Or... was it new? Jack had known Wyn was fae for years before she had. Maybe it was an old insult between them. Jack had only lately grown comfortable enough in her presence to swear. Should she consider that progress?

"How did he look?" Hetta asked her brother, who was still lost in thought. "Marius?"

"What?" He came out of his abstraction with a start.

"I asked how Wyn looked," she repeated patiently. "Although from your demeanour I gather he wasn't on his last legs, at least."

"No," Marius said slowly. His expression was still shuttered, a queer light in his eyes as he took her in. "Where are you going?"

She threw her hands up in despair and began to walk away. "The kitchens, numbskull, as I said barely thirty seconds ago. It's nice to know you listen when I talk."

"I'll come with you," he said, quickly descending the stairs to fall in beside her.

A heavy silence prickled between them as they made their way through the house. Drat. Hetta could hardly go and be appropriately soppy over Wyn with her older brother in tow.

"Hetta," Marius said as they neared the kitchen. "Is there something going on between you and Wyn?"

17

ACCUSATIONS

HETTA STUMBLED AND Marius reached out a hand to steady her. His eyes widened. "There *is* something going on between you and Wyn!"

"Ah—" There didn't seem to be much point in denying it, but Hetta found herself oddly tongue-tied. It was different, facing Marius cold, than it had been when Jack and Caro walked in on them. Besides which, Hetta was the same age as the other two, whereas Marius was older. And her brother. Which didn't normally matter at all and yet somehow seemed to matter quite a lot when facing his shocked expression. "Yes," she finished. She wasn't ashamed of anything, she told herself. "Yes, there is." To her irritation, it came out sounding defensive.

Marius's reaction was, in many ways, the opposite of Jack's. Jack had leapt quickly from shock to anger with characteristic decisiveness. Marius, in contrast, didn't seem to know how to react. He went quiet, grey eyes wide.

"How long have you— What exactly—" he began inelegantly.

He paused, took a deep breath. "How sure are you of his motives?"

"How can you ask that?" she whispered, low and furious. "You know Wyn—"

"Do I?" Marius said, voice rising. "Do I know him?"

"Yes!" Aware both that their voices were reaching a level that would travel and of the proximity of the kitchen and its occupants, Hetta dragged Marius into the nearest room. This turned out to be a storage closet, filled with buckets and brooms.

Hetta glared at her brother. "What in Prydein did you mean by that remark?"

Marius crossed his arms and glowered down at her. A mop-end was propped up next to his shoulder. "Just that. How sure are you of his motives? It seems mightily convenient that he's courting you just when he most needs sanctuary."

"Oh, thank you for your faith in my judgement! And his! You must know he'd never do that!"

"Must I?" There was something hard and brittle in his voice. "I've known him as long as you, Hetta. Longer, really. All those years you were away—I was here. Wyn was here. Before you came back, I would've said I knew him better than anyone."

"Honestly, Marius, it's not like he's transformed into a completely different person! He's the same man we grew up with!"

"He's not a man at all!"

Hetta didn't understand why Marius was being so petty. "Does it matter so that he's fae?"

"It matters more that he lied to us about it for so long. I don't understand how you can forgive him so easily!"

And with a twist of perspective, Hetta suddenly saw the past through her brother's eyes. Wyn was the nearest thing Marius had to a best friend. He'd trusted Wyn with his greatest secret—a secret he'd only admitted to Hetta under duress. And it wasn't Hetta he'd turned to for help when his ex-lover tried to blackmail him. Wyn had been the person he trusted more than his own family. No wonder the revelation that Wyn had been keeping his own greatest secret close had shaken the foundations of their friendship.

"I forgive him," Hetta said, speaking more softly, "because I know he didn't do it with malicious intent, and I know he regrets it." She shuffled her position so that the door handle wasn't digging into her back. It was an awkward room to argue in, with Marius only two feet away.

"He might regret it, but don't you dare say he wouldn't do anything of the sort again, because we both know he would if he thought it best."

Jack's scandalised objections had been a lot easier to deal with, Hetta reflected. There was too much truth in Marius's words for comfort.

Marius didn't wait for her response. He shook his head. "And look at us now, fighting over something he's convinced you to keep secret! It was his idea, wasn't it?" Hetta didn't deny it. "I will strangle him," he said, and his fingers flexed as if he were truly considering it.

"You most certainly will not!"

"Secret relationships might seem exciting," he said, biting off each word, "but they are anything but." Marius's gaze turned inward, and she knew he was thinking of his ex-lover. "You should have someone who wants to show you off, not keep you a secret."

"Forgive me for keeping my less-than-two-weeks-old relationship from all my nearest and dearest! Particularly when you of all people know the awkwardness of Wyn's situation."

"Two weeks, eh?" Marius became suddenly forbidding, tall and aristocratic, peering down his long nose at her. "He'd better not be taking any—any *liberties*."

Hetta burst out laughing. "Liberties? That's almost as bad as Jack's accusations of 'canoodling'!"

Marius was already scowling, but at this he straightened further. "Jack?"

"He...ah...inadvertently encountered the fact of our relationship two days ago."

"What do you mean, *encountered*?"

Hetta gave Marius a sardonic look. "Do you really want a detailed answer, brother mine?"

His attempt to glower intimidatingly down at her was rather less effective when he blushed beet red and made a choking noise.

"I'd no idea my male relatives were such prudes," Hetta continued, unable to resist. "Jack made a very similar sound."

"I'm going to *murder* Wyn," Marius grit out.

It belatedly occurred to Hetta that there was a kind of code between men regarding sisters and their supposedly being sacrosanct. She relented and was about to admit that she and Wyn had barely done anything more scandalous than holding hands—Marius didn't need to know about the kissing, obviously—but again Marius spoke before she could.

"What if there were a child, Hetta? Did you even think about that when you—" But even he wasn't quite game enough to go there. There was a horror in his expression that had nothing to do with Wyn and everything to do with imagining his sister as anything other than an utterly chaste human being.

Hetta was torn between laughter and irritation at both Marius and her own embarrassment. "Oh, Marius, much as I'd like the earth to swallow me up and transport me literally anywhere else in the world right now, I do appreciate the depth of your affection. You must love me, if you're willing to contemplate such topics!"

The corner of his mouth twitched, and his eyes softened. "Of course I love you, Hetta." He breathed out a long sigh. "I'm just worried about you."

"Wyn and I haven't done anything that could result in children," Hetta admitted, her cheeks feeling unusually warm. "But there are precautions one can take, if we ever do."

"You'd better bloody well not need to use them!" Marius spluttered, completely unable to meet her eyes.

Of course, it was at precisely this moment that the door to the broom closet opened, revealing their younger half-sister Alexandra.

"Not need to use what?" she asked, frowning from Marius to Hetta. Her blue eyes were wide and innocent, and with her guinea-gold hair hanging loose down her back, she looked about twelve rather than the nearly sixteen that she was.

"Never mind," Marius said quickly.

"And why are you hiding in a broom closet?" she asked, her frown deepening. She took in her siblings' flushed faces and shrank into herself. "Is everything all right?"

"Marius is merely giving me a dressing-down," Hetta said cheerfully. "But I think he's done. Were you looking for one of us particularly?"

"Um. Yes. I was looking for you, Hetta." Alexandra examined the two of them curiously, looking for a hint of what their disagreement had been about.

"Well, you've found me," Hetta said. "Would you mind very much letting us out of the closet first, though?"

"Oh, of course!" Alexandra scrambled to get out of the door. Hetta and then Marius emerged back into the hallway. Marius gave Hetta a meaningful look that said he wasn't done with the conversation. Hetta ignored it, since she very much *was* done, and raised an expectant eyebrow at her sister.

Alexandra hesitated.

"Spit it out, Alex," Marius said, though his tone was gentle.

"Um, well, it's about Gwen," she said in a rush. "You said her court helped you—the Court of Dusken Roses?"

"Well, someone from her court," Hetta said. "It wasn't Gwendelfear, though. It was Princess Sunnika."

Alexandra's face fell. For reasons Hetta didn't understand, a friendship had formed between Gwendelfear and Alexandra. It had saved Alexandra's life in the end, when Gwendelfear had healed her after an accident.

"You haven't been seeing her, have you?" Marius asked sharply.

Alexandra gave a guilty start, and Hetta looked at Marius in surprise. It would never have occurred to Hetta to ask—a reminder of how much she still had to learn about her younger siblings. The gap created by her six-year absence from their lives hadn't yet been filled.

Hetta turned her attention back to Alexandra. "You *did* go to see Gwendelfear."

"No, I didn't!" Alexandra looked everywhere but at her older siblings.

"Alex…" Marius said with a sigh. "You're a terrible liar."

"Well, I only saw her the once!" Alexandra protested. "I just wanted to thank her for saving me. I never got to say thank you when she came."

"What happened?" Hetta asked tiredly.

Alexandra shuffled her feet and then confessed in a rush, "We didn't speak for very long." There was a note of hurt in Alexandra's voice. "She told me I shouldn't have called her."

"And it was just this once?" Marius asked.

"Yes, I—well, the truth is that Wyn caught me on my way back, and he persuaded me not to do so again without telling him." Alex hunched slightly under the weight of Marius's disapproval. "You're not angry with him, are you? I thought you'd be pleased he talked me out of it."

"I *am* pleased," Marius said.

Alexandra frowned. "You don't *sound* pleased. You're angry he didn't tell you I'd been to see Gwen, aren't you? But I made him promise not to, so you shouldn't blame him for keeping it a secret!"

This comment, obviously, didn't improve Marius's mood at all, and Hetta decided this was a politic moment to intervene. "Is that all you wanted to know, Alexandra? Whether Gwendelfear was the fae who helped us?"

Alexandra shook her head. "No, not just that. I mean, what I wanted to say was...have you seen..." She bit her lip. "Have you seen the creatures in the house?"

There was fear in her eyes, and Hetta realised abruptly that Alexandra was half-afraid she was going mad, seeing things that weren't there.

Hetta rushed to reassure her. "The housefae, you mean? Brownies and so on." Hetta hadn't actually seen them, as such, for they were quick-silver fast, but she could feel them moving about.

Alexandra sagged with relief. "I think so."

"What are you talking about?" Marius asked, frowning. "Creatures in the house?"

Hetta explained about the housefae, wondering why Alexandra had seen them but not Marius—and if any of her other relatives had noticed the small fae. She rather thought not, since no one had mentioned it in the hall.

She should ask Wyn about it when he was awake again. That thought sparked another: why spend all this time wondering about the fae when they could simply *ask* what was going on? Alexandra had summoned Gwendelfear; Wyn had summoned his godparent. Couldn't they just summon up Gwendelfear again, or even Princess Sunnika, and ask what in Prydein was going on? Hetta would like to know what Princess Sunnika had meant by helping them at the bank. She was sure that she and Wyn would've found a way out of the situation...somehow, but it had still been a very convenient rescue. Hetta didn't particularly like feeling obligated to Wyn's old fiancée.

That trick Wyn had pulled with his godparent—it hadn't sounded too difficult in theory. She itched to try it but reflected that it would be foolish to go summoning potentially hostile fae without backup. She reached out to touch Wyn's presence. Focussing within the house was slippery and disorienting, as always, but eventually she found him, so deeply asleep that he didn't even give his usual flare of acknowledgement when her awareness brushed over him. She sighed. She hated waiting.

"Are you all right, Hetta?" Alexandra asked.

"Ah, yes, thank you. I've just remembered something I need to do," she lied, excusing herself before Alexandra could leave her alone with Marius again.

UNEXPECTED CATS

WYN WOKE IN a frenzy of electrified awareness. He wasn't alone. Fear thrilled through him, and he leapt to his feet in a rush of storm magic and protesting muscles.

"Hmmmmmrrowww?" Plumpuff the cat peered up at him curiously. Her eyes gleamed in the dark, reflecting the starlight coming through the open window. Wyn hadn't bothered to pull the curtains before collapsing.

Wyn sank back onto the bed, heart pounding. "How," he said to the cat, "did you get in here?"

Plumpuff butted her head into his leg—fortunately, his uninjured one—and then bounded up onto the bed beside him. His heart rate, which had been quietening, sped up as he spotted the small black bundle nearby. Carefully, he began to systematically search through the bedclothes. The three kittens had been tumbled among the sheets by his abrupt movement but appeared otherwise unharmed. He blew out a long breath of relief and gathered the furry bundles into a pile next to their mother.

Plumpuff settled down beside her progeny. They wormed their

way towards her, tiny paws kneading as they nursed. Meeting his eyes, regal as a queen, she seemed to ask, "What are *you* looking at?"

How had they gotten in? Plumpuff would've had to carry her kittens one by one, which meant three separate breaches of his wards had failed to rouse him. Never mind the remnants of yarrow, iron, and lug-imp venom in his blood; that should've been impossible. He drew on his leysight to examine his wards and found them hanging as tangled as poorly stored yarn in the room's corners. How had they unravelled without him noticing? Had he really been that insensate?

No catshee could've unravelled his wards. He reached for Ivy's cane and levered himself off the bed with a wince. The dull ache of his calf sharpened as he put weight on it, but the limb held. Satisfied, he limped over to the door, where he could reach out and touch his wards. Touching wasn't technically required, but he found it easier to work magic this way, particularly since he didn't wish to take his fae form again just now. Losing control of his shape yesterday, and having Jack, Marius, and Caro unable to keep themselves from goggling at his strangeness had been...discomfiting. It reassured him to hold this mortal form he'd inhabited for so many years now, despite how it constrained his magic.

He tugged one of the tendrils of the ward back into position, and Stariel pounced, jerking it away. Faelands didn't typically express emotion as lesser creatures would understand it, but as Stariel crouched like a cat waiting for his next move, he swore the land radiated smugness. *Does that make me the mouse in this situation?* He reached for the ward again, only to have Stariel flick it out of reach once more. *Apparently, yes.*

"Dammit," he growled. "That's *mine!*" A fierce surge of magical possessiveness surged up and outwards, so strongly that he could almost feel phantom wings flex. Stariel flopped back, much like a puppy knocked off balance.

Wyn was almost as startled as Stariel, but he quickly braced himself for the faeland's reaction. What was he thinking? Hadn't he learnt anything from last time? *This is not a good time to try out insanity, Hallowyn!* he told his subconscious sternly. He had as much chance against Stariel as a gnat; he shouldn't challenge it. Why was he having so much difficulty remembering this fact of late?

Stariel didn't react straightaway, circling him with the unsettling focus of a hawk. So Wyn stretched out his fingers and grasped the end of the unravelled ward. It was that or stand there twiddling his thumbs. Stariel let him slot the ward back into place, though its presence strengthened. Why had it decided to undo the wards on his room? Perhaps it simply had a soft spot for wandering cats.

Or—he frowned and expanded his senses. The leylines brought unwelcome news; *all* his house spells had been shredded to some degree or other. Stormwinds only knew what state the ones on the wider estate were in. They were all small weavings, but they were numerous, and it would take him time to repair them all. *If* Stariel let him repair them.

<Stay away from my spells!> he snapped at the faeland in another display of ill-judgement. Stariel didn't respond, which was probably better than the alternative. He took a long, deep breath, reining in his temper and bristling magic. Stormwinds, the Wintertide had never affected his judgement so badly before, but that was no excuse for losing control. *Less than a week to go*, he consoled himself. After the longest night, the power of the season would begin to ebb. He could keep himself from unravelling for that long, couldn't he?

When he'd smoothed his emotions back down again, he limped around the room fixing the rest of his wards. Stariel remained impassive, but the hairs on the back of his neck stood on end. He ached, but he doubted he'd be able to go back to sleep with Stariel watching him so intently, so instead he made his way to the wash-room and filled the basin with warm water. Scrubbing the residue of Mrs Thompson's mixture from his skin was so deeply satisfying that he wondered that he'd been able to sleep at all with it still on him. Each pass of the cloth quietened the off-key jangle of the anti-fae substances.

Should he remove the bandages? Hetta would probably scold him, but he eyed their now less-than-pristine appearance with distaste and began to unwrap them anyway. The soapy water stung as he washed his forearm, and he had cause to regret his decision as the wound began to bleed sluggishly again. He grimaced but persevered, then pressed a dry towel to it. The laundry was going to be hellish for the laundry maid this week. He made a note to make sure the extra service was rewarded.

The cleaning ritual steadied him, and he limped back to his bedroom feeling much less pathetic. Plumpuff raised her head when he came in, decided he wasn't worth the trouble, and settled back to sleep. Stariel weighed on his shoulders as he found a clean shirt, but it hadn't unravelled his wards in his absence. Maybe his possessive outburst had made it rethink undoing his spells again. He hoped so. Otherwise, his job had just become substantially more difficult.

He eyed the cat and her litter but decided to leave them be for now. He would bring up a box for them when he returned. The need to sieve through the implications of the attack at the bank had him restless, and he always thought better in motion.

By the time he was halfway down the first set of stairs, he was having second thoughts about the wisdom of leaving his bed. Besides the stabbing pain of his leg, all his muscles felt weak and watery. He stopped on the landing to rest. Each panted breath echoed in the silence of the house, the cool shifting of the night currents. At least the one benefit of it being so near to Wintersol was that it would increase his healing rate; he was already tired of limping.

It was darker here away from the windows, dim enough that he had to lean significantly on his fae nature to see. He should take care—using his fae abilities to augment his night vision would make his eyes glow if he wasn't careful, and that would certainly surprise any of the staff making an earlier-than-usual start to the day.

But he could hear no footsteps from the belly of the house. Clarissa and the other kitchen staff would not be up for another hour.

His muscles warmed as he moved, and he was almost able to ignore his leg by the time he made it to his office, but it was still a relief to drop into a chair behind his desk. Closing his eyes, he tried to concentrate, but his thoughts whirred towards unpalatable conclusions and he opened them again almost immediately, seeking distraction. A large map of the estate was spread out on the table before him—he'd borrowed it from the map room two days before, to better plan the improvements the bank's loan should fund. He traced the small black blobs denoting cottages, guilt and frustration following in his finger's path. Had he permanently spoiled Stariel's chances with the bank?

Footsteps sounded outside, and Hetta came in carefully balancing a plate, accompanied by a bobbing light made from her own magic. She took in his position, lips quirking, and came into the room.

"Cake?" he asked.

She put the cake down on the desk beside the map. "You always did have a sweet tooth, and if fae magic works anything like human magic, you ought to be starving."

He was, though his other concerns had pushed it from the front of his mind.

"Thank you," he said formally. "Any particular reason why you are awake so early?"

"I asked Stariel to wake me when you were conscious." She frowned. "It's reacting very strangely to you."

Wyn paused. "I think it might be jealous of me."

She blinked. "Well, it shall just have to learn to share." Reaching out, hesitantly at first, she began to trail her hands lightly over his shoulders and down his arms, as if reassuring herself that he was whole. "You look much better than you did last night."

He leaned into the caress. "I still feel wretched. You should definitely pet me some more to make me feel better."

Her laugh was deep and throaty, but she obliged, smoothing strands of his hair. "I came to scold you for getting out of bed."

"Excellent scolding," he said, eyes half-lidded. "Continue."

"Hmmm," she said, but she didn't stop.

"How did last night go?" he asked, snaking his good arm up to twine his fingers with hers. She let out a surprised 'O' as he pulled her into his lap.

"You're supposed to be resting!"

"There's nothing wrong with my knees."

She rolled her eyes but didn't otherwise protest. Instead she carefully arranged herself to avoid his bad shoulder and summarised the discussion with her family. She made a face. "Aunt Sybil is particularly unimpressed with my leadership skills. So much so that she's invited her friend's son to give me advice, of all things!" Her eyes glittered with indignation, but a shadow passed over her face, a doubt he wasn't used to seeing in her, one he hoped would fade with time as she grew into her role—because if he was sure of anything in this world, it was that Hetta would be a good lord to this land and her people. More than good—great. *Unless I jeopardise that with my presence.* He shied from the thought; he didn't want to think of it, not with Hetta here and warm against him.

"*Are* there other mortal faelands?" she asked quietly when she'd finished working through her annoyance with her aunt.

"I don't know," he admitted. "If there are, there can't be many, I would think." He answered the question she hadn't asked. "I don't know how faelands act when their rulers are new. My father"—his heart skittered just saying the words, as if the mere mention of King Aeros might summon him—"has ruled the Court of Ten Thousand Spires for many mortal lifetimes. He is one of the oldest faelords of Faerie. I don't know what it was like when he ascended. And Stariel isn't the same as a normal faeland in any case. It's a shame you're the target of Lady Sybil's persistence, but perhaps some useful advice will come out of it. But even if it doesn't, there is always trial and error. And you're already proving a better ruler to Stariel than previous ones."

She sighed, but the shadow in her eyes had receded. "Well, not that I wouldn't have liked more information on the subject, but it's also sort of nice to know you don't know *everything*."

He walked his fingers over her collarbone, just above the thick lapels of her dressing gown. "What particular piece of my apparent omniscience has irked you most recently?"

Her voice was breathier than usual when she replied. "Alexandra," she said, giving him a Look.

Wyn froze.

"Yes," Hetta agreed as if he'd spoken. "She said she'd talked to Gwendelfear." She shook her head. "I'm not angry at you about that, actually. I know you take other people's secrets seriously. I wouldn't expect you to break such a confidence."

He leaned his head back so that all that he could see was the peeling plaster of the ceiling. It was far from the only ceiling in the house so affected. When would they be able to afford a plasterer, given their failure at the bank? "You want to talk to Gwendelfear too," he said heavily.

"Can you think of a better way to find out what's going on? Don't tell me you came here at this hour merely to brood over the household accounts. I know you'll have been trying to untangle everyone's motives from yesterday. But it seems much simpler to *ask* rather than *guess*." Her eyes were fierce and penetrating. "And don't tell me that you're thinking of leaving so there's no point in asking them."

"I'm often here at this hour," Wyn said mildly.

Her expression softened. "I don't appreciate you enough."

He laughed. "Hetta, do not fall for my attempts at deflection. I am quite ruthlessly manipulative when I'm avoiding a subject."

She burrowed into him. "Yes, I know, but still, it doesn't seem fair to me how much we all expect from you. Those cleaning spells—you mentioned them as if they were nothing, but the house wouldn't run with so few staff without them, would it?"

"Well, it may have to learn, if Stariel persists in interfering with them." He told her about Stariel shredding his wards, and her expression grew distant as she communed with her faeland.

"Well, I'm fairly sure I've told it not to do that again," she said apologetically after her eyes refocused. She shrugged helplessly. "Sometimes it has its own opinions on what constitutes good ideas."

He leaned his head against hers, enjoying the warmth and scent of her so close. The dark currents tugged at him, tempting him to start an entirely different tactic of distraction, but he ignored them and said instead, "It's not an entirely terrible idea, to try to uncover DuskRose's motives. But I would like to wait until after Wintersol before we try to summon anyone." He was only delaying the inevitable, but he couldn't seem to make himself let go. Not yet. And maybe there was something he was missing, some way out he hadn't yet seen.

There was a deep silence in which the tick of his wall-clock was suddenly audible, the little metal clicks of the gears slicing time. Wyn was moderately certain they were both recalling Hetta's words from earlier: *I won't forgive you if you leave.* Could he leave, knowing that?

"Why wait?" Hetta challenged.

"This is a time of…seasonal magic. It will reach its zenith in a few days, at Wintersol. Fae can be…unpredictable at such a time. And your family won't plan to leave the bounds till after that in any case. It should be safe."

She tilted her head. "Does the unpredictability include you?"

He smiled and spread his hands. "I am fae." Much though he might wish otherwise. "In any case, I think it likely you will receive an emissary from DuskRose soon, regardless. It would explain why Princess Sunnika aided us, as a prelude to negotiations." He tightened his arms around her. "Although it's also possible that she feared I was about to expire and was merely acting to prevent my oath from becoming void in order to maintain the imbalance of power between the courts."

Hetta disentangled herself so that she could meet his gaze. "What does that mean?" Her eyes were as dark as wet river stones.

He kissed her, deep and full of all the things he didn't know how to say without sounding ridiculous. Her mouth resisted his for perhaps a half-second, refusing to encourage this change of subject. And then her lips softened with a quiet sigh and she leaned into the touch. Her hands went to his neck, winding in his hair. The world became a tangle of sweet, piercing sensations, warm breath and cool fingertips, the texture of cloth and soft, exposed flesh. It wasn't until her hands began to wander somewhat lower that he pulled back, leaning his forehead against hers in a soft rebuke. They were both panting, little huffs of warm air against each other's skin.

"You don't care to take this somewhere else?" Hetta said, her voice quiet but steady. It was an offer more than a question. Wyn gave a minute shake of his head, grappling to form a coherent sentence without much success. Hetta didn't argue, merely making a regretful noise and then re-buttoning her way up to his throat. Her fingers rested lightly on either side of his neck, smoothing tiny circles.

"Perhaps you should get off my lap," he suggested.

Her smile was wicked. "Am I bothering you?" She wriggled suggestively, and his breath caught, body tightening in a way she could not be unaware of. She laughed but slid obediently off him, depositing herself in the neighbouring seat. "But you make a good point. Before you distracted me so ably, I was demanding an explanation. Emissaries? Have we become a sovereign nation, to host ambassadors?"

Wyn spread his hands, still painfully aware of how close she was, of how little effort it would take to bridge the distance between them. "In a word: yes."

Hetta looked thoughtful. "Well, that will certainly be something of a surprise to Her Majesty."

"There's a reason mortal lords have to swear fealty to your Crown, though they've largely forgotten it."

"I haven't sworn mine, yet, though," Hetta pointed out. "I was planning to go down to Meridon in the New Year and sign all the official documents and suchlike." Her eyes sparkled. "Does this mean in the interim I'm running a kind of rebel state?"

He smiled. "If you like."

Hetta shook her head. "Fascinating as these revelations are, we're getting distracted again. This is about oaths, somehow, isn't it? I remember you said that fae are bound by their word and that they forfeit power to break it."

He squeezed her hand. "Yes." He sighed, cold seeping into his soul, as if her warmth against him had been the only thing holding it at bay. "Yes. I am...not all that I should be. Fleeing a marriage I had promised myself to lessened me. But it didn't affect only me. The Court of Ten Thousand Spires made that same promise also." A memory taunted him, of his younger self, trembling but hopeful, trying not to stumble over his words as he spoke the oath. He remembered staring at the back of Princess Sunnika's head, wondering desperately what she was thinking and what this promise of a new beginning meant to her. The ink-black and cherry-pink strands of her hair had gleamed beneath the faelights.

Hetta pursed her lips as she absorbed the information. "Your father lost some of his power too," she guessed. "When you broke your oath."

Wyn remembered the wrenching pain of it, the snap of something inside his soul as he made that final, desperate decision to run. "I believe so. How much, I don't know, but perhaps enough to shift the balance with DuskRose should hostilities between the two courts recommence. My father and Queen Tayarenn were closely matched in the last conflict. I suspect DuskRose has been testing his power ever since, but they cannot openly attack without directly flouting the High King's command."

Hetta frowned. "So this isn't just about punishing you. Your father wants to get his power back, doesn't he? *Can* he get it back?"

"Yes. Most obviously, by forcing me to fulfil the promise." Wyn ticked the thoughts off on his fingers. "Secondly, he could repay DuskRose a price equal to that of the broken promise, but I doubt he would choose to do so. DuskRose will exact a heavy price to discharge the debt—they will have no desire to see my father's power returned. Thirdly—" He paused. "The oath is void if I am dead."

"Hence the lug-imps," Hetta said grimly.

"Hence the lug-imps," he agreed. "My sister Aroset sent the lug-imps, but it was almost certainly with my father's blessing." He thought of Lamorkin's information. "I think she was Plan A, as it were. I believe my brother Rakken may have suggested an alternative approach to solving the oath-debt, one less favoured by my father. That would explain why Rakken deliberately sabotaged Aroset's attempt—to give himself the chance to win the game himself."

He knew what she was about to ask; her quick mind was one of the things he loved about her. But he wished she would be a little less quick in this one instance. He didn't want to hear her say—

"Can I buy your debt from ThousandSpire without DuskRose's agreement?"

He put his hands flat on the desk and pushed himself to standing, wincing as his injured leg took his weight. He persevered and limped over to the window.

"Wyn?"

He knew she was debating whether to come to him. His fractured reflection rebuked him from the diamond-patterned windows. The night was dark without even the promise of dawn; the sun wouldn't rise for at least another four hours, this close to Wintersol.

"I don't want you to have to pay for me," he said, finally. Storms take it, she'd homed in on the loophole that could free him, but how could he burden Stariel with his oath-debt, given what he'd already cost it?

She made an impatient noise, and he turned back to face her.

"Are you done brooding? Because obviously I don't want to bargain with the fae either, but I will if it solves the issue. I know you don't like it, but do you have any better ideas?" Her eyes blazed a warning. "And don't say that you could leave Stariel. Or at least, don't you dare say that you'll leave Stariel for my own good. If you're going to run away, leave me out of it. This relationship has to go both ways, Wyn; that means we solve this *together*."

The silence drew out between them. *I love you*, he nearly said again, but it would still be unfair to say it, not unless he could add, *and I promise I won't leave* to the end. And he couldn't make that promise, not when he didn't know what the fae might ask of her.

But as if she had heard him anyway, she closed the space between them and rose on her toes to kiss him. He pulled her closer, warmth to hold against the deepening cold, the terrifying reminder of all he stood to lose. When they broke apart, her eyes shone as bright as stars, a wordless reflection of his own depth of sentiment.

"Let me bargain," she murmured.

His arms tightened around her, a wordless, instinctive negative. "You should remember your children's tales, Hetta: it's unwise to bargain with the fae. You will not like their prices."

"Well, if it reassures you, remember I don't *have* to agree to anything your relatives demand. But surely it can't hurt to at least try?"

It didn't reassure him nearly enough. She didn't understand, not truly, what she was contemplating. Jack's words simmered in his mind. How could he call this protecting Stariel, bringing the worst of fae machinations to bear upon its lord? But she was right; he had no other suggestion to offer. Or at least, none except that which she'd already dismissed. The need to protect warred with the desire to stay, the proverbial immovable object meeting irresistible force until something had to give, the merest inch of compromise. Was this weakness? It didn't feel like it.

"Promise that you won't agree to anything without asking me first. *Promise me*, Hetta." She hesitated, and he met her gaze, unflinching. Her clear grey eyes struck straight at the heart of him, but he would not back down. Not on this.

She wrinkled her nose. "All right. I promise. Are the fae fond of sheep?" she asked lightly. "I think I could part with one or two. We need to update our breeding stock anyway."

He laughed, brittle as hoarfrost, but the hard knot of terror eased a little. She had promised. If they truly were going to attempt to bargain with ThousandSpire, he would need to map out every possible contingency, define the hard limits of what could be offered. The cost of his debt would not be monetary, but guilt still clawed at him as he thought of the incident at the bank.

"So," she said, stepping back. He released her reluctantly. "Our working theory is that your brother has persuaded your father to let him try to bargain with me for your debt instead of simply trying to kill you outright?" When Wyn nodded, she added, "And you think DuskRose will want to send us an emissary for the same reason? To bargain with me for your release?"

"Perhaps," Wyn said slowly. "Or perhaps not. Perhaps they will try to persuade you to cast me out, or not to deal with ThousandSpire. I imagine DuskRose wouldn't be entirely unhappy for the current state of affairs to continue."

"But if DuskRose don't want you to marry their princess either, doesn't that make them oathbreakers too?"

Wyn shook his head. "Intent is not action. So long as Princess Sunnika remains unwed and professes willingness to marry me, they have kept their side of the bargain."

"She can't marry anyone else without breaking her oath too?" An unfamiliar expression crossed Hetta's face. Jealousy, he identified with a startled jolt.

"You are jealous of her?" he asked, unable to keep the incredulity from his tone.

"It's all very well for you to tease me about it," Hetta grumbled, "but you might have mentioned that your fiancée was fantastically beautiful and well-endowed enough to set up her own dairy farm."

He should not find jealousy endearing, and yet he did, if only because it wasn't an emotion he'd seen from her before. That had to mean something, didn't it? "*Former* fiancée," he emphasised. "And I am not sure when precisely you think such a comment, voiced by me, would have been well-received on your part." She narrowed her eyes and he chuckled. "Do you need me to praise your, er, dairy farms?"

That did coax a reluctant huff of laughter from her. "I'm being ridiculous, aren't I?"

"A little," he agreed. "Though I am happy to indulge you. I hope, however, that this gives you a greater appreciation for my past sangfroid upon witnessing your obvious admiration for Lord Penharrow's person."

"I didn't admire—" Hetta began but stopped when he raised a cynical eyebrow. She slumped in defeat. "Well, perhaps I did. You never let on that it bothered you!"

"It was very understandable that you admired Lord Penharrow's... physical attributes. He is, after all, a most finely built man. Though I think not, perhaps, as handsome as I am."

She laughed, delighted, and his heart lifted.

"All right," he said, when her amusement had quietened. "I am finished brooding; let us plan."

EMBROIDERED PEACOCKS

WYN ASSEMBLED HIS troops early the next morning. It was a less inspiring sight than it should have been, given Stariel's understaffed nature. Hopefully, that was another thing that would change with Hetta's lordship. Though changing it with any speed would depend on securing the bank loan. Which he'd obviously done a marvellous job at so far.

Still, at least the existing staff were worth their weight in gold. They were typical Northern folk, inclined to speak their minds, allergic to formality, dedicated workers, and loyal to the bone. He looked down the long table in the servants' hall, meeting everyone's eyes in turn. Some, like Clarissa, he'd known since he'd arrived. Others, like Lottie the housemaid, were more recent additions to the household.

"I want to thank everyone for the hard work you've put into keeping the household running smoothly, particularly this last week. I know it's a difficult task with so many of the family home and not as many staff as I'd like," he said frankly. "But I'm proud of how you've risen to the challenge. Now, some of you will already have heard this news from Lord Valstar, but I want to repeat it now, for clarity. You are a largely sensible lot, and I trust you will treat this information with that same attitude." He laid out the broad details of his and Hetta's encounter with the lug-imps yesterday. From the staff's reaction, they had already had a chance to absorb the news.

Ms Whitlow, the most senior housemaid, pursed her lips and then said, "I've heard Lord Valstar said there would be talismans available for the family. What about us?"

There was a general murmur of agreement.

"You will get them also, if you want them," Wyn promised. Curse the Maelstrom. Lady Philomena's anti-fae talismans wouldn't do much more than inconvenience greater fae, and he thought it unlikely that the staff would be targeted anyway, but he couldn't begrudge them even a small bit of added protection. But this was going to make his job more difficult. His spells would begin to fray the longer they were exposed to anti-fae talismans unless he poured more power into them. "But I do not think you will be at risk. My understanding is that the Valstars' connection to the estate may make them the more attractive targets."

"*You* were attacked," Ms Whitlow pointed out.

"As was the bank manager," Wyn agreed. "A one-off occurrence, I hope. In any case, it was fortunate that Lord Valstar was there. She is a powerful mage in her own right and saved us both. In any case, you should all be safe so long as you remain within the boundaries of Stariel."

"But what do the fairies want?" Lottie piped up. One of the gardeners scowled at her. As one of the youngest staff members, she should not have spoken out. "Why have they appeared now?"

Wyn considered her for a long moment before addressing the wider table. "A reasonable question. As to why the fae have reappeared now…" He shrugged. "It is clear the world is changing. But mortals and fae lived alongside each other before, if you believe the tales, so perhaps they can do so again." The staff didn't seem entirely reassured, and he berated himself for getting too philosophical. "In any case, I have complete faith in our Star. Please do come to me if you have any further questions, or if you see anything that concerns you," he said. "Now, I will run over today's schedule…"

Clarissa lingered after he'd sent everyone on to their various tasks. "Should you be up and about?" she asked, frowning at him.

He still had Ivy's spare cane, though he was leaning on it less than the night before. "I am recovering rapidly."

Clarissa, unfortunately, knew him. "You shouldn't be standing so much though."

"I intend to spend some time with paperwork," he assured her. She harrumphed but left.

He made his way through the house and up to the floor that contained most of the family's bedrooms with trepidation. He would've liked to have come bearing gifts, but he couldn't hold a tea tray on his injured arm whilst leaning on a cane with the other, so the small bribery would have to be dispensed with. It probably wouldn't have made much difference anyway.

After repeated knocks and a minute and a half of waiting, Marius's door opened. He was wrapped in a thick green dressing gown embroidered with peacocks, and his black hair was a tufty, lopsided landscape. He blinked rapidly behind his spectacles, adjusting to the sudden light. When he saw who it was, his bemused expression changed to a scowl.

"Wyn," he said flatly.

It stung, this distance between them.

"I have a favour to ask." Wyn let his gaze fall on the embroidered peacocks. "It will require you to be awake and dressed, however."

"What time is it?"

"Seven o'clock," Wyn apologised.

Marius ran a hand through his hair, making it stick on end. "What is it? The favour."

"I need someone to pick up the car from Alverness. I thought you might catch the nine o'clock train down from Stariel Station."

Marius stared at him.

"I know it seems trivial," Wyn said. "But someone needs to pick it up, and my driving abilities are impaired at present." He waved the cane for emphasis.

"Are you trying to ship me off and out of your hair for the day?" His eyes narrowed. "I know about you and Hetta."

"I know." Hetta had told him last night. Even if she hadn't, the anger in Marius's expression would have clued him in. "But no, I'm not trying to get you out of my hair."

"That's it?" Marius's mouth formed a grim line. "That's all you have to say for yourself?"

"You're quite welcome to rail at me, but would it be too much to ask that you get dressed first and that we refrain from arguing in the hallway?" Wyn said mildly.

Marius glared. "Damn you," he said, and shut the door.

"I'll be in my office," Wyn told the solid oak between them.

A QUARTER OF AN hour later, just as Wyn had decided which field to suggest to Hetta for a drainage experiment, Marius appeared. His hair now lay mostly flat, though one curl had escaped his ministrations and bounced untidily next to his right ear. He wore a dark grey morning suit with a salmon pink tie and carried a hat, which told Wyn that he'd at least half-committed to carrying out Wyn's errand.

Their eyes met. Marius came in and shut the door with a snap.

"I'm angry with you," he said without preamble.

"Good," Wyn said. This brought Marius up short, and he halted a few feet from the desk where Wyn was seated.

"What do you mean 'good'?" he demanded. Like Hetta, the grey of his irises tended to lighten when he was agitated. Right now they were as pale as frost.

Wyn stood with a slight wince. "It means you care."

"Of course I care! She's my sister!"

"I meant that you still care about me," Wyn clarified. "I comfort myself that our friendship cannot be irreparably broken, if I still have the power to hurt you so."

Marius glared at him, fists clenched. "Don't try to make me feel guilty."

Wyn allowed the point with a nod. "You shouldn't feel guilty in your treatment of me. I have deserved it wholly. You trusted me with your own secrets while I hoarded mine. You welcomed me into your family and I have repaid you by endangering them. And now I court your sister in secret, as if I am ashamed of her. I have caused a great deal of trouble."

"What am I supposed to do with that? Punch you in the face?"

"You may, if it will make you feel better," Wyn said with a slight smile.

Marius's eyes flashed. "What will you do if I tell you to stay away from her?"

"Probably not stay away from her," Wyn admitted. "Are you sure you don't wish to punch me?"

"Don't tempt me," Marius said darkly.

"I love her," Wyn said, a soft relief coming from finally being able to *say* the words aloud, even if they were not to the person he most wanted to say them to. "I know you have good reason to doubt that sentiment, but please trust me when I say that there is nothing you can do or say that would make me more determined to do right by her. I am already determined to the utter limit of my capacity."

Marius's lip had curled at the word 'love'. "Love is for fools, Wyn." His shoulders slumped.

The hairs on the back of Wyn's neck rose—it was eerily close to the old fae saying: *Love is for fools and mortals.*

But this was not about him. Wyn dared to reach out and rest a hand briefly on Marius's shoulder. "Don't let John's shadow leave a permanent mark," he murmured. John Tidwell had been Marius's recent lover. It had ended badly.

Marius shook him off. "That has nothing to do with this!"

"And you are fortunate you aren't bound to speak no falsehood." But he turned away from Marius's glare and went to the key rack. From a large square board hung keys for every door in the house, each neatly labelled. They glinted in the soft lamp glow, and Wyn selected the large triangular key that belonged to the kineticar.

He held it out to Marius. "Will you run my errand for me?"

Marius didn't move. "Why didn't you ask Jack?" The question revealed more than Marius probably intended. It had been hard for him, growing up with a father who preferred his nephew over his oldest son. Mostly Marius managed to keep that resentment from spilling onto his cousin, but several events recently would have exacerbated that already tender spot. Jack had known Wyn's secret for years—years in which Marius had considered Wyn more his friend than Jack's. In truth, that was a symptom of the same issue: Lord Henry had told Jack about Wyn because he expected him to inherit. And, most unfortunately, Jack had found out about Hetta and Wyn's relationship before Marius. On top of that, it wouldn't have escaped Marius's notice that Hetta had summoned her cousin and not her brother for aid yesterday.

Wyn owed Lord Henry much, but he didn't know if he would ever forgive him for his role in Marius's insecurities. "I would rather send you than Jack. You've a better hold on your temper than he does and you're more intuitive. I'd like you to talk to the staff at the bank, see if you can ascertain both Mr Thompson's health and exactly what story is being spread about. I fear Jack may simply get people's backs up if he doesn't like what he hears."

Marius blinked. Wyn wondered how long it had been since someone had compared him favourably to his cousin.

"And," Wyn added, waving the key for emphasis, "you've more native resistance to enchantment than most of the other Valstars."

Marius appeared as nothing so much as a startled owl. "I do?" Marius had only a weak land-sense, and he'd foolishly equated this to his own worth. *Oh, Marius, there is no lack in you, nothing that should be changed.*

"You do," Wyn said. "It makes you resistant to compulsion."

Marius's eyes narrowed. "And exactly how do you know that, *Mr Tempest*?"

Too quick by half. Wyn spread his arms placatingly. "I was young, in fear of my life, and had no idea how the mortal world worked. In my first weeks here, I set a low-level compulsion so that people would be inclined to view my rapid insertion into the household in a positive rather than negative light. Low-level compulsion is very mild—it cannot force someone to act against their nature. It is merely…a kind of charm."

Marius folded his arms. "And now?"

"With one exception, I haven't compelled any mortals for years now."

Marius abruptly deflated. "John."

"Yes." He'd done it at Marius's request, though in fairness Marius had not known exactly what he'd asked for. Wyn thought a change of subject in order. "In any case, I wouldn't ask you to go if I truly thought you were in danger. I think it's very unlikely the fae will attack anyone associated with the Valstars just now, when they're trying to figure out how to negotiate with Stariel."

"It's not your leg stopping you from going, is it?" Marius said, with characteristic insight. "They'll try to kill you again if they catch you outside the bounds, won't they?"

"Maybe," Wyn admitted. "Probably."

Marius's expression softened. "That rather neatly puts my problems into perspective, doesn't it?" He took the key from Wyn. "At least my family isn't trying to kill me."

"A consoling thought to hold on to during particularly dull monologues from certain of your relatives."

Marius didn't smile. "Don't think this means I'm all right with any of this. I'm not. Not Hetta, and not the compulsion. But I'll get the dashed car." And he turned to leave, shoulders stiff again.

"Thank you," Wyn said. "For what it's worth, I'm sorry that I did not trust you sooner."

Marius paused. When he spoke, his voice was so low Wyn had to strain to catch it.

"I'm sorry too."

HEATHER AND SNAPDRAGONS

MARIUS WATCHED STARIEL Village disappear as the train rounded a bend, taking his land-sense with it between one breath and the next. He used to relish that loss because it meant he was outside his father's power. Now he tried to pretend he wasn't afraid without the land guardian watching silently over his shoulder. He dug his fingers into the seat and tried to reassure himself. Wyn had said he was resistant to compulsion. Resistant, though—that was hardly the same as *immune*, was it? Why hadn't he asked for further clarification on that point? He shuddered. Was there anything worse than the idea of someone else controlling you? *You asked Wyn to do that to John, though.* Not asked—he hadn't known Wyn had magic when he'd come to his friend, in heartbreak and panic. *But you didn't say no when he offered, did you? Not a lot of moral high ground to claim, is there? Hypocrite.*

At least Marius now knew Wyn hadn't ever compelled him, something that had been preoccupying him ever since he'd found out about his friend's abilities. *But you're not entirely reassured by that, are you?* a tiny, treacherous voice pointed out. An idea had been growing in him ever since John's departure and the reveal of Wyn's true nature—if Wyn could bind John not to speak of Marius, then maybe he could bind Marius not to be…what he was. But if Marius was immune to compulsion, then there went that idea.

He snorted. *I should've known it would never be that simple.* Outside, the train passed a stripe of heather with silvery-grey foliage, contrasting vividly against the darker browns of the more common varietals. Did the colour breed true or would the resulting hybrid be merely a paler brown? The snapdragons he'd grown last summer had turned out a disappointing pink, despite their parents blooming crimson and white.

Thinking of his experiments brought his other recent botanical research to mind. He'd applied to return to Knoxbridge in the New Year, but he carefully hadn't mentioned this particular line of research to the department. An uneasy mixture of shame and excitement swam in his belly as he contemplated the passing countryside. Was it traitorous to investigate plants rumoured to have anti-fae properties? Surely it was simply good sense? After all, Grandmamma's talismans were based on such things, and Wyn thought them a sensible precaution. Wyn wouldn't be angry with him for pursuing this line of inquiry. Would he? Why did he even *care* if Wyn would be upset at him for it? Wyn *deserved* to be upset.

Marius shifted irritably in his seat. There was no one else in the carriage, which would ordinarily delight him because it meant he could stretch out his legs and read without feeling self-conscious, but today he found it unsettling. His book remained in his satchel, unopened.

Of course, it was quite hard to stay properly angry at Wyn when his family was trying to kill him. *Oh, how rational of you to find his tragic backstory irritating because it makes him harder to villainise.* But he didn't want to feel any sympathy, didn't want to let go of righteous anger. At least being angry at Wyn provided some kind of variety. If Marius let it go, he'd be right back at the bottom of his personal and entirely tedious well of sadness. He was so tired of being sad, of every other emotion feeling as thin as wallpaper on top of that base.

Fuck John, he thought with sudden venom, glaring at his own reflection in the window glass. Did John think about him at all? He probably didn't. He'd probably shacked up with someone else already. Someone younger and better looking, with more social graces. Someone interesting and complicated.

"You're boring, Marius. You just want to talk about the same bloody things all the time, and the only time you have anything new to say, it's from some bloody book or other! You never DO anything!"

He got up and stretched, restless with the barbed memory of John's words. It wasn't helpful to think about them. He knew it wasn't helpful, but they pricked at him nonetheless, round and round like a pebble lodged in his shoe. It didn't matter if John had found someone else. He could be going at it with someone new every night and it still wouldn't matter. Well, rather, it *shouldn't* matter. Why couldn't he just be over him already? He *wanted* to be over him.

"It will take time," Wyn had said. "Sometimes the heart takes a while to catch up to what the mind knows." But what would Wyn know about such things? When had he ever faced heartbreak?

Well, he did have to deal with his father plotting to kill him. He probably didn't process that with perfect equanimity, despite that unruffled face he shows. Marius's burst of anger faded, leaving only a tired, foggy greyness behind.

The train slowed for the Deeplake station, and Marius nearly groaned aloud. Alverness was still an hour away, and he thought he might go mad, left alone here gnawing on his own thoughts. Desperate for distraction, he pulled out his notebook and began forcing himself to list all the plants he'd so far identified as potentially having anti-fae properties alongside ideas for preparations and concentrations. Grandmamma had been frustratingly vague about quantities when he'd tried to pin down exactly how she made her anti-fae talismans, but careful experimentation ought to be able to give him better data.

WHEN THE TRAIN ARRIVED in Alverness and Marius had found his way to the solemn stone edifice of the bank, he wished he'd spent the last hour planning what to say rather than categorising herbs. He glumly examined the grand entrance with its decorative columns. What was he supposed to say? *'So, how is everyone feeling about that fae attack yesterday? Anxious? Pleased? How interesting.'*

Stop procrastinating, idiot, he mentally berated himself. He supposed he would do what he always did: muddle through on a wave of his own awkwardness. Stiffening his spine, he marched up the stairs into the bank.

He veered away from the tellers and found the receptionist, who was female, thank the nine heavens. He found women so much easier to talk to than men. *And isn't that the very definition of irony?*

"Good morning," he said to her.

"Good morning, sir," she said with a polite smile. "How may I help you?"

"My name is Marius Valstar, and I'm here on behalf of Lord Valstar. Would you be able to give me news of Mr Thompson, by any chance?"

The woman's friendly expression changed to uncertainty. "Mr Thompson is unwell."

"I know he was injured yesterday," Marius said. "That's why I'm here, really; to check that he's all right. Well, that and to pick up the car. Do you know where that might be, by the way?" He leaned on the counter and smiled at her. "Sorry, I'm a bit scatter-brained this morning, bombarding you with questions and just assuming you know what I'm talking about. Do you know what I'm talking about or should I backtrack a bit and explain?"

She smiled. "Perhaps a little explanation would help."

He didn't know why, but his general scatter-brained aura often made women warm to him, and thankfully it seemed to be working on the receptionist. Maybe it was just his rakish good looks—*ha!* After a bit of back-and-forth, she relaxed slightly and told him Mr Thompson was at home and no one knew when to expect him back. The kineticar, it transpired, was currently parked behind the bank next to its stables.

Marius thanked her. "My apologies for causing such a bother."

The receptionist—who by this point Marius had learnt was named Ms Hutchins—bit her lip and then blurted out, "What *did* happen to Lord Valstar yesterday? We were all in a flutter with Mr Thompson unconscious, and I could have sworn I heard a gunshot… but then they were gone."

"Ah," said Marius intelligently. Why hadn't Wyn been more explicit about what story he wanted Marius to tell? *You're the one who wanted people to stop keeping secrets on his behalf*, his inner critic pointed out. But it was one thing to say this and quite another to do it. He couldn't just…coldly out Wyn.

Wyn never told my secret to anyone, Marius told his inner critic firmly, to which it responded: *Funny how you forgot to mention that when you were arguing with Hetta…*

The receptionist's expression was beginning to go blank at the edges, and he realised he'd been silent for too long, distracted by his own internal debate. *Say something! Anything!*

"Ah—I don't know all the details," he said cautiously. "Lord Valstar was very upset by the…altercation." There. That was vague enough, wasn't it?

"Mary said—she got there first—she said she saw…things. Creatures." Ms Hutchins pursed her lips. "And Mrs Thompson, she said…"

"What did she say?" Marius prompted, but Ms Hutchins shook her head, apparently reluctant to say the word 'fae' aloud, though he could practically hear her thinking it.

"It's nothing," she said. "Shall I get someone to show you where the car is?"

"It's clearly not nothing, though," he said, trying to look as unintimidating as possible. He smiled at her sheepishly. "I said I'd try and find out what kind of chaos my sister and our steward had left in their wake. I'd rather know than be left guessing! Creatures, you said?"

She nodded. "Yes. One of them bit Mr Thompson. And Mr Tempest—although he did not seem so badly affected. I trust he is well?"

There was something in her tone that made Marius suspect Mrs Thompson had said something about Wyn to the staff.

"He's recovering," Marius said. "Is Mr Thompson—do you know how he's doing?"

She shook her head but then reached out to pat him reassuringly on the arm. "But he was already doing better yesterday, by the time Mrs Thompson took him home. I'm sure he will recover."

"That's good," Marius said. "Please pass on my—and Lord Valstar's—best wishes. If there is anything we can do…" He shook his head. "Um…also, I think our accounts books are still here. Mr Tempest asked me to fetch those as well while I was here."

Again, that flicker of something in her expression at the mention of Wyn. Some species of cat had clearly been released from its bag, though it was hard to say if it was merely a tomcat or a fully-fledged lion. *That was a dreadful metaphor.*

Marius didn't pursue it, and the receptionist found him a clerk to fetch the accounts books and show him where the car was parked. The clerk did a double-take at Marius's name too. Just what, exactly, was being said about the Valstars and Stariel in this establishment?

"I gather my sister caused something of a stir yesterday," he said to the clerk as he was escorted through the panelled hallways of the bank. The boy looked barely older than Gregory, all awkward angles and oversized feet.

"You wouldn't believe what Mary said! Said there were some kind of creatures in Mr Thompson's office, but I didn't see anything." He sounded disappointed.

"Did anyone else?"

"No." He paused. "But Mr Thompson's wife, she was yapping about that other man, the steward. She didn't like him much."

And still no one had said the word 'fae'. Marius couldn't blame them. A few months ago, he would've been reluctant to voice the word either outside of fiction. How strange though, that everyone knew what the fae were whilst simultaneously not believing they were real. *How quickly we forget and things become mere children's tales.* How would the world change now that the fae were back? A deep uneasiness filled him. People would talk about this incident here, at the bank, even if they were currently reluctant to talk to Marius about it. *Pebbles that start avalanches*, he thought, feeling hopelessly out of his depth.

Marius was distracted by this line of thought while the clerk went to look for the accounts books and returned frowning. "I'm sorry, Mr Valstar, but they seem to be missing."

Marius blinked at him. "What do you mean, missing?"

"I think Mr Thompson may have taken them away with him." The boy didn't seem to know what to do about this. "We could send them up in the mailbag when he comes back, if you like?"

"Er...yes, I suppose that would be fine," Marius said, not sure what to do about it either.

The clerk seemed relieved at his reaction and rushed to deposit him in the stableyard, where the kineticar had been parked forlornly in the back corner.

"Do you mind if I leave you here, sir, if that's all you need? Only I've got to finish a ledger before lunchtime."

"That's fine. Thank you," Marius said, and the boy left. Gods, the boy was barely an adult and already working his way into a profession, and what could Marius do? Identify a tree at ten paces? How had he gotten so old while remaining so incredibly useless? *I'm not that old*, he reassured himself, hand going self-consciously up to touch his hair just above his ears. The silver stripe there was only getting wider, to his despair. Aunt Sybil kept gleefully reminding him that Father had gone completely grey before the age of thirty-five, which gave Marius less than a decade, assuming he suffered the same fate. *At least Father wasn't balding*, Marius consoled his vanity.

He sighed and leaned against the metal of the kineticar, staring moodily around the stableyard. He wasn't sure what Wyn had been hoping he'd achieve here, but it didn't feel like he'd achieved it.

The bank shared a stableyard with the buildings next to it, and it was a hive of activity completely unconcerned with his presence. Part of the yard had been converted into garage and parking space for the new kineticars, but there were still horses coming and going as well, interspersed with delivery boys on bicycles. Everything had a purpose, was in motion, apart from Marius.

Except…across the courtyard a woman stood stock-still, watching him with the single-eyed focus of a predator. No one else had noticed her, even though she had a singularly striking appearance that should've made heads turn towards her. She was tall, taller than any woman Marius had met before. Her hair was a blond so pale it was nearly white, contrasting sharply with the brown of her skin, and it was arranged in a nest of elaborate braids. Everything about her was faintly not-right, out of place not just for a stableyard or for Alverness but for, well, *everywhere*. Her dress wasn't a dress at all, but some kind of strangely cut long tunic paired with elegant black boots and trousers that narrowed at her ankles.

She seemed familiar, somehow, but before he could really process what he was seeing, she was moving towards him across the courtyard, quick and smooth as a blade. No one looked at her, although one delivery boy did abruptly veer to avoid crossing her path, without appearing to notice her presence.

Marius scrabbled at the roof of the kineticar, but she was in front of him before his brain had caught up. She was only a little shorter than he was, and this close he could see her eyes were a pale brown that was almost gold. There was no warmth in her expression, even when she bared her teeth in a smile.

"Marius Rufus Valstar," she crooned.

It was like having an ice cube tipped down the back of his shirt, every conflicting inner-voice suddenly aligning to shriek the same word: *Danger!* He took an involuntary step back. Wyn had been wrong about the fae not approaching him.

Her smile widened. "Be pleased to see me. Be very pleased." She tilted her head expectantly.

"Sorry—what? Who are you?" he said, heart hammering. What had Wyn called the sister who'd sent the creatures? *Aroset*. Was this her? How many sisters did Wyn have, and were all of them of the murderous sort?

The woman frowned, and Marius's temples began to throb.

"Are you pleased to see me now?"

"Sorry, I'm not sure that I am, exactly. I don't think we've been introduced." He felt unreasonably angry that Wyn had failed to predict this encounter, leaving Marius without a script for it. What did probably-Aroset want from him?

Anger flashed across the woman's eyes, and his headache became splitting, as if a swarm of bees had become trapped inside his skull.

Compulsion, he realised with horror. She was trying to compel him.

"Oh, leave off, Aroset, before you burst the mortal's brain," came a drawl from behind him. "I'm here to tell you Father has now put this business into my hands to deal with. Your…'help' is no longer necessary."

Aroset spun towards the voice, fury in her every line. *Iron*, Marius thought, taking advantage of her distraction to wrench open the door to the kineticar and slide inside. His headache snapped out of existence, and he locked the doors to the kineticar with shaking hands.

RED AND BLUE

MARIUS'S ABSENCE HUMMED at the back of Wyn's mind as he went about his duties; a small unease that wouldn't settle until Wyn knew he was safely back. Fortunately, he had plenty to keep him occupied, as preparing for Wintersol would've kept even a fully staffed household busy. Wintersol was one of the most important festivals in the mortal Prydein calendar. The fact that it was also of importance to the fae certainly made it…more interesting than he would have preferred. For mortals, it was a celebration of rebirth, of the sun's return after the longest night. The fae knew it as Wintertide, when the power of the dark courts reached its zenith. Already cold energy crackled over his skin, a blessing and a curse. It sped his healing rate whilst simultaneously waking parts of his nature he preferred to keep dormant.

He had to take extra care to measure his words rather than snap them; to listen patiently to Lady Phoebe's long list of anxieties instead of rushing to his next task; to calmly repeat instructions rather than snarl them when one of the staff forgot something; to suppress a burst of anger when the the still unfixed pipe in the lavender bathroom burst in a new and exciting location. He didn't especially like this wilder, meaner, and more impatient version of himself, but it would pass. It wasn't a sign, despite Lamorkin's words about his bloodfeathers. He was *not* becoming his father. But not for the first time, he reflected that it must be nice to be mortal and unaffected by the shifts of seasonal magic. *I have weathered this before; I will this year too.* He didn't think about what he'd agreed to undertake with Hetta, after Wintersol.

"Are you sure you ought to be standing, Wyn? I can't think it good for your leg," Lady Phoebe asked with a frown when he came into the green drawing room to find Hetta. He'd given the cane back to Ivy after luncheon, finding it was beginning to hinder more than it helped.

"It's much better, thank you," he tried to tell her, but she pressed him down into the chesterfield before he could protest. He didn't need to rest, but he had a pang of helpless fondness for Lady Phoebe's characteristic kindheartedness nonetheless.

Hetta grinned at him from the other end of the seat. She and her grandmother, stepmother, and three younger half-siblings were making up boxes to go out to the cottages. Little Laurel, who was only nine, sat on the floor next to the coffee table, carefully affixing labels under the watch of her brother Gregory, who seemed cheerfully resigned to the situation, though both their hands were now ink-stained—as was the table. Magic tingled under Wyn's fingertips, itching to magically remedy the situation. *Not the time*, he told himself firmly. Though magic would probably be necessary— nothing stained wood quite as badly as ink.

Lady Phoebe followed his gaze and made a noise of dismay, abandoning Wyn for her children. "Gregory! Laurel! For goodness' sake put some paper down if you're going to dribble ink everywhere!"

"You're nervier than usual," Hetta murmured, recalling Wyn's attention.

"I am," he acknowledged. She raised an eyebrow at him, and he spread his hands in a gesture of unrepentant vagueness.

Hetta glanced towards the window, though this drawing room didn't face the driveway. The day had shadowed into the afternoon, but the hour was not yet so advanced as to cause concern over Marius's return.

"Are you worried about Marius?" she asked.

"I would not have sent him if I thought he was in danger," Wyn said, a reassurance to himself rather than Hetta. "Though I confess I'll be easier once he's back." He changed the subject. "Sunrise is at 8:57 a.m." The Kindlemorn ceremony was held at daybreak.

Her nose wrinkled. "The joys of a Northern winter. Though I can't claim surprise, given that the sun rose at roughly the same time this morning."

"Well observed," he said lightly. Then, more seriously, "How are you finding it?"

"The Northern winter? Boxing jars of cough remedy and sloe chutney?" She lowered her voice. "The thought of fae royalty descending upon us?"

"Any and all of the above."

She sighed. "It's cold and dark, and I swear the sun rose an hour earlier when I lived in Meridon."

"That was almost fae-cryptic, though I'm unsure whether to congratulate you on that."

She smiled. A stray bit of hair had fallen against one cheek, and without thinking he reached out and tucked it behind her ear.

Behind Hetta, Alexandra shot Wyn a puzzled glance. Stormcrows, he was playing with fire. He raised an eyebrow in return, heart racing, and she frowned and looked away.

"This is getting foolish," Hetta said in an undertone, echoing his own thought.

"It is," he agreed, equally quiet.

Her expression sobered. "After Wintersol."

"A promise or an ultimatum?"

She blinked, surprised, and he realised his words had come out more aggressive than he'd intended. He took a long, deep breath, trying to settle the strands of dark energy vibrating over him.

There was a pause in which she weighed him, grey eyes dark and thoughtful. "Yes," she said eventually. "Yes, it is."

He gave a short, tight nod. She was right. One way or the other, this had to end. Stitching his self-control back together, he adopted a normal speaking tone: "So, my Star, about the schedule…"

Hetta accepted his cue, and they each withdrew to their respective ends of the chesterfield. They talked of small domesticities, ignoring the invisible, magnetic force humming between them. Hopefully it truly *was* invisible. Alexandra's attention continued to slide towards them periodically, but no one else seemed to have noticed anything amiss.

They spent several enjoyable minutes arguing about how long it really took to walk to the Standing Stones from the house—Hetta maintained he was being too conservative whilst Wyn pointed out that a desire for more sleep didn't magically shorten the distance just so that she could get up later.

"I'm not going to sleep through Wintersol Eve!" she said indignantly. "When did I ever do such a thing before?"

"Well," he said apologetically, "I've heard that in Meridon the sun rises nearly an hour earlier. And this will be the first time in seven Wintersols that we are together. I don't know precisely what you got up to on the other six."

Her eyes sparkled, and the invisible line grew tight enough that he could hardly breathe from resisting the urge to pull closer.

"It is, isn't it?" She folded her arms as if to stop her own hands wandering. "But I can assure you I haven't outgrown the tradition yet." Her eyes went suddenly distant, her fingers spasming. Pine bloomed in the air, and the hairs on the back of his neck prickled. "Marius has just crossed the boundary."

A weight slid from his shoulders despite his earlier assurance.

Hetta was still staring beyond the drawing room. "He's upset." She blinked and came back to him, the faint scent of pine dissolving. Her eyes widened as she processed her own words, and she gave him a slightly panicked look. He had to stop himself from reaching for her. Instead he tried to will reassurance across the space between them.

"But unharmed, if he's driving?" he said.

Hetta took a deep breath, steadying herself. "Yes. Yes, you're right."

"Then we should see what he has to say." Wyn got up, his leg taking his weight with a twinge.

Hetta rose with him. "Don't get into too much trouble without my supervision," she told her younger relatives, who were mostly too distracted to notice her exit at all.

She was quiet as she followed his limping exit. Giving in to temptation, he slipped his hand into hers once they reached the hallway.

"For someone intent on keeping secrets, you take a lot of risks," she said wryly, but squeezed back.

"I have very acute hearing."

"Hmmm." Her gaze turned inwards as they walked, Wyn keeping an ear out. Hetta was right; he was taking risks, and he wasn't sure he could blame it entirely on the season. He waited until they were passing down the long gallery to ask, "Are you all right?"

She took a beat to answer. "I didn't know I could get a read on my relatives' emotions like that."

"It's not compulsion," he said quickly, knowing this would be her key concern. "You're just…a bit more connected to them than you used to be." He thought of his own connection to the Court of Ten Thousand Spires, long quiescent.

"That's not entirely reassuring." The long line of ancestral portraits stared down at them, strangely appropriate to the subject of conversation. "I wish I knew more about this lording business."

"After Wintersol," he said impulsively, prompted by the worry in her eyes. "Let's go out on the moors, away from everyone, and practise."

"Practise what?" she said, lips curving.

"I'll show you my magic; you show me yours," he said suggestively down at her. "I know you want to experiment more with your land-sense, and that would be a good place for it. My knowledge of the bond between lord and faeland is imperfect, but I may be able to offer advice."

Her eyes sparkled. "You're very transparent when you make peace offerings, trying to distract me with magic experiments. But yes, let's."

He smiled. "I wasn't trying to be subtle."

The offer did seem to have successfully distracted her from her anxiety. She looked thoughtful. "I wonder if my new-and-improved land-sense can mimic the effects of some of your house spells?" she mused.

Footsteps sounded nearby, and he released her reluctantly, stepping back to a respectable distance. "Company," he muttered just as Lottie rounded the corner carrying a tray. He smiled in acknowledgement of the housemaid, who blinked at them, measuring the distance between him and Hetta with interest, before bobbing her head and carrying on her mission down the length of the long gallery. *Oh dear*, he thought, feeling he might have just added further fuel to the smoking embers of household gossip.

They met Marius striding down the long hallway from the kitchens—the stables and garage were at the back of the house.

"What happened?" Wyn asked, trying to wring meaning from Marius's agitated hand motions—usually a sign of stress.

"Your sister," Marius said, and Wyn's stomach dropped like a stone. His gaze flicked over Wyn as if he were seeing someone else. "Or at least, I think it was. She looked like you. Aroset, the other man—fae—called her."

"Come out of the hallway," Hetta said grimly.

They went to Hetta's study. All the way, Wyn berated himself. How could he have so misjudged the situation, exposing Marius to danger? Marius didn't seem hurt, at least, but what had happened? Wyn doubted Aroset had only wished to talk to Marius; it would never occur to her to simply *talk* to a mortal.

Hetta's study had once been her father's, but it had altered considerably since she'd taken possession of it. A painting of the Sun Theatre where she'd lately worked had replaced the previous one of a racehorse, and the antlers that had taken pride of place above the large square desk had been banished to the attic. There was still a slight undertone of tobacco smoke, but it was overlain now with coffee, ink, and the subtle scent of the perfume she preferred.

Wyn spoke as soon as they entered, closing the door impatiently. "Hetta, can you ask Stariel to check if there's any fae magic on him?" There was no scent of storm magic on Marius that Wyn could detect, but he wanted to be sure. The faeland would be able to pick up more subtle influences, though it was a good sign that it hadn't roared up in alarm already. Faelands were too big to pay attention to individuals, generally, but Stariel was possessive of its Valstars. As Wyn had reason to know.

Marius whirled from where he'd been about to sit down next to the window. "How do you know your sister tried to compel me?"

Wyn grimaced. "A guess. I can't smell any magic on you, so I assume your own native defences held, but I'd rather be sure." Aroset was the most powerful of his siblings, but he hadn't lied to Marius about his natural resistance to compulsion.

Hetta's eyes went distant again. "There's... Something strange tried to touch him but hasn't touched him." She blinked, coming out of her daze. "If that makes any sense to you. What happened, Marius?"

Marius collapsed into the chair. "Nothing," he said. "When you come down to it. Nothing happened." He told them about Aroset's attempted compulsion before she'd been interrupted by someone he hadn't seen—someone Wyn suspected was his brother Rakken, given what Marius had overheard. "When I got the kineticar running, they were gone. I didn't see where they went."

"What about the people at the bank?" Hetta asked.

Marius frowned. "Well, no one would come out and actually say 'it was fairies that did it', but I'm pretty sure they were thinking it." He nodded in Wyn's direction. "There was definitely a lot of hostility towards you, particularly."

"You did well," Wyn said, the cold terror of might-have-beens drawing icy tendrils around his heart. He sent a silent thanks to the mortal gods, for it didn't seem right to give any part of Faerie credit for this. "I'm sorry for my error in judgement, and even more sorry for my sister's behaviour."

There was something curiously penetrating about Marius's grey stare. "It wasn't your fault." He gave a short, ironic laugh. "You said you thought it would be safe. Truthfulness doesn't always mean right, does it?"

"No."

"Well, you were right anyway. I'm safe. It's fine."

Wyn was pretty sure that it wasn't fine, that Marius was still badly rattled, but he just as clearly didn't wish to talk about it anymore. So Wyn leaned back against the door and drawled,

"Also, in the interests of accuracy, I would like to point out that your comment that I look like my sister is not particularly correct. Aroset and I have a similar hair colour, that is all."

"Obviously a highly salient fact," Hetta said, shooting him an exasperated look.

But Marius laughed, the nervous energy in him settling a fraction, and Wyn took this as a cue to continue in this vein. "Besides, her wings are full-red, and mine are—" A month ago he would have said 'white', but he thought of his blood feathers coming in and what Lamorkin had said and knew that that could not be entirely true anymore. Perhaps they already resembled the red-and-white patterning of his father's.

"White and blue," Hetta said absently. "Yes, we know. I think you're straying from the main substance of the issue, though. And if we've digressed to discussing your relatives' hair colours, we'd all better get back to work."

Wyn froze. "What did you say?"

Hetta raised her eyebrows. "That we all have work to be getting on with. Or at least—I certainly do. Now that the car's back, it'll be a lot easier to get round to all the cottages."

"No," Wyn said. He had to force the words out, his throat was so tight. "Before that. What did you say about my wings?"

Marius, who had fallen into abstraction, now looked up sharply.

"She said they were white and blue. Not red like your sister's."

"How…?" He trailed off. Had he misinterpreted Lamorkin's words? Feverishly, he shrugged out of his coat and flung it atop the desk. The knot in his bowtie resisted for a second before coming loose. He was halfway down the buttons on his waistcoat when Marius objected.

"I say—what are you doing!? You can't just—"

Wyn ignored him and tossed the waistcoat on top of his coat, nimbly unpicking buttons, impatient to be free of his shirt, to know for sure.

He glanced up as he finally rid himself of that last layer of fabric to find both siblings' attention firmly fixed on him. Hetta's mouth was trembling with the desire to laugh, her eyes tracing down his bare chest, and Marius was both glaring and blushing furiously.

Wyn gave them a sheepish smile and changed, self-conscious for reasons that had nothing to do with his state of dress, but he had to know. A second later he was trying to crane his neck to see between his shoulder blades, but it was impossible to twist his wings in such a fashion, and he merely performed an inelegant pirouette making the attempt.

Hetta laughed. "Are you trying to see your own feathers? I promise you, they're blue just along your spine. And, well, in fairness 'silver' seems a better descriptor than 'white' everywhere else."

"You can't just go undressing in front of people!" Marius said, as Wyn grasped hold of his uninjured wing and tried to bend it round to see better. "Especially women," he said with a sharp glance at Hetta.

"I don't have any objections." Hetta grinned.

"That's very much not the point! I'd like to register my extreme disapproval, though I can see neither of you cares!"

"I do care what you think, actually," Wyn said, giving up the attempt. His injured wing ached, but there was no impairment of movement when he flexed it in and out. He ran a hand through his hair and was slightly disconcerted when it met horn. It unsettled him, the strangeness of his own body. "Are you sure they're blue, Hetta?"

Her amusement dimmed as she absorbed his expression. "Yes. You truly didn't know? Hang on—I think I have a mirror here somewhere." She went around her desk and opened a drawer with a click. "Here." She emerged with a small mirror-compact and instead of handing it over, walked behind him and held it up. "Can you see?" she said, angling it.

"Yes." He stared at the tiny reflection. He wasn't sure exactly which bit of him was being captured except that it was right next to the warm brown of his skin, but the colour was clear enough. "That's not red, not by any stretch of imagination." There was a distinct line of tiny blue coverts, the deep saturated colour of lapis lazuli.

"Is it important?" Marius asked.

"I don't know." The little piece of heaviness he'd been carrying at the thought of sporting his father's colours transformed into, well, a little piece of confusion instead. Was that an improvement? What did it mean?

SNOW MOON

F OR SIX YEARS, Wintersol had been a bittersweet night for Hetta. At no other time had she felt so alone, her family and heritage quite so far away. As counterpoint, at no other time had she been so forcibly reminded that she was free of her father's narrow-minded rule. Now Lord Henry was dead, and Hetta stood in her father's shoes here at Stariel, his ghost lurking in every sight and sound.

The main festivities would be tomorrow, beginning with the all-important Kindlemorn at sunrise. It wasn't required, exactly, but it was something of a tradition for the younger members of the house to see the longest night through on Wintersol Eve. Those who considered themselves too old, too young, or simply too tired went to bed as usual and woke early instead.

Hetta wasn't a teenager anymore, but she had been last time she'd been at Stariel House. *How the world has shifted since then.* She was tempted to push all her concerns aside and lose herself in the merry-making of her relatives. A dozen of them had already marked out the ballroom and cajoled cousin Ivy into getting out her fiddle so that they could dance all the old country dances. Hetta suspected the phonograph would be making an appearance later in the night, after the aunts had retired—Aunt Maude in particular disapproved of 'modern music'. The spice of mulled wine permeated the air.

"The world won't end if you regress to your rebellious youth for one night," Wyn murmured from behind her as she stood vacillating on the threshold to the ballroom, thinking of all the other things she ought to be doing ahead of indulging her craving for nostalgia.

"Does that apply to you too then?" she said without turning.

"How do you know the world does not depend upon my maintaining a sober and dignified mien at all times?" he countered. His breath tickled in her ear.

"Because it would already have ended more times than I can count."

"Hetta!" Her younger brother Gregory had noticed her standing there. "Are you going to stay up with us?"

"It's tradition," she intoned, though it was peculiar to be asked this by Gregory, who'd been too young and thus made to go to bed early last time she'd been home for Wintersol.

"I want to stay up too!" little Laurel said firmly to her brother, and Hetta realised the age difference between Gregory and Laurel was nearly the same as that between Hetta and Gregory. This was the same scene as six years ago, more or less.

"You can stay up till you fall asleep," Gregory told Laurel.

"I won't fall asleep!"

Hetta had another flashback, to bundles of smaller relatives curled into cushions and blankets in Carnelion Hall, lit only by the flickering embers of the great hearth fire. She turned to see Wyn's expression, but he'd vanished.

"Come dance with us!" Laurel said, tugging at her hand.

"All right," she said, letting herself be pulled into the ballroom.

HOURS LATER, HETTA SAT in Carnelion Hall watching the embers flicker. In the next room she could hear the low murmur of voices—Gregory and Alexandra, she identified from the pitch. Laurel was asleep, curled into an armchair, having refused to be put to bed by her mother two hours prior. Most of her older relatives had sought their beds, including Marius.

Something deep and primal was moving in the night. If she closed her eyes, caught on the edge of sleep, she could almost comprehend it. She lay back against the cushions, feeling strangely here-and-not-here. Stariel was—she reached for the word—dozing off. The sensation was akin to an eiderdown being laid upon the land.

The act of analysing the sensation distanced her from it. She shook off the drowsiness and sat up. It was very late—or very early, depending on how one judged such things—and the house felt hushed, despite the few people she could still sense moving about. Driven by instinct, she rose and went to the great glass windows to look out.

The sky was clear, and the full moon hung suspended in a wash of stars, throwing cold light on the landscape below. Snow was falling lightly and had already blanketed the ground. The combination of snowfall, clear skies, and full moon was at once beautiful and entirely eerie. *Snow Moon*, she thought. *The change of seasons.* This was the first snowfall of winter, and to Stariel it marked the first of the dark days ahead.

Although the land was slipping deeper into slumber, Hetta felt wide awake. She hugged her dressing gown around her and quietly slipped out of the hall, summoning a small magelight as she did so. It bobbed along beside her, just enough to make out the edges of things. She could've summoned a brighter light, but it seemed out of keeping with the season's shift.

She followed that tug of *something* through the house to the tallest tower. She had to briefly cross the courtyard outside to do so, and cold radiated up through her slippers. The air was bone-chilling and absolutely still, with snow falling soundlessly from the cloudless sky. The hairs on the back of her neck rose.

She opened the door to deep shadow. The only illumination came through the narrow slits of the windows, throwing pale moonlight onto the narrow, winding stairs. Hetta felt her way along the wall, trusting her land-sense to tell her the depth of the stairs. Her fingertips ached with the cold.

When she emerged on top of the tower, she found herself no longer alone. If her land-sense hadn't warned her, and she didn't know the architecture of Stariel so well, there might've been a moment where she thought he was simply a particularly lifelike statue, perched as he was on the parapet. He was poised as if he'd been about to take flight but had changed his mind at the last second. Bare to the waist, he stood with wings half-furled, white-gold hair loose and fluttering about his pointed ears and dark horns. The snowflakes made tiny hissing noises as they hit his skin, but he didn't appear to register them.

She knew he'd heard her come up, though he didn't move. He was staring over the landscape—holding vigil, was the phrase that came to mind. Could he fly with his injured wing? He was awfully close to the edge. His recent injuries showed as angry red scars, jagged but still astonishingly well healed given the timeframe.

She burrowed her hands deeper into the pockets of her dressing gown and carefully picked her way towards him. The tower stones were slippery with snow, and her slippers made small muffled sounds in the night's emptiness.

Wyn still hadn't looked at her, staring out at the world with the intensity of a hawk watching prey. She came as close as she dared, and would've halted, but he raised one of his wings and Hetta took the gesture for the invitation it was. She ducked under his feathers until she stood below and beside him, her back enveloped in wings.

He radiated heat, like standing next to a hot water pipe, and she had to resist the urge to snuggle against him, worried he'd lose his balance. The ground was far below.

Sometimes it was easy to forget Wyn wasn't human. But under the white light of the moon with the snow falling silently and strangely around him, he couldn't be mistaken for anything merely mortal. There was a wildness in him that she rarely saw so close to the surface. The faint itching sensation at the back of her mind suddenly made sense: it wasn't just Wyn.

Stariel was a faeland, which meant that underlying the everyday world of humanity was another reality, populated by creatures of legend. In Stariel, the two realities—human and Faerie—lay close together, but—and Hetta realised this only now—still distinct, and usually with the human side face-up, as it were. Tonight, the fae side of Stariel was in ascendance.

She reached out, carefully, not wanting to be dragged under by the deep and ponderous thoughts of the land. Her hunch was correct: the wyldfae that she was always aware of, on some level, were unusually *present* tonight. They acknowledged her awareness with brief flickers of obeisance as she brushed over them. There were a few inside the house now as well as the wider estate. Most of Stariel's native fae were small things—lowfae, a handful of lesser fae, and the dim smudges of the half-fae kittens.

Wyn wasn't one of Stariel's wyldfae, and he wasn't just greater fae but a prince, bound to a foreign land much as the Valstars were bound to Stariel. His presence blazed like a beacon. The part of Hetta that was most in tune with the land, a part that didn't recognise human rules or social niceties, wanted to flare up in response to the power she sensed in Wyn.

She felt rather than saw Wyn quiver under the scrutiny, but to her surprise he didn't back down. The bright inferno of his presence didn't *quite* challenge Stariel, but nor did it falter. It simply said: *I*

THE PRINCE OF SECRETS

am here, this is what I am. I won't lessen myself. Stariel bristled a bit at that, and Hetta gave it a stern talking to.

<I have room for *both* of you in my life, you know. This jealousy is silly; you're a land, not a child!> She'd *make* room for them both.

Hetta didn't know what they were waiting for until, abruptly, she did.

The world shifted, the infinitesimal moment when the tide turns. And in that turn, there was power. It crackled in the air, and through Stariel she felt the sparks of the wyldfae shimmer as they drank it in. It tasted cold and solemn, with hints of savagery but also of deep patience. Her senses filled with pine, snow, and bitter berries.

Wintertide, she thought distantly as she braced herself: the power of the darkest season. It washed over Stariel and through her, infusing her with strange and conflicting desires. She was the bear, asleep in her mountain den, the growing bulk of cubs within her. She was the fox, lean and fierce with hunger, the copper-rich tang of blood on her fangs. She was a thousand trees, sap flowing ponderously under her bark, and seeds beneath the snow, waiting patiently for the sun to return. And she was the night, inexorable and endless.

She surfaced slowly and sensed the change in her companion. He turned towards her, eyes dark and *other* as he stepped from parapet to stones in a single smooth motion, so they were suddenly at the same level. There was something predatory in the way he moved, sending a frisson of excitement through her.

He wrapped his wings around them both, cocooning them in feathers, and pulled her to him. His lips were hot and shockingly demanding, and Hetta threw her hands around his neck to support knees gone suddenly weak.

He brought one of his hands up to clasp the back of her head, deepening the kiss. None of his usual restraint was evident. She came up for air with a gasp, heart beating jack-rabbit fast as he laid claim to her throat, kissing and nipping his way down to the sensitive spot above her collarbone. Heat flared, fire under her skin despite the chill air around them, a heat that only increased when he let his other hand fall through the loosened ties of her dressing gown, to the hem of her nightgown. She shivered, with anticipation rather than cold, as the dressing gown slid from her shoulders and he teased his way up beneath the nightgown, splaying his fingers possessively over her bare stomach.

She touched him back, savouring the touch of his bare skin. His muscles were incredibly defined under her hands, the skin almost feverishly hot. She could've lost herself exploring him, but he bent to bring his mouth to her breast, licking through the thin fabric of her nightgown, and she abruptly forgot what she was doing, forgot everything in exquisite, gasping pleasure.

Before she could catch her breath, he spun them effortlessly and walked her backwards until her back pressed against the tower, cushioned on his feathers. Turning her head, she rubbed her cheek across the silk of them, rewarded by a soft hiss of breath from Wyn. She took the opportunity to distract him further, running her hands over his chest, up to the corded muscle of his shoulders. He made a sound she'd never heard from him before—a low, startled noise halfway between pleasure and distress. Her heart melted, and she cupped his face so she could press a soft kiss to his mouth.

It didn't stay soft. The world blurred, coherent thought impossible in the twist of sensations: heat, flesh, lips. Over and through it all crawled the cool tingle of winter magic. Their own magics rose to meet it, until Hetta couldn't distinguish the physicality of Wyn from how Stariel perceived him. His power manifested as spice and the smell of earth recently touched by rain. Her own magic was tightly wound with Stariel's. It tasted of cold mountain streams and pine, the dark damp of loam, laced with the faintest trace of coffee. The magic grew thick as water, and she realised with a shock that Wyn was glowing faintly, lighting their feathery cocoon with the luminescence of his own wings and skin. When their mouths met, the different magics seemed to flow between them, mingling and growing stronger for it, intoxicating, until Hetta wasn't sure whose desire was whose.

She'd never seen Wyn like this: almost feral with need, utterly without control. This wasn't her slightly shy partner, anxious over his own inexperience. This was the part of him he usually hid; the part that commanded rather than persuaded. There was nothing innocent about him now, caught in a dark tide.

That same dark tide stirred something equally primal within her. She let her hands wander south, down the flat planes of his stomach. Lower. Wyn went rigid, made that same small distracted sound again, low in his throat, and kissed her with increased fervency. He tugged at her nightgown, demanding, and she obediently lifted her hands above her head so he could remove it. There was no bite of cold; the sheer force of the magic swirling around them was heating the air.

Wyn pulled his wings back and stared at her hungrily, his eyes hot and black in the low light. The heat woke an answering flame in her, and she dragged a fingernail over his chest and down to his belt, holding his gaze while she undid it. The storm of magic around them grew wilder.

Hetta had seen more men naked than her relatives would've approved of—though that wasn't hard when the approved number was *zero*. Some men, she'd found, were oddly coy under a woman's appraising gaze, awkward in their own skin. Not Wyn. There was a trueness to him like this, in his fae form. He was astonishing under the starlight, too beautiful, too erotic, to be quite real.

When she touched him, skin-to-skin, he shuddered, and crackling energy surrounded them. The dynamic between them changed. Where before he'd been the pursuer, now she took the lead, running lightly over the hard length of him. He threw back his head with a groan.

We could have him, she thought, *claim him down to his bedrock as he comes apart under our hands.* Their magics were already entwined; now they could swallow his magic as he unravelled, make him truly theirs, this foreign prince with his foreign magic. She shivered with lust at the thought.

"*My love.*" His voice was low and harsh, nearly unrecognisable from his normally polished tones. "*Hetta.*" They were the first words either of them had uttered, both a benediction and a plea.

It wasn't unlike waking up, so deeply was she immersed in the magic. Stariel was no longer slumbering; instead its awareness burned in her, focussed with fierce intent. Her thoughts thrummed with unsettling plurality, and she understood in a single shocked second that she was channelling more than her own desires. The winter magic wasn't only affecting the fae; she too was being swept away and taking Stariel with her.

Shaking free was like pushing her way up-river through chest-deep water—*warm, tempting water.* Her body ached with desire, and everything in her—including Stariel—resisted as she made herself step away from Wyn. She shook her head, as if the physical movement would clear it of magical entanglements, and thought of frozen lakes, the touch of ice, and the barely flickering movements of trout sheltering under deep riverbanks. The magic fought her, wanting to continue its crescendo, but she hadn't become a master of illusion by giving up easily. With iron willpower she slowly and inexorably broke her way out. <Sleep,> she told Stariel. <It's the beginning of the deep cold; now is the time for sleeping.> With extreme reluctance, the weight of the land's focus began to subside.

Carefully, she drew another long breath and took another step away. Now she had only her own and Wyn's lust to deal with, a tightrope of her own desire. A misstep would summon Stariel back in an instant, ready to swallow Wyn's magic whole—whatever that meant. It didn't sound good.

Wyn had stilled, sensing something shift, but he was still under the full sway of the magic, and there was more feral wild creature than sentient man in his glittering gaze. Her blood stirred, and she wondered if it would truly be so terrible to give in to temptation? A small, shameful part of her pointed out that with Stariel extricated from the mix, it wouldn't be some kind of disturbing metaphysical claiming; it would just be the two of them, flesh to flesh. Knowing Wyn, he'd probably forgive her even if she slipped from the tightrope and accidentally helped Stariel do...whatever it had been trying to do.

That was the sticking point, of course. He might forgive her, but she wouldn't.

"Oh, Hallowyn Tempestren, what am I going to do with you?" She spoke his name—his true name—aloud. She saw its effect—the faintest beginnings of a frown—and stepped back again, further from the temptation he presented.

"Hallowyn," she said, surprised at how easily the name came to her lips. She'd never used it before. "Hallowyn, come back to me."

He trembled like a leaf in a high wind, and then she saw awareness seep back into his gaze, a softness that had previously been missing. His wings fanned in and out once, twice, and then he blinked slowly, glanced down at his naked self and up to meet Hetta's eyes.

"Well," he said, his voice deeper than usual. "This is...a little awkward. I don't suppose you remember what you did with my trousers?" He seemed to be trying but failing not to look at Hetta's own nakedness, which she found as endearing as it was ridiculous.

Her voice quivered only slightly as she said, "I think I may have tossed them over the parapet."

"Ah. Well, excuse me a moment." He ducked his head, turned, and in one swift motion had unfurled his wings and leapt off the tower. So he *could* still fly then.

The night's cold came back in full force with the magic dispersed, and she hurriedly gathered up her clothing, tying the knot of her dressing gown just as Wyn reappeared, a good half—sadly the most interesting half—of his own nakedness remedied. His form shimmered slightly as he shifted back to his more familiar human shape, wings vanishing in a rustle of feathers. There were snowflakes in his hair. He swallowed, somewhat at a loss for words, but he rallied quickly, mustering a self-deprecating smile to disguise his embarrassment. *No, not embarrassment*, she realised with a start. That was her superimposing what a mortal man might have felt in this situation. There was something more complicated going on here, because the emotion Wyn was trying to hide looked disturbingly like fear. Fear of what, exactly? Had he felt what Stariel had been trying to do to him?

"Now I must merely remember where I left my shirt," he said lightly.

"Wyn," she said, fixing him with a stern look. Oh, he was so good at burying any feelings he thought he ought not to have. His armour settled back into place, his eyes full of nothing but mild inquiry. As if they were merely lord and butler. It infuriated her.

She made a frustrated *humph* and then simply went and wrapped her arms around him. He tensed, but she persisted, and he sighed and relaxed fractionally, though he didn't hug her closer as she'd expected.

"I'm—I am not yet fully in control of myself," he said, and she could hear the strain in his voice. "I appreciate the sentiment, but… *please*, Hetta."

She unwrapped herself but didn't move away. "Why did the magic pull you under so badly?" she demanded.

"I am not…certain." He hesitated in his word choice, and their eyes met. They both knew there was a world of wriggle-room in that statement. He gave the ghost of a smile. "No, don't call me on it. I wasn't trying to evade the question, truly. It's just that I can think of several reasons, but I'm not sure which one applies, or if any of them do." He took a step back, and she noticed his hands were held in loose fists, as if he didn't quite trust himself not to reach out if he left his fingers to their own devices. He swallowed again, and his tone when he spoke was clinically detached. "First, it could be that the Iron Law being revoked has increased the power of the Wintertide in the Mortal Realm. Second, it could be because I have not often taken my fae form at Stariel until recently. I'm more sensitive to magic in it, but I'm also somewhat out of practice. My powers have changed since I was a youth. It's possible that inexperience made me vulnerable. And third…it could be in some part due to the relationship between us. Stariel's recent hostility…I don't know. Perhaps it is testing me."

"Stariel was here tonight. I mean, more than usually present. I think it may have been influencing me." She found herself reluctant to say the next words but made herself do so. "We wanted to see if we could ensnare you." Was this a *normal* lord problem to have? Hetta's thoughts unwillingly went to her father's relationship with her stepmother and immediately recoiled. She was *not* asking Lady Phoebe anything even tangentially related to the subject.

Wyn didn't seem as alarmed as he should've been by this confession; he was still watching her the way men who are mentally undressing a woman do, his eyes lingering on her curves. It was immensely distracting, and she gave herself a shake.

"Go and get dressed and come and find me in the green drawing room. I'll make us some hot chocolate. We need to talk."

"I can—" he began but she held up a hand to stop him.

"Yes, I know you can, but I, quite frankly, could use the distraction, and although you may not be impressed with my cooking abilities, I'm quite capable of finding the chocolate."

A smile. "As you wish." He hesitated, and she knew he was considering whether to shift forms again in order to take the swifter method to the ground below. But in the end he ducked past her and down the tower steps. He was still so deeply uncomfortable with being seen in his fae form, and she wasn't sure how to change that. In truth, she still found it disconcerting too.

With him gone, the air was colder but a lot more plentiful. She let herself sag back against the tower for a few moments, using the cold shock of it to try to cool her own libido. *Gods above.*

23

THE STARCORN

HETTA WASN'T A great believer in chastity, and if the choice had been hers alone, she and Wyn would've already consummated their relationship—frequently and with great vigour. She hurriedly wrenched her mind back from those fantasies and thought determinedly of snowstorms instead. Wyn had wanted to wait, had pointed out that this change from friend to something else was still so new that neither of them had quite settled into the shape of it yet. She'd known, deep down, that it was really because of his own uncertainty about his future at Stariel. While she couldn't say she was precisely *happy* about that, she'd understood, and had been prepared to give them time. Wyn was right, in some ways; it *had* only been two weeks since their relationship had shifted. It only felt longer because she'd known him for so many years before that.

But tonight—tonight had made her think there was something more going on here, something that she couldn't quite puzzle out as she made her way down the tower and through the house. After a moment's consideration, she detoured to her room to collect the package that had arrived with yesterday's mail. Stuffing it under her arm for safe-keeping, she made her way down to the kitchen. It took her a little time to find the correct pan to heat the chocolate, and she used it to draw up another layer of calm.

She arrived in the green drawing room and deposited the package safely out of sight underneath the armchair's skirt in case she changed her mind. She'd just finished setting up the chessboard when Wyn appeared, hair slicked back and dressed like an elderly and conservative butler.

"Protective armour," he said with a gleam of amusement, correctly interpreting her expression. He raised an eyebrow at the chessboard. "Is this an ardour-cooling exercise?"

"If you like," she said.

Hetta was a decent chess player, but not a brilliant one. Wyn was. It was one of the only times he let her see the cold, calculating part of his mind, the part that thought ten moves ahead and ruthlessly sacrificed any piece necessary to achieve the ultimate goal. They played in silence, and Hetta was even less attentive to the game than usual.

"Checkmate," Wyn said softly, and Hetta flicked over her king with a finger. "But your mind was barely in the game tonight." He paused, then reached out and covered her hand with his. "Thank you. I'm more myself now."

"All right," she said, leaning backwards in her seat. "I think we need to talk then."

A shutter closed in Wyn's eyes, though he shrugged carelessly. "About what, precisely?"

"Gods, I want to shake you when you do that," Hetta said. "Stop pretending it doesn't matter, that you don't care. It does and you do. *Talk to me.*"

A tiny spark of anger in his eyes. Good.

"I *am* talking to you," he pointed out, his tone still mild.

"Do the fae particularly value chastity?" she asked bluntly.

His lips curved. "No. The opposite, if anything."

"Well, do *you*, then?"

"I admit I was glad of it in the case of the lug-imps, but otherwise, no. My choices have not been driven by Prydinian morality, Hetta."

Well, that was a relief, at least, to know that the fear she'd glimpsed wasn't about that. She hadn't really thought it was, but the recent revelation about his inexperience had made her question her previous assumptions.

"Then tell me what you're so afraid of," she said. "And try and tell me that it's not fear driving you, because I don't think you actually can."

He stiffened, and his fingers curled into the armrests, making small divots in the green fabric. "I am not afraid of you," he said, enunciating each syllable with clipped precision. His eyes were dark, the russet of them rich and sensual as wine. "And I'm not afraid of sex, if that's what you're referring to." His words carried the barest hint of earth-and-rainstorm, and Stariel stirred restlessly in response.

"Well, if we wait for you to list all the things you're *not* afraid of, we'll be here some time. I want to know what's going on in your head, Wyn. Are you going to tell me, or am I going to exhaust myself talking in vague circles till dawn?"

Abruptly he let the tension go, collapsing back into his chair, magic fading. "I wanted so badly to get this right, and I seem to be making an absolute mull of it instead." He snuck a sideways look at her. "If you make some remark about my manipulative tendencies, I will, I will—" He growled in frustration. "I will be mildly and momentarily put out."

Hetta giggled; she couldn't help it.

"It's not very nice to make fun of my inability to use hyperbole," he groused.

"It *is* quite funny, actually," she said. "Why didn't I notice your deliberate avoidance of such sentence constructions before now?"

"Several of the villagers do think me painfully literal," he admitted.

"Well, I think it's very good for you to realise that there are limits to your own omnipotence. You can't control *everything*, Wyn. And I'm a little concerned that you think of me as something you ought to be able to manipulate according to your own goals."

"I wasn't talking about controlling *you*." He paused. "I know you worry about Stariel influencing you, but note that of the two people on that tower, you were the one who found your way back to yourself, not me. If it was a test, I'm not sure I passed. I could not control the magic. I am not *safe*. You haven't seen my father's court, Hetta. You don't understand what he is capable of; what *I* might be capable of."

Hetta stared at him, nonplussed. "I'm beginning to think I have a much greater idea of what you're capable of than you do, if you're truly worried about that."

It had never occurred to her that Wyn's self-doubt would take this particular form. Him fearing he lacked self-control seemed particularly ironic given that Hetta had been waging an unsuccessful campaign to get him to shed his self-restraint.

But Wyn shook his head. He moved, supernaturally fast, and suddenly he was in front of her armchair, hands on the armrests, caging her in. Their faces were only inches apart, his eyes cold and boring into hers. The smell of thunderstorms spiked thick enough to choke on, and when he spoke his voice held dark echoes of the night.

"I am stronger than you, faster. I could snap your spine if I wished. I know fae magics that would let me ensnare your senses, bind you to do my bidding. I am not *tame*, Henrietta Isadore Valstar."

She leaned forward and kissed him and, in direct counterpoint to his harsh words, his lips were soft and hesitant. She had to coax the kiss from him, and even when she managed it, he refused to let it deepen, just holding himself over her and letting her brush butterfly kisses over his mouth. She pulled back a little and rubbed her nose against his affectionately.

He gave a deep sigh and sagged down to the floor. "And apparently, I'm not even scary."

She petted his hair, and he leaned into the sensation like a cat. "Well, it was a good effort," she said consolingly. "But as I've seen you carefully transfer spiders to the garden rather than squash them, it was rather a pointless one. You can't be heartbroken over kittens and still expect people to see you as the big bad wolf."

He made a grumpy sound, delighting her. She kept twining her hands through his hair and he let her, settling back against the chair.

"If we're going to have further arguments, I think I ought to win at least some of them," he groused.

"Of course, darling," she said, trying out the pet name. *My love*, he'd said to her twice now without her returning the sentiment. But Wyn couldn't lie; Hetta could. That meant she had to be very, very sure of what she said before she said it. "Though…as my next argument is going to be that you should tell everyone what you are, I would prefer to win that one too." He stiffened under her hands. "I think you underestimate them. After all, who knows already? Me, Jack, Marius, Caroline. Gregory," she added. "And Grandmamma. It's getting silly pretending it's really even a secret anymore, isn't it?"

He was so still and silent that she couldn't tell what he was thinking except that he wasn't enjoying it much.

She worried at her lip. "In any case, I have something for you. Under the chair." She gave him a prod with her toe.

His lips quirked, and he gave her a curious look but obediently extracted the wrapped package for her. She shook her head when he tried to hand it to her.

"It's for you. Happy Wintersol."

Wyn blinked. "We agreed we don't do gifts."

"Ten years ago," Hetta pointed out. Wyn had been the hall boy then, the agreement a way to navigate the difference in their respective positions. After she'd left for Meridon, the question had become moot. "Don't worry; I'm not going to sulk because you didn't get me one. Open it!"

Her enthusiasm made him smile. Gently, he untied the strings of the package, the brown paper rustling as it fell away to reveal the garment. She knew the moment he realised what it was, his fingers stilling on the extra seams.

"I asked one of my costuming contacts in Meridon," Hetta said, trying not to immediately launch into *What do you think? Do you like it?* "She does a side-line in unusual requests." And heavens knew what she'd made of Hetta's, but she hadn't questioned it.

Wyn held up the shirt, shaking out the fabric so that the extra slits in the back gaped open—the space for wings. Maybe Hetta wasn't yet used to him in his fae form, but that wasn't going to change if he kept hiding it from her.

His expression had gone unreadable. Was he annoyed? "This wasn't an attempt to railroad you into revealing yourself. In case you thought that it was," she added.

He looked up, eyes brimming with amusement. "*Hetta*," he said accusingly.

"All right, maybe it was a *tiny* bit of a railroad attempt, but think how much less awkward it'll be if you need to give my family a demonstration of your other self! But that wasn't the *only* reason, you know. I don't want you to feel you have to hide from me. Or that you have to leave me because of what you are."

Amusement deepened to something warmer as he set the shirt aside and rose, reaching for her. Sadly, he aborted the movement as he remembered himself, perching on the arm next to her instead and twining his fingers with hers. "I...thank you."

"I hope it fits," she said lightly. She hesitated, a panicky feeling fluttering in her chest as she added, "And that you have reason to wear it." He'd agreed to let her bargain, but Hetta wanted more than that slim inch of compromise. *After Wintersol,* she'd said, and meant it. She couldn't keep dancing to this uncertain tune forever.

Wyn fingered his bowtie. "Well, I would try it on now, but that would rather defeat the purpose of my protective armour."

Hetta was about to suggest that protective armour was vastly overrated when he paused and said quietly, "Actually, I do have something that I would like to give you also."

He swallowed, looking uncharacteristically nervous, and released her hand. Reaching into the pocket of his coat, he withdrew a feather.

It was Hetta's turn to blink as he handed it to her. It was one of his, unmistakably; no bird she knew had feathers so large or so obviously magical. It glimmered with faint luminescence, the silver frosting each white filament catching the light as she turned it in her hands.

Wyn watched her intently; clearly there was some significance here that wasn't immediately apparent.

"Thank you," she said. "It's lovely."

His solemn manner fractured, and he began to laugh.

"That was a compliment!" she protested.

"I know," he said, eyes bright. And he kissed her swiftly, there and gone before it had really begun, as if he couldn't help himself. It made it quite hard to be annoyed with him.

She held the feather up. "All right, what does it mean, then? Is this the fae equivalent of giving someone a lock of hair as a token?" Though wasn't that something people did when they anticipated being *apart* from each other?

His gaze turned thoughtful. "It's a stormdancer tradition. It denotes a depth of…sentiment," he said, skittering around the word he'd clearly intended to say in its place. "Of trust."

She thought suddenly of how he'd destroyed the remnants of his blood from the office at the bank. A sufficiently skilled illusionist could use a piece of someone's essence to personalise a spell, though it was considered a slightly old-fashioned, distasteful branch of the magic. What if fae magic could work in the same way—fae magic of a much more destructive sort than illusion? What would it mean, in Faerie, to voluntarily give someone a piece of yourself, to hold that power over you?

A depth of sentiment indeed, she thought, brushing her fingertips over the softness of the feather. "Oh."

He looked down at her, weighing something. "Tomorrow," he said suddenly. "I will tell your family tomorrow."

Her heart burst with relief, but before she could respond, he tensed and pulled away from her hands. There was something in the movement that put her on instant alert. She scanned the room instinctively and found the wyldfae he'd reacted to lurking behind the chesterfield across the room.

<What is it?> she asked Stariel, and the answer came dismissively: lowfae/one of ours/not a threat/not worth our time. To her surprise, for Stariel rarely gave her actual words, there was a name attached to the response: *Starcorn*. The name was familiar; something from her childhood. Starcorns were Stariel's answer to tales of unicorns. *One of ours*, Stariel had said, but she only understood what it meant when she felt for her land-sense and examined the lowfae with it. A feeling of possessiveness welled up. The starcorn was *hers*, just as much as the people, trees, and rocks.

"Come here," Wyn said to the wyldfae, his voice deep and commanding, shivering with a thread of compulsion. She wasn't sure he even realised he'd reinforced his words with magic until he repeated the words, this time without the compulsion. Interesting.

Something shuffled out from behind the sofa, and Hetta found herself staring into a pair of overlarge indigo eyes.

"Oh!" she said, entranced despite herself. Her exclamation startled the wyldfae, and it ducked out of sight. She made her tone softer. "Please do come out."

Slowly, it emerged from the safety of the chesterfield. It was about the size of a collie and had a dog-like quality to its face. The long streamers from its mane and tail and many-tufted ears gave it the appearance of moving within a cloud of fine sparkling mist. Its fur was a deep cobalt, run through with shimmers of purple and silver. From the centre of its head rose the reason for its name: a shining curved horn about a hand span in length.

Hetta couldn't help the small noise of delight that escaped her. "Hello," she said, stretching out her hands towards it. "You are *adorable*."

"*Hetta*," Wyn chided, but he sounded amused rather than alarmed, so she paid him no heed.

"Can you understand me?" she asked the small creature as it picked its way towards her, nose outstretched and trembling. "I'm sorry if the 'adorable' remark offended you, by the way."

"They don't speak," Wyn said. "But they understand intent. She knows you're admiring her."

"It doesn't seem to like you much," she observed, for the starcorn stopped and eyed Wyn balefully. Wyn sighed, levered himself up, and walked over to the far wall. The starcorn blinked at him for a bit before deciding he was at a safe enough distance. It shook itself and trotted happily over to Hetta on delicate hooves and proceeded to snuffle her palms. It was hesitant at first but grew bolder as Hetta crooned to it. "Oh, aren't you a beautiful thing?"

There was a statue of a starcorn at the bottom of the house's main entrance, which she now realised was startlingly accurate, though the sombre grey stone hadn't done justice to the riotous colour of the little creature, nor to the soft texture of its fur. It accepted Hetta as a long-lost friend, wriggling under her hands like a cat, demanding attention.

"I thought unicorns had a fondness for virgins?" she couldn't resist saying, shooting Wyn a sly look.

He wasn't ruffled by the sally. "That is a starcorn, not a unicorn," he said from his position against the wall. "And they've a fondness for innocents, not virgins."

"It thinks I'm innocent?" Hetta frowned down at the starcorn, not sure how to feel about this.

"*Unicorns* have a fondness for innocents. That's a starcorn. They're far more worried about intent than their larger brethren. She knows you mean her no harm, that you are her lord and feel a degree of responsibility towards her."

"Don't tell me *you* mean her harm?" Hetta couldn't imagine anyone wishing ill upon the beautiful little creature, least of all Wyn.

"No, but she can likely tell that I'm fighting an urge to strangle my brother." When she looked up in question, he folded his arms and nodded at the starcorn. "That's who sent her to you. Rakken's always had a gift for making the lowfae do his bidding willingly. Starcorn are very intuitive; she won't understand our speech, but she knows I'm not feeling particularly happy with the person who tasked her with carrying a message."

"Message?" She ran her hands over the starcorn. "It's not like she has pockets, and if she can't speak...?"

"Ask her," Wyn said.

"All right, lovely," she said to the starcorn. "Do you have a message for me?"

The starcorn stopped rubbing itself against her to lift its head and blink big eyes at her. Then it snorted, and a small puff of dense green smoke appeared, smelling strongly of tangerine. Hetta sneezed.

When the smoke faded, a single piece of parchment lay on the carpet, and the starcorn was gone.

"It's good to know you come from a long line of melodramatics," Hetta commented as she picked up the parchment, making Wyn chuckle. She read the letter aloud:

"*Forgive me my stratagems, Lord Valstar. I assure you they are intended to extricate my brother from this mess alive, which I presume is a goal you also desire? I shall look forward to seeing you again. I will of course abide by guestright.*"

"It's the pact between host and invited guest," Wyn explained before she could ask. "Basically, both parties agree not to harm or dishonour the other for the duration of a visit. It's an old law in

Faerie, and about as sacred as anything gets there. It's so ingrained that most fae would not bother to spell it out, but he's making a jab at me and my broken oath." He sounded tired.

"But I haven't invited him," Hetta pointed out.

"No, you haven't." He looked troubled. He glanced at the curtained windows. "It's nearly time to wake everyone."

"Kindlemorn in the snow—is that a good omen or a bad one, do you think?"

"Regardless, I'm glad I planned a vast quantity of hot drinks."

PEOPLE WOKE WITH A mixture of excitement and feigned reluctance. The nostalgia of the night before returned in full force. By the time they made their way up to the Standing Stones, the snow was falling thick and fast and the sky had become a vast whiteness. Hetta stared up at it thoughtfully and then mentally suggested to Stariel that it could fall somewhere other than where everyone was walking. To her satisfaction, the faeland accepted this request without a blink, and the snow parted before them, creating strange white waterfalls in the air to either side of the path.

The reactions to this ranged from shocked to delighted. The younger family members thought it was a great trick and ran to the side of the path with outstretched hands, catching the diverted streams of snowflakes. Aunt Sybil made a clucking sound of generalised disapproval. Jack merely looked thoughtful.

Dawn was still some time away, and the way was lit by Hetta's bobbing magelights. The snow had a muffling effect, and they proceeded in a cocoon of humanity amidst the vast emptiness of the dark estate.

The last time Hetta had been to the Standing Stones had been for the Choosing Ceremony. She'd stood alone in front of a crowd of Stariel's people, having overturned every expectation of who would inherit the lordship. It hadn't been a particularly pleasant experience. This morning, she was once again the centre of attention, but the crowd's focus was much less hostile than that night.

Outside of Stariel, Kindlemorn was usually done with candles, but here their own variation on the tradition went back as far as the Valstars did. Hetta was abruptly aware of that long weight of history, of that unbroken chain all the way back to the first lord of Stariel. He'd dealt with the fae too, as had all the lords after him up until three centuries ago. What did it mean that the fae were coming back again now, for the first time in generations? And why had the High King made them leave in the first place? *And why am I the lucky lord who gets to deal with them again?* Had Stariel really known what it was doing when it chose her?

She pushed the unhelpful musings aside as they reached the Stones. A fire had been laid on the central plinth, as yet unlit. As dawn approached, the general murmuring of the crowd—composed of Valstars, staff, and villagers—began to hush. Those bearing torches, lamps, and light-spells made their way to the front, and as the sun came over the horizon, they began to douse them, one by one.

Hetta reached out with her land-sense. All across the estate, those who weren't gathered here were following suit, dousing fires across the land. In the heart of winter, this was an act of faith that humbled her. For a moment, she worried that something would go wrong, that she wouldn't be *able* to complete the tradition, that the power of the Valstars would end with her. Which was ridiculous; she was a fully-fledged mage in her own right and thus probably the *most* prepared of all the lords in living memory. The others would've had to rely purely on Stariel's magic.

She felt the last light extinguish, somewhere deep in the estate. The cold dawn spread over the land, so diffuse through the snow-laden sky that it was impossible to accurately locate the sun. She took a deep breath and drew upon her magic, wondering just how she was supposed to explain to Stariel what needed doing.

But Stariel needed no explanation. It knew exactly what was required of it, and it grasped hold of her like a parent drawing a child to the correct path. She could only follow, the magic spooling out, through her, and into the land. She breathed in her people, their lives so small and fragile, all of them reaching out for her in return. It was eerily similar to the small flares of acknowledgement from Stariel's fae denizens the previous night. It should have shaken her, to realise how many lives she was responsible for, but instead something inside her steadied.

All over Stariel, the fires rekindled, symbolising the return of the sun, that they had passed the darkest hour and yet lived.

<You are mine, and I will do my best for you,> she sent out into that great web, knowing that no one would probably hear it, but needing to say it in any case. It wasn't an especially elegant promise, but she'd never meant anything quite so seriously before in her life. She met Wyn's eyes across the circle and saw his eyes widen. He, at least, had heard her sentiment if not her words. It came with that same deep feeling of possessiveness the starcorn had woken, a powerful urge to protect that which was hers. *<You are mine.>*

24

LORD FEATHERSTONE

THE DAY AFTER Wintersol, Wyn sat in his office, where he and the head ranger were keeping track of all the roads that needed clearing. Hetta could prod Stariel into doing it, but she needed to know where to prioritise her efforts; they'd learned that the land didn't much like interfering with natural processes. Hetta had so far coaxed Stariel into shifting the snow off the main roads, but the smaller tracks to the outlying cottages still needed attention. Villagers had been traipsing back and forth all morning, and Wyn now had a fairly accurate idea of what was needed where. He'd already sent down extra heatstones to the most vulnerable cottages, though thank the stormwinds his insulation spells were still mostly intact. Fae magic was less efficient than human technomancy for such things, but also far less expensive. He'd nearly repaired all the shredded spells in the house, and though he'd felt Stariel lurking over him, the faeland had so far left them alone.

The snow had given him a brief stay of execution, but he'd agreed to let Hetta try to summon Gwendelfear tomorrow, to try to find out DuskRose's motivations in all of this. It would give them a stronger bargaining position when it came to ThousandSpire. Guilt and fear needled around his rib cage, but Hetta had *promised* him, he reassured himself, even if it already felt too late to pull out of the dive.

He paused, pen poised over the map of Stariel. That just left the Valstars and the secret of his identity. But Hetta was right; that secret was already creaking at the edges, especially given what Marius had reported of the reaction at the bank. Further rumours were no doubt already vining their way across the countryside in the wake of that.

Anger, blooming between heartbeats, and not his own. *Stariel's* anger, surging over him. The pen went clattering across the desk, and he clutched wildly at the wooden surface, seeking an anchor as the world shook with snow, pine—and coffee. For once, the hostility wasn't directed at him; this was a directionless echo of its lord's emotion, the faeland's focus far from here. The tremor passed as quickly as it had come, and Wyn could abruptly breathe again as the leylines steadied. Whatever had occurred, Hetta had quickly damped Stariel's reaction after that initial jolt of alarm. Which meant she wasn't in immediate danger, at least.

He looked up to see the head ranger frowning at him. Wyn had missed what he'd just said.

"You all right, Mr Tempest?" The disturbance had occurred only on the magical plane.

"I am well," Wyn assured him, retrieving the pen. Ink had splattered across the map's surface, though fortunately not on any crucial details. He pulled a handkerchief from his pocket and began to dab the worst of it away.

The ranger raised an eyebrow at the inky mess. "Not like you to be clumsy. Your arm still paining you?"

Wyn shrugged. "A momentary lapse." What had prompted Stariel's roll of sudden rage? Hetta had gone with Aunt Sybil to meet Lord Featherstone at the station.

He froze. Lord *Feather*stone. Stormcrows, he was so *stupid* some-times, and Rakken's sense of humour so warped. How had he failed to make the connection? *I shall look forward to seeing you again*, he'd said outright!

"All right, then," the ranger said. He sounded as unconvinced as Clarissa had earlier in the week, though the similarity wasn't sur-prising. The couple had been married longer than Wyn had been at Stariel.

Wyn tried to shake off the dread seeping into his bones, or at least to hide it. If he was to face his brother, he needed to be in control of himself.

"Where were we?" He put the handkerchief to the side and tried to concentrate on finishing the map. But his senses stretched south-east towards Stariel Station and Hetta, and he struggled to make meaning of the inked lines in front of him. Minutes—or possibly years—later, his ears pricked at the faint but unmistakable sound of the kineticar on the gravel of the driveway. He excused himself, and the ranger gave him a look that said his distraction hadn't gone unobserved.

Heart hammering, he made his way through the house, strug-gling not to break into a run. Would Rakken truly dare such an entrance? Uncle Percival startled as Wyn passed him in the corridor, and he knew he'd moved a little too swiftly to be quite natural. He tried to slow down, to move at a more human pace, but he could not find the correct rhythm, not with apprehension swelling in him like the sea in storm. He careened out the front door, down the steps, and skidded to a halt just as the kineticar swept around the last bend before the house.

Heads turned towards him, wordlessly querying his frantic entrance. A small knot of Valstars were waiting, including Jack, Marius, and Caroline, huddling against the chill wind. The wind had flung Caroline's bright red hair into disarray. Jack had his arms folded and was clearly impatient to be off doing something more useful than greeting titled guests. Aunt Sybil would of course have requested her son make an appearance in the welcome party.

Wyn jerked his head, unable to explain, torn between reassuring them and telling them to flee, *now*, before Rakken arrived. *But Hetta rules here; she can protect them, if need be.* He tried to will calm into himself. Calm; he had to be calm.

Marius frowned at Wyn. "What—" But the car pulled to a stop with a crunch of gravel, distracting him.

Hetta got out barely a second after the engine turned off, haste making her clumsy. She met Wyn's eyes with a grimace, and the word *Sorry* blazed across the space between them, nearly audible in its force. Aunt Sybil emerged next, blissfully oblivious to any undercurrents. She seemed happy, or as happy as Aunt Sybil ever really got. And then…

He was a decade and a thousand miles away, except that the memory of Rakken *then* jarred with the sight of Rakken *now*, in mortal form, on mortal soil, the two worlds surreally colliding. Rakken's ears were human-round instead of coming to points, the angularity of his usual fae features subtly softened. And strangest of all—no wings. It was as if someone had made a good but imperfect facsimile of his real brother, and for a wild moment Wyn thought it possible he was merely having a particularly vivid dream.

His brother wasn't quite as graceful as he should have been getting out of the car—as Wyn knew well, it took time to accustom oneself to the lack of wing-weight at one's shoulders. Standing, Rakken scanned the crowd with a careless smile. For the merest instant, his gaze met Wyn's, and his smile sharpened before he passed on, pretending he hadn't yet seen him. His face might not be the one Wyn was used to, but that fleeting expression—that mixture of arrogance and sardonic enjoyment—was so familiar it carved furrows in his chest.

"Lord Featherstone, this is my son, Jonathan," Aunt Sybil said, waving at Jack. But Rakken ignored her, meeting Wyn's eyes again, this time with a deliberate and exaggerated double-take.

"Brother?" he said with deliberate surprise.

A frisson of speculation shot through the crowd, and everyone turned towards Wyn. He froze, and his mind went utterly, unhelpfully blank.

"Whatever are you doing here?" Rakken pushed his way through the crowd as Wyn stood paralysed, scrambling to find his place in this new script. Rakken appeared every inch the delighted relative, unexpectedly reunited with someone he'd thought long-lost. Concern warred with relief in his feigned expression, playing to his audience, but Wyn knew the glimmer in Rakken's eyes for the tell it was. Rakken was enjoying the fruits of his manipulations. At least Wyn hadn't lost that, the ability to read his brother despite his many masks.

Rakken didn't actually think Wyn would let him embrace him, did he? But apparently, he did, for he approached Wyn with that intent clear in his movements. Sheer distaste at the prospect broke Wyn's immobility, and he moved, evading the gesture. Rakken gave him a stage-perfect hurt expression.

"What, no hug for your big brother, Hollow?" he said in a tone too low to be overheard by non-fae. "Haven't you missed me?"

Hollow. The nickname rang strangely in his ears. With a distant jolt, he noticed he and Rakken were now precisely the same height. Would Rakken notice? Why did it matter if he noticed? Of course Rakken would notice; he wasn't an idiot. But Wyn couldn't help wondering if their wingspans would match now too.

"You...know our steward, Lord Featherstone?" Aunt Sybil said after a beat.

The crowd's silence deepened, forming an expectant vacuum.

"Your steward?" Rakken blinked between Aunt Sybil and Wyn

with wide, puzzled eyes. "But how can that be? This is my youngest brother, lost to us for years."

"I thought that Lady Featherstone's youngest lived on the Continent..." Aunt Sybil said uncertainly.

Rakken shook his head and sighed, as if preparing to reluctantly unbury old hurts. The stormwinds take Rakken and his play-acting!

"I'm afraid the case is more complicated. Wyn and our father had something of a falling-out that caused him to depart abruptly without notice. We spent years looking, but we had all but given up hope of ever finding him again..."

Everyone was looking at Wyn expectantly, and all Wyn could think was how strange it was to hear his assumed name from his brother's lips. None of Wyn's family had ever called him that before, which was precisely why he'd chosen it.

He swung to Hetta, seeking he wasn't sure what. One of her hands still gripped the driver's door, and her eyes blazed with anger on his behalf, but she, too, was waiting for his direction. His glacial thoughts stuttered back into motion. Stormcrows, he didn't want to dance to Rakken's tune—but what was the alternative? Even knowing that Rakken intended to come across as the gracious one here, the dutiful older brother set against the rebellious black sheep, it was difficult not to reinforce that narrative. He *felt* rebellious, off-balance, as if Rakken's presence had made him a child once more.

He straightened and met his brother's eyes. He wasn't a child, and Rakken was the one on unfamiliar territory here, not Wyn, even if he'd caught Wyn unprepared. *Ride the winds that are, not those you wish for.*

"I did not expect to see you here...brother," Wyn said stiffly.

There was a collective intake of breath. The Valstars hadn't believed it, quite, without Wyn's confirmation.

Aunt Sybil looked at him as if he'd sprouted wings and horns there on the front steps of the house. "You are *Lord Featherstone's* brother?"

"I am *his* brother," Wyn said, indicating Rakken with a nod. "Forgive me for deceiving you."

Hetta slammed the car door and took charge. "Well, this seems something that the two of you will need to discuss. You must both come up to my study. I'll see the rest of you at dinner." And she marched purposefully into the house before any of her relatives could object. Rakken raised an eyebrow at Wyn but obediently followed her.

Wyn looked helplessly around at the Valstars' mixed expressions, incredulity being foremost among them. "I...will explain later," was all he could think to say before he turned and scrambled back into the house after his brother.

Hetta was stalking up the entry stairs as if she held each one personally responsible for the situation. Rakken walked a step behind her, and Wyn had to strangle down panic to see him so close to Hetta's exposed back. It was irrational—Rakken would not break guestright after going to such lengths to get himself into Stariel under a mortal alias—but Wyn still had to swallow the urge to throw himself bodily between them. Focus! He could not be this panicked, flighty creature.

"A fine old house," Rakken remarked as they passed the painting of Hetta's grandfather, Lord Marius II. The old lord stared imperiously down at them. Both Hetta and Marius-the-younger had inherited his long nose and piercing grey eyes.

"If you say absolutely anything else before we get to my study," Hetta said without turning around, her voice low and furious, "I'll singe your dashed eyebrows off!"

Wyn's heart jerked. Would Rakken take offense? But Rakken's mouth curved in amusement, and Wyn nearly sagged with relief. Rakken's anger was harder to provoke than Aroset's, but it was as cold and implacable as mountains. Ironically, at court, people often assumed Rakken was hot-headed simply because of the contrast between his manner and that of his more taciturn twin sister, Catsmere. They were wrong; it was yet another mask.

No one spoke until they reached Hetta's study. Hetta jabbed a finger at the seat beneath the window. "You," she said, glaring at Rakken. "Sit. Explain your little display out there. I thought the entire point of this guestright business is that you do no harm to me and mine." She threw Wyn an apologetic glance. "Sorry, Wyn. I was sorely tempted to reveal him for what he was down at Stariel Station, but he said he could see you free of your oath and…"

She hadn't wanted to out him, hadn't wanted to rob that choice from him.

Rakken folded himself onto the seat, languid as a cat. "You should be thanking me, Lord Valstar. You've been searching for a way to legitimise your *affaire* with your servant lover to your family without revealing his true nature, and I've just handed you a neat solution, don't you think?" A quick flash of teeth. "I scarcely think I harmed you and yours; rather the opposite. And, technically, he's not *yours*. Not yet." He shrugged. "Besides, you yourself noted the apparent similarity in our appearances. How else did you propose to explain that?"

Hetta thought he and his brother similar? Did she think Rakken was attractive? Wyn couldn't help recalling how in ThousandSpire Rakken's lazy sensuality had drawn lovers as effortlessly as a flame draws moths. Why on earth was he worrying about such a petty thing? *Focus*, he told himself sternly.

Hetta collapsed into the chair behind her desk and crossed her arms. "It wouldn't be necessary to explain anything at all if you hadn't seen fit to smuggle yourself into my house under false credentials. And don't say I invited you, because I'm not in the mood for fae technicalities."

"These negotiations should prove interesting, in that case." Rakken stretched an arm along the back of the settee, utterly relaxed. "But you should be thankful I represent ThousandSpire's interests in this. Hallowyn's death profits me nothing, and I cannot say the same for the alternative ambassador you might have had in my stead."

"Instead of Aroset, you mean?" Hetta said flatly. Rakken inclined his head.

Negotiations. Wyn went to stand beside Hetta after an internal struggle. It was irrational, but it was still reassuring to be between her and his brother.

"What do you want, Rakken Tempestren?" he said, putting a touch of emphasis on his brother's name. It wasn't a threat, not really. More a reminder to them both that Wyn wasn't some lesser fae to be commanded. He might not be all that he should be, but he wasn't a youth anymore either.

Rakken smiled, showing teeth rather than mirth. "So you do have a backbone after all, Hallowyn Tempestren." Power shivered lightly over Wyn's skin as Rakken named him.

He smiled, with a similar lack of mirth. "Tacky, Rake, to copy my posturing."

Rakken's eyes gleamed. "Poor-spirited, *Hollow*, to plead fatigue when you started the game."

"I admit I've not much taste for such things."

"So impatient, little brother. Running to mortal time, are we?"

"If it has escaped your attention, let me remind you that Stariel is a mortal faeland. We *all* run to mortal time here."

Hetta glanced between the two of them, a V forming between her brows. "Are the two of you quite finished?"

"I do not know," Wyn said. "*Are* we done, brother? Or shall we find further irrelevant tangents to bat back and forth between us?" He put a hand on Hetta's shoulder and she covered it with her own.

Hetta smiled up at him. "Remind me never to fault you for your lack of plain-speaking again; I can see you've vastly improved on your upbringing." There was a question in her eyes: Was he all right? He squeezed her hand in silent reassurance. Rakken's abrupt arrival might have knocked all his previous plans out of alignment, but of one thing he remained sure: he would not let Rakken harm Hetta or Stariel. That thought steadied him.

"You are fortunate that I'm in a tolerant mood, Lord Valstar," Rakken said. "Or I might choose to be insulted. You'll note that I *did* apologise for my stratagems in advance. That, to my mind, is good manners." He observed the interplay between Wyn and Hetta with interest, trying to judge how entangled Wyn's emotions were. Wyn knew Rakken; his brother's hypothesis would be that Wyn had seduced Stariel's lord to further his own position. Should he reinforce that idea? It would be safer for Rakken to think he had no emotional stakes in this, even if Wyn rebelled at the prospect.

The door opened with a thud, and Jack, Marius, and Caroline tumbled into the room, all clearly half-expecting to encounter a battle-scene. They drew up short at the sight of Rakken lounging on the settee beneath the window.

Jack, never one to let a good bluster go to waste, rapidly regrouped. "What's going on?" he demanded of the mid-point between Hetta and Rakken.

"This is Wyn's older brother, Rakken."

"*Prince* Rakken Tempestren," his brother corrected. "Of the Court of Ten Thousand Spires." Wyn watched him quickly tot up the three new Valstars. Jack, he noted down as the leader of the trio. Caroline, he wasn't sure what to make of. Marius, he dismissed, a judgement that both irritated and relieved Wyn. It was better not to draw Rakken's attention, but it irked him to see Marius undervalued yet again.

There was a beat of silence, and then Marius said in a strange tone, "Prince?"

Oh. Of course. Wyn hadn't spelled out the full details of his origins to the others. It had seemed an unnecessary complication. "Ah…yes. Did I forget to mention that?"

Marius gave him an incredulous look. "How exactly do you forget that?"

Caroline's expression had much in common with Marius's, and from the slightly bemused curve of her lips, Wyn felt moderately certain she was replaying their earlier conversation about his employment prospects.

"It did not seem important," Wyn apologised. The incredulity didn't lessen.

Rakken laughed. "So they do not know exactly who's been sweeping their floors and taking away their plates for all these years? It seems some introductions are in order." He flourished a long-fingered hand at Wyn. "This is His Royal Highness Prince Hallowyn Tempestren, stormdancer and youngest child of King Aeros of Ten Thousand Spires."

"In any case," said Hetta, "that is quite beside the point." Her fingers tightened on Wyn's and she took a deep breath. "Tell me what you want for Wyn's release." When Jack tried to interject, she held up a hand to stop him. "Not now, Jack. Questions later. I want to know this now."

Jack shuffled angrily to slouch against the wall, glaring at Rakken and Hetta in equal measure. Rakken shrugged, unruffled, and the late morning sun picked out the gold threads in his dark curls. Caroline and Marius were both transfixed by the sight, and Wyn fought the urge to choke. Apparently at least some Valstars *did* find his brother attractive. Wyn couldn't help meeting Rakken's eyes to see if he'd noticed. He had, of course, by the sardonic gleam there. Stormwinds.

Rakken considered Hetta, tilting his head so that the contrasting sun-and-shadows sharpened the planes of his face, bringing them closer to his usual fae appearance. It filled Wyn with deep unease. Rakken might look mortal, but if Father had truly appointed him ambassador, he brought the weight of a fae court with him here, to this household of mortals completely unprepared for such things.

A hard knot formed in Wyn's chest.

Rakken spoke evenly, enunciating every syllable with slow, cut-glass deliberation. "This is my father's offer. In exchange for my brother's oath debt, you swear fealty to him and Stariel becomes a vassal state of ThousandSpire. Beyond the oath of fealty, he is willing to let you retain management over your own lands and people."

Wyn moved so fast he even surprised Rakken. "Be thankful I am near certain you have no intention on following through on that offer. The Valstars gained their right to this land direct from the High King; do not pretend you think it is wise to try to subvert that." Standing over his brother, he let his magic rise, petrichor and cardamom blossoming in the air. He might not be all that he was meant to be, but he was still stronger than he'd ever been. Strong enough to give Rakken pause, he hoped.

"I'm not negotiating with *you*, Hallowyn, but with Stariel's lord. She's the one who asked the price of your oath-debt," Rakken said coolly past Wyn, ignoring the wash of magic. "And if you care so greatly about the High King's decrees, you shouldn't have left the Spires."

Wyn didn't move, though the remark stung. If he'd stayed in the Spires, he'd be dead. He had let himself be cheered too much by Rakken's current preference for him living over dead, let sentiment make him forget the lessons of the past.

"Well, regardless of which of us you're negotiating with, the answer is the same: No," Hetta said firmly, and relief at the quick refusal made the knot in Wyn's chest ease a little. "What point would there be in freeing Wyn from ThousandSpire's yoke only to put Stariel under the same one? No, thank you. Wyn is right: you can't possibly have thought I'd accept that. Ask for something sensible." She frowned at Wyn, the question in her eyes mirroring his internal debate between pride and reason—*Are you going to let me do this?*

Wyn bit back the instinctive negative and instead gave a tight
nod. It was rational to at least try to bargain, now that they were
here, he told himself sternly. But, oh, he hated it every bit as much
as he'd expected, and his magic thrummed under his skin.

And then Marius said quietly, "Wyn, he doesn't know."

There was silence, or as much silence as four humans and two
fae in a small room could contain. The windowpanes rattled with a
particularly strong gust of wind.

"I assume you are referring to me, Marius Rufus Valstar?" Rakken
said with extreme dryness. Wyn shot him a narrow look for the use
of the full name. None of the mortals would know he was being
rude, but that was no excuse.

But Marius wasn't paying any attention at all to Rakken. His
focus was entirely on Wyn, expression intent, trying to communicate…something, biting his lip to keep from blurting it out. Marius
wasn't sure whether his intuition would help or harm, and he didn't
want Rakken to know it before Wyn did.

What did Rakken not know?

Oh. The taste of cardamom faded from the back of Wyn's tongue
as he let his magic fizzle out. *Oh.*

"You don't know," he said to his brother with a kind of wonder.
Rakken's eyes narrowed.

"It would be helpful to establish which *specific* thing your brother
doesn't know," Hetta said, her voice trembling with a familiar note
of fond amusement.

"He doesn't know the reason Wyn left. He doesn't know his father
was planning to kill him," Marius said, unable to keep the words
in any longer.

Rakken's eyes widened fractionally, and his lips moved as if he
wanted to say something, but he held himself back at the last second.

Wyn gave the confirmation Rakken's pride would not let him
ask for. "It's true," he told him. "What Marius said is true. Father
was planning to kill me after I married Princess Sunnika and frame

DuskRose for it." He had to give his brother credit; he adjusted to unexpected information quickly. Probably no one else in the room realised how disturbed he was. Wyn could not help it; he grinned at his brother like a loon. "You don't want me dead."

Rakken rolled his eyes. "I've already said your death profits me nothing. To repeat the sentiment seems excessive."

"That has to be the lowest bar for familial affection I've yet encountered," Caroline said. "Ah...not to take away from what is clearly a sentimental moment for the two of you."

Rakken shrugged and turned back to Hetta. "In any case, it does not change my offer."

"Hmm," Hetta said, weighing him up. "Well, if that's the case, you can dashed well get out of my house. I'm going to leave the two of you here alone for half an hour." She fixed Wyn with a meaningful look. "And when I come back, I shall expect you to have either come up with a better proposal, or you can leave." She rose.

Rakken rose with her. Hetta's impatience irritated him, but he didn't let it show in the unruffled tone of his voice. He brushed a stray lock back from his forehead, as leisurely as if he had all the time in the world. "I shall...consider whether there might be an alternative offer I could make. But I'm not sure what purpose leaving me alone with my brother serves, Lord Valstar. I assure you, it's unnecessary."

"I'm not doing it for you, Your Highness," Hetta told him.

"Hetta—" Wyn began, but she cut him off. They exchanged a heated look, in which Hetta said in no uncertain terms that she trusted him to keep his brother occupied for half an hour while she spoke to the others away from Rakken's interested gaze. In answer, Wyn tried to convey that Rakken not wanting him dead didn't mean he and Rakken would be playing happy families any time soon. He wasn't sure whether she got the message.

"All right, everyone. Come away and I'll explain some of this to you." And for the second time in not so many minutes, Hetta swept out of a doorway before anyone could object. Jack, Marius, and Caroline trailed her out. Caroline shut the door with a thoughtful glance at Wyn.

Rakken examined the closed door for a moment before collapsing back onto his seat with a sigh. "Mortals are so impulsive, aren't they?"

"If you didn't want Hetta angry with you, you shouldn't have deliberately provoked her," Wyn said calmly. "You can scarcely complain about a result you set out to achieve. Are you satisfied with your little test, or do you mean to continue to be a curiously disagreeable ambassador?"

Rakken smiled, and this one was sincere, softening the mask. "So playing with mortals hasn't made you entirely foolish."

"They're not as easy to manipulate as you think," Wyn warned.

"Perhaps you're not as clever as you would like to think, then, if you find it so difficult." Rakken raised an eyebrow at Wyn, still standing. "Are you intending to loom over me for the next half hour?" He somehow managed to imply that Wyn was the one being childish, even though Rakken was the cause of this entire charade.

"How long has this 'Lord Featherstone' business been going on for?" It was the least of what Wyn wanted to know, but perhaps beginning somewhere small might be more effective.

"Really, brother, do you expect me to divulge all my secrets merely for the asking?" A spark of humour lit Rakken's eyes.

It was going to be a very long half hour. "At least reassure me that the real Lord Featherstone is alive and well."

"So soft-hearted, still? But yes, since you ask. He is." By Rakken's standards, this was an expansive mood, so Wyn pushed his luck.

"What do you want, Rake?" He went and perched uneasily on the desk, not nearly as far away from his brother as he'd like now they were alone. "Really?"

Rakken smiled, the proverbial cat with cream. "Directness. What a novel approach."

"Well, what else do we have to talk about?" Wyn pointed out. "Other than your less-than-hilarious attempt to not kill me."

"It was *entirely* hilarious, I assure you. And you should definitely thank me for that. Aroset is so unoriginal sometimes. She would have sent draken again without my prompting, and I know how you detest collateral damage."

Wyn thought of Mr Thompson, curled up in agony against the wall. "The bank manager was wounded also." What Marius had reported had only partially reassured him; what if Mr Thompson didn't fully recover from the poison?

"For which you had an antidote on hand, thanks to me." His eyes gleamed, daring Wyn to point out that he'd provided only sufficient antidote for *one* person, if Wyn had not already had his own.

Wyn refused to react to his brother's needling. "Mortals do not heal as quickly or as well as fae. The bank manager is still recovering, and the fact that more mortals weren't injured was due in large part to luck."

Rakken shrugged. "Don't tell me you would rather Aroset had set the town alight with drakkenfire."

Wyn pressed his lips together but didn't argue. Rakken was right, in a way; one could only channel Aroset's destructive tendencies, not remove them. But he'd never agree that the harm of innocents was acceptable.

Rakken read him easily enough and shook his head. "Ah, sentimental little Hollow. Is that why your lord has left us here together, do you think?"

"I think she thought I might be better able to cut through your attempts at obfuscation without an audience to impress. She *will* kick you out, you know, if you stick to Father's original offer and refuse to budge." Wyn held that reassurance close.

Rakken waved a hand. "Oh, don't be disingenuous, Hallowyn. Of course I knew she wouldn't accept that."

"Then you may as well tell me what long game you're playing."

"I may," Rakken allowed, the amusement draining from him. "But I won't. Not yet." He searched Wyn for something, but Wyn didn't know if he found it. "Give me a little time. I need to...consider alternatives. You may of course assure Lord Valstar I will mind my manners in the meantime."

What game *was* Rakken playing? He might be here nominally on behalf of their father and ThousandSpire, but Rakken would always act firstly to promote his own self-interest.

Wyn sighed. He still had, by his estimation, at least twenty-eight more minutes to try to extract something useful from Rakken, but all their interactions so far had only emphasised how badly out of practice he was at that.

He looked past Rakken, out to the view of Starwater. The wind had whipped small white caps in the lake's surface. Beyond that the forest was dusted with snow, the white growing thicker as the terrain rose to the west. He thought of the roads still to be cleared, of the news they'd received of the infant born down in Stariel Village during the night, of the plumber due to come out to the house this week. He thought of the way Hetta's skin had looked under pale moonlight, the delicate curves and lines of her, of the way her pulse had fluttered in the hollow of her throat. *My love*, he'd said to her, a truth as inevitable and inarguable as gravity.

"I do not want to leave," he said eventually. "But I will, if the price is too high to stay." He took a deep breath, let it out, met Rakken's eyes. "And if I have to, I will kill you to prevent you harming Henrietta Valstar." The vow shivered in the space between them, potent with the lightning-and-rain scent of his magic.

Rakken's eyes widened, but that was the only outward sign of shock he showed. Wyn could feel his own pulse racing, though he didn't break eye contact with his brother, letting the challenge sit there without explanation or apology. He had meant the words; he could not have said them otherwise. And yet...what kind of creature did that make him?

After a moment Rakken looked away. "*Love* then, is it, Hallowyn?" He said the word distastefully, as if handling something noxious. "How terribly cliché of you." A warning hint of citrus in the air. "You may be more useful to me alive than dead, but my tolerance *does* have limits, Hallowyn." It wasn't an idle threat; Rakken was considerably older than Wyn, and age brought power, in Faerie.

Strangely, the trading of threats made Wyn relax. Perhaps it was merely a relief to speak plainly, or as plainly as things had ever been spoken between him and Rakken. He smiled. "It's good to see you, brother." Rakken was right; he *was* sentimental.

Rakken grumbled. "It's unreasonable to expect me to say the same less than ten seconds after you have *threatened* me."

"Oh, don't pretend to be such a fragile flower; I did not say I *wished* to kill you. And we wouldn't be having this conversation if I thought you actually intended harm to Lord Valstar. I'm merely laying out the limits of what I will tolerate. You should thank me for making your job as ambassador so much easier."

"I'm not sure I like what mortality has done to you," Rakken complained. "You used to have more respect for your elders."

Wyn thought of the other siblings he'd left behind and, irrelevantly, of the Valstars gathered around the Standing Stones, and, despite everything, a thread of...*something* plucked at him. It wasn't nostalgia; he didn't have the necessary fond memories to draw upon for that. He had no illusions that his family had developed any degree of warm connection in his absence, and it would be foolish to yearn for it. But whatever the feeling was, it prompted him to ask, "Speaking of, what have I missed in the last decade in ThousandSpire?" He tried to tell himself it was only a desire for information that might aid Stariel. "Has Aroset maimed anyone else? Has our mother returned? Is Cat still..."

Rakken's eyes narrowed. "Still what?"

"Still Cat, I suppose." Catsmere was the sibling Wyn had been closest to. This was possibly the one point he and Rakken had in common, since Rakken's twin sister was the only person Rakken truly cared about. Cat had always had a gruff fondness for Wyn, though she also thought him too sentimental. Wyn wondered if Catsmere's affection would influence her twin at all.

Rakken had clearly shared the same thought. "Trying to manipulate me, brother? Cat has little sympathy for oathbreakers." He made a thoughtful noise. "Though she may have more now, when she learns your flight was not as unreasonable as we thought."

It had never occurred to Wyn that his siblings might not know why he'd fled. They'd always appeared so much more knowledgeable about everything than he was—particularly Rakken, with his vast network of lowfae informants. Which reminded him: "The catshee was yours, I assume?"

Rakken frowned. "What catshee?"

Interesting. Maybe it *had* merely been coincidence that Wyn had needed to take down the housefae-repelling spell only two days before he'd been attacked. "And Mrs Thompson? Was she yours too?"

A small crease formed between Rakken's brows. "I take no responsibility for the spontaneous and foolish acts of mortals," he said in disgust.

"I did try to tell you that you can't always control what they do," Wyn pointed out. If Rakken hadn't been responsible, who had? It seemed too subtle for Aroset, involving the bank manager's wife.

"You take far too much delight in my not being in control of a situation that ended with you shot with iron," Rakken countered. He was right, though Wyn wouldn't admit it aloud. Rakken watched him for a moment. "Aroset has not maimed any more of us," he said abruptly, coming back to Wyn's original question. "Irokoi is still as he was."

Irokoi had had the misfortune to be the oldest of them. Fae usually gained in power as they aged, and Aroset had taken it upon herself to rid herself of a potential rival, with the result that Irokoi was…damaged.

"Our mother remains conspicuous in her absence," Rakken continued. "And Father…" Darkness flickered in his eyes, and he didn't finish his sentence. A chill fell over the room, one that had nothing to do with temperature.

"So things are much as they were, then," Wyn said flatly. "That is Faerie, Rake: where change comes slowly if it comes at all."

Rakken smiled, the nonchalant mask back in place as if it had never slipped. "Are you trying to persuade me of the benefits of mortality, brother? Where the humans flicker in and out of existence like fireflies?"

"At least fireflies *live*. The fae just…exist."

Rakken's eyes turned knowing. "Do you think if you play at being human for long enough, it will become truth?" His smile sharpened. "Oh, Hallowyn, you fool."

Wyn didn't respond, and Rakken shook his head, dismissing him. He tilted his rings this way and that so that the light made the gemstones glow with inner fire. Wyn thought of the gem-studded walls of the capital, Aerest. ThousandSpire was rich in mineral wealth.

"Here is a change of note for you, then," Rakken said after the silence had lengthened, the minutes ticking away. "Torquil defected." He sat back casually, as if he had not just lobbed an incendiary into the quiet study. Torquil was the sibling nearest in age to Wyn, though they weren't close in any other sense.

Wyn couldn't hide his shock. "Defected to where?" Torquil was rigidly dutiful—probably the most so of any of them. It beggared belief that he would do something so dishonourable as defect from ThousandSpire. Or that their father had allowed it.

For a moment he thought Rakken would not answer; he looked pleased with Wyn's reaction, and it would be like him to revel in Wyn's ignorance for as long as possible. But eventually he said, "EdgeSmoke. He thought he would be more at home in one of the light courts. Perhaps you are not the most naïve of us after all."

Wyn ignored the jab. "And Father?" He didn't need to specify what he meant; that Father would tolerate a defection was more incredible than Torquil choosing to do so.

Rakken steepled his fingers, again weighing Wyn for some unspecified quality. "Hmmm."

"Was that supposed to be an answer?"

A faint smile. "You've been among mortals too long, Hallowyn, if you expect all answers to be spelled out plainly."

Wyn was about to respond when he sensed it through the leylines: ripe cherries and beeswax. Rakken went as still as a hunting hound catching a scent.

"DuskRose," he growled, at the same time as Wyn said,

"Princess Sunnika."

PRINCESS SUNNIKA

"WHAT DO I have to say to make the two of you understand that the fae aren't something to be treated lightly?" Hetta scowled at her younger brother and sister in exasperated wrath.

She'd just finished explaining the situation to Jack, Caro, and Marius when Stariel had alerted her to the new presence within her borders. She would've immediately repelled it, but Alexandra and Gregory had come rushing into the room with cries of: "We can explain!" so she'd held off.

"Don't blame me!" Gregory said indignantly. "This wasn't my idea! And I already told Alex it was a stupid one!"

"This isn't my idea either!" Alexandra said hotly. "I'm just passing on a message!"

"Yes, but you shouldn't be passing on messages on behalf of the fae at all!"

Hetta was inclined to agree with him, but she stepped in before the two of them could devolve into further argument.

"Never mind!" she said. "Just what is this message and what has it got to do with Princess Sunnika popping up in the Home Wood?"

"It's from Gwen," Alexandra said. "She just sent me a message saying it was urgent and that her princess was about to visit us and that I should warn you in case you thought she was attacking us or something."

"And just how is Gwendelfear sending you messages?" Marius said, standing shoulder to shoulder with Hetta, equally displeased with their younger siblings.

"Um," said Alexandra. She took refuge in petting Plumpuff, who'd been asleep on the sofa arm and gave a conversational meow at the touch. Some of Hetta's irritation transferred to the cat. Shouldn't she be down in the kitchen with her kittens, anyway?

"Gwendelfear gave her a locket that sends messages!" Gregory said, earning him a glare from his younger sister.

Hetta held out her hand imperiously, and Alexandra reluctantly undid the necklace she was wearing.

"It warms up if she has something to say," she said, not meeting Hetta's eyes. "But she can't say much because not much writing can fit on the inside of the locket. You see?" She showed Hetta the tiny script on the inside of the metal shape. It was as Alexandra had said: *Princess arriving. Not an attack. Warn Lord V. Urgent! Sorry.*

Hetta found the apology the most interesting part of the message. Gwendelfear had struck her as a singularly unapologetic personage, but her fondness for Alexandra was apparently sincere. Or possibly merely a useful conceit. Alexandra took the locket back, shoulders hunching as if she thought Hetta would refuse. Hetta considered it but decided it was an argument best had another day. She wasn't her sister's keeper, and Gwendelfear *had* saved Alexandra's life.

"And how did you get embroiled in this, Gregory?" Hetta asked.

"Well, I was with Alex down in the stables, and she yelped and grabbed at her necklace, so of course I made her tell me what was going on!"

"Well, I suppose we ought to go down to the Home Wood, then."

Hetta didn't see anything else for it but to ask the source of the disturbance herself.

"We're not inviting another fairy into Stariel, surely?" Jack objected. He'd been pacing off his agitation at the earlier revelations on the other side of the room, but at this he came over to glower at Alexandra too.

Alexandra and Gregory said, nearly in unison, "*Another* fairy?" And Hetta realised they'd been absent for the entirety of Prince Rakken's dramatic entrance and apparently no one had told them anything about him yet.

Gregory's expression darkened. "Do you mean Wyn?" he said, half-defiant, half-ashamed.

"*You knew Wyn was a fairy too?*" Alexandra exclaimed.

Caro looked up from where she'd been sitting quietly at the other end of the sofa, a rueful smile twitching at her lips. "So who exactly *doesn't* know yet, then?"

Hetta rubbed at her temples. "Most of the family, present company excepted." Keeping track of who knew what was becoming exhausting. She turned back to her siblings. "In short, no, I wasn't referring to Wyn. I was talking about his brother, who's assumed the identity of Lord Featherstone for reasons best known to himself."

This necessitated rather more explaining than Hetta had patience for, but fortunately Marius took over the bulk of it and she was able to get them all moving at the same time.

"Should I get my gun?" Jack quietly asked Hetta as they swarmed out of the entrance hall.

Hetta stumbled and righted herself. "What? No!"

"I don't doubt your magic," Jack said, "but what about the rest of us?"

"I'm not an expert on the fae, but I'm fairly certain that threatening their princess with an iron weapon would be extremely likely to offend them."

Jack looked unconvinced. "Am I supposed to care about that?"

"You're supposed to care about Wyn, and this is one of the courts that has it in for him. Antagonising them is unlikely to make matters better."

Jack grunted but didn't argue further as they pulled on coats and boots from the nook next to the entrance.

Hetta thought of Alexandra seeing the housefae and said thoughtfully, "Also, you might all think of yourselves as magic-less, but you actually aren't, you know."

Jack made a wordless sound of disagreement, grimacing.

"Most people aren't magically connected to their homeland," Hetta pointed out.

"That hardly counts," Jack said, pulling on an ugly woollen hat that Grandmamma had knitted.

"And it's not like any of you have ever been properly tested for magegift," Hetta continued as if he hadn't spoken. "My own talents were strong enough that they were rather hard to ignore, but not everyone's magic manifests so obviously."

"You think we might have magic?" Alexandra said, overhearing them. Her eyes shone. Hetta had a jarring realisation that to her younger sister, Hetta and her gifts were something to *aspire* to.

Jack certainly looked less than thrilled at the idea. Of course, Jack was of an age to remember the shouting matches between Hetta and her father on the subject.

"As I've been telling Jack, you already *do* have magic," Hetta said. "With the land-sense. Whether you might have more, I don't know, but it seems to me it might be worth getting you all tested."

"Wouldn't be any point," Jack said with a shrug, keen to get away from the subject. "Wouldn't change anything for me."

Hetta thought her cousin was lying to himself as much as her, but she conceded that perhaps now wasn't the time to pursue the matter.

THE PATH THROUGH THE Home Wood had been cleared of snow, but away from the path, the snow lay fluffy and undisturbed but for the occasional tracks of small animals, giving the atmosphere a curiously muffled feeling. Dark tree trunks stood in stark contrast to the overwhelming whiteness. The native forests of Stariel included a lot of evergreens, but the Home Wood had been planted with more decorative deciduous trees from the South. On the other side of the Home Wood were the equally uniquely named Home Farm and Home Orchards. Hetta assumed one or other of her ancestors had decided that being able to see people actually working spoiled the view from the house and had so begun the Home Wood to hide that unpleasant reality; subsequent ancestors had added to it.

How was Wyn getting on with his brother? Her stomach twisted itself into knots as she remembered Wyn's expression at the sight of Prince Rakken. He would stay, wouldn't he? He'd *agreed* to let her bargain, but what if this was the point where he decided the risk was too great and that they'd all be better off without him? She'd known they couldn't keep on like this, dancing on the knife edge of maybe, but she'd thought they'd have more time to sort it all out between them before the fae descended on them.

Distracted as she was by these thoughts, the sudden appearance of Princess Sunnika next to the path made her jump. Stariel had warned her, but it wasn't quite the same as seeing with her own eyes. The fae woman hadn't teleported, but she might as well have, so smoothly did she coalesce from the shadows beneath the trees. How did the fae *do* that? It wasn't glamour, if Wyn was right about Hetta having the Sight now. Maybe fae just got lessons in sneaking.

"Lord Valstar," Princess Sunnika said, inclining her head.

The others all jumped as well. Princess Sunnika was in her fae form, and it was hard not to stare at the sleek points of her ears or the curl of her tail.

"Princess Sunnika," Hetta said evenly, giving a much smaller curtsey than one really ought to give visiting royalty. Instinct told her not to treat Princess Sunnika too deferentially. This was *Hetta's* faeland they stood on; Princess Sunnika should be the one seeking her favour, not the other way around.

The princess surveyed Hetta's family without a change in expression. They didn't appear to intimidate her, though there were six of them to her one, and they were all taller than her—even Alexandra. Hetta's one brief encounter with Princess Sunnika hadn't been sufficient for Hetta to realise quite how short she was. Hetta had been assuming tallness was a fae trait, based purely on Wyn and his brother, but that clearly wasn't the case.

"Why are you here?" Hetta asked when it seemed like the fae woman was in no rush to explain herself.

"I am here, Lord Valstar, as an ambassador from the Court of Dusken Roses to the Court of Falling Stars."

"And you decided now was the perfect time to drop by?" The timing was too neat to be coincidental; she must be here because Wyn's brother was here. Here to make sure Hetta didn't 'buy' Wyn's debt from ThousandSpire? "And this has nothing to do with oaths and debts?"

Her relatives shifted, curious glances passing between them, but didn't interrupt. She hadn't got as far as explaining the full tale of Wyn's debt to them yet—hadn't, in fact, decided if it was her place to tell them or not. But the time for secrets was fast disappearing; Wyn would just have to live with that. The knots in her stomach tightened.

Princess Sunnika smiled. "It has been remiss of us to let relations with this faeland lapse, and my queen is most anxious to ensure we make the most of the opportunity to renew them."

"I'm glad to hear it," Hetta said. "I'm very keen for the fae to stop attacking me and my staff."

"It wasn't DuskRose that attacked your staff," Princess Sunnika said pointedly. "Lord Valstar, I appreciate your caution, but I am not used to being so insulted as an emissary."

"I'm not sure how I've insulted you." If only Wyn was here—this was his area of expertise, not hers. Heavens knew she hadn't yet grasped her new role in *human* politics, let alone fae ones. But she supposed it was rather too much to expect Wyn to be in two places at once, and she had a feeling that keeping Prince Rakken away from Princess Sunnika might be important.

"Is it because we haven't invited you in?" Marius blurted. He shot Hetta an apologetic look, but she moved to squeeze his arm, grateful both for his insight and the reminder that she wasn't entirely alone in this.

Princess Sunnika considered Marius with cool eyes. Her long hair hung perfectly straight and glossy despite the slight breeze, and for the first time in many years, Hetta had a pang of regret for the short hairstyle she'd adopted within three days of leaving home at eighteen. But hair that perfect couldn't be natural, she consoled herself. It must be magic of some sort. Maybe Hetta could learn it too.

"You have offered guestright to an ambassador of another court," Princess Sunnika said eventually. Hetta took that as a 'yes' in response to Marius's question. How had the princess known Prince Rakken was here? Had there been fae eyes watching the borders?

"If it makes you feel any better," Hetta said, "I didn't particularly wish to invite Prince Rakken in either."

There was a sharp intake of breath from both Gregory and Alexandra, and Hetta realised she'd again lost track of which pieces of information were known to who. It only bolstered her determination to make a clean breast of the whole affair as soon as possible. This was getting silly. And she didn't like the way Princess Sunnika's dark eyes tracked her younger siblings' reactions like a predator looking for signs of weakness.

Princess Sunnika's tail drew an idle shape, like a fern frond swaying in the breeze. "DuskRose has never acted with hostility to the Court of Falling Stars—a stance that ThousandSpire cannot claim."

Jack made an exasperated noise. "What are you talking about and what do you want?"

Well, Hetta supposed it had been too much to hope that her audience would remain silent forever. And she broadly agreed with Jack's impatience.

Princess Sunnika's eyes flashed, but her voice remained level when she spoke: "I had thought the word 'ambassador' carried a similar meaning to mortals, Jonathan Langley-Valstar. I am here to further the interests of my court and my queen. As at this moment, we bear FallingStar no ill will." Unsaid was that that could change.

"You're here for Wyn," Marius said flatly.

"We have an interest in one who claims sanctuary here," Princess Sunnika allowed.

"What would it take for you to give up your claim on him?" Hetta asked. She'd promised Wyn she wouldn't agree to anything without him, but surely it couldn't hurt to ask?

Princess Sunnika blinked, taken aback by their bluntness. Did the fae find plain speaking as disorienting as Hetta found their roundabout phrases? The princess' eyelashes were ridiculously long, another tiny unfairness. The longer Hetta looked at her, the more she wondered if Wyn had looked forward to marrying this beautiful fae princess, before his father's plot came to light. She grew irritated with herself in equal measure for wondering about such a trivial thing. It didn't matter what he'd thought of his fiancée ten years ago, not when Hetta knew he loved *her* now and not some foreign princess. Unfortunately, this encouraging thought didn't make Princess Sunnika's eyelashes any less irritatingly luxuriant.

"I do not know you or FallingStar well enough to know if you have anything of sufficient value to trade for such a debt," Princess Sunnika said after a pause. There was a hint of sarcasm in her next words. "Perhaps I would be better able to make such a judgement call if I spent some time here. Under guestright. Such as is usually extended to ambassadors from foreign nations."

Hetta shook her head without meaning to. She wanted both royals out of Stariel as soon as possible. She could *make* them leave, of course—Stariel was bristling at them already, waiting for the slightest encouragement to bear down on them with the full force of its displeasure. Greater fae or not, Hetta was pretty sure no one would be able to stand up to that for long. But wasn't this opportunity what she wanted? A chance to free Wyn from his previous entanglements once and for all?

"Can you and Prince Rakken be in the same house together without starting a war?" she asked.

Princess Sunnika's expression grew haughty. "I make some allowance for your mortality, Lord Valstar, but as a guest one does not shed blood in the house of one's host. DuskRose respects the laws of hospitality. Whether other courts do so is beyond my ability to predict."

Right. Sending monsters to kill people was fine, but not while you were having tea with them, so long as they'd invited you. Hetta supposed it was only slightly less ridiculous than some of the social constructs of the upper classes. It helped a bit to think of it like that, although Hetta didn't have much patience for the social niceties of the aristocracy either.

And Princess Sunnika was right—of the two courts, DuskRose was the only one that hadn't tried to hurt anyone here. Yet.

"Will you promise to abide by guestright?" Hetta said.

Princess Sunnika's tail lashed, and Hetta had the feeling she'd offended her by spelling it out. "I will."

"You can't mean to invite her in—" Jack objected. Hetta silenced him with a glare. His eyebrows drew together mutinously.

"You may come in," Hetta said to the princess. She turned to Gregory and Alexandra. "Go and tell Cook to send up morning tea to the green drawing room." Alexandra looked like she was about to object to this summary dismissal, but something in Hetta's expression stopped her. "Now."

26

GUEST WRANGLING

"**D**O YOU MEAN to leave her alone with a *shadowcat*?" Rakken demanded when Wyn moved to block his exit from Hetta's study. "You haven't secured the boundaries against breach?"

Wyn didn't appreciate the criticism, especially since he'd thought much the same thing only a few days ago when he'd summoned Lamorkin. "I do not mean to leave *you* alone here, and I'm not letting you rush off to reignite a war with DuskRose on Stariel's lands."

"I have no intention of doing such a thing." Rakken had abandoned his languid manner, now tightly coiled with predatory intent, and there was a brief, faint tang of storm in the room, disappearing as Rakken masked his signature. It was worrying that Princess Sunnika hadn't done the same, her presence blazing along the leylines like a firestorm; it meant she wanted them to know she was here.

"You don't think the sight of Prince Orenn's killer might anger his cousin?" It wasn't an accident that Wyn was ThousandSpire's sacrificial lamb on the altar of marriage; there was too much DuskRose blood on his other siblings' hands to make them acceptable candidates. Well…apart from Irokoi, but he would've been just as offensive to DuskRose for entirely different reasons. Rakken and Catsmere held the dubious distinction of 'most hated' for their part in the death of DuskRose's crown prince. That had been the act that had driven the High King to intervene in the war.

Rakken's eyes narrowed. "And are you happy to let your beloved play both sides of this game? To negotiate on your behalf? You think DuskRose won't do everything in its power to stop ThousandSpire from passing its debt to another court?"

"If you're so worried about ThousandSpire's debt, why not give it to Hetta freely?" Wyn snapped.

"For someone you claim to love, you are very keen to saddle her with a heavy magical burden."

"For a faeland you claim to represent, you are very reluctant to *un*burden it!"

They'd drawn closer as they argued, but at this Rakken took a step back and said softly, "I am indeed here for ThousandSpire." Again, there was some deeper meaning there, a subtext Wyn was missing.

He knew that standing on home ground, Hetta was far more capable of defending herself and Stariel than he was. But the faint trace of Sunnika's magic made him wish desperately to be out there at Hetta's side.

Time crawled. He extended his senses as far as they would go, trying to get some idea of what was happening. There was no point asking Stariel for information; the faeland was far too preoccupied with all these foreign fae within its borders to have time for him. At least its low-level restlessness meant nothing truly terrible had happened yet—because Stariel wouldn't stop at that if someone threatened Hetta or any other Valstar within its borders.

Rakken folded his arms and leaned against the wall opposite, an eerie mirroring of Wyn's position. Deliberate, of course. Rakken always knew exactly how to rile him. "And does she love you as much as you love her, this mortal lord?" he asked as the silence stretched. "You don't know, do you? And it bothers you."

"If you think I am going to give you any information *at all* about Hetta, you are greatly mistaken." Wyn stared at the unchanging view of Starwater as if he could will it to tell him what was going on elsewhere on the estate—or where exactly Hetta was. It was hard to read the leylines amidst Stariel's agitation.

Rakken continued as if Wyn hadn't spoken. "That's rather tragic, actually. A fae prince willing to give up immortality for a mortal he's not even sure feels the same depth of affection. Love is for fools and mortals, dear Hollow—it's not an emotion one can rely on."

"You love Catsmere," Wyn pointed out. "Don't tell me you don't rely on that."

Rakken shrugged the words off as if a fly had settled on his shoulder. "Far be it from me to judge your relationships, brother, but if Lord Valstar loves you like a sibling, you're doing something terribly wrong."

"A childish misinterpretation, Rake."

Before Rakken could answer, a knock sounded at the door. Wyn hastily removed himself from the doorframe as it opened to reveal Marius. He blinked as he absorbed Wyn and Rakken's adversarial positions.

"Oh good; you haven't killed each other then." Marius's gaze settled on Wyn, troubled. "Hetta wants you in the green drawing room. Princess Sunnika is here. I'll babysit him." He indicated Rakken with a curt gesture.

Wyn thought this was an incredibly bad idea, but he understood Hetta's reasoning. Jack might punch Rakken in the face if he irritated him, and whilst Wyn had no issue with that, it would break guestright.

"I do not actually require babysitting," Rakken said dryly. "I have sworn to abide by guestright."

Wyn and Marius both ignored him.

"Don't let him get under your skin," Wyn advised. He shot Rakken a look before he left. "And do try to control your childish urges."

EVEN WITHOUT MARIUS'S WARNING, Wyn would have known another greater fae was present in the house. Housefae barely made a dent in the currents of magic, but greater fae… Rakken had clearly decided to cease masking his signature, because Wyn could feel his brother in Hetta's study, hopefully not provoking Marius (a foolish hope), and ahead, in the green drawing room, the princess.

As he drew closer, that awareness sharpened, a lingering taste of cherries and beeswax in the air. He found her standing outlined in sunlight next to the windows. There was no sign of Hetta. He paused on the threshold. What was going on?

Princess Sunnika turned in an unhurried motion, so that her hair rippled like water down her back. "Prince Hallowyn," she murmured. Her dark eyes took in his appearance. "In mortal form."

"So are you, Princess," he said. It was the first time he'd ever seen her so, and it was just as disconcerting as it had been with Rakken. Perhaps more so because Sunnika's human face and petite stature made her appear almost harmless, and Wyn knew that she was anything but.

Princess Sunnika smiled but made no move towards him, no move to summon her magic. It didn't stop every hair on his body from standing on end, the fear of DuskRose's powers going bone-deep. And this wasn't a general fear but a specific one, informed by his own recent experience: Princess Sunnika had teleported him and Hetta miles across the country as if it had been no great effort.

She could be at his side in an eyeblink and outside Stariel's bounds in another. He deeply regretted not prioritising anti-translocation wards for the faeland; in hindsight it probably should've taken precedence over the lavender bathroom's plumbing issues.

"Why are you here alone, Princess?" he challenged, to disguise his unease.

"Perhaps you are not as deep in Lord Valstar's confidence as you thought."

"Did you ask to speak to me alone?" he said, suddenly confident that must be the reason. "In exchange for the favour you did us?" What did Hetta think he had to say to Sunnika that he couldn't say with Hetta present? He narrowed his eyes. "Though I will debate the obligation."

"So did she." Sunnika's smile cut off abruptly. "Do not mistake my calm for lack of anger, Your Highness. Lord Valstar has been attempting to persuade me that you did not intend your betrayal of our betrothal vows as a personal insult to me, and yet you do not seem pleased to see me."

"Ah. My apologies; my concern is for FallingStar's future. I owe this court a debt." *And I am not at all pleased to see you*, he added mentally.

"You owe a debt to the Court of Dusken Roses."

"I do." He didn't see how acknowledging the debt could make things worse. "Lord Valstar spoke truthfully; my leaving had nothing to do with you personally," he added, marvelling yet again at his failure to consider how his actions must have looked to everyone else. It was so easy to forget that the fae weren't omniscient; they did such a good job at pretending to be.

She made a thoughtful noise and came towards him. It took everything not to step back, the impulse irrational given her powers. The pink tips of her hair swished as she moved. She seemed a lot shorter than he remembered, although perhaps that was merely in comparison to Hetta.

"Yet it has affected me very personally," she said, halting a mere arm's length away. She had to tilt her head back to meet his eyes. "Perhaps I should kill you where you stand, for the insult."

"I intended no insult." He didn't flinch from her gaze, trying to read her mood. It didn't seem murderous, despite her obvious anger. That was something. "I ran from my father, not you."

She scoffed. "DuskRose has stood fast against all your father's efforts for centuries, Prince Hallowyn. It was not necessary to hide yourself away in a mortal court to evade his grasp."

"And you would have trusted yourself to the care of an enemy court, if the situation was reversed?" It would've been fantastically easy for his father to frame DuskRose for his murder, given the degree of antagonism between the courts.

"The entire point, dear prince, was to change 'enemy' into something else." Even Princess Sunnika wasn't optimistic enough to use the word 'friend'. Did she truly care about cementing the peace only the High King's edict had forced? Perhaps she did. He didn't *know* her, couldn't judge.

"I'm sorry," he said.

Her eyes narrowed. "Yet I hear no words from you to make good on what you promised."

Where in the high winds was Hetta? "Will I marry you, you mean? Is that really what you want?"

"It is not a matter of want. I am not an oathbreaker."

He made himself think about it, though everything in him screamed a negative. Perhaps she was right. Perhaps he could evade his father's wrath by remaining within DuskRose's bounds. Perhaps his father would even abandon his initial plan to kill Wyn and pin the blame on DuskRose, now that the element of surprise was gone. That would leave Wyn with only the pit of vipers that was the Court of Dusken Roses. It would mean a return to every word carrying an undercurrent of meaning and threat, to watching over his shoulder for those who would betray him without a second thought if they thought it would benefit them. He would be an outsider at DuskRose, one of the hated stormdancers, which would make it even harder to slide beneath the surface, unnoticed. And Princess Sunnika was Queen Tayarenn's heir; he would not be able to escape the court politics, not as her consort.

But perhaps Stariel would be safe, if he patched over his broken oath. Perhaps the fae would lose interest in this mortal faeland without him in it. But what if they didn't? When had the fae ever let go of something if there might be some gain to be had from it? And there was the revocation of the Iron Law to consider; it changed things in ways he couldn't predict.

And Hetta would never, ever forgive him.

"No," he said, something in him shifting as he made the decision, the hollowness his broken oath had left seeming to reverberate beneath his sternum. "I'm not confident that my reception at DuskRose would be any less hostile than in the Spires. And there remains my debt to FallingStar." A debt that was emotional rather than magical, now, but there was no need to specify that. "I should like to try to repay at least some of my debts, even if yours remains outstanding. I'm sorry, Your Highness, but you should go."

He found Princess Sunnika hard to read, but something that looked like surprise flickered in her eyes—followed swiftly by anger. He replayed his last words. Ah. Perhaps telling his ex-fiancée he placed a mortal's claim above hers had not been very diplomatic.

Princess Sunnika tsked. "So dishonest."

"The fae cannot lie."

She didn't dignify this with a response. A trace of smugness flickered in her expression. "And why should I go? You assume *you* are my only business here?" She laughed. "I am here as an ambassador to the Court of Falling Stars."

Heaviness filled him at her words; he'd been right. He felt Hetta's presence and turned to find her watching him and Princess Sunnika with an inscrutable expression.

"I take it she hasn't convinced you to become a blissful groom again." Hetta said it lightly, but he wasn't an idiot; she was relieved.

"No." Anger spiked, shocking in its intensity. How could she doubt him? Didn't she know how much she meant to him? But the emotion collapsed just as quickly. How could she *not* doubt him, when he'd never fully committed to staying? He closed the distance between them and linked his arm with hers, not caring what Princess Sunnika might think.

He turned back to the princess. "What will it take?" he asked. "For you to release me from my oath?"

Princess Sunnika's gaze rested on where Wyn's hand intertwined with Hetta's. "Lord Valstar has granted me guestright that I may better ponder that very question."

"And how long, exactly, do you plan to ponder it for?" Hetta said. "I may have invited you in, but I'm not at all inclined to let you stay long."

Wyn squeezed Hetta's hand, overwhelmed with sudden fondness.

Princess Sunnika looked the opposite of fond. "I do not know," she said evenly. "How long is ThousandSpire's emissary intending to be here?"

RUMOURS

THEY BEAT A tactical retreat to the map room to discuss the situation, leaving Jack and Caroline with Princess Sunnika in the drawing room and Marius with Rakken in Hetta's study. Wyn had never been more conscious of the house's occupants as they made their way up. He could not avoid overhearing snippets of conversation in which his name was mentioned.

"Did you hear? Lord Featherstone called him his brother! In front of half the Valstars!"

"—he's always had a certain manner about him. Like he wasn't raised one of us, you know?"

"Do you think he'll go back to Featherstone?"

Wyn knew he couldn't hide from the questions or the stares for long, but he hadn't yet decided how to handle them. The larger questions of his brother and ex-fiancée loomed over that smaller uncertainty.

Hetta closed the door behind her and raised her eyebrows. Before he could think too much, he pulled her into a crushing embrace. She let out a soft sound of surprise as he pressed her into the door. Desperation lent a pure cutting edge to sensation, and he buried himself in physicality, ignoring the flaring leylines in the house. Some wild part of him thrashed its wings, trying to escape the collapsing house of cards. He kissed her until they were both breathless and shaking.

"*Wyn*," Hetta complained up at him. She was so close that he could see the ring of darker grey close to her pupils.

"Ah, yes. Possibly not the time. Sorry." At some point in the earlier interplay he'd captured her hands and pinned them above her head. He released them now and tried to step back, but she held on to his shoulders, stopping him.

"Well, it's not as though I weren't willing." Her eyes sparkled; he nearly kissed her again. "Are you all right?"

"No," he said, surprising them both. "No, I am very far from all right." He wrapped his arms around her and tucked her head against his neck. "They are *here*, Hetta. At Stariel. In this house."

"Yes, I noticed." Her words were muffled, but their dry tone was unmistakable.

"One of my worst fears is playing out as we speak, and you are not taking it seriously enough."

She wriggled so that she could look up at him. He didn't like allowing her even this space, though it was irrational to think that if he just held her tightly enough he could protect her.

"One of your worst fears is two fae taking tea with us?" She paused as they both contemplated the mental image of Aunt Sybil seated next to Rakken on the chesterfield. "This *is* me taking it seriously. You don't think I've invited them in for the sheer entertainment value? You said you'd let us try to negotiate with them. Are you going to back out of that?"

"Don't you see? There's no way to extricate you neatly from this now, even if I were to leave Stariel this very moment and swear never to return. Stormcrows, even if I were to marry Sunnika tomorrow, I could not make them leave Stariel be. You've intrigued them, and they'll never stop pushing for an advantage now, even if I were out of the picture. I'm a fool. I should have left the second they found me. I should never have come here in the first place!"

Hetta stilled, and an entirely different fear kindled in his chest—a fear that he had said something unforgivable.

"And what about us?" she said, her voice low and dangerous. "Do you wish you'd never met me? Do you wish you didn't *love* me?"

The word reverberated through the bond between them, old friendship and new romance, and Wyn feared that the wrong words could shatter it. Yet he couldn't stop himself from saying with cold, clipped precision, "I imagine it would make things considerably easier for both of us if I did not." What was he doing? What was he trying to achieve? What was *wrong* with him?

She balled her hands in the fabric of his shirt and made a wordless noise of frustration. "Stop being an idiot."

"I fear it may be an integral part of my character."

"I love you, but sometimes I just want to shake the martyr out of you!"

He froze. It was like stumbling into an unexpected thermal, warm air buoying him upwards to dizzying heights. He shouldn't let himself be distracted by sentiment, not with fear for Stariel and Hetta thrumming through him, but he wanted to kiss her all over again. At the same time, it terrified him. *Don't love me*, he wanted to say. *They will use it against you if you love me. Don't let me make you weak.*

Hetta sighed and shook his shirt for emphasis. "Yes, I do love you, you foolish and entirely idiotic man. Don't pretend you're surprised."

"You've never said it before," he pointed out. "I wasn't...sure."

"Well, I was trying very hard not to love you because you kept threatening to leave! And you still are! And I've been putting all my wants and hopes on hold so as not to frighten you off, so as not to force you into anything!" She gave an angry laugh. "As if anyone has *ever* managed to make you do anything you don't want to do! But I don't want to pretend anymore, Wyn." The anger in her faded, quick to burn out as always, leaving something cold and sad in its wake.

"What *do* you want, love?" he murmured, and it was such a relief to *finally* be able to say it properly, without needing the excuse of pain or magic.

She released her death-grip on his shirt and smoothed it down. "I want us to not be a secret from my family anymore. I want them to know who—and what—you really are. I want you to stand beside me as an equal. And I want everyone to appreciate you properly."

"It may be difficult to simultaneously fulfil—" But she put a finger to his lips.

"I haven't finished yet. I want you freed from your old oaths. I want to know no one is going to try to kill you. I want to not have to worry about the fae attacking my people." A wry note flickered in her expression, and the hand that had been smoothing at his shirt grew somewhat more possessive. "I want to take you to bed. And for the bank to give us a loan."

"Are these items ordered in terms of priority, may I inquire?" he asked huskily.

"Shush. They are in the order they are occurring to me. I want you to stop trying to put everyone else first or wallowing in self-pity about what you *should* want or do, and instead admit what you *actually* want. And I want you to fight for that."

"I'm beginning to wonder why you love me," Wyn said, still enjoying the shape of the words. "I sound frightfully wishy-washy in this description."

"You're deflecting."

"Yes." He paused. "I don't like the idea of dragging your name through the mud if I'm not in a position to make the promises I should to you."

Her eyes widened at the oblique reference. "Wyn, I really don't care one whit for my good name or otherwise."

"I do," he said. "I care that the bank won't lend you funds if they think someone untrustworthy is at the reins. I care if people think you're not a good lord. I care if people think I've taken advantage of you, or if they think you've taken advantage of me."

"*Do* they think I've taken advantage of you?" Hetta asked, diverted.

"Caroline said something a few days ago that made me think— but we are getting off track again," he said sternly. "The point is that if word of us gets out, *you* will be the one judged most harshly for it, not me, and I cannot help caring about that. Mortal culture here is…unfair to women."

He shook his head before she could try to talk him out of it. "I want to talk to my brother again, see if I can prise his ulterior motives out. Sunnika may not know what she wants, but I'm convinced Rake knows exactly what he's here for." He tightened his arms around her, heart racing. "But first, I want to tell everyone what I am."

28

SECRETS

ETTA HAD NEVER seen Wyn wound quite so tightly as they walked down the hallway from the map room. She took his hand. He squeezed it briefly without looking at her but didn't keep it.

"I'm not going to *make* you tell people," she said. "You don't have to do this, if you don't want." Why was she trying to talk him out of this? She wanted him to do this! This love business was…a kind of madness.

He gave a huff of amusement, his russet eyes fond.

"Didn't you recently claim that you couldn't *make* me do anything? This is my own choice. Besides, the ball is in motion. The details of my past have spread too far now to take back. And—" His expression hardened. "I will not give either Rakken or Sunnika further ammunition to use against me here. They will only exploit any secrets I leave unrevealed."

They made a detour first so Wyn could change shirts. "Let's not outrage your family's sense of modesty alongside everything else," he said wryly as he slipped quickly into the specially cut shirt Hetta

had given him, revealing only the briefest glimpse of coffee-colour-
ed skin in the process.

She liked the intimacy of watching him dress. It woke a yearning
in her that had nothing to do with lust. Or, well, not *everything* to
do with lust. Their eyes met just as he fastened the top button, and
she saw that same yearning reflected there. For a moment, he wasn't
a fae prince masquerading as a servant and she wasn't the Lord of
Stariel. She was sixteen, and he was her dearest friend in the world,
vexing and amusing by turns. She'd never looked at him in a romantic light as a teenager, which seemed slightly incredible now. Why
on earth had she wasted so much time nursing a girlhood crush on
Angus Penharrow, the neighbouring lord's son?

Hetta had never before had the desire to help a man with his
tie, and Wyn certainly didn't need such help, but she found herself
moving to do it anyway. It amused him, but he didn't try to stop her.

"To battle then," he said when his clothing was in place.

On the two occasions Hetta had needed to make a dramatic
announcement to all and sundry, she'd called everyone together and
gotten it over with as quickly and efficiently as possible. It shouldn't
have surprised her that Wyn's approach was entirely different.

He began with Aunt Sybil, Aunt Maude, and Lady Phoebe.
They'd clearly been discussing him, because the conversation
died the instant he crossed the threshold of the sitting room. Her
aunts brightened, and Lady Phoebe looked anxious. She hated
confrontations.

Wyn bowed his head. "Ladies. Forgive me for interrupting, but
I'm afraid I owe you something of an explanation after my brother's
arrival this morning."

An anticipatory ripple passed through the assembled women at
the promise of interesting gossip to come.

"May I sit?" he asked.

"Yes, of course," Lady Phoebe said. "How is your leg?"

But the conversation wasn't to be so easily derailed. Aunt Sybil said bluntly, "You're the son of old Lord Featherstone?"

Wyn hesitated, and Hetta could practically see the thoughts cross his mind in rapid succession, the temptation to spin truth in a wholly false direction. With a sigh, he seemed to master the urge. "My brother has misled you. Neither of us has any connection to Featherstone. He adopted the persona of Lord Featherstone in order to gain entry to this house."

This was interesting gossip indeed. The aunts leaned forward.

"He *is* your brother though?" Aunt Sybil pressed.

"Yes. But more importantly, he is not human. And neither am I. We are both fae." A beat of silence followed, and then Lady Phoebe tittered. Wyn folded his hands together and smiled. "I am not joking, though I understand your surprise."

"You can't be a fairy," Aunt Maude said authoritatively, as if this would make it so. Aunt Maude considered herself something of an expert on folklore.

"Nonetheless, I am." He was so calm, and so mild, that even Hetta was almost fooled. "Will you take my word for it, or would you like me to prove it?"

"Lord Featherstone is a fairy?" Lady Phoebe asked.

Wyn smiled. "Well, my brother is. I make no claims one way or the other for the real Lord Featherstone; I do not know him."

"I always thought you had good sense, Mr Tempest," Aunt Sybil said. "But I don't know what's got into your head now. Lord Featherstone a fairy!" She made a sound of disgust. "That is ridiculous." Her gaze went to Hetta, and she nearly groaned aloud; of course Aunt Sybil would target her if possible. She'd always distantly approved of Wyn, but the same didn't apply to Hetta, who she thought far too headstrong and improper. "Is this your idea of a joke, Henrietta?"

"I do not joke, Lady Langley-Valstar," Wyn answered in her stead. He stood. "Thank you for taking this so calmly." He smiled again, and even Aunt Sybil softened a fraction in the face of it. Wyn had a singularly charming smile when he wanted to. "Thank you for your support. But I must be getting back to my duties now."

Hetta had to hurry to exit with him.

"What was that?" she said when they were out of earshot. It wouldn't have occurred to her to make such an announcement so casually, thank everyone for their acceptance of it, and leave. On the other hand, it never would've worked if she'd tried it; she lacked Wyn's aura of persuasive self-assurance, as if there were simply no other way for the world to be.

"A defusing tactic," he said. "They'll all mull over that and approach me one-on-one later. Crowds are always more volatile and harder to handle than individuals."

That made sense, Hetta supposed, though she doubted she'd have the patience for it as a general approach. But this wasn't about her. "What now?"

"The older cousins, I think."

"Not Uncle Percival?"

"No. He comes later. With, preferably, at least some of Aunt Maude's youngest children present."

"Obviously," she said, though this order of events wasn't obvious to her at all.

"He will moderate his own reaction according to his audience," Wyn explained.

"You are the single most manipulative person I've ever met."

He flashed her a quick grin.

The older cousins were a different kettle of fish. They were Hetta's age peers, and they saw Wyn as somewhere between friend and social inferior. Most of them would've said they didn't care at all about social class, but the truth was that they did, unconsciously, and they were rattled by the thought that they'd treated Wyn as a servant when he might've come from similar privilege to them.

The fae business they were inclined to treat as a rather poor joke, which Wyn dealt with by removing his coat, handing it to Hetta, and changing.

Hetta's cousins went improbably silent. The previously spacious billiard room was suddenly crowded as Wyn stretched his wings to their fullest and everyone got out of the way. The movement was mesmerising in its slow grace. He held the position briefly, a pendulum at the top of its arc, and then feather and bone shifted and compressed until he was only himself again. Or, Hetta thought with a frown, still himself, but the less feathery version of it.

"I hope you are now convinced of my truthfulness," he said dryly. "Or would you like me to do it again?"

It was fascinating to watch how Wyn took control of people's reactions. With the aunts he'd framed the situation as imparting a slightly embarrassing but not terribly important fact; with her older cousins, as a revelation that they could assure themselves they'd all secretly suspected anyway.

Hetta would've found it exhausting to approach all her relatives in small groups and one-on-one, to tell the same story over and over, to respond to the same outbursts with patient tact. Moreover, she couldn't have stood the scrutiny the way Wyn did, as if it didn't bother him in the least. It made her want to shout that he wasn't a carnival attraction but a living, breathing person. But though she accompanied him in silent endorsement, she let him manage the show. She could give him back this bit of control.

With her younger relatives, he let the revelation become something wondrous and didn't rebuke little Laurel when she reached out to touch his feathers.

"Can you fly?" Laurel asked, eyes wide.

"Of course he can fly," Willow said scornfully. "Why else would he have wings?"

"Chickens have wings," Laurel pointed out. "And they can't fly."

"That's because their wings are clipped, silly. Everyone knows that. If they weren't clipped, they could fly."

Wyn met Hetta's eyes with a firm message: *do not ever compare me to a chicken*, and she had to press her hand to her mouth to keep from laughing aloud.

All in all, it went far better than Hetta had hoped. Oh, she knew as well as Wyn that this was the calm before the storm. Already some of her relatives looked at Wyn differently, and not in a good way. As if he were…not just inhuman but *sub*human. But it was such a relief to have things out in the open at last. Surely from here things could only get better? Well…some things out in the open. He'd not even hinted to her family that there was anything between him and Hetta.

He showed his first and only sign of fatigue when they were alone once again, rubbing briefly at his temples, after having extracted himself from her youngest relatives' hands.

"Are you all right?" she asked him.

He shook his head and grimaced. "I need to talk to the staff. This will go better without you there. They're too intimidated by you."

Hetta hadn't realised she intimidated anyone at all, least of all locals that she'd known for most of her life.

"Oh," was all she could think to say.

He glanced quickly up and down the hallway and then pressed the merest flicker of a kiss to her forehead. "It's not a bad thing. It's just…there is a divide between staff and family. The staff consider me theirs, but this story they've heard about Lord Featherstone will have shaken that, and you appearing at my shoulder will only shake it further."

"You're not theirs," Hetta said. "You're mine."

Wyn's eyes danced, but he managed to check his laugh, just. He nodded instead. "My Star."

AN ENTIRELY AWFUL PLAN

HETTA WENT TO poke at Prince Rakken while Wyn was speaking to the staff. To her relief, Marius looked bemused rather than stressed when she reached her study. Prince Rakken remained languorous as a jungle cat, once again stretched out on the settee beneath the window.

"Lord Valstar," he said, getting up. Apparently some manners were universal. "Your brother has been"—he paused, and amusement glimmered in his green eyes—"enlightening."

Marius, to Hetta's astonishment, didn't seem at all fazed by Prince Rakken's barb. "Yes," he said with a sigh. "I enlightened him as to the key characteristics of snapdragon varietals. I figured that was a safe topic of conversation."

Hetta let out a peal of laughter. She'd thought the day had reached its utter limit of absurdity, but she really ought to stop making such predictions.

"I am, indeed, now most enlightened on this subject," Prince Rakken said dryly.

"Well, you did *say* you wanted to learn more about the mortal world," Marius pointed out. "Snapdragons are mortal. Or do you have them in Faerie too?"

Prince Rakken ignored him. "Lord Valstar, I would like to speak to you alone."

Marius glared. "Are you planning on trying anything nefarious?"

Prince Rakken didn't seem to know what to make of Marius's directness. He canted his head at her brother. "Do you truly expect I would tell you if I was?"

"It's all right, Marius. I'll let Stariel eat him if he tries anything." The land had been quivering protectively since Prince Rakken's arrival; it wouldn't take much to unleash it. But he *had* sworn guestright. Marius gave a narrow-eyed nod and left them.

"Sit," she said to Prince Rakken. Was she supposed to offer him refreshments? As if the thought had been a summons, a knock sounded at the door and the housemaid Lottie appeared carrying a tea tray. Her eyes sparkled as she took in Prince Rakken, and Hetta knew that Wyn had already told at least some of the staff what was going on. It was typical of him to organise refreshments even while under stress.

Prince Rakken seemed faintly amused when Hetta offered him tea after Lottie had left, but he took a teacup without comment and settled back. He was so…metaphorically glittery that he made everything around him seem shabbier in comparison. Was this what Wyn had meant by fae allure?

"You said you wanted Wyn free of his oath," Hetta said.

"So I did," he agreed easily.

"Was that just so I wouldn't toss you out straightaway or did you actually mean that? Because if you're sticking with your completely outrageous request from before, you can leave as soon as you've finished your tea."

This seemed to amuse him further. He tilted his head, the gesture eerily similar to Wyn's. "I see now that my dramatic entrance into this house has not endeared me to you, and I apologise. I was testing your mettle, I will freely admit, but I'm not always so antagonistic. Ask my brother."

"Don't you dare try to make Wyn feel some kind of familial obligation to defend you!" Hetta flared up.

"Very well: I retract the suggestion. Do not ask Hallowyn. Tell me instead what words I may say that will reassure you of my good faith."

"The words: 'we will release Wyn from his debt, go away, and promise not to attack anybody here ever again' would be an excellent start."

He threw back his head and laughed, that chocolate-rich sound that she couldn't help finding attractive even as it irritated her.

"These are times of change," he told her, sobering. "The High King has lifted the Iron Law. What will come of that, I do not yet know. But you can be certain of one thing—my people are not going to simply go away, not now that we have remembered how interesting the Mortal Realm can be."

A chill went down Hetta's spine. He spoke of something much wider than Stariel and the two courts Wyn owed a debt to.

"So you see, it is more important than you thought, the relationship between your realm and mine." He swirled his tea thoughtfully. "An alliance with another faeland could benefit your people, in this changing world; an alliance with a mortal faeland could benefit mine."

The door opened again and Wyn appeared, expression slightly harried. He shut it behind him and glanced between his brother and Hetta.

"I think your brother is doing his best to be as cryptic as possible," Hetta summarised. "He was saying something about the fae coming back to the world and talking of alliances as if we were staging a medieval war."

Wyn's gaze locked onto his brother, and some message Hetta didn't understand passed between them. Whatever it was, it alarmed Wyn, and he said, voice tight, "Hetta, how many housefae are nearby?" His eyes burned with silent meaning. Why didn't he simply *tell* her what he was getting at? But then she understood: he was worried about eavesdroppers. Hadn't Prince Rakken said a similar thing back at the pub? "*I do not care to air my name about for those who might be listening.*"

What a horrible level of paranoia to live with! But Hetta obediently reached for Stariel and felt about for the tiny sparks of the housefae. There *were* an abnormal number of them in proximity to her study, and she pressed down upon them and suggested that they should move along. They did, squawking objections.

<Can you stop anyone from hearing what we speak of in this room?> she asked Stariel, trying to convey the concept of secrecy. The faeland paused and sent back an image of a cocoon, quiet inside while outside the storm raged. <Er...yes, I think that's what I mean. Or rather the reverse of that: inside, storm raging; outside, no sound.> Understanding flickered from the faeland, and she felt something shift.

Hetta opened her eyes. "No one is now listening to us," she said, keeping a heightened connection open to Stariel. "So you can say whatever melodramatic thing you felt you couldn't say before. But who are you keeping secrets from?"

Wyn and Prince Rakken exchanged another meaningful glance.

"Our father," said Wyn uneasily, as if he didn't like saying the words aloud despite her reassurance. "King Aeros."

"I thought you were here on his behalf?" Hetta asked Prince Rakken, confused.

Prince Rakken glanced thoughtfully around her study. The faint scent of citrus and storms pricked the air for a heartbeat as he reassured himself that no one was listening.

"I am here on behalf of the *Spires*," he said, emphasising the last word.

Wyn froze. "You cannot mean..."

Prince Rakken's lips quirked into a crooked smile. "Oh, Hallowyn, you always were far too easy to shock."

Despite Wyn's stillness, or perhaps because of it, Hetta knew that he was afraid. Hetta was too confused to be properly alarmed.

Prince Rakken saw it, the fear, and gave a bitter laugh. "How well Father's lessons have stuck with you, little brother. Even now, you blanch to think of him."

"You cannot..." Wyn trailed off again. He wrapped his arms around himself as if he were suddenly cold. "You are not alone?"

"I am not alone," Prince Rakken said meaningfully. Or at least meaningfully for Wyn; Hetta was still entirely at sea.

"Are either of you going to actually explain what you're talking about?"

"You will not involve Hetta in this," Wyn said to his brother, voice low and menacing, as if she hadn't spoken at all. "You will not involve Stariel in it."

"Oh, Hollow, if you did not want them involved, you should never have come here."

Wyn didn't flinch, but she knew the jab had to have hit him hard. "What if I leave?" he said slowly, without looking at Hetta. Her stomach dropped.

Prince Rakken's gaze was pitying. "You think that will make the fae lose interest in this faeland and its rather fascinating mortal lord now? Perhaps I wasn't clear: this is happening, with or without your involvement. All it affects is the timing. You said you would kill for this mortal lord; why do you flinch now?"

"*What are you talking about?*" Hetta got up and put herself bodily between the two of them.

Wyn sagged against the door. "He is talking about treason. And, I think, murder?"

Prince Rakken didn't answer, watching Hetta's reaction intently.

Hysterical laughter threatened to bubble up, and she checked the urge to cry: "*What are you talking about?*" yet again. Hetta had dealt with some fairly unexpected things in the last two months, but this was…

"I think," she said, trying to collect her scattered thoughts, "that you had better tell me exactly what you are proposing, without all the hedging about."

"I am proposing…" Prince Rakken paused and looked at his brother.

Wyn made a 'go-on' sort of gesture. "You won't convince me you can successfully stage a coup, Rake, if you can't even bring yourself to speak the words aloud."

"It is *because* I watch what I say aloud that I *will* successfully stage a coup," Prince Rakken said.

And Hetta finally, finally, understood what they were talking about. "You want to depose your father and take over the Court of Ten Thousand Spires."

Prince Rakken nodded.

Wyn's facade fractured for a second as he burst out, "It is *madness* you speak of!" He turned wild eyes on Hetta. "You don't understand. Our father…his power is stronger than any fae I know bar the High King. Even Rake and Catsmere together do not stand a chance against that. Even *all* of my siblings together do not stand a chance!"

Prince Rakken removed an invisible speck of dirt from his shirt collar. When he spoke, his voice was low but firm as steel. "Your broken oath did not stunt only your own power, Hallowyn. ThousandSpire labours under the weight of an unfulfilled promise also. Our father is…not all that he should be, not what he once was." He smiled. "And I am *more* than I was."

"That is still not *enough*, Rake. Or has the Maelstrom granted you powers beyond your age?"

Prince Rakken shrugged. "Facing the Maelstrom with no guarantee of outcome…that *would* be madness. I am not yet so desperate." His focus sharpened on Hetta, eyes brilliant as spring leaves. "But facing my father, on a faeland not his own, with four of his children and, perhaps," he shot a look at Hetta, "a powerful pyromancer at my side…that is *not* madness."

"Four?" Wyn said sharply. "You have talked Irokoi into this as well?"

Hetta was struggling a little to keep up with all the names and references, but she understood well enough what Prince Rakken wanted.

"Let me get this correctly: you want Wyn and me to help you kill your father?" It didn't sound any better when she said it out loud.

"You want a way to free this one of his oath; a way to keep your land free of ThousandSpire's influence," Prince Rakken said, as calmly as if they were discussing the weather. "And I do not require you to do the deed." He shot her a mirthless, dagger-sharp smile. "Cat and I will take care of that. I merely require a compelling reason for Father to leave his faeland."

Wyn laughed. "And why would he do that?"

"Because," Prince Rakken said smugly, "he can hardly expect FallingStar's lord to agree to swear fealty to him by proxy. Lord Valstar would be within her rights to demand a face-to-face meeting, on her own territory."

"And then you…what? Murder your own father?" Hetta said. *What am I becoming?* she thought, faintly horrified that she could even contemplate such a thing and yet apparently not horrified enough to discard the idea out of hand.

Wyn was roiling with agitation now, as if he would pace if not constrained by the dimensions of Hetta's study.

"Don't make me a party to this, Rake."

"It's actually Lord Valstar's participation I need most, not yours," Prince Rakken said, meeting Hetta's eyes. An awareness passed between them, as if Rakken recognised the bit of Hetta's soul that didn't recoil from the things that it ought to, a shared understanding that they would cross lines if necessary to protect their own. Hetta didn't much like that piece of herself. "Help us, and we will give you Hallowyn's debt if Cat or I gain ThousandSpire's throne. The blood will not be on your hands," he added, soft and persuasive. "This is my plan, not yours. And, if it helps, even my soft-hearted brother here cannot tell you the world won't be better off without our dearest father ruling the Spires."

"Maybe talking about killing people is a perfectly normal thing where you come from, but it's definitely *not* normal or acceptable here," Hetta said.

"I do not suggest this course of action *lightly*. I assure you I have no wish for it to become normal behaviour for any of us. But I told you, Lord Valstar: this is a time of change. And is your true concern here maintaining a semblance of normality?" He shot a look at Wyn. "Or is it my brother's conscience that holds you back?" Hetta caught the subtext, loud and clear, and wasn't especially happy with it, though it was probably true. In his bones, Wyn was *good*, despite his secrecy and tendency to manipulate, good in a way that Hetta wasn't sure she could lay claim to. The irony of it bit at her as she met Wyn's eyes and he jerked his head in a fierce negative.

"Well," Prince Rakken said, as if the tension in the room hadn't ratcheted up a thousandfold. "I can see you have much to discuss." He shrugged. "But I have business elsewhere in any case. I will give you twenty-four hours to persuade my brother to set aside his weakness. I will see you tomorrow."

"I haven't agreed to it," Hetta said.

Prince Rakken ignored this, pausing before he got to the door. "And Lord Valstar…be careful what words you speak aloud. The world has ears."

THEY ARGUED AS HETTA felt the spark of Prince Rakken's presence disappear from the estate.

"He's planning this *anyway*, Wyn. I don't like it either, but tell me you don't think it could work!" Hetta's stomach roiled. How could she even be considering this? It was awful; everything about it was awful. But she couldn't forget the draken Wyn's father had sent, nor the lug-imps Aroset had let loose on his command; King Aeros had been perfectly happy to murder his son. If King Aeros was no longer around, Wyn would be safe, finally, and so would everyone else. A fierce, protective bit of her hummed at that, Stariel rumbling agreement.

"That's not the point!"

"What *is* the point then? Your father wants you *dead*, Wyn! Tell me that you don't want your brother to pull off his coup!"

Wyn's mouth thinned into a line, the rest of him simmering with the same tension. "I don't want Stariel to be a venue for murder, Hetta. That *is* what we're talking about here. Murdering *my own father*."

It did sound much worse in those terms, but Hetta still refused to shy away from it. "Yes, and he seems perfectly happy to murder you! How is it better to wish your brother success but not help him just so we can keep our moral high ground?" Was she really arguing in favour of this? Stariel's awareness swarmed around her, drawn by her distress, and she soothed it.

"I don't wish to be like my father!" For an instant that expression was back, the same fear she'd seen on the tower under the snow moon, and it made her want to shake him until he saw sense.

"Don't be foolish; you aren't at all like your father, and you have to know that."

He tucked his fear away with an attempt at a wry smile. It looked a lot like a grimace. "Well, in fairness, Hetta, you haven't met him."

"I don't need to." But she could see his point, even if she disagreed with the comparison. She sagged down onto the seat Wyn's brother had so recently occupied. "Is there some other way to depose your father, then, without killing him? Because it seems like that might solve a lot of this."

Wyn sank down beside her with a sigh. "The bond between faeland and ruler is permanent, once formed, so far as I know."

It was both reassuring and not. Hetta reached for Stariel, feeling the pulsing energy of the land as if it were her own heartbeat.

He put an arm round her, and she leaned her head on his shoulder. "I don't know what to do. My not-so-brilliant plan to leave if this all got too dangerous for Stariel has collapsed in on itself, and so I am left with no plan at all."

"Well," she pointed out, "we have a whole twenty-four hours to think about it." She paused. "I said I wouldn't do anything without your agreement, and I meant it. We'll find some other way."

His arms tightened around her. "Thank you. That is…more reassuring than you know." She felt him sigh again. "I wish I could bring something other than trouble to Stariel. As a prince, I have only brought you danger. And I seem to have failed to do you any good at all in my role as steward. All I seem to be able to do is rack up obligations. And scandalise bank managers."

Hetta frowned. "Well, it's not as if the bank was ever very convinced by my lording, anyway, so I think it's a bit much to take the responsibility for that entirely on your own shoulders. It also doesn't change the fact that this estate would fall apart without you—would have fallen apart long since!" Finances would just have to wait, though that creeping sense of guilt stole over her again. Shouldn't a good lord prioritise the estate's interests over individuals? Her soul rebelled, refusing to compromise. Why couldn't she have *both*?

He paused. "Regardless, it seems we have twenty-four hours of breathing space in which no one is trying to kill me. I would like to use some of that time to resign my position." Hetta immediately un-burrowed herself so she could glare at him properly. He held out a placating hand. "Hear me out, please. If I am not your steward, then the bank will probably give you a loan."

"That is honestly the least of my concerns right now. We can worry about the bank later, after we've figured out this *life or death* situation."

He continued, relentless. "Now that your family and the staff here know what I am, the news will spread. Very soon the district will know, and soon after that, the entire North, possibly the entire country. If that comes to pass, you won't get the treatment you should get. *Especially* if I am still employed here." He paused. "And...if somehow, miraculously, I escape from this bloody oath, I would have us be other than liege lord and supplicant," he said, echoing her own words back to her.

"I would still put you to work, you know."

He smiled. "I know. But I do not like loose ends, and someone warned Mr Thompson of my identity. I would like to know who, and why. Rakken claims it wasn't him." He paused. "And I would like to assure myself that he truly *is* recovering."

The sound of the gun going off, the sudden red flower blossoming from his wing. "If you—"

"I promise to do my utmost to avoid being shot again. Mrs Thompson caught me off-guard last time," he said persuasively.

She narrowed her eyes, though she could already feel herself being talked into this madness. "And what about our resident princess?"

Wyn spread his hands, the words dragging reluctantly from him. "You can try if you will to discover what she considers a fair price for me."

Hetta appreciated that he trusted her to bargain on his behalf, even if her interactions with Princess Sunnika so far hadn't made her optimistic about getting a straight answer. "Is she going to be offended if I don't sit by her side and babysit her?" Hetta had no intention of leaving Princess Sunnika unsupervised, but it wasn't as if she had nothing else to do, and Stariel could supervise perfectly well from afar. Maybe she should enlist Marius's help in that; so far he'd been much better at seeing through fae motives than she had.

Wyn looked out towards the lake, and something seemed to harden in him. "I think it may be wise to remind Faerie that mortal affairs do not necessarily revolve around it."

She made one last attempt at protest. "I still think this is a terrible idea and that we could find better uses for our day of grace." Prince Rakken's plan loomed over them, filling all the spaces between words.

His eyes were very dark. "I just…let me do this one thing for the good of Stariel, my love." He set the word down with the fragile, testing weight of a snowflake, and a taffy-soft emotion swelled in her in answer.

"Oh, very well then, you impossible man," she grumbled. "Go and martyr yourself in the name of finances."

STEWARD OF STARIEL

W YN SET DOWN outside Mr Thompson's home the next day with only a few awkward steps to take his momentum, boots scuffing the pavement. At least he hadn't ended up in a tumble of wings this time. He was getting better at landings, flexing long disused skills.

The street of terraced houses was deserted, most of its occupants already elsewhere on the grey, cold morning. *Am I being foolish, spending my day of grace so?* he wondered. But he had no other brilliant ideas, and this felt like something he needed to do, a small thing that was still within his power to control.

It had been easy enough to acquire Mr Thompson's address from the bank, though the experience of wandering its austere hallways winged and shirtless, unnoticed by primly dressed secretaries and bankers, wasn't one he'd soon forget. Human sensibilities had apparently rubbed off on him, for he'd felt self-conscious even though no one could see him through his glamour.

A set of steps led straight from the street to Mr Thompson's front door, the iron guardrails to either side distorting his leysight. He folded his wings back and changed, pulling on the shirt he'd brought with him—an ordinary one; he hadn't wanted to ruin Hetta's gift with exertion. But before he could move from the pavement, the door opened. In its shadowed frame stood Mrs Thompson, glaring belligerently down at him, a pistol in one hand.

Wyn quickly held up his hands in supplication. "Please don't shoot me again." Even though he currently didn't *have* wings, the recent memory of the bullet scraping against bone spiked through that phantom location.

"You!" The pistol didn't waver. "I know what you are!"

"Yes, yes, I know. I am fae," Wyn said, keeping very, very still.

This took some of the wind out of her sails, though the gun didn't drop.

Her eyes narrowed. "What do you want?"

"I wanted to reassure myself that your husband was recovering from the poison."

"So you can finish him off! I warn you, this is loaded." She brandished the pistol in a worrying way; they were unreliable things, from what Wyn knew of them.

"Mrs Thompson, I have no doubt of that after our last interaction, but I do not wish any harm to you or your husband. I was not responsible for the attack, but I am in part to blame for his injury. The creatures that bit him were intended for me; he was merely in the wrong place at the wrong time. May I come in? I would like to talk to you both."

"You think I'm going to let you in the house?" But she lowered the pistol slightly. Progress.

He risked a smile and spread his arms, slowly so as not to startle her. "Well, as only you can see me, it may look a little odd if we continue to converse on your doorstep."

Her eyes narrowed. "What have you done with your wings?"

"I'm a shapeshifter, a true one." He'd been right; she'd never met a greater fae. "May I come in? I promise to abide by guestright." A house wasn't a faeland, and her invitation would have no effect on his ability to enter, but manners were still important.

"Who is it, Mabel?" came the bank manager's voice from the townhouse's interior.

Mrs Thompson hesitated, and Wyn saw her suddenly become aware of the quiet street, of the fact that her neighbours would hear her extended conversation with no one.

He waited, hands still spread wide. A postboy on a bicycle turned into the street and barrelled past Wyn without pause, his tyres juddering over the cobblestones.

"It's Mr Tempest," she said eventually. "He says he means no harm. He wants to come in."

"Tell him to come in then."

Wyn didn't move. Mrs Thompson fixed him with a long, slow look. "If you do anything I don't like, I'll put another bullet in you without hesitation."

He nodded carefully. "I would expect no less."

She shook her head and yanked the door open, backing away from it while still holding the gun. At least it wasn't pointed at him anymore, though her stance made it clear this remained an option.

Pretending not to be acutely aware of the weapon's location, he made his way into the house. Mrs Thompson warily led him through to the sitting room, where Mr Thompson sat at a writing desk in the corner, leg propped up on a footstool. The bank manager was paler than he should be, with deep circles under his eyes, but he was upright and appeared to be in possession of his usual faculties.

Relief flooded Wyn, heady as malt whiskey. Marius's report from the bank had suggested the antidote had probably done its job, but Wyn had needed to see it for himself to make sure.

"Forgive me for not getting up," Mr Thompson said with a vague gesture at the thickness of bandages distorting his trouser-leg. His gaze flickered over Wyn, looking for signs of injury. "You don't appear any the worse for wear."

"I heal very fast," he apologised. "Though the bullet hurt considerably." He raised an eyebrow at Mrs Thompson, who put the pistol down on a sideboard, still within arm's reach, and scowled at him as if sheer ill-wishing could cause him to vaporise.

"Will you sit down?" Mr Thompson said when it became apparent his wife wasn't going to do the honours.

Wyn sat carefully on the pink-and-tan-striped sofa. "I want to apologise for the injuries you suffered." He repeated what he'd said to Mrs Thompson.

The bank manager's expression was difficult to read, but he seemed puzzled rather than alarmed. Mrs Thompson remained stony-faced.

"So you admit it then—that you're not human?" Mr Thompson asked at the end of the explanation.

It was becoming easier to say it aloud, with repetition. "I am fae." Maybe soon he would be able to drop it casually in conversation without first pausing to prepare himself for the reaction it might cause. "I'm curious to know what gave me away." Had it been Aroset's doing? It seemed both too subtle and too human a gambit for her, since neither of the Thompsons bore any signs of compulsion.

"The former steward of Stariel wrote to me," Mr Thompson said. "He was bitter at the loss of his job and claimed you'd framed him."

"That is untrue." And also made even less sense than any of Wyn's other theories; the former steward, Mr Fisk, hadn't known Wyn was fae. Or at least, so he'd thought. Could he have misjudged? Wyn's mind raced. Mr Fisk had run after it was discovered he'd been skimming from the estate's accounts. "I cannot even claim to be responsible for his fraud being discovered." He wished he *had* been responsible; it stung that Mr Fisk had been quietly sabotaging Stariel's accounts for so long without Wyn noticing what was going on. But Mr Fisk had always jealously guarded his books.

Mr Thompson added, "He claimed you had unnatural powers to make people believe what you wanted them to, and that's why he ran."

Wyn's threads of speculation multiplied. Setting aside just how Stariel's former steward knew Wyn was fae, how did he know he was capable of compulsive magic? Only greater fae could compel. Could Mr Fisk somehow have found out about Wyn's compulsion on Marius's ex-lover? Or the binding he'd placed on Gwendelfear, to keep her from speaking his true name while she'd been imprisoned at Stariel House? But Wyn was nearly certain Mr Fisk hadn't been aware of either of those when he'd fled. Had one or other of them contacted Mr Fisk after he'd left, as revenge on Wyn?

If it had been Gwendelfear, she would scarcely act without her princess's knowledge. Sudden suspicion spiked in him. There had been that moment in the library with Sunnika, a moment of personal rather than political anger at Wyn's attachment to Stariel. If his mortal reputation was blackened such that he had to leave Stariel, then Hetta would have no reason to negotiate with ThousandSpire for the release of his oath. Which would leave ThousandSpire still indebted to DuskRose. It would be a neat way for the princess to seem to keep her own hands clean, a tactic prized by the fae courts.

Mr Thompson was eying him guardedly. "Well?"

Ah, yes. He still needed to answer the actual question being posed him. The problem, of course, was that Wyn *did* have powers of persuasion, even if he'd never used them on Mr Fisk. Wyn somehow didn't think the Thompsons would find that answer reassuring.

"I have no unnatural powers of persuasion," he said, the sharp technicality of that truth catching on his teeth. Compulsion wasn't unnatural, for greater fae. "I like to think I'm a reasonably persuasive person, but if I could make people believe anything I wished, then my recent injuries seem curiously masochistic." Wyn smiled at Mrs Thompson, who did not smile back. Her husband, however, nodded and relaxed fractionally, convinced by this argument. Guilt twisted in Wyn's chest. *Do not trust the fae*, he wanted to say. *For we will deceive you with truths.*

"How many of you are there?" Mrs Thompson demanded abruptly.

Wyn had to resist giving a very fae answer to that; he knew what she meant. "Have you been seeing lowfae?" he guessed. "Little creatures, mostly." Most lowfae had basic don't-see-me glamour, but Mrs Thompson had pierced the glamour of a royalfae with ease; lowfae should prove no difficulty to her.

Mrs Thompson rolled her lips around. "There have been more of them, of late." And she was worried about it—which would have made the Thompsons ripe for suspicion against anything fae, not knowing the reason for the change. The Iron Law had never technically applied to lowfae, but they didn't thrive cut off from the ambient magic of Faerie, so they had largely retreated with the lesser and greater fae.

Wyn hesitated, but this was something the Mortal Realm would need to adjust to, sooner or later. It might as well begin here. "There will be more. The fae have been kept from this realm for a long time, but that is no longer so. This is a time of change." Rakken's words came back to him, uneasily. He saw that same uneasiness in the Thompsons and couldn't blame them for it, but he set it aside, along with the problem of exactly who was responsible for Mr Fisk's accusations. "In any case, my reason for coming here—other than to check on your health—was to inform you that I am resigning my position as steward of Stariel. Therefore, there will be no reason to fear granting Stariel a loan because of my influence there." The words tasted acid, but he spoke them calmly enough. "I can assure you that the figures I presented you with were solid, but you are welcome to re-examine them, of course. Lord Valstar is perfectly numerate and likely to become more so with experience. I do not agree with the bank's prejudices against females, but Lord Valstar has many male relatives who may aid her in the interim if it remains necessary. I have drafted a notice for my replacement, but I'm not sure how long it will take to bear fruit."

There was a long pause in which Mr Thompson considered him, again with a faintly puzzled expression. Eventually he shook his head and said, "I'm sorry to hear that," surprising his wife nearly as much as Wyn. "As fae or no, you seem to have a good head for figures." He glanced towards his desk. Perched on the glossy black surface were Stariel's missing accounts books. "The business case you and Lord Valstar put together is solid, as you say."

Wyn had never been quite so touched by a compliment, but Mr Thompson wasn't done. "I'm persuaded to make a case for the bank to grant you an initial loan, when I am well enough to return to work. Which will be soon, I think," he said, reflecting on his propped-up leg. "As I have not fallen asleep so far today."

Mrs Thompson plopped down onto the ottoman. "He's a *fairy*!" she reminded her husband.

The bank manager shrugged. "That isn't the bank's concern so long as he isn't ensorcelling people. I'm merely concerned that he is a suitable steward for the estate's finances." He frowned at Wyn. "The bank will need to be assured that the predicted cashflow from the rents of the Dower House can indeed be achieved on the timeline you put forward before the greater part of the loan will be granted."

Wyn laughed. He couldn't help it. The world had tilted on its axis again, shifting a burden with such suddenness that it left him giddy. It had been so long since he'd felt like he'd done anything right, since he'd felt like he'd made matters better rather than worse. It felt like the first ray of dawn after the longest night.

"That is…thank you," he said when he found his voice again.

Mr Thompson flicked his thanks away. "I hope you will reconsider your resignation."

"Ah, there are other considerations, but may I take the accounts books back?"

Wyn left the bank manager's house feeling oddly anti-climactic. He hefted the accounts books under his arm, considered the long road stretching to either side, and shrouded himself in glamour. Removing his shirt and coat whilst holding the books required a certain amount of juggling, but he managed not to drop them.

He'd changed back and forth between mortal and fae form so much recently that the contrast was, if not less jarring, more familiar. All the iron of the street did strange things to his fae senses, warping the leylines around the streetlamps and guard railings. He wrapped the books carefully in his shirt and coat before placing them in his satchel and affixing it in place. It didn't hang as neatly as he would have preferred, and he thought again of the specially designed harnesses of the fae.

Frigid air worried under his feathers as he rose, nips of snow-flake-promises. Flying through sleet for the return journey seemed a fitting accompaniment for his mood, though he hoped it would hold off for the accounts books' sake if nothing else. Would Hetta's exasperation be softened if he turned up dripping and woebegone on her doorstep? The small victory of the loan would probably do the trick, regardless. That thought buoyed him up briefly, but the attempt to distract himself didn't survive long in the cold clarity of the snowbound sky, the world spread small below him.

What was he going to do about Rakken's plan? He couldn't drag Hetta into murder. Or a coup, for that matter. *And myself? Can I drag myself into it, if need be?* He had run for ten years and across realms to escape bloody familial betrayal, and it hadn't been long or far enough. Tonight, Rakken would return for an answer to the unanswerable. *You are weak, Hallowyn.* His father's words taunted him, ironic given the subject under contemplation. What did weakness *mean*, here?

It happened between heartbeats, a psychic shock so powerful it jerked his wings out of rhythm. One second he was arrowing smoothly through the clouds; the next, he was falling. Gravity wrenched at him, his stomach dropping before he righted himself. Every hair stood on end.

Someone was invoking his name. Someone he loved, invoking his name in fear.

He hadn't built a portal in nearly a decade, and only the greatest of mages would attempt to build one aloft. He knew this, but still the magic rose up in a wave, shivering with urgency. No. Ripping himself apart through reckless impatience would benefit no one. Folding his wings, he plummeted, willing gravity to strengthen, not flaring out his wings until the last possible second. He hit the hard earth with a crunch, the impact juddering his bones as he stumbled through a half-dozen steps, falling to his knees as the momentum dispersed.

He didn't take the time to stand before thrusting his hands out and tearing at the fabric of the mortal plane. Words he hadn't spoken in years streamed out of him, clumsy on his tongue as he focussed on the resonance his name had invoked.

I am Hallowyn Tempestren.

He poured magic and will into the spell, but it was like trying to make the ocean boil, a vacuum absorbing power without end. His only reward was the lightning smell of ozone, a hint of metals and dust. The signature hit him like a struck gong, fear ringing through all the dark places in his soul. He knew it as he knew the span of his wings—or perhaps even better than that, given how little time he'd spent in his fae form in recent years.

Even if he hadn't, there was only one place that was so tightly and specifically warded against translocation. He rose to his feet, staring at the space in the air that remained relentlessly unmagical, showing only the half-frozen field he stood in, strewn with the sad remnants of swedes.

He could be mistaken. Maybe it hadn't been Hetta summoning him. Maybe the summons hadn't come from where he'd thought. And maybe bluebirds would begin nesting amid tonight's snowstorm.

He launched skywards, driven by new urgency; he had to get back to Stariel. What had happened? She was supposed to be *safe* at Stariel. Sunnika had sworn guestright; Rakken had promised them a day of truce. Straining wingbone and muscle to their limits, drawing on air magic without concern for the cost, it seemed to take both no and too much time to reach the estate.

The instant he crossed the border, he felt the *wrongness*, Stariel's alarm soup-thick. His senses stretched to breaking point but couldn't locate Hetta, even as he closed on Stariel House. Wings burning, he flew straight to his own room, over the balcony and in without pause, and slammed into the wall opposite, taking the impact on his palms. He smelt the intrusion before he turned: copper and old-fashioned roses caught in a storm.

"Mrow?" Plumpuff stared up at him from the box he'd set up for her and her kittens beside his bed.

Aroset's signature was strong enough to choke on, and his gaze fixed on a brilliant spot of crimson next to the cat. In moments he had it in his hand, a crisp blood-red note. Plumpuff grumbled at him as he tore it open.

There were only two lines, in his sister's tight copperplate. He could almost hear her crowing as he read.

Come and get her, little Hollow. Did you like the kittens?

GODPARENT'S GIFT

AROSET, NOT RAKKEN, not coincidence, had been responsible for the half-fae kittens. Wyn put a hand on the cat's head and *reached*. Plumpuff was only an animal, and he went through her mental shields as easily as tissue paper. She made an uncertain grumbling noise, but he ignored it as he searched for the threads of compulsion. There were none. Or—wait, the barest hint of copper, so subtle it was hardly there at all. Subtler than he would've given Aroset credit for. So subtle he'd missed it. It was inactive now, but he was sure it had once been a passive listening spell. That was why it hadn't thrown up any of his alarms; it had no compulsive or aggressive capabilities. But information was power. What had Aroset managed to learn, through Plumpuff's ears or through those of the housefae Wyn had let back into the house because of her kittens?

Wyn plucked the copper thread out of Plumpuff. The cat blinked suspiciously at him before settling back to wash her kittens. He was a weak-hearted fool, and Aroset had known and used it against him. How could he have been so foolish as to assume his eldest sister would accede meekly to Rakken when her first plan fell through?

He stood, gripping Aroset's card so tightly it crumpled in his fist, but it didn't relieve the awful pressure building in him. Aroset had Hetta. *Aroset had Hetta.* Which meant...*his father had Hetta.* Lightning shivered under his skin. He had to get her back. He would burn the *world* down if he had to.

Stariel hit him with a wordless demand for information. His knees buckled, and he stumbled against the wall. Clear skies above, how did Hetta bear being bound so closely to the faeland? The insides of his skull reverberated with the implied threat as Stariel bore down, its need such that Wyn could nearly discern words: Tell it where Hetta was *or else.*

He snarled and pushed an image of ThousandSpire at it. <She's there. They've taken her. I'm going to get her back.>

Stariel, to his astonishment, answered him with an image of the Maelstrom overlain with a swinging blood-red pendant.

He hadn't realised it had understood any of his encounter with his godparent. <Yes. I am going there.> Lamorkin had said their spell would take him to the Maelstrom. The Maelstrom lay on the doorstep of the capital city, where he was certain he'd find Hetta. He hoped, desperately, that 'to' meant the spell would deposit him *beside* rather than *in* the storm, or at least to its edges and not its centre. He could probably escape the edges of the Maelstrom. Probably.

The faeland paused, and Wyn braced himself. Stariel's answer came as a soundless pulse of force, a swell of fierce resolution, and then nothing but the lingering taste of pine on the back of his tongue. He blinked. On the one hand, it wasn't the attack he'd feared, but on the other...what had Stariel done?

He retrieved the lockbox where he'd stored Lamorkin's amulet and threw back the lid. The magical object that stared up at him was not the same one he'd deposited. What had been a teardrop of red stone when Lamorkin had given it to him was now deep blue, glittering oddly. It reminded him strongly of star indigo, a rare mineral found only within Stariel, and its signature too was an odd mingling of his godparent's magic and the faeland's.

"What are you up to, Stariel?" he asked it softly. There was no response. "If you have broken this…" But he could not think of an adequate threat. He hung the altered amulet around his neck, but before he could stand, the door burst open and Marius flung himself into the room.

"Wyn! You're all right! I thought…" He came to a screeching halt at the sight of Wyn's fae form. His eyes widened, darting from feather to feather.

"Thought what?" Wyn said, rising in one movement, icy foreboding crystallising at the point of every quill. "Where's Hetta?"

Marius re-focused with a sharp breath, worry making his face gaunt. "Gone. There was… Alex and Hetta, they went riding, but Jack just found Alex, and she can't remember what happened except that they went outside the boundaries. I thought something must have happened to you, that Gwendelfear had told Alexandra something through that damned locket, but if you're here—"

Marius's eyes were wild, and he rubbed his temples with the heel of his hand. Marius's land-sense was weak, but Wyn wasn't even connected to Stariel and *his* head was throbbing with the faeland's anxiety. It would be worse for the Valstars.

Wyn stared down at the crumpled note in his fist. Aroset had tried to use compulsion on Marius and failed. What if she'd succeeded on another Valstar? That damned locket indeed. How easy it would have been for Aroset to subvert a spell set by a lesser fae, to lure Alexandra out to meet her with some plea sent in Gwendelfear's name. What falsehood had she made Alexandra tell, to make Hetta leave the safety of Stariel? Oh. *I thought something must have happened to you,* Marius had said. If Hetta had thought he was in danger… Oh, he *was* a fool.

"Is Alexandra all right?"

"She's pretty shaken, but she's not hurt except for Stariel giving us all headaches. I've never felt it like this before. It won't—was it compulsion?"

"Maybe. Probably." Wyn thought of Hetta's younger sister, that bright-eyed innocence coming face to face with Aroset's sadism, and his chest constricted. Forgetfulness was relatively easy to induce, but the fact that Alexandra *knew* she'd forgotten something meant it had been done hastily, with brute force rather than skill. If Aroset had damaged Alexandra…

"What's going on, Wyn?"

Wyn closed his eyes and took a deep breath before opening them again, the ice forming a cage around the lightning shivering in his veins.

"Aroset has taken Hetta. I am going to get her back. Watch Alexandra carefully." He turned towards the window, but Marius grabbed hold of his arm, stopping him.

"What are you doing?"

There was no time—and if Wyn were to face the Maelstrom, he couldn't afford softness. He pushed past the other man, breaking out of his grip without effort.

"Wyn!"

"I am sorry, Marius, but I need to go."

And he wrapped a glamour around himself, obscuring his form, and flung himself from the balcony. Behind him, Marius swore a blue streak, but Wyn didn't look back as he flew towards the mountains.

Resonance made all types of translocation easier, and the Indigoes were the closest match for the Spires within a reasonable distance. In theory Lamorkin's translocation spell should be powerful enough to work regardless, but the amulet would give him a single chance to breach the wards of ThousandSpire, and he couldn't afford to waste it. *Please let Lamorkin not have thought it a good idea to make the translocation take me directly into the Maelstrom's heart. Please let me be lucky, this once.*

The amulet burned cold against his throat as he flew, absorbing heat without ever warming. It fit with the winter landscape, the snow drifts deep this high in the mountains. Arctic cross-winds buffeted him, and storm magic crackled over his feathers.

He landed in a snowdrift above the tree line with a soft, graceless thump. Pulling himself out, he shook the snow from his wings.

It had been a long, long time since he'd thought deeply of his homeland, but he thought of it now, closing his eyes and letting the mountains' cold seep into him. Aerest, the capital, would be cold and dry in this season, bitter winds screaming through a thousand narrow openings and rattling the bridges. The sun was setting here, the Indigoes already in deep shadow, but in ThousandSpire the city would be set afire with the reflected light from the many gemstones embedded in its buildings.

He gripped the pendant tightly and drew in the power of the storm, feeding the resonance into Lamorkin's spell.

"Take me to the Maelstrom," he told it. Translocation magic sprang from the stone, creating a brief, temporary connection between here and there, opening up around him and sucking him through.

He emerged falling through churning sky. Gravity and wind wrestled to claim him, yanking him down and sideways and over. Violent magic swamped him, blurring his leysight to a blinding tangle till he had to close his eyes against it.

His hope of avoiding the Maelstrom's touch had been futile. He wasn't just close to the Maelstrom; he was *in* it. How far in? Probably he could escape from its edges. Probably. He *had* to escape; he hadn't come this far to fail, not now. Scrabbling desperately for his air magic, he tried to stabilise his fall, but the winds here were not tame things to be so commanded. They punched through his magic as if it were nothing, shredding and tangling what was left. He tumbled, helpless as a dandelion seed, losing all sense of orientation as he fought to find *up*, to beat his wings against the relentless *down*. His vision flashed white even through his closed lids: lightning.

He had to get out, now, but as his wings buckled, he knew, deep down, that it was already too late. Feathers ripped and tore free, and his gut clenched in sheer animal terror as the wind whipped his wing around to an angle it was not meant for.

For one horrible, endless moment, he bent. And then, with a snap of bone, he broke.

THE MAELSTROM

HETTA PACED THE circular cell, furiously. The alternative was to pace fearfully, and she'd rather not encourage that emotion just now, stuck in a cell atop a mind-bendingly high tower. The cell's shell-pink rock floor and ceiling were held apart by narrow, evenly spaced white bars that went all the way round. They were disturbingly tooth-like, and the wind cut straight through them. Was this the fae version of a dark dungeon, or a special privilege reserved just for her? She wrapped her arms around her chest, wishing she hadn't lost her hat. Her ears ached with cold.

The Court of Ten Thousand Spires. The land was alive, but she felt no connection to it. Was this how non-Valstars felt in Stariel? Its alienness thrummed up through the rock, a vast, unsettling presence. She reflexively reached for Stariel for reassurance, but there was only a faint, worried echo along the bond.

Her tower lay on the outskirts of a city big enough to rival Greymark, the largest city in the North. And it was only one piece of what felt, from the vastness of ThousandSpire's presence, like an entire country. *It's so much bigger than Stariel,* she thought, feeling very small as she looked out on the forest of rocky towers. *And I'm probably the only human in the whole of Faerie.* She hadn't quite grasped the scale of what she was grappling with before. Prince Rakken was right—this went beyond just Stariel, beyond just her and Wyn. She hugged herself tighter.

The titular Ten Thousand Spires that made up the city varied in height and girth. Had anyone counted them or was the name merely poetic exaggeration? Buildings bristled atop some of them, and others had doorways in their sides. The whole was criss-crossed with alarmingly improbable bridges spun out of threads so fine they looked like toffee turned to stone. It was all very well for creatures with wings, but the sight gave her a horrible sense of vertigo.

Inevitably, her gaze slid to the *other* side of her tower, and her stomach lurched. There, the rocky terrain fell away steeply to a vast plain with a bristling storm whirling in its midst, deep purple and flashing with non-stop lightning. It was much too close for comfort. This had to be the Maelstrom Wyn had spoken of; it definitely deserved a capital letter. The horrifying vortex spun, ever-moving and yet strangely anchored in place. *It hasn't gotten closer in the last five minutes*, she reassured herself. *It must keep its distance from the city.* They wouldn't have put her here just to be eaten by an oversized storm, surely?

She swallowed and turned away from the Maelstrom. She needed to focus on getting out of this cell. How fortunate that anger always seemed to bolster her pyromancy, for without Stariel to draw on she would need everything she could muster.

Hetta glared out through the bars, stoking her anger. How dare Wyn's sister have played that trick, luring her out of Stariel through Alexandra? She'd taken Alexandra with her out on the estate, and they'd been far from the house when Alexandra had received an urgent message from Gwendelfear. Except it hadn't been from Gwendelfear, clearly. As soon as she got home, Hetta was destroying that dashed locket; if only she'd taken it off Alexandra in the first place! Was Alexandra all right? The last thing she remembered between there and waking here cold on the cell floor was a woman with blood-red wings and the sudden heart-sinking realisation that she'd stupidly walked straight into a trap. Then everything had gone dark. But the fae woman—Aroset, it had to have been Aroset—had seemed entirely focused on Hetta, and if Alexandra wasn't here in the cell with her, hopefully that meant she was safe back home?

Hetta tried not to think of Wyn. He was almost definitely fine, probably still immersed in banking mundanities. After all, Aroset wouldn't have needed to capture Hetta if she'd already had Wyn, would she? But that wasn't a helpful line of thought, to know that she was in all probability being used as bait to lead Wyn to his death. Or to use against Stariel, somehow. Maybe the price of her release would be the terms Prince Rakken had laid out earlier, giving Stariel over as a vassal state.

Anger threatened to tip over into fear, and she hurriedly built it up again. She refused to let the Court of Ten Thousand Spires intimidate her. She took off her gloves, tucking them into her coat pocket. Her chilled fingers brushed the silvery feather she'd been keeping there, and she closed her eyes for a moment, taking a deep, shuddering breath to steady herself. She *would* find a way out of here.

Opening her eyes, she removed her hand from her pocket and let heat pool just under the skin of her palms as she turned purposefully towards the locked door. It was made of the same white bars as the walls, though these ran the full length of it. She ran her fingers down one to try to work out what it was made of. The texture was more like ceramic than stone, but she didn't notice much more than that because the bar zapped her.

She jerked back, and her fireball was more instinctive outrage than escape attempt, but it hit the slanting bars and fizzled out. As it snuffed out, the threads of a spell lit up. Sight and excellent visual memory notwithstanding, even she needed more than a split-second to properly examine something. She conjured another fireball and flung it at the bars, this time deliberately trying to take a mental snapshot of the fae spell as it illuminated.

The threads were peculiar, in the same way that Wyn's house spells had been. *Well, it's not as if it's surprising that these are fae spells.* She took a breath and concentrated on the threads of the spell. If she stood on Stariel soil, she could've leaned on the faeland for knowledge and understood them, but here she was on her own, and this fell outside everything she knew of human magery. Still, they seemed familiar somehow. They reminded her of the air magic Wyn had used to sweep the lug-imp corpses into a heap. *Air magic*, she thought with a blink. Air magic, defusing fire. Fire needed oxygen to burn. What if the spell were somehow designed to take that away?

Could she overwhelm the spell, somehow? She had a *lot* of anger. She raised both her palms and let it boil out of her. Fire hit the bars with a disheartening sizzle. The temperature warmed a little, but the icy winds carried most of the heat away. She poured magic at the bars until she wobbled and had to cut off the flame, panting. The bars didn't look even slightly singed. Her heart sank. She put a hand in her pocket, wrapping it around the silvery feather again for comfort.

Before she could decide her next move, footsteps sounded below. Hetta peered as far as she could through the bars of the door, careful not to touch them. The staircase wound around the outside of the rocky spire, and there was no handrail. Her stomach gave a worrying tilt of vertigo, and she closed her eyes briefly. She wasn't afraid of heights, but still!

When she opened her eyes, she caught a flash of pale hair, and her heart lifted in sudden hope, only to immediately plummet. It wasn't Wyn, though it was, without a doubt, another one of his brothers. There had been a resemblance between Wyn and Prince

Rakken's features, but it was even stronger with this man—this fae. His white-gold hair hung longer than Wyn's, obscuring half his face, but the main difference was his wings, black as a moonless night. His horns were the same shade.

He drew closer, and Hetta saw that his eyes were pale gold to Wyn's deep russet, his features an otherwise eerily similar reflection of Wyn's. He didn't speak as he drew up to the door, tilting his head curiously.

"You must be either Prince Irokoi or Torquil," Hetta said, picking through the names and genders of all of Wyn's siblings when it became clear he wasn't going to say anything.

The stranger stared at her for a long moment. Had he heard her? She was about to repeat herself when he spoke.

"Aroset calls me Irk. It's not very nice of her, is it? If one must be shortened, I much prefer the fish-end."

"Er...I'm sorry?"

"The fish-end," he said earnestly, the pale gold of his eyes bright with anticipation, which slowly faded at her lack of comprehension. "You don't understand me," he said heavily. "You're the wrong one. The other one—they would know."

"The other one," Hetta repeated faintly.

But the stranger was shaking his head. "Stupid, stupid, Irokoi. They do not even look alike! Wrong person; wrong *time*!"

He appeared to be conducting an argument entirely with himself, and Hetta took a cautious step back from the bars. Wyn hadn't told her one of his brothers was mad.

Her movement broke him out of his self-recriminations, and he looked up sharply, his hair falling away from his face.

Hetta gasped. A smooth white scar ran from his temple to mid-cheek, directly through his right eye. That eye wasn't the pale gold of its partner but a shattered arctic blue, beautiful and, she realised after a second, blind.

Blind or not, his gaze was disconcertingly penetrating. "Ah, you have observed Aroset's gift." He waved unnecessarily at his mis-matched eyes. "Maimed creatures are upsetting to look upon, are they not?"

"Ah—" she began uncertainly, but he shrugged.

"I *am* Prince Irokoi," he said with a slight bow. "I unnerve you. I am sorry." He brushed his hair back across his face, covering the scar. "Is that better?"

"I…it's fine," she said. "I was just startled. But you don't have to hide it. I don't mind."

Another slightly too-long pause. "You *do* mind," he said. "But I appreciate the lie." He abruptly put his wings back against the tower wall and slid down to ground level. The stairwell wasn't wide, and his chosen seat meant his legs dangled over the edge.

She swallowed. It was a long way to the ground. *Aroset's gift?* Her stomach twisted again in sudden horror as she realised what he meant.

"I thought I might be less hideous to mortal eyes," Prince Irokoi said conversationally, gazing out over the vista. He shot her a sly look. "Do you feel sorry for me yet?"

"A little," she said. "Though not because you're hideous. You're very handsome, as I'm sure you must be aware." Flattery couldn't hurt, though it was true enough. "It's just—did you say your *sister* did that to you?"

"You think I'm handsome!" He beamed at her, but then his face fell. "Is it because I remind you of Hallowyn? We always did look alike, although more so before Aroset filleted me like a fish. Ah! Fish! A recurring theme tonight." He laughed, silvery and delighted, but stopped as he read her expression. "You don't think it's funny."

Hetta didn't think it was at all funny that his sister had appar-ently blinded him, but she didn't know if saying so would offend him. "Can you help me get out of this cage?" she asked him instead. Hadn't Prince Rakken said his other siblings—bar Princess Aroset—also wanted their father gone? Maybe that meant this one would be on her side.

He huffed, wings shifting against the stone. The ink-black feathers merged softly into the shadows. "You *do* realise that you're asking a prince of the court that's imprisoned you for help? Did I forget to say that part when I introduced myself? Irokoi *Tempestren*, eldest prince of Ten Thousand Spires."

"It seems like that would make you a person well placed to offer me help."

"I bear you no ill-will, Lord Valstar, but why would I cross my father for you?" Prince Irokoi rustled his feathers uneasily. "Or Aroset. What could you offer that I would value more than my remaining eye?"

It sickened her, that he needed to fear such a thing from his own sister. Gods, how had Wyn made it out of this court alive and intact? Prince Rakken hadn't prepared her for this—he'd been calculating and self-interested, yes, but not sadistic.

"Is Prince Rakken here?" she asked. He would have to be worried about Hetta telling his father about his plans; maybe that meant she could convince him to help her escape.

"You would prefer a saner sibling to speak with?" Prince Irokoi shook his head. "Fair enough, but I'm not sure exactly where he is." He brightened. "Rakken Tempestren! Rakken! Rakken! That ought to get his attention, though he does hate being teased. But he likes you. Perhaps he will be brave enough to risk father's wrath for you." He sighed. "It doesn't sit well to be shown up by one's younger siblings for bravery, but there you have it."

Lightning-quick mood swings and refusal to help her aside, Hetta couldn't help liking Prince Irokoi. There was something very open—very *human*—about him, she realised with a start. Of all the fae she'd met, he was the only one who'd made no effort to hide his feelings.

"Where am I, exactly?" If he wouldn't help her, maybe he would answer her questions.

"Why, in the tower with the best view of the Maelstrom," Prince Irokoi said, waving at the awful vortex in the distance. "As far as intimidation tactics go, it's a crude but effective one."

"Wyn told me people sometimes go in there," Hetta said, looking at the storm doubtfully. It looked like a good way to die a swift and violent death.

"Yes, little Hallowyn! The winds are very fierce inside, and the lightning is also quite troublesome. I hope he's all right. He has a kind heart. I was glad when he found shelter at Stariel, despite the blood and sorrow there."

Hetta blinked at him, nonplussed. She had a feeling that asking for clarification wouldn't help. Prince Irokoi pulled his long legs away from the stair-edge to sit cross-legged and propped his head up on one hand, completely mesmerised by the Maelstrom to all outward appearances. The wind had whipped his hair away from his face again, revealing the mismatched eyes. It was less shocking now Hetta was prepared for the sight, though the scar was still a dramatic pale slash against his brown skin.

He didn't turn his head but said conversationally, "It mainly affects my depth perception. Which is, obviously, a thing that is particularly useful when flying. Hmmm." He pursed his lips. "He came in closer than I'd hoped."

Hetta followed his gaze and clutched the bars in horror. The zap knocked her back a step, but she barely noticed. Against the dark roil of the Maelstrom, a pale winged shape was visible: Wyn. He fought the winds for long, agonising moments, before he crumpled and dropped like a stone. Something was horribly wrong with his wings.

Fire roared out of her, snuffing out at the cage's boundaries. She clenched her fists in helpless terror. "Help him!"

"Hmmm, yes," said Prince Irokoi. "Probably a good idea." He

made a strange clutching gesture and drew back his arm as if the air had real resistance in his grasp. Wyn's fall abruptly ceased, and Irokoi began to make a hand-over-hand motion on the empty air, drawing Wyn towards him as if he was at the other end of a long, invisible rope.

Hetta's heart hammered in her throat as Wyn drew closer. She knew immediately how he'd come here, the amulet gleaming darkly against his skin. His body hung limp and unmoving. Most of his feathers had been ripped out, and his wings hung askew like a broken bird's. Oh gods. She dug her fingernails into her palms. He had to be alive. She would burn this whole dashed city down if he wasn't.

Prince Irokoi made a sympathetic noise and glanced around at the narrow staircase thoughtfully. Then he straightened. "Ah, Mossfeathers, you have impeccable timing," he greeted Prince Rakken as he winged his way into sight. Prince Rakken in his fae form. His wings were dark bronze, tipped with vivid green, the whole threaded through with gold. His mouth set in a grim line as he took in Wyn's suspended body, but he hoisted him into his arms without comment.

"I've got him, Koi," he said. "Bloody fool." He met Hetta's eyes, expression unreadable. "He's alive," he added shortly, and then turned and winged away from the tower.

KING AEROS

EVERYTHING HURT. PAIN came in splinters with each breath, scissoring through Wyn's chest and radiating out to his wingtips. The Maelstrom's magic shuddered through him, sparking and short-circuiting where it touched his innate magic and feeling remarkably like a swarm of angry hornets had taken up residence in his bones, all stinging their disapproval.

Something wrenched at his wings and everything, impossibly, hurt *more*, sending his thoughts into blank free-fall until the pain ebbed a fraction. Coming back to himself felt like slamming to earth. On the up side, this meant he probably wasn't dead.

He opened his eyes and found he was lying on his belly on a hard, cold surface. The shell-pink of the wall in front of him told him he was in one of the outer spires.

"That was a singularly stupid course of action," a voice said tightly from somewhere beside him. *Rake.* Wyn twisted his head towards his brother with a groan. "You'll be earthbound for months, healing this." Rakken tapped meaningfully on Wyn's wingbone. The touch sent a wave of fresh daggers, and Wyn let loose a string of profanities in storm-tongue, which Rakken ignored. "You should thank me for setting it. What in the High King's name possessed you to try your luck in the Maelstrom? Even I would not risk it, yet, and you are little more than a child in comparison."

"I didn't *intend* to go into it," Wyn protested. His voice came out distorted, and he swallowed unpleasantly, tasting blood. The violent storm's energy ached at the back of his teeth, ran up and down his wings in jagged flashes. Rakken had splinted them tightly, which helped with the pain, but it was hard to feel thankful. Nothing took longer to heal than wingbone and feather. "And I don't know how you and Cat hope to succeed if you're afraid to face the Maelstrom."

Rakken stilled. "Be careful what you say, brother."

Wyn knew what he meant. They were in ThousandSpire, where their father had ruled with an iron fist for longer than anyone could remember. You never knew when he might be listening. Wyn shouldn't have needed Rakken's reminder, not with his bond to ThousandSpire active for the first time in years, but he'd lost the habit of caution.

Wyn touched the bond, familiar yet unsettling, filling an emptiness he hadn't been aware of carrying, humming a sense of homecoming completely at odds with his heart. He and his kin were bound to ThousandSpire much as the Valstars were to Stariel, and ThousandSpire was glad to see him. It had always liked him, despite his father's attitude. The faeland snuffled over Wyn's aching skin like a dog inspecting him for strange smells. Its attention sharpened on the amulet around Wyn's neck.

"ThousandSpire doesn't like the whiff of FallingStar on you," Rakken observed just as Wyn reached a similar conclusion. "Tell me, did you really think you could bring a piece of a foreign faeland into the heart of the Spires?" He tapped Wyn's collarbone next to where the amulet rested, as if he was loath to touch the object too.

Interesting. Wyn didn't know exactly what Stariel had done to the stone, but if Rakken said it held a bit of Stariel, it did. Rakken was by far the better sorcerer of the two of them. It should help with the resonance, at least, which was good news if he could just get it into Hetta's hands. Both of them would need to be touching it for the translocation spell to take them back.

"Where is Lord Valstar?" he asked, deliberately not answering Rakken's question. Rakken was right; better to be careful what they said aloud. Seven stormcrows, his wings hurt, an unpleasantness compounded by the trapped feeling of the bindings strapping them tightly to his back. He ignored the urge to try to flex them; that would most definitely *not* help. Thank the High King he hadn't been conscious when Rakken set them. The tiny pricks where his feathers had torn free were almost negligible in comparison to the stabbing pain of the broken bones, though they added to the humiliation. He must look like a trussed chicken.

"She's in the storm cage," Rakken said. "She had a front-row view of your fall."

Wyn winced. "Is she all right?" The power of the Maelstrom still buzzed behind his eyes. If this was what it felt like just to brush the surface, what would the heart of the storm have done to him?

"Brother, our previous interaction may have given you the impression that I am on your side. I am not on your side, Hallowyn. Whatever mad belief you have in your head, rid yourself of it."

"Is she all right?" Wyn repeated, levering himself up onto an elbow. *Ow.* The limb appeared functional, however. Thank the high winds. He wasn't entirely sure which parts of him still were. From the spikes with each breath, at least one of his ribs was broken.

With some difficulty, he slid off the stone, trusting that his legs would probably hold him. They did, but the shock of his weight punched pain up from the soles of his feet, hard and punishing. *Ow.* He wobbled and grabbed the edge of the table for balance.

"She was significantly *more* all right before your dramatic entrance. Just how well do you think she'll do now you've turned up and given Father such an excellent bargaining chip against her?" Rakken sounded furious, though he was trying not to.

"Careful, brother," Wyn said. "Or I might think you care." He laughed, a rasping cough of a sound that only made him laugh harder.

"What is *wrong* with you?" Rakken took hold of Wyn's shoulder and shook him. Little knives twisted where he'd lost feathers, and he laughed again. Rakken cursed and released him. "Has the Maelstrom made you as mad as Irokoi?"

Wyn had to admit he was edging into hysteria territory. He suppressed another inappropriate giggle and took a deep, steadying breath. "I've never been convinced that Irokoi *is* mad, though," he said after a pause to collect himself. "He sees things. Like Hetta, now. She was always an illusionist, but lordship has given her the Sight." Maybe it would prove useful for Rakken to know that. He wasn't sure how, exactly, but he was going to need every bit of advantage he could muster, to get him and Hetta out of here alive and intact.

"You're babbling," Rakken said in disgust, but a spark lit in the green of his eyes. He'd understood the coded message.

Dizziness overcame Wyn suddenly, the half-second's warning of a 'port. Only one person was exempt from ThousandSpire's wards against translocation. It had taken his father slightly longer to retrieve him than expected, actually. At least he was standing. It would have been worse to face his father on his belly.

The 'port was thick with King Aeros's magic—lime leaves mingling with rain falling on sun-scorched earth, overwhelming even the taste of Wyn's own blood on his tongue. Wyn held fast to his pain-inspired giddiness; it was his only defence now against the terror threatening to rise up and paralyse him, and he could not afford that. Not with Hetta at stake.

Wyn staggered as the 'port spat him out onto the marble floor of the throne room. He'd never liked the large, ostentatious space, and he liked it even less from this vantage point directly below the dais. The massive hall was open to the elements on one side and above for the length of the rectangular skylight down its centre. Artificial shade or shelter was added with magic when King Aeros was feeling beneficent; when he wasn't, supplicants below his raised dais stood under baking summer sun or freezing winter snow. Immense rounded columns ran down each side of the hall, and every surface glittered with gems and precious metals.

The court lined the walls, whispering. Not all the court were stormdancers, and the shapes and colours of lesser and greater fae were a form of decoration in themselves. Their presence probably meant Father intended a spectacle rather than a swift death, which meant Wyn might be able to buy time, if he could just *think* properly. The world still swam with the Maelstrom's energy, sound and leysight coming in and out of focus.

Wyn's two sisters were at the front of the crowd, beneath the raised dais. Catsmere was dressed in her customary dark tones and standing in the relaxed, watchful pose she could hold for hours if needed. Aroset jittered with anticipation, her robes a pure frost that matched her hair and emphasised the blood-red of her wings. Catsmere didn't react to the sight of him or Rakken, but Aroset smiled in a deeply disturbing way, showing teeth.

But Wyn spared them only a glance, for there was only one fae in the room who really mattered here, the fae whose power eclipsed the others so utterly they might have been mere tinder-sparks against the blaze of the sun.

King Aeros sat on a throne on the raised dais, his eyes gleaming guinea-gold as he considered Wyn. The gems inlaid on the throne and wall behind were designed to best frame ThousandSpire's ruler. Diamonds and rubies featured heavily in the design, almost as brilliant as the silver and scarlet of King Aeros's wings, as if blood had been gilt with the shining metal. His silver-white hair hung long and intricately braided over one shoulder.

"Ah, my youngest," King Aeros said with satisfaction. Dread washed over Wyn, an instinctive response to the sound. His father chuckled. "You seem somewhat worse for wear than when I last set eyes on you."

"When you were planning to kill me and blame DuskRose for my murder, do you mean?" Wyn said, marvelling at how cool and clear his voice sounded. There was a ripple in the assembled crowd, but the King appeared unconcerned.

"Hallowyn," King Aeros chided. "Such a lack of loyalty to your own blood!"

The compulsion hit him, swift and stunning in its strength. Wyn buckled and fell to his knees, biting his tongue to keep the words of obeisance from spilling out. Every sinew shuddered under the compulsion, but it seemed muted compared to what he remembered. Rakken was right; King Aeros's power *was* weakened. Or perhaps even his father's magic paled compared to the Maelstrom's energy still ringing in his ears. It was all he could do to kneel and pant silently, teeth clenched, but ten years ago he would have been begging and writhing on the floor, so that was progress of a sort.

Compulsion was a nasty loophole in the fae inability to lie; compulsion could make you say *anything*. The flipside was that you couldn't make oaths under compulsion; only freely given words had the power to bind.

King Aeros gave no outward sign that his compulsion hadn't been quite as effective as he'd intended. Narrowing golden eyes, he asked, "And what is this whiff of FallingStar I detect about you?" He turned his attention to Rakken, who'd stood quietly to one side throughout the exchange.

Rakken walked calmly—almost languidly—towards Wyn. His expression was faintly bored.

"It's this, Father," Rakken said and leaned down to pull Lamorkin's amulet over Wyn's head. Wyn jerked at the feel of Rakken's magic. He'd masked his signature completely, so Wyn only sensed the glamour because it was literally touching him. Shock held him frozen for a heartbeat. Surely Rakken wouldn't *dare?* He was a gifted sorcerer, but their father was a *faelord* of one of the most powerful courts in Faerie, older and stronger than any fae Wyn knew bar the High King.

But apparently Rakken *would* dare, because he lifted a facsimile of the amulet over Wyn's head while the cold weight of the true amulet still pressed against his skin. Wyn scowled, playing his role, though his heart beat fast as a hummingbird's. *I suppose this is the time for risk-taking.* He hoped Rakken wouldn't suffer for it.

"Some sort of token, I think," said Rakken, holding up a facsimile of Lamorkin's amulet. How in the high winds did he hope to get away with it? King Aeros didn't have the Sight, but the glamour would never hold against their father's close inspection. But Rakken didn't move to hand it over. Instead he tossed it into the air with the timing of a showman and summoned a contained ball of lightning to destroy it. Sparks flew, white-hot and blinding, as the fake amulet appeared to burn away to nothing. Rakken shot a glance at Wyn. "Though perhaps he has *mingled* with FallingStar deeply enough that he may still carry the scent even now." He wrinkled his nose fastidiously.

Wyn fought a sudden urge to laugh, oddly reminded of Jack's use of 'canoodling'. *Mingling indeed.* Hetta would roll her eyes at the euphemism. Was she all right, in the stormcage? The winds would be fierce up there. She would be cold.

King Aeros shifted in his seat, propping his head on one hand to consider Rakken. Wyn had to give his brother credit; Rakken remained impassive under the scrutiny.

"You make an excellent point, though; we do seem to be missing someone," King Aeros said eventually, and lazily snapped his fingers. Citrus and desert air swelled, and two figures appeared in front of the dais: Irokoi and Hetta. Hetta stumbled, and Irokoi's black wings flapped briefly in startlement.

Hetta. Wyn strained to go to her, but a hard shield of air as well as compulsion pressed him down. Damn his father. He met Hetta's gaze and for an instant everything else faded away. There was no throne room and no power holding him in place. There was only the grey of Hetta's eyes, blazing with anger and distress. He tried to convey all that she meant to him along with a warning against all that she should be careful of, but it wasn't a particularly effective communication method. She stepped towards him, but Aroset grasped her forearm and jerked her back.

Hetta, of course, didn't take this passively. She lit up like gunpowder, and Wyn felt the wash of heat even from where he was kneeling. Aroset shrieked, but there was a reason she was the heir presumptive. She stole the air around Hetta without loosening her grip, and the fire snuffed out. Hetta gasped and clutched at her throat, struggling to breathe. Wyn fought his way to one knee before the bindings dug into him again, preventing him from rising.

"Aroset," King Aeros chided, and Hetta abruptly inhaled. Wyn felt as if his own breath had returned with hers. Her harsh pants were the only sound as the King turned his attention to her. "My daughter has poor manners, but I trust the message was still received? You are in *my* court, Lord Valstar, and Hallowyn is *my* son, not your vassal. You have no claim on him." He paused, and his smile grew edged. "Unless you would like to bargain for one? I believe Prince Rakken outlined my terms."

Wyn laughed then. "Trade me for Stariel as a vassal state, you mean?"

His father turned towards him, eyes cold. "I did not ask you to speak." Compulsion bit into Wyn again, and he dropped his head, unable to hold his father's gaze. King Aeros turned back to Hetta. "But yes. What say you, Lord Valstar, to my terms?"

Hetta hesitated, and Wyn's blood froze in his veins. *No.* No, she mustn't consider it. He raised his head to glare at her from across the room. She'd drawn lines around their relationship, things she could not countenance. This was his line in the sand. *I will never forgive you if you do this*, he tried to tell her, suddenly furious and terrified both. *I will never forgive you if you let me weaken you, if you let me cost you everything.* The thought of Stariel's people at the mercy of his father's rule…it hardened something in him, sent the Maelstrom's energy dancing to a new, higher frequency.

She gave him a small, sad smile and nodded slightly before turning back to his father. "No," she said, her voice quiet but clear.

His heart began to beat again, and he slumped in relief. Thank the Maelstrom. They were still in precisely the same situation as before, but his worst fear was now alleviated. Hetta's strength was part of why he loved her, but it had never been tested like this before.

His father didn't seem surprised by her answer. "This is how much your lover values you," he said, as if he expected Wyn to be hurt rather than thankful. *He still doesn't understand me.* "That is the love of mortals for you, little Hallowyn."

"I believe we are in fact the same height now, Father." How strange to notice that now, of all times, another small similarity he could do without.

Hetta gave him a Look that asked if now was really the time for levity, but he saw her regain a measure of calm at his words and could not regret them. The amulet lay cold against his throat underneath Rakken's glamour. How could he get it to Hetta?

King Aeros ignored him. "And that is the sum total of effort you will expend on bargaining for my son, is it? I thought he meant more to you." His wings rustled. "How disappointing."

Hetta shrugged, though the motion was constrained by Aroset's grip. She raised a contemptuous brow at Wyn's sister, surprisingly similar to the expression she reserved for the village councillors when they were being particularly ridiculous. "I'm willing to give quite a lot for him, actually, but you already know that. I, however, have no idea what you want that I'm prepared to give, so it's your turn to provide information. I'm not sure what else you were hoping for, other than to draw out the suspense."

Wyn choked back a pained laugh. Had she just matter-of-factly told the ruler of Ten Thousand Spires that he was being ridiculous? Of course she had. But he needed his father's anger to focus on him, not Hetta, so he added, "Stariel has many sheep, for example. I am certain Lord Valstar deems me worth a few."

King Aeros rose then, coming to his feet with a lion's sleek grace. He shook out his wings, and the light from the jewel-encrusted walls fell upon them, picking out the fine silver filigree edging each blood-red primary. Lamorkin's comment snagged at Wyn. *Your bloodfeathers are coming in. Very like your sire's they will look when they are done.* How could his godparent have lied? He might hate it, but King Aeros was definitely his father. Setting aside his bond to ThousandSpire, they looked alike. Even Wyn could see the echoes of his own features in the King's. He hoped Hetta did not. Assuming an optimistic outcome here, he didn't want his face to remind her of his father. That would definitely put a damper on things.

King Aeros sauntered down from the throne without hurry, supremely confident in his power, and paused at the foot of the dais to consider Hetta, who met his guinea-gold eyes without fear, head high.

"I don't think you truly understand, Lord Valstar, what I am capable of," he said thoughtfully. He went to tilt her chin up and she flinched away, but Aroset held her in place.

A deep rage burned in Wyn, for all the good it did him, kneeling here in helpless servitude. The Maelstrom's aura vibrated in response. ThousandSpire, too, twitched, alert to his distress but answering to another master. And lastly, a hint of pine and frost stirred against his chest. His anger was nothing to Stariel's, distant and frustrated though it might be. The cold ferocity of it burned through the amulet.

If he could just get the amulet to Hetta. He wasn't sure exactly what Stariel had done to it, but it clearly carried some connection to the faeland. It might boost her magic, but in any case, it could get her out of here. One trip each way, Lamorkin had said.

King Aeros's eyes flicked briefly to Wyn. "*You* know," he said, voice ripe with amusement. "Don't you, my son? And yet you have dared to try to defy me." He moved so swiftly that Hetta had no time to avoid him, his hand abruptly around her throat. He lifted her casually off her feet and threw her upwards with a swirl of air magic. Hetta kicked in midair, awkward and panicked, as his father's magic held her effortlessly above the floor. "Come, Lord Valstar. Let us see if I can find another way to convince you." He turned and strode towards Wyn, Hetta bobbing helplessly along in his wake.

His father was right; she didn't understand what King Aeros was capable of, not in her bones. Wyn didn't want her to understand, didn't want to strip away that warm human naiveté. He struggled against the compulsion, but the only thing that moved was the Maelstrom's energy, skittering wildly over his skin.

King Aeros's smile grew razor-sharp as he stalked towards Wyn. Wyn made another effort to stand. He drew on his anger, burning cold as the midwinter depths of Starwater, cold as the frozen air high above the Indigoes, where only fools flew. And in the heart of that winter, the Maelstrom's energy abruptly caught, flooding him with icy, borrowed strength, hardened to diamond chill. He rose, panting, wings protesting, the power of his father's will threatening to make him buckle with every breath. King Aeros's smile grew, if anything, even sharper, the throne room humming with storm-scent.

His father was deliberately drawing things out, savouring the anticipation of pain. Wyn did his best not to think about what might be coming, of all the ways his father might hurt him to try to persuade Hetta to do what he wanted. He balled himself up, ready to become a pebble in a river once more. Perhaps this could buy time, time in which he could figure out how to breach the tantalisingly short distance between him and Hetta. She was only a few strides away now, her arms flailing for balance in the air magic's grip, but it was all he could do to remain upright under the weight of his father's displeasure. If he lifted a foot to step, he'd fall. But maybe if his father were distracted…

"Oh, little Hallowyn. Always so very good at boxing away your fear. Is it because you have hope?" And without warning King Aeros whirled, the blast of air catching Rakken dead-centre and whirling him straight into a column in a crash of bronze and green feathers. "Ah, disobedient sons. Did you really think you could fool me with your pitiful magic, Rakken?" He smirked at Catsmere, who'd drawn her blade instinctively. "Or that I was unaware of you and your sister's plans?" Catsmere would have rushed for Rakken, but he held up a hand to check her advance and she halted, bristling.

Rakken shrugged, as if he weren't sprawled beneath the pillar, a thin line of blood dripping from his head where he'd hit.

"You cannot blame me for trying, Father," he got out. His voice was huskier than normal, but his smile evoked the same dagger-sharp humour as King Aeros's.

King Aeros eyed the twins speculatively. "I will deal with the two of you later. For now…" He turned back to Wyn, and his smile broadened. "Did you hope that this would save you?" he asked, tapping a finger on the amulet, as if the glamour were simply not there at all. "Did you hope to give it to her?" He laughed. "You're a fool, Hallowyn." Hetta's eyes were wide as she spun helplessly in the air behind him. King Aeros wrapped a hand around the amulet to lift it away.

"FallingStar," Wyn said, releasing the storm of anger and magic inside him. The world tore in two, pulling him and his father with it.

34

OATHBREAKER

THEY TRANSLOCATED ONTO cold stone and snowy mountainside. Wyn had braced for the disorientation, but there was still a moment of breathless confusion where he wasn't sure which way was up, the world cast in the unfamiliar shadows of the setting sun. He choked on pine and frost, and Stariel's anger rose up through his feet, consuming him, spreading out through his veins and into the broken pieces of his wings. The faeland's demand for Hetta hit him with the force of a typhoon, and Wyn fell to his knees for the second time that day, eardrums reverberating.

King Aeros turned on Wyn with death in his eyes, wings flaring out to their full extent. Ozone hissed, sparks washing over his wings, and the pressure plummeted as the storm answered his father's command, jagged lightning crashing its way over the mountains. Thunder boomed overhead. But the storm magic was a beacon for something else, something that here was stronger even than one of the oldest faelords in Faerie, for they stood on Stariel's soil.

<Him,> Wyn said to the faeland. He knew, in a single hard moment, exactly what he was doing, exactly what it would cost, and it did not stop him. *<Him. He took Hetta.>*

The swelling charge redirected with Stariel's rage. Its fury burned as hot as stars and as old as mountain bones, relentless as the swell and dip of lake water, full of the shaking of branches in a high wind, the sharp taste of blood. Wyn had been in the Maelstrom, but this magic was the might of a faeland, focused on a single point, overwhelming his leysight.

Lightning forked from the sky, but the earth rose up to meet it with a roar. The world shuddered as the wave of earth broke, crashing over his father and swallowing him whole.

Something snapped in Wyn's chest—a blood tie suddenly cut loose. He staggered, knowing that all his siblings would be feeling the same sharp knowledge, the death of ThousandSpire's ruler a shockwave reverberating out along their shared bloodline. But he had no time to process, because Stariel turned its attention to him.

Wyn smelled of ThousandSpire, and Stariel was in a killing rage against that court. The earth quaked again, and Wyn could not breathe as leylines glowed and writhed like a sea of agitated snakes. Hetta belonged to it, and Wyn's blood had taken her. It wanted her back. Now.

Wyn's temper shattered. His father was *dead*, and the Maelstrom had broken something more than just his wings. Something sharp and feral came loose in his chest in a painful, knife-sharp fury that seared through the ice in a sudden roar. <*She is MINE as well!*> He poured magic into the leylines, wrenching them out of Stariel's grip, heedless of the cost. He didn't care that Stariel was bigger and older and stranger than him. <Hetta is still in danger, and I am going to get her back! So stormwinds take your jealousy! You're a faeland, not a child!>

It shouldn't have worked. Stariel hadn't even *noticed* King Aeros's opposition, and Wyn's magic was a mere shadow of his father's. But Stariel quivered as if struck. For the space between heartbeats, the faeland *paused*. And then, with a rush of wind, it wrenched the leylines back from Wyn and—

"What the fuck are you doing?" Jack said.

The universe froze, and Wyn froze with it, trembling with magic so hot and potent he couldn't even feel his broken bones. And then, with a release of breath, Stariel's anger eased back from the trigger. It still seethed in the air around him, but Wyn no longer stood on a knife edge between life and death.

Wyn sagged and let the storm charge in the air fizzle out. "Challenging a faeland's wrath, fool that I am. Thank you, Jack."

He turned. He and his father had arrived in a small gully on the lower slopes of the Indigoes. Or possibly it had been a ridgetop moments ago and was now a small gully. He'd been too disoriented to pay much attention to topography before the earth had shifted. Jack stood on the crest of the nearest ridge, staring down at Wyn incredulously, scarf flapping about his neck, hands tucked in his greatcoat. He wasn't alone. Barely a breath later, Marius appeared beside him, looking uncomfortable out-of-doors in the exposed weather.

Wyn stared at the two of them. They looked so normal, so very human and so very…Valstar. Affection swelled up, love for this land and its people, and he knew that the fae were wrong; love wasn't a force of weakness. Not this sort of love, that didn't soften anger but hardened it into something unyielding.

"Alexandra?" he asked.

Marius's face was pale. "Fine. I mean, not fine, but, well, you know what I mean. Not any worse." He sketched the distorted shape of Wyn's bound wings. "What's going on? Why did Stariel try to…" He trailed off, looking disturbed. The Valstars weren't used to thinking of their faeland as anything other than wholly benevolent.

Wyn took a deep breath and began to piece together a rapid plan. There was no time to waste now. "The Maelstrom. My father. It does not matter much, now. I need to get back to ThousandSpire immediately. We need to get Hetta back." He rose to unsteady feet, the ache of broken bones once more making itself known. He changed to his mortal form and it helped, a little, though the loss of magic made the world as dull and thick as soup.

"Get back to ThousandSpire?" Jack asked.

"Yes," Wyn said. "I'm going to need a lot of Valstars."

THE TWO MEN TRAILED him back to the house, and he could feel their disquiet. He was having trouble re-assuming his old skin. Marius tried to question him about his physical state and seemed faintly surprised when he answered bluntly and without prevarication.

"Your wings are…broken?" Marius said as if he could not quite believe what Wyn had just said.

Why had he chosen a resonance point so far from the house? How much longer till they reached it, and how many Valstars were still in residence? Wyn did a quick calculation and came to a total somewhat less than what had been here for Wintersol. That would have to be enough. Using people for a resonance was generally a bad idea. People were too fleeting to really change the nature of a place, but enough Valstars in one place might be enough. He would *make* it be enough, combined with his own feathers and blood and the itch of the Maelstrom's magic. Thank the High King he'd given Hetta one of his feathers.

"Are you sure you should be racing around like this?" Marius said hesitantly. "I mean, you don't look…" He was slightly out of breath at the pace they were keeping. Wyn would've run, but he wasn't sure he could get far enough without collapsing. Besides, he needed these two Valstars as well. He was going to need every Valstar he could get, now that the amulet's power was sucked dry.

"It doesn't matter what I look like," Wyn said with a shrug he regretted, since mortal form or no, his shoulders were strung tight with pain. "Your sister is a foreign power in a faeland that has just lost its lord. Exactly how safe do you think she is?" The earth rushing up to swallow his father...

"Lost its lord...?"

"My father. He's dead. Stariel killed him." *I brought him here so it could kill him*, he did not say, though the words clawed at the ice around his heart, seeking entry.

He realised he'd left the others behind and turned impatiently. "Come on. If you're going to pause in shock at every surprising revelation, I shall cease answering your questions."

"Your father's dead?" Marius said, his expression unsure. "Are you...are you all right?"

"No, Marius, I am not all right. But my state of mind is not important right now. Come." He wished he could teleport them all to the house, but that wasn't a stormdancer skill and he wasn't the lord of this land. Hetta would want to know if she could teleport within Stariel now that she'd seen his father's abilities. Usually he would say it wasn't within the scope of human magery, but he'd learnt not to underestimate Hetta. He would teach her anything she wanted to know, spill any secret he could think of if only he could have her here and safe.

Jack shook himself but started forward again. Marius fell into step after a pause. "All right. But you still haven't really explained what you're planning."

"Madness," Wyn said. "But it's the best I can think of right now. We're going to need the Star Stone." He addressed this comment to Marius, who narrowed his eyes but nodded.

"I've always wondered what it would take to make you angry," he said quietly.

"I'm not angry at you, Marius," he said, trying his best not to snap it.

"I know," Marius said. "You're not the only person who loves her, Wyn. We'll do anything to get her back too."

The words were good ones, and they loosened the tightness inside him a tiny fraction. But they were still so far from the house, and he didn't know how much time they had. Who knew what chaos ThousandSpire would be in, how it might lash out at a foreign lord. King Aeros had ruled the Court of Ten Thousand Spires for so long. Wyn didn't even know how old his father was, and he had no idea how the faeland would react. Stariel was so much more accustomed to the fleeting lives of humans, to being without a lord for a time. If ThousandSpire *was* still without a lord. Aroset would waste no time trying to wrest control of the Spires. He hoped Rakken and Catsmere had some sort of plan for that. He didn't trust any of them, but at least the latter would probably not be actively trying to kill Hetta.

Cherries, ripe and jarring with the season. Wyn froze and spun, abused muscles protesting at the speed of the movement. But Princess Sunnika made no effort to hide as she appeared in front of them. She was in her fae form, her ears twitching as she tilted her head thoughtfully, her hands on the curves of her hips. Her gaze met Wyn's. She would have felt the magical upheaval up in the Indigoes.

"Princess, will you please take us to the house?" he asked, closing the distance between them.

"You do not look well, Your Highness." Her tail switched from side to side.

Wyn repeated his question.

"In exchange for...?" she said.

"Put it on my account. I believe you've some experience with banking debts."

Her eyes widened at the word 'banking'; he'd guessed true, then, about her interference with the Thompsons. He could see her weighing factors, deciding it was worth the opportunity to demand answers from him. "You have a poor debt collection history. But very well." And she held out her arms commandingly. "You'll all have to be touching me," she told the others, with special emphasis for Jack, whose harrumph didn't hide the slight flush on his cheeks.

Her hand was smooth and warm despite the air's chill. They shared a glance, and Wyn was moderately certain they were both reflecting on the strangeness of two fae from opposing courts willingly holding hands.

Between one breath and the next, the world shifted in a tangle of beeswax and cherries and then they were abruptly standing in Stariel's library. Wyn didn't much like teleportation. It reminded him too forcibly of his father's habit of summoning people on a whim. But he was still more accustomed to such a method of transportation than the Valstars, who staggered in disorientation as they arrived.

"Wow," was all Marius could find to say, righting himself with a hand against a bookcase. "That's... Can you take us to Hetta?"

"Teleport to the heart of the Spires from the Mortal Realm half a world away?" Princess Sunnika shook her head. "No."

"Teleportation and portals are two different types of translocation magic," Wyn tried to explain. "Teleportation shifts the individual—or several individuals—in space. Most can only do it within line-of-sight." He nodded an acknowledgement at Princess Sunnika. "Portals connect one place to another, and as long as the portal stays open, one can pass through it. But to connect two places together, especially strongly individualised locations such as faelands, they need to share a resonance. That's why I need as many Valstars as possible. You're all bound to Stariel, and you all share blood with Hetta. And the Star Stone—anything that might help."

"All right," said Jack when Marius would have asked further questions. "Where do you want us to shepherd people?"

"The Standing Stones." Wyn had been wracking his brain for a likely location. They would never get everyone up to the Indigoes in time. The Standing Stones were only a few fields from the house, and the rocky forms of them at least had something in common with the Spires, in shape if not in scale.

Wyn would have scattered with the Valstars, but Princess Sunnika prevented him.

"Prince Hallowyn," she said in an undertone as the others left, "I would have a word with you."

"This isn't an ideal moment," Wyn said. "But I suspect you already know that. Speak your word, Princess."

She stood next to one of the windowseats, the angle shadowing her features, but he could still see her wide smile. "You have excellent manners. I do not think we would have dealt all that badly together. You are a touch reserved, but I am very good at provoking a reaction." She smoothed a lock of hair behind her ear, the motion a deliberate one.

"You felt it," Wyn said. It wasn't a question.

"The shattering of half an oath? Yes," she said. She looked out to where the dark shapes of the Indigoes rose. "The promise between DuskRose and ThousandSpire no longer stands."

"The one between you and me, though…"

"Still intact."

Wyn gambled. "I release you from your promise to me, Princess Sunnika of the Court of Dusken Roses."

She whirled, shocked out of her composure, her eyes flying to his face in search of answers. "You're trying to manipulate me into reciprocating," she said incredulously.

"Yes."

His answer made her laugh, the sound as silvery as bells, and she shook her head. "Oh, Prince Hallowyn, I could have liked you. But I think you are foolish to give up your hold over me so easily." She considered him, weighing her choices. "I don't much like featuring as the villain in your martyr attempt. Tell me," she said, "before this… Did you ever want to marry me?"

"You are beautiful," he said. She was, objectively, even by fae standards.

She flicked his words away with a tiny shake of her head, as if to dislodge a fly. "And that is not an answer."

Wyn could feel the ice under his feet, treacherously thin. What had he thought, before Stariel, before Hetta, when he'd thought he might be married to the woman in front of him?

"The day I met you," he began slowly, remembering, "Queen Tayarenn could not even bring herself to look at me." Queen Tayarenn had stared straight ahead throughout the engagement ritual, her expression one of deep loathing. The agreement had been signed within DuskRose's borders, and the air had warped menacingly around Wyn with the force of its queen's emotion. "But you... you met my eyes, and you did not look at me as if I were a monster. You looked brave and determined. It gave me hope."

Princess Sunnika's eyes widened fractionally before her cool façade slipped back into place. "Do you think I'm so easily manipulated?"

"No—I'm gambling with all the truth that I have in me."

She smiled, but it didn't quite cover the brief flicker of something sad and fragile in her features. Then she straightened. "Very well, Hallowyn Tempestren." Her expression dared him to challenge her use of his full name, unadorned, but he let it pass. "I will give you what you want—but in return you will owe me a favour."

Relief was a heady thing, making him light-hearted enough to say, "I was under the impression that I already did. You teleported me twice when I had need of it."

Her gaze cooled, her tail switching dangerously. "You cannot equate this with those trifling debts."

He bowed his head, accepting the rebuke. Hetta would have rolled her eyes at his levity, but Princess Sunnika wasn't her, and he could push her only so far before she would take offense. In truth, she'd already shown more flexibility than he'd expected. "My apologies. Of course I do not equate the two." The teleportation, whilst convenient, had only a minor value compared to his broken oath. "I will accept the bargain you offer."

She smiled. "Then I release you from your promise to me, Prince Hallowyn Tempestren of the Court of Ten Thousand Spires."

Such a small collection of words to repair a broken oath, and yet power swelled in their wake, immediate and immense. His magic boiled up, filling spaces he hadn't known were hollow, overflowing until it hit the Maelstrom's energy still crackling in his veins and combined with the force of an inferno. His knees buckled, and his broken wings strained under his skin, breaking free as he lost control of his shape.

The accompanying pain snapped him out of the raging storm of magic. He knelt on the rug, panting, the carpet fibres pressing into his palms, lightning shivering under his skin. *I am ending up on my knees rather a lot today.* Hopefully that wasn't an omen of anything. He looked up to find Princess Sunnika staring at him with open shock, her ears flat against her skull. So she hadn't expected that surge either.

Is this what I should have been? he wondered, still humming to the Maelstrom's frequency. *Or is it something...more?*

It didn't matter right now. He rose, folding himself back into a mortal shape with an effort of will. The pain eased and so did the hum of magic. He found himself grateful for the limits of his mortal form—his control felt slippery, and accidentally summoning lightning because he couldn't leash his power would be beyond unhelpful.

"Thank you," he said to Princess Sunnika. It was appropriate to thank her, an acknowledgement of the debt he now owed.

Her expression was thoughtful. "Go rescue your mortal, then." She smiled, dagger sharp. "And do not forget the favour you owe me."

THE STANDING STONES

NOT HALF AN hour later, Wyn stood at the Standing Stones in a crowd of confused Valstars. Jack and Marius together had alarmed their relatives enough to rouse them into action without Wyn's aid. It helped that they were all connected to Stariel, and Stariel was roiling with distress.

Wyn surveyed the crowd and tried to settle the energy crackling through his veins. He still hadn't found the shape of himself in this new, untested power, like a fledgling before his first flight. *Let us hope I do not shock anyone literally as well as figuratively today.* Stormdancers had a high tolerance to charge, but mortals didn't, and he didn't quite trust the currents shifting through him.

The Valstars stared at him, still processing the revelation of his true nature from earlier, intently examining his back and head as if wings and horns would burst free at any moment. Wyn had never addressed them like this, as an equal rather than an inferior. *I ought to thank Rake for his little charade.* Rakken's fabricated title had paved the way for the Valstars to re-evaluate Wyn's social status, even before he'd told them he was fae. Of course, that re-evaluation was

countered by a hefty dose of disapproval. They didn't like that he'd
deceived them for so long. No one liked to be made to feel foolish.
I suppose I had better tell them about the royalty aspect as well. But that
could wait for later. It would only cause a scene now that he did not
have time for. How long had passed in ThousandSpire since he'd
left? Time didn't move quite the same in Faerie and Mortal.

He drew in magic, cardamom and petrichor, so vivid he could
see as well as smell it. How strange to know that he alone on this
hilltop could. *Or perhaps not quite alone*, he amended, taking in
Alexandra's wide eyes tracing the patterns of the leylines. She was
still shaken from her earlier encounter with Aroset but had been
determined to come anyway. At least she didn't seem to have taken
any physical harm. He gave her an encouraging smile and made a
mental note to talk to her later privately. Assuming there was a later.

His wings itched for release, but he held grimly on to his mortal
shape. The pain of the broken bones would probably offset the
increased ability to work magic in his fae form, and he could not
afford that. Yet he'd never before felt this powerful, in either form.
Could he have broken the oath, all those years ago, knowing now
what it meant to give up this piece of himself? *I have been a shadow
of myself without realising it.* He thought of his father's murderous
expression, and the chill still gripping him deepened. *But what am
I becoming now?*

"Jack and Marius have told you that Hetta's in trouble," he said,
loud and clear. "She's trapped in Faerie, in a foreign faeland. I am
going to try a...spell to get her back." He expected them to demand
to know more, but Stariel's distress clanged even in his ears, and
there was minimal protest. They all knew something was very, very
wrong. And they knew that Wyn was at the centre of it, somehow.

He arranged them around the stone circle, holding hands, the
Star Stone dead centre, then he took a deep breath and *pushed*. The
magic surged up in a hammer and hit what felt like solid iron: the
wards of the Spires. But there were so many Valstars, and the King

of Ten Thousand Spires was dead. And Wyn…Wyn had ties to both courts, and he'd never been more full of magic.

His magic streamed out, storm and spice thick enough to choke on, reaching between the home he'd chosen and the one his blood bound him to. Far in the distance, thunder rumbled, out of season, and the air bristled with static. Lightning tried to answer the summons, but Wyn held it back, pouring magic into the stones until they seethed with potential. He thought of his blood, *there* splattering the stone where Rakken had tended him, *here* rushing in his veins, and Hetta's blood, linked to the Valstars surrounding him, the feather of his she'd thankfully kept on her person.

Stariel understood what he was doing. He'd almost forgotten what it felt like to have the land working *with* rather than against him, but he forgave Stariel for all its recent hostility when it leaned its weight in concert with his own.

It was like trying to force the wrong ends of two magnets together, the energies sliding and repelling, ThousandSpire's wards ancient and impenetrable, the land curled and defensive without its lord. But Stariel's desire aligned with Wyn's. It wanted Hetta back, and it pushed with Wyn and the Valstars. The Valstars, who despite everything, were fiercely loyal to their own blood.

The pressure built and built, unbearable against his eardrums, until finally something *gave*.

The portal snapped into place between two of the stones. It rose high enough for a person to pass through, its edges strong and unwavering. Through the stone frame, the brilliant gems of the throne room glowed in the setting sun instead of the darkly forested hills that had been visible a second ago. Wyn didn't pause to see the Valstars' reactions. He hurtled through the portal, unsure how long it would hold, and the world tumbled with the transition.

But the tumbling didn't stop as he hit the marble floor, and he realised it wasn't the portal causing the disorientation. The Court of Ten Thousand Spires was shaking, both physically and magically.

An ice-storm of grief slammed down Wyn's connection with it. Of course; it had just lost its lord.

Where was Hetta? The magical cacophony swamped his leysight as he tried not to lose his footing. *There*—the tiniest hint of coffee, nearly lost in the typhoon. He stumbled towards it as the tangled magic of ThousandSpire flailed, vast and confused and alarmed. It was sheer instinct to reach back along his bond and try to comfort the faeland. *Stupid* instinct, because the moment he tried, the Spires grabbed for him, seeking a place to anchor.

Wyn tried to shove it aside, but the faeland was having none of it. It swarmed up through his bones, dust and rain and spice, melting away his mortal form. His wings screamed into being, and magic roared through the broken bones, agony and ecstasy. He felt his bones knitting under the onslaught, feathers re-growing at unnatural speed, pushing through skin in hundreds of tiny pricks. He fell to the floor with a cry. *Again.*

<Let me find Hetta!> he told it.

But the faeland was impossibly strong, impossible to resist, and it only snarled in raw possessiveness, a wave of magic trying to claim him for its own. <No!> he thought, panicked, scrabbling at the stone floor as the threads of connection started to form. <No, I do not want this! I do not want YOU!>

But then hands were on his shoulders and another force was there, shouting at ThousandSpire, stubborn as the roots of the Indigoes and smelling of coffee and frost: <You can't have him! He's OURS.>

A new sort of magic washed over him, familiar and steadying, pouring through the portal to counter ThousandSpire. He was hauled back, away from the raging clutches of the Court of Ten Thousand Spires, falling through the portal to Stariel.

HOMECOMING

OR A LONG moment, he was too disoriented to process anything. The first thing he became aware of was Hetta's hand, warm in his. He squeezed it. Things couldn't be that terrible if he was holding Hetta's hand. The second thing he became aware of was the sky above, heavy with stormclouds. The portal was gone.

He sat up, still holding Hetta's hand. His head swam with the afterimages of the Spires' violent magic. Hetta sat up next to him, looking similarly dazed, and he found himself drowning in the grey of her eyes. She was alive. She was safe. He pulled her close and kissed her.

It wasn't lust. It was something fiercer and gentler and altogether terrifying, and it threatened to break him in ways the Maelstrom couldn't. *What is happening to me?* She would tell him he was being melodramatic, but if he'd lost her... He had smothered his fears under a layer of ice, but now her warm shape moulded to his, familiar and perfect, and the ice thawed in a rush of heat. Stormwinds, more than thawed. He *burned.* He'd been wrong; there was definitely lust in the mixture.

Stariel swirled around them, possessive and unsettled, and for the first time in months there was no hostility in its attitude towards Wyn. It felt, if anything, almost…affectionate. Hetta pulled away from him, her attention going to her faeland as she reassured it. Then she looked back at him and smiled.

"Wyn," she murmured, "look at your wings."

He followed her gaze and choked out a laugh. The riot of magic had accelerated his wings' healing rate, and the broken pinions were now interspersed with immature fluffy pin feathers. But the new feathers weren't white. Instead, they were an intense, iridescent blue. The relief from the pain of broken bones was welcome, but he looked ridiculous, like a moulting piebald parrot.

It was at this moment that he became aware of the fact that he and Hetta were sitting inside a circle of Valstars. Who had all just seen him kiss Hetta. Quite passionately. In his glorious half-moulting fae form. *Seven stormcrows.*

Hetta had just noticed the same thing, and she began to laugh. He recognised the mix of hysteria and giddiness, since the same bubbled up in him. He beamed at Hetta's assorted relatives, who mostly did not beam back. Mainly they stared in stunned disapproval, though they did at least look relieved to see Hetta safe and well. *I suppose it's been a strange day for them too.*

He rose and offered Hetta a hand up, not releasing it even when they both stood on their own two feet. The Valstars continued to stare in crowded silence as he flexed his ridiculous half-fledged wings. Hopefully they'd look somewhat more majestic when they'd finished growing in, but the colour of the newest bloodfeathers still lifted his heart, reminding him of star indigo. Surely that was a good omen? He'd thought, from the way that ThousandSpire had grabbed for him, that he might be torn from Stariel and Hetta's side. A shiver of unease chilled down his spine. *But I am safe now. We are both safe. The Spires cannot reach me here.* But he wasn't sure if he could say the words aloud, not sure if they were truth or merely a good attempt at denial.

"Good news, everyone!" he told the Valstars. "We have successfully saved Hetta from wicked fae."

It was perhaps fortunate that the thunderstorm he'd summoned earlier chose that moment to break, removing the need for speech in favour of everyone urgently seeking shelter as the skies opened. The Valstars streamed back towards the house, squawking like a flock of indignant chickens.

He kept his wings spread and let the rest of Hetta's family pull ahead, savouring the rain on his feathers.

"What are you *doing?*" Hetta made an exasperated sound, though she hadn't let go of his hand. She waved an arm commandingly, and Stariel diverted raindrops to create an umbrella above the two of them. Her already wet hair slicked against her skull. He ran a hand over it and bent down to kiss her again. "You're in a very strange mood," she grumbled, though she pressed herself tight against him, as if she too were trying to reassure herself that they were whole and together.

"It's been a very strange day. My father is dead, ThousandSpire is in uproar, and who knows what your family are going to say when we reach the house now I've done such a spectacular job of scandalising them, but I am *free* of my oaths, Hetta, and you are safe. Stariel is safe. And I am home." He tilted his head back and laughed, letting the storm magic crackle between his feathers.

AUTHOR'S NOTE

Thank you for taking the time to read my book! I hope you enjoyed it.

The Prince of Secrets is the second book in the Stariel Quartet. The next book in the series is *The Court of Mortals*, which should be released in 2019. Keep turning the page for a sneak peek of the first chapter. If you'd like to be emailed when it's released, you can subscribe to my mailing list on my website www.ajlancaster.com.

Please consider reviewing *The Prince of Secrets* on Amazon or Goodreads, even if you only write a line or two. Reviews mean a lot to authors, and I appreciate every one!

SNEAK PEEK: THE COURT OF MORTALS

"I won't forgive myself if I electrocute you," Wyn said.

"Well, don't electrocute me then," Hetta replied calmly. She was perched on one of the great flat rocks inside the circle of Standing Stones and the two of them were blessedly alone in the countryside—a state that was becoming harder and harder to achieve these days. "I have complete faith in you," she said, drawing her feet up and crossing her legs. The day was unusually warm, and she shucked off her coat and put it neatly beside her.

Wyn narrowed his eyes from the opposite side of the circle, weak spring sunshine glinting in the white-blond of his hair. He stood a few feet from two of the taller stones.

"I'd rather you sat on the ground, if you must treat this so lightly."

Hetta doubted it would make much difference where she sat, but she slid off her stone obediently and extended her land-sense towards the soft earth. The magic of Stariel Estate came at her call, and even after three months of being Lord of Stariel, it still filled her with wonder. Focusing, she encouraged the water to drain away from the top inch of soil, creating a wide dry circle around herself.

There were still so many things she didn't know about being lord, but she'd discovered this particular trick a few weeks ago. *And very useful it's been, given recent weather,* she reflected wryly as she arranged herself on the grass. She preferred not to get the seat of her trousers damp.

Wyn took a deep breath and measured the distance between them. "I don't trust my control in this form." He shrugged out of his coat, folding and placing it on top of the nearest stone. His expression was carefully neutral, which meant he was feeling self-conscious, but he didn't let it show as he returned to his previous spot and changed. Between one moment and the next, he shed the proper butler and became fae, complete with wings, horns, and pointed ears. It changed the aspect of his face subtly, his features sharpening, the colour of his eyes deepening. Hetta found the transition disconcerting, as if he'd donned a costume on top of his real self. Except this was his real self. It remained hard to think of it as such, particularly since she could count on one hand how often she'd seen it.

But he was still Wyn, still the man who made her heart sing, and the prickle of unease settled under that weight of familiarity.

"What a pity I had all those shirts specially made for you," Hetta reflected. The shirts she'd given him as a Wintersol gift were made to accommodate wings and meant he didn't need to go bare-chested when he changed shape. Why had she thought that would be a good idea? She'd relied on her costuming contacts from her old theatre days for the unusual request, back before anyone other than her immediate family knew about the fae. Wyn's supply of such shirts had increased over the last few months, so he'd clearly commissioned more, probably feeding the spreading rumours about him, inside the estate and out. But still not any modified coat. Perhaps he didn't think it worth the bother to get one tailored.

"Love, I'm about to undertake a potentially dangerous experiment that depends not only on my focus and self-control but on your quick reflexes if something goes awry, and you're complaining about a missed opportunity to ogle my shirtless self?" His wings shifted restlessly. He was easier to read in his fae form, unable to keep his feathers betraying his emotions.

She leaned her elbows on her knees and took a moment to consider. "Yes, that's exactly my complaint."

His eyes danced. "*Hetta.* You aren't helping my concentration."

"Isn't that the whole point of this exercise? Isn't that why you've been torturing us both with your self-imposed celibacy these past few months while you practiced? So you could prove to yourself you wouldn't lose control of your magic under pressure?"

He scoffed. "Not entirely self-imposed, love. You're conveniently ignoring Stariel's contribution."

"Well, figure out your part of it first and then we'll tackle Stariel's," Hetta said. "It has to calm down eventually, doesn't it?" This last was a skyward plea to her estate, which had been nearly as troublesome as her relatives when it came to her and Wyn's relationship—only where they were opposed, Stariel was now rather too enthusiastic. "Who knows, perhaps it's only been so troublesome because it needs reassuring that you're not about to explode into a lightning storm the minute you get excited."

He mock-glowered at her choice of words, though the corner of his lips twitched. "The minute *I* get excited?" he teased. "Are you maintaining that *your* emotional state has no effect whatsoever over *the land you are magically bonded to*?" He eyed the space between them again and sighed. "Would you be willing to move fifty yards further away?"

"No," Hetta said without hesitation. "Stop procrastinating."

A hint of spice coloured the air, out of place amongst the meadow-scents of crushed grass and warm stone. It was gone before Hetta could identify the exact composition, but she knew it was Wyn's magic, rising with his temper and disappearing as he wrestled it under control.

"Do you realise exactly how unpredictable and powerful my

magic has been these past months? How dangerous I could be if I lost control over it?" In direct counterpoint to his ominous words, a bumblebee weaved drunkenly around one of his horns before deciding there was no nectar to be had there and continuing on its way.

"I'm perfectly aware, but don't try to tell me you would've agreed to try this if you weren't certain you could control yourself, or at least certain that I wouldn't be in danger."

Wyn sighed and capitulated. "Not *no* danger. There is no such thing, in this world. But, yes, I'm very sure I won't harm you."

"Then why are you delaying?"

He rubbed his horn. "Very sure is not *completely* sure. I worry."

"You worry too much. Think of the rewards, instead!" She put her hands behind her head and leaned back against the flat rock, knowing the position would emphasise the curves of her breasts against her blouse. Wyn tracked the movement, unable to help himself.

"You're doing this on purpose," he accused.

"Well, if your control over your magic is fractured by only very mild flirting, you're of no use to me," Hetta pointed out.

"I intend," he said, voice gone deep, russet irises nearly swallowed by black, "to be of very great use to you, my Star."

She shivered as their gazes locked. "Stop delaying then," she said. "Or with our luck, our 'chaperone' will turn up before you've begun."

Wyn's nose wrinkled at the reminder that Hetta's cousin Jack was more likely than not to come hunting for them. Jack had taken it upon himself to guard Hetta's virtue, whether or not she wanted it guarded. And whether or not it actually needed guarding. Wyn's erratic magic and Stariel's attitude were perfectly adequate chaperones without additional help, she thought sourly.

"Very well." He smiled, a hint of wickedness in it. "But next time we test your lord-powers, I reserve the right to interfere with your concentration similarly."

"Done," she agreed.

Wyn closed his eyes and drew a deep breath, fanning out his wings. They lit up in the sunshine, hundreds of overlapping jewels. They were blue now, though little flashes of iridescent purple, indigo, and even emerald caught the light as his feathers rustled in the slight breeze. Silver frosted each wing tip. It was a recent change. They'd been silvery white before he'd gone to the Court of Ten Thousand Spires to rescue her, through the Maelstrom. He'd come out with his wings broken and feathers torn free, humming with power. His wings were healed now, but the feathers had grown back with an entirely new colouration. Hetta chose to take it as a sign—blue, after all, was Stariel's colour, and after the events at the Spires, he no longer owed an oath-debt to the fae courts. Surely that meant they didn't have to worry about Faerie politics anymore?

She knew, deep down, that there was no way that could be true, and not least because they still didn't know who ruled in ThousandSpire. They'd heard nothing from Wyn's homeland since their escape. Was no news good news?

Hetta pressed her fingertips into the earth and burrowed a little deeper into Stariel than she normally would, ready to react if something went wrong. That was how it had gone the first time Wyn's new magic had surfaced unexpectedly: lightning on a clear day, and Stariel snapping it out of the air like a dog catching a stick, both of them wide-eyed with shock, hair standing on end with the static remnants.

"You'll do fine," Hetta said. *And Stariel and I will catch it if you don't*, she added silently.

He unfurled his wings to their full extent, and a feral wildness rose in him, bringing with it the smell of dust after rain and the thick spice of cardamom. His skin grew faintly pearlescent, the strands of his hair into a liquid metal that matched the silver filaments on his blue, blue wings. Pressure beat against Hetta's eardrums, and she swallowed.

In that moment, Wyn looked exactly what he was—a prince, full of strange magic, alien and inhuman. The Standing Stones made an appropriate backdrop, connected as they were with Stariel's most magical ceremonies. Last year, when Hetta had been kidnapped by King Aeros, Wyn had used the stones to forge a portal between Stariel and the Court of Ten Thousand Spires. The remnant of that passage was still visible behind him, in a line of dead grass between the two tallest stones.

Power swelled in the air, and though the sky was clear, in the distance Hetta felt clouds respond to Wyn's summons, a storm trying to begin with him at its centre. Leaning in to Stariel, she discouraged the unnatural weather. It felt remarkably like taking handfuls of grain and scattering them, only to have the wind whirl them back into piles as quickly as she could throw.

Wyn corralled the effect with visible effort. The gathering of distant stormclouds ceased and the power shifted to the here and now, rippling in the air in front of her.

Wyn glowed, and lightning—or at least its lesser cousin—curled around him in blue-white snakes. He opened his eyes, and Hetta gasped. In the russet of his irises, tiny bursts of lightning flickered, as if the storm was looking out. Goosebumps broke out on her arms, every fine hair standing on end. Stariel crouched just beneath her surface, waiting to pounce. She held her breath.

Wyn smiled and drew a smooth shape in the air. The lightning wound down his arm and pooled in his hand, a stuttering ball of blue-white charge. He laughed and held it up, joy shining in him.

"Pretty, isn't it?" he said, letting the ball spin slowly.

Hetta exhaled and let her grip on Stariel ease. The land still watched, of course. It was aware of everything within its borders, but it saved special focus for events outside the ordinary. Before ThousandSpire, it had viewed Wyn's magic with suspicious jealousy, but those events had changed its attitude completely. It curled around him like a cat, as if it would scent-mark him if it could.

<Yes, I know.> she told the faeland. <You've decided you like him

now. But you can't keep interrupting us just because you can't bear to leave him alone for five minutes together!> She'd probably caused this too, somehow. *I need to know more about being lord of a faeland,* she thought, not for the first time.

"Can I come closer?" Hetta asked, getting up.

Wyn transferred the blue orb from one hand to the other. "Slowly," he warned. "People carry their own elektrical field. They start to interfere with each other and I need to adjust for that."

Hetta took one tentative step forward, then another. The air on the grassy hilltop grew dry and thick with ozone. All her instincts screamed danger, but she ignored them and kept going. The storm in Wyn rippled in response to her movement, contained but churning. She took several more steps and felt the moment the magic began to unravel.

"Stop!" he said. His chest heaved with exertion, primaries spread wide. Little sparks arced from feather to feather. His silver hair stood on end, rippling in response to currents not caused by wind. The lightning in his eyes almost obscured the russet. He'd never looked less human, an unearthly creature of storm and wind. "I'm going to have to ground the power," he said slowly, shifting his stance wider.

"I'm ready," Hetta said, gathering up Stariel again. The land bristled under her skin, heather and pine and bluebells. Wyn nodded.

The power slammed into the ground at his feet in a rush, and Stariel leapt, swallowing it in a single gulp. For a moment, Hetta was blinded by the sudden assault on her magesight, and she stumbled. Strong arms steadied her, and she found herself crushed against a warm male chest.

"Hetta," he said. Just that, just her name, but there was such a wealth of affection in it that the two syllables sounded like something far more important. The lightning was gone from his eyes. He smiled, though she could feel his heart pounding under her hands. "Do we call that a success or a failure?"

She was about to answer when the world shuddered. They both

gripped each other for balance before realising simultaneously that the world wasn't literally shaking; something was disturbing Stariel's magic. Hetta reached for Stariel for an answer and received it between one breath and the next. *There.* She turned instinctively towards the source of the disturbance.

Between two of the stones, where Wyn had made a portal to the Court of Ten Thousand Spires a few months ago, the line of dead grass was spreading, reaching towards them. Not them, Hetta realised in horror. Reaching for Wyn.

The dead grass was just the visible sign of the searching tendril of foreign magic creeping into Stariel. It tasted of storms and minerals and blazing heat and Hetta recognised it: ThousandSpire. In the space between the stones, hints of another landscape glimmered in and out of focus—a city built of towering rock needles.

Anger not all her own blazed up, and for a heartbeat her and Stariel's desires were one.

<Get out!.> She wasn't sure if the words came from her or the estate, but both of them meant them. She shoved power at the incursion, her own magic entwined with Stariel's.

ThousandSpire was bigger and older and probably stronger than Stariel, but they were in the heart of Stariel's territory. She and Stariel forced the incursion out, inch by inch, until the space between the stones settled to show only the forested foothills of the distant Indigo mountains that bordered Stariel.

She wobbled with the sudden release of tension. Wyn stood a few feet closer to the old portal than he'd been, and he looked down at himself and back up to where ThousandSpire had tried to reach through, slow horror creeping over his face.

"It wants you," Hetta said. "The Court of Ten Thousand Spires."

"Yes," Wyn said, folding the horror under a mask of composure, though every feather was still raised.

"Why?" Hetta asked, though she feared she already knew the answer.

Wyn opened his mouth to speak, but at that moment Hetta's cousin Jack came rushing into the stone circle like a red-headed dervish.

"What in blazes was that?" he said, spinning around and searching frantically for danger. He spotted the line of dead grass making an arrow from the two stones towards Wyn's feet and whirled on Wyn. "What did you do?" he demanded. A quick glance at Hetta and he added, for good measure: "And what do you two think you're doing, wandering off alone together?"

"In order: I don't know; Wyn was experimenting with his magic; and none of your business," Hetta said. Jack bristled. He was a broad-shouldered man with brilliant red hair, but when he bristled he looked like nothing so much as a bulldog with a bone.

"What do you mean, experimenting?"

But Hetta had no patience for her cousin right now. She put a hand on Wyn's shoulder. He started.

"I thought the wards we set were supposed to stop portals from forming inside the borders?" she asked him quietly.

"The resonance here must be stronger than I realised," Wyn said, staring at that line of pale grass only a few feet from the tips of his boots. "Or ThousandSpire more desperate. My magic just now must have strengthened the link."

"Could it happen again?"

Wyn frowned at the Standing Stones. "I don't know," he admitted. "I never expected ThousandSpire to make another grab for me. I cannot think of a precedent for two faelands warring in such a way."

Jack glowered at where Hetta's hand rested on Wyn's shoulder.

"It's not appropriate, Hetta," her cousin burst out, unable to help himself. "The two of you lollygagging off together without a care for what people think. You know the rumours are spreading."

"If anyone knows the two of us are up here alone," Hetta said, "It will be because you told them."

"That's not the point and you know it, Hetta! I don't like it and the gods know the family doesn't like it, but you better bloody well be planning to marry him, the sooner the better! Either that or send him away!"

She glared at Jack. He glared back. *Marriage.* Neither she or Wyn had said it aloud, but Hetta had felt it circling them for two months, becoming ever more conspicuous in its omission from their conversations.

"That's a conversation for Hetta and I, not you." Wyn said with deceptive mildness. He was angry from the way his coverts stiffened down against his spine. "But was that the only reason you came up here, Jack?"

Jack narrowed hard grey eyes at Wyn. "No, it wasn't." He turned back to Hetta. "There's a royal courier for you down at the house."

Made in the USA
Middletown, DE
12 August 2023

36585762R00220